Darling Girl

ALSO BY LIZ MICHALSKI

Evenfall

Darling Girl

A NOVEL OF PETER PAN

LIZ MICHALSKI

DUTTON

DUTTON

An imprint of Penguin Random House LLC

DUTTON and the D colophon are registered trademarks of Penguin Random House LLC.

ISBN 9780593185636

Printed in the United States of America

Book design by Nancy Resnick

For mothers everywhere,
and for Bill, my second star to the right

Darling Girl

Prologue

In a very tall tree sits a girl. The tree is perhaps fifty feet high, and the girl rests with her back nestled against its trunk. If a person passed beneath the tree and looked up, it is unlikely they would see her. The color of her dress blends perfectly with the leaves around her. Her face is pale, as if the sun has not touched it in days.

The girl swipes a hand across her nose. A bee is buzzing somewhere. She has been in this tree for a long time, much longer than anyone would believe possible. Her arms and legs are stiff, and there are bruises on them; she can tell by the way they hurt. A tear slips from her right eye and she catches at a fragment of memory. Once, she sat in a tree with someone whose eyes were the exact shade of the sky. She wore a blue dress, one that brought out the color in her own eyes. A blue silk ribbon tied back her hair. When the boy told her she could fly, she laughed.

"Of course you can, silly," he had said. "How do you think we got up here in the first place?"

She remembers the crack of the branch when she stood, the way the cool air spun up through her dress, rushed across her skin. It had felt so good. She wants to feel that way again, not like the broken thing she is now. She remembers the boy's instructions. He'd recited them from the storybook, the one she'd been reading to him. The one their mother didn't like.

"Don't look down," he'd said. "And don't doubt. The moment you doubt whether you can fly, you cease forever to be able to do it."

A second voice had echoed him, tiny and excited, like the tinkling of golden bells.

Now she hears those bells again. She stands up on the branch, edges away from the trunk while keeping one hand on it. Bounces gently on her toes, like a diver at the edge of the board. Now that it's come to the moment, she's afraid. But if she stays much longer, she'll never get down from the tree. She won't be able to. She may even become a part of it.

In a stone house in the English countryside far below, there is another girl, mirror image to the first. This one also wears green, but it is the green of a hospital gown. In her room, machines beep and chime, make quiet hissing sounds. A nurse sits in the kitchen, drinking tea and listening to classical music. A gardener mows the lawn, and the buzzing noise incorporates itself into the girl's muzzy, drug-soaked dreaming. She is waiting for something deep inside of her, whether she is aware of it or not.

In the tree far above, the girl perches on her branch, takes a deep breath, lets the wind wash over her. She closes her eyes and jumps.

The girl in the house opens her eyes.

Chapter One

The Darlings age well. Everyone says so, and they say it especially about Holly Darling. They whisper it when they pass her in the halls at work; they murmur it when they see her at galas and fundraisers. Everyone wants to know her secret. Everyone wants to be photographed with her. But Holly's almost never in the glossies if she can help it, and she turns down most of the invitations she receives. Those people didn't know her before; they'd never understand who she really is now.

So when people ask, Holly simply tells them it's in her genes. And it's true. Her grandmother Wendy looked fabulous until the day she died, and Holly's mother, Jane, could pass for someone decades younger. On her trips to London, Holly is always surprised to see how little her mother has changed. A few more lines around her eyes, maybe, another streak of silver in her hair, but overall, the same cool, beautiful Jane.

Of course, Holly's also in the business of looking good. Thousands of women all over the world rely on Darling skin cream. At her shiny headquarters on Fifth Avenue, marketing routinely suggests that she model for the line. What better face for the brand than her own wrinkle-free one? With her sleek blonde hair and Pilates-honed frame, Holly embodies what most of her customers want to be. Plus, there's her famous name, an added allure. But Holly always refuses. She doesn't want the extra publicity.

Or the scrutiny that comes with it. It's bad enough that she's done what she swore she'd never do when she was a child—use the Darling name to get ahead. She hadn't made the choice lightly, but the cosmetics industry is cutthroat, and Holly's not stupid enough to waste such a big advantage. But she draws the line at putting herself out there.

This morning, as she's walking down the hallway to the conference room, a handful of people poke their heads out of cubicles and offices to wish her good luck. Holly nods and smiles, but her focus is on the meeting ahead.

When she reaches the conference room, she takes a deep breath to gather herself, then pushes open the door. A half dozen faces turn to look at her.

"Are we set to go?" she asks, crossing the room to her seat at the head of the table. There's the faintest hesitation to her steps, as if she's dragging one leg. It's the remnant of a car accident she suffered in her twenties, back when she was young and foolish and believed love was enough to protect those she cared about. A naivete that cost her one child and almost another, not to mention a husband. When she's cold, or tired, or stressed like today, the limp is more pronounced.

"Marketing dropped off the mock-ups," Barry says, taking her abruptness in stride. Barry's been with Holly since the beginning. Today he's wearing his lucky blue suit, a pink silk handkerchief peeking out of his breast pocket. On anyone else, it might have been overkill. On Barry, polished to such an extreme that even his bald head shines, it looks good.

The team talks strategy for a few moments. They've done one or two of these deals before, where the Darling name is loaned out for a special product launch—though never one of this magnitude. Today they'll combine their brand with the country's leading cosmetics company to create a highlighter called Pixie Dust. The conference phone rings, and Barry answers it.

"Send them up," he says. Then, to Holly, "They're here."

A low buzz fills the room as the four staffers turn to one another, aligning marketing materials that are already perfectly straightened, doing a last-minute check on water glasses and chairs. Only Barry seems relaxed. His eyes roam the stark white conference room, the sole hint of color coming from the bouquets of pink peonies dusted with golden glitter that are arranged in the center of the table. He grins widely, teeth gleaming.

"We're ready for this," he says. "We've got this, people."

A few minutes later Holly, Barry, and the rest of the team stand as Holly's assistant ushers in a woman and two men. The woman reaches out to shake Barry's hand, then leans in to hug Holly, who proffers her own hand instead.

"Lauren," Holly says smoothly, covering any awkwardness. "So nice to see you again."

"It's wonderful to see you too, Holly. You look amazing, as always. How's Jack?"

"He's great, thanks. Still living for lacrosse. His sophomore year is flying by."

"He must be itching to get his driver's license," Lauren Lander says. "I'm telling you, hold him off as long as you can. Once they start driving, you lose all control. Teenagers behind the wheel are an accident waiting to happen."

"I can imagine," Holly says with a tight smile. She can tell when realization hits Lauren; she glances involuntarily at Holly's leg, a horrified expression crossing her face.

"And your two?" Barry says, stepping in to do damage control before Lauren can make it worse. "I heard your son made the golf team at Eckerd. You must be so proud."

"We wish he was closer, but at least we have a warm place to visit," Lauren says, clearly grateful for the change in topic. "Ashley's already planning on heading there for spring break."

She turns to Holly. "We should introduce Jack and Ashley sometime. It would be so thrilling for her to meet a Darling."

"That would be great," Holly says. Her eyes meet Barry's.

"She'd be so excited," Lauren continues, letting out a very unprofessional giggle. "She's fascinated by your family. Peter Pan was her hero for years. Though it's always a shame when you realize your literary crushes aren't real, isn't it?"

Holly's lips thin. "Tragic."

There's no chance in hell she'll make that introduction. She's worked too hard, for too long, to keep Jack safe to blithely put him in the path of a party girl like Lauren's daughter.

Holly moves to the table and Lauren follows, still chatting. A folder filled with mock-ups of Pixie Dust ad campaigns rests at each place. Each folder is topped by a tiny pink glass bottle of the powder that glitters in the light. One bottle is slightly off-center, and Holly frowns until the marketing director hurriedly adjusts it.

"Adorable!" Lauren says. "This is going to fly off the shelves."

Barry gives Holly a triumphant look, but she's not ready to celebrate quite yet. She taps a finger against her folder, and Barry gets the hint. "Let's take a look at the terms," he says, opening his up.

"Oh, but before we get into that, I want to *see*," says Lauren. She cracks open the glass bottle, sniffs. "Smells like . . . lemon. No, sarsaparilla. No, that's not it. But it's . . . something effervescent. Am I right?"

Holly's staff freezes. Holly's known for her strict adherence to the agenda, and she's been known to explode when someone goes off schedule. Even Barry's giving her the side-eye, but Holly surprises them all.

"Think of it as . . . the scent of springtime," she says, shrugging almost imperceptibly toward Barry. For the amount of money on the line, she can afford to play nice.

"I like that. How does it work?" Lauren asks, tapping a tiny bit into her hand.

Holly nods at the marketing director, who cues the video. A wide shot pans to a beautiful young girl by the banks of a frozen lake. Ice covers the ground. A glass bottle floats through the night sky. The girl catches the bottle, opens it, and blows the contents into the air. As the golden powder swirls above her, her face brightens, as if lit from within by stars. She turns to the camera, radiant.

"All you need is faith, trust, and a little Pixie Dust," a man's voice intones. The screen fades to black.

"Oooh," Lauren breathes. She tilts her head up, blows the dust in her palm into the air, closes her eyes as it settles on her face. "It feels . . . tingly." She turns to the man next to her. "How does it look?"

The man inspects her face as if he's looking at a spreadsheet. The powder has disappeared, but there's a slight sheen to Lauren's skin, a radiance that wasn't there before. Her skin looks taut and even. "It's subtle, but there's a definite glow. It's quite pretty. More to the point, it looks completely natural. Honestly, it's like nothing we've seen out there."

"Exactly." Barry grins. "And you won't find anything else like it, either."

"How does it work?"

"We use a proprietary blend of light-refracting pigments, combined with the best masking and camouflage agents in existence."

"And it's nontoxic?"

"Of course," Barry says. "We at Darling Skin Care have been the leaders in that area for quite some time."

He points to the deputy marketing director, who produces a hand mirror emblazoned with a large *D*. Barry passes the mirror to Lauren, who stares into it.

"Wow," she says. "Your guys are really, really good."

"Thank you," says Holly. She's particularly practiced at keeping the edge from her voice on this one, but Lauren must catch a hint, because she stops looking in the mirror and glances over.

"Sorry," she says, and has the grace to blush. "It's hard to remember you're a scientist on top of everything else."

"It's quite all right," Holly says, although it's not. This is one of the reasons she decided early on to partner with Barry—strictly in the business sense, after those first few nights—since even in this day and age there are some people who can't seem to believe that a woman who looks like she does could also be a real, hands-on scientist. But Pixie Dust is every bit Holly's baby, in more ways than one.

"Well," says Barry. "If you'll look in the folders in front of you, you'll find a standard—"

There's a knock on the door, and Holly's assistant pokes her head in. "Dr. Darling, I am so sorry to interrupt, but I need you for a minute."

Holly makes an effort not to scowl. She has a habit of running through assistants, and this one is so new Holly's struggling to remember her name. "Can it wait?"

The assistant shakes her head. "I'm afraid not."

"Excuse me a moment, everyone," Holly says. "I'll be right back." She pushes her chair out, stalks around the table. She runs through the list of what it could possibly be, stops short when she gets to the most likely. *Jack.* There's one thing her assistant would interrupt her for right now, and that's her son. His is the only call she'll take no matter what she's doing. But he knows what a big day today is for the company. He wouldn't bother her unless it was an emergency. Her pulse pounds in her ears, and she hurries outside.

"What is it?" she demands. Her voice is brusquer than she'd intended, and the girl flinches.

"I'm sorry, but the caller said it was urgent."

Barry has left the conference room too and come up behind her. His face is so worried it's clear he's had the same thought as Holly.

"Is Jack okay?" he asks, putting a hand on Holly's arm.

"It's not Jack," the girl says, and relief rushes through Holly. She inhales deeply, aware for the first time that she'd been holding her breath.

"Then why the hell did you interrupt us?" says Barry. "If it's not about Jack, whatever it is can wait."

"It's not Jack," the girl repeats. "It's about your daughter."

"Her daughter? Holly doesn't have a daughter. She has Jack. Everybody knows that," Barry says. He glares at the girl, who looks as if she'd like nothing better than to flee. "Come on, Holly. We need to get back in there."

But Holly's not moving. Her limbs have grown cold. She feels sick and shaky, as if she might faint. Barry takes one look at her and wraps an arm around her for support.

"Holly?" he says. "What is it?"

For once, Holly's iron self-control deserts her. Because the truth is, she does have a daughter, a secret clutched so tightly to her heart that no one here, not even Barry, knows about her.

"What did they say?" Holly manages to ask.

"Holly?" Barry's looking at her, his eyebrows raised in disbelief even as he holds her up, but she can't answer him right now.

The girl shakes her head. "Just that you should call right away. They left the number."

Holly doesn't need to look at the slip of paper the girl is holding. After ten years of calling that number, she knows it by heart.

"Then get them on the phone," Barry barks. He may not know what's going on, but the good thing about Barry is he's always on Holly's side. "We'll take it in there." He points to an unused office a few doors down from the conference room and guides Holly into it.

Once there, he paces around the small space, his large form making it feel even tinier. "I don't understand, Holly. How could you not tell me you had a daughter? I mean, Jesus, we're like family."

"I'm sorry," Holly says wearily. She's been waiting for this call for over a decade, and now that the initial shock has passed, she's exhausted. She wonders if all her preparation will be enough. But there's nothing she can do now. She takes out her own phone and tries the number. It clicks straight to voicemail, so she hangs up.

"It's just . . . I found out I was pregnant after the crash. The pregnancy was a struggle the whole way." *The truth. But not all of it.*

"But how could you not tell me? Why haven't you ever talked about her? For Christ's sake, what's her name?"

"Eden. Eden Estelle. Her birth was . . . complicated," Holly says. She hits redial. Still nothing. "And then, a few years after, she had an accident. She and Jack had been playing. They climbed a tree and she fell . . . The doctors didn't think she would survive. She's been on life support ever since." *Also true, in its own way.*

"Oh, Jesus, Holly," Barry says again, but his tone has softened. "I wish you would have let me help."

"I didn't talk about it because I couldn't bear to go through it again." And that is true, completely. Losing Robert, and Jack's twin, Isaac, and almost Jack . . . if Eden had died that day, she's not sure she would have recovered. Even now, with all the years she's had to prepare, all the time she's spent already mourning her daughter, there's a deep well of sadness opening at her core. If she's not careful, she'll fall back in. "Losing Eden has never been a matter of if, just when. Being here, at work, helped me forget at least part of the time."

"What do you mean, losing? Maybe she's sick. Pneumonia or something. Kids get sick all the time."

Holly shakes her head. "I have round-the-clock care for her at our old house in Cornwall. I get an email update at the end of every day, and talk to the nurses at least once a week. They wouldn't call if it was anything but . . . but this."

She doesn't say what "this" is, but Barry has always been talented at reading between the lines.

"I'm so sorry. Do you need me to call Jack?"

"He doesn't know, Barry."

"Doesn't know?" His face is puzzled.

"Doesn't know about Eden. At all. And I want it to stay that way." Holly's firm on this.

Barry stares at her in disbelief, as she'd known he would. "Yeah, but Holly, come on, this is his sister you're talking about. He has a right to know about his family."

Barry is knowledgeable about many things—contract law, fine whiskey, and, back in the day, mutually agreeable sex—but he has no idea what he's talking about on this particularly complex subject. "Jack doesn't remember her—he was still so little, and he's repressed so much from that time. I wanted to shield him. I *still* want to shield him. He's been through so much already."

Barry starts to respond, but the assistant pokes her head around the door, exhales hard. "I've got her," she whispers to Holly. "Please hold for Dr. Darling," she says into her headset, then points with her chin to the phone on the desk next to Holly. "I'll put her through whenever you're ready."

Barry waits, but Holly motions to the door. "Go. You need to get back in there and close the deal."

He looks at her, uncertain.

"I'm okay, Barry. I promise," she says. "I've been expecting this. The surprise is that she lasted as long as she did. I mourned Eden a long time ago. The call took me off guard, that's all."

He hesitates. "If you're sure . . ."

Holly makes a shooing motion with her free hand. "Go. I'll try to come back in if I can."

"All right," he says dubiously. "You're the boss." He squeezes her shoulder before he leaves.

She's finally alone, and in the few seconds she has, she thinks of Eden as a baby, as the precociously beautiful child she was before the fall. She thinks of the girl who never sat still, instead of the one who has not been able to move for ten years. And then she takes a deep breath, because she knows before she even picks up the phone what the nurse is going to say.

Which is what makes the actual words so astonishing.

"Dr. Darling? I'm so sorry," the voice on the other end of the line says. It hesitates, then continues. "But your daughter? She has vanished. We cannot find her anywhere."

Chapter Two

The nurse is talking, a deluge of words. Holly's brain tries to catch at them, but she's drowning. *Your daughter has vanished.*

Vanished.

"Stop," Holly says. "Slow down. I can't understand you. Tell me what happened."

The nurse, having conveyed her point, gets her speech under control. "Eden was in her room at breakfast. I checked on her after tea. Her room is empty! No sign anywhere!"

A hard knot forms in Holly's chest. She grasps at any possibility that could explain what happened. "Did you check under the bed? Could she have fallen and rolled beneath it?"

"I checked everywhere! Under the bed, in the closet! She is nowhere!"

Holly tries to think, but all she can see is Jack, leaping with catlike grace across the lacrosse field, radiating good health and vitality from every atom of his being. Jack, smiling at her, the scars that once crisscrossed his face nearly invisible. How will Jack survive if his sister is gone?

"What about the other nurses? Did they see anything?"

"I have asked them all. I have called the gardener. Nothing. But . . ."

The voice on the other end of the phone hesitates. "The window in her room was open, and I am sure I left it closed."

The knot in Holly's chest changes to a fist, squeezing her heart. She sees a shining head framed against the dark sky, mischievous eyes watching her. The scent of springtime. And then bruises blossoming against her skin like dark flowers. She swallows hard. "Are you certain?"

"Yes. But the ground outside is damp, and there are no footprints."

The room, Holly notices with a detached kind of interest, is growing black, crowding around the edges of her vision. It's a panic attack, a bad one, the kind she hasn't had in years. She focuses on a poster that's hanging on the wall. It is of a woman on a beach using Darling Skin Care sunscreen, and Holly tries to imagine the waves, to see herself there, but instead the thudding in her head becomes a thundering roar, overpowering her ability to speak.

"Ma'am? Should I call the police?" A pause. Then uncertainty. "Ma'am? Dr. Darling?"

If only that were an option. "No." Holly works to get air into her lungs. "I'll come as soon as I can. Until then, keep looking." She hangs up.

Minutes or maybe hours later, she hears the conference room door down the hall open. Voices laughing, receding footsteps. She's bent over and staring at the carpet, trying to breathe. The office door opens. Barry's hand is on her back, he's yelling, sending someone for ice, for a wet cloth, a paper bag. The scurry of feet. And then he's picking her up as if she is weightless. He's moving like the linebacker he was in college, carrying her farther down the hall to her own office. He's kicking the door open with his foot, depositing her on her white silk couch. The fabric is so soft it's as if she is floating.

But of course, she's never been the one who could do that.

A shock of cold on her neck brings her back to herself, makes her sit up and open her eyes. She reaches up and finds the ice pack Barry has applied. He thrusts a paper bag at her.

"Here. Breathe into that."

She tries to push it away, but his hand won't move.

"Breathe."

She breathes into the bag, five deep long breaths, five slow exhales.

"Again."

At last he pulls out the bottle of Irish whiskey Holly keeps in the bottom drawer of her desk for celebrations and pours them each a finger, neat.

"You look like shit," he observes. He hands her a glass and sinks onto the couch beside her.

"I feel like it," she admits. Her hands are shaking. She takes a sip of the whiskey, holds it in her mouth and lets it burn, then swallows.

"I'm sorry, Holly. I wish there was something I could do. You want to talk about it?"

She shakes her head, her long blonde hair curtaining her face. *Not even a little bit.*

"Will there be a service? Do you need help planning it?"

"I . . . ," she starts. She doesn't mean to lie. But there's no way to tell him the truth, nothing that he'd believe. "I kept Eden in Cornwall because I thought she'd be safe there," she says, deflecting the question. "Even after the company took off, and I moved to the States, I kept her at the cottage there because . . ." She trails off. *Because she loved the sea and the sky and the cold air so much, and she would hate it in the city. Because Robert and Isaac are buried there, and I wanted her with family. Because I could protect her better there.* "I was wrong."

Barry looks at her. "Is that a no? On the service?"

For years, Barry has fixed every problem she's encountered. That's his job, and he's very, very good at it. She wants to unload, tell him everything, throw herself on his mercy and beg for help. But at best, he'd think she is crazy. At worst, he'd accuse her of child abuse. So she simply nods. "No service."

"I suppose that's smart—I can already imagine the headlines. 'Secret Darling Family Daughter Dies Under Mysterious Circumstances,' or some such. The London press would love it."

Holly winces. This is one of the reasons she fled to New York after the accident. For over a decade she's imagined the same sordid stories— or worse. Unlike Barry, her imagined headlines are based on past experience with the tabloids. "Awfully Sad Adventure: Darling Daughter Loses Spouse, Child in Car Crash," "Darling Daughter, Twin, Hover in Neverland Between Life and Death," And that's just her own life. It doesn't include the paparazzi that have dogged her family for years. She downs the rest of her drink.

"I'm sorry," Barry says, running a hand over his shiny scalp. "I didn't mean to sound flippant. What do you need?"

What she needs is to get back to England, fast, and find Eden. Wherever she is. She thinks of that open window, of the black sky and the crashing waves beyond it, and shudders.

"Holly?" Barry's looking at her again, but this time, his gaze is more searching. He has what she calls his lawyer look on. It's as if she's a contract, and he's found the line that's not supposed to be there.

"Yes. Sorry." She gives a bitter little laugh. "You were right. The phone call—hearing the news—was tougher than I thought." She closes her eyes and leans back against the couch, more to keep her thoughts from him than because she's exhausted. "I need a flight home, as soon as I can get one. And I need a safe place for Jack. Can he stay with you?"

"Jack's always welcome with us, you know that. Minerva and the kids will be thrilled. But what do you mean, a safe place?" That lawyer tone again.

"I need someone to watch over him," she says. She can't think about all the ways it can go wrong for Jack right now. "I'm not planning on telling him about Eden, but in case something comes out, I want him with someone I trust. I could leave him at the apartment with the housekeeper, but I'd rather leave him with you."

"Of course. But . . ."

She sits up, opens her eyes. She's not having this conversation, not letting Barry make her second-guess her choices. "I'll make out his schedule for you," she says briskly. "Lacrosse is about over, so it won't be that complicated."

Barry takes the hint. "How long do you think you'll be gone?"

How long does it take to find a missing daughter? She has no idea. "At least a week, maybe more."

"Don't worry about it," he says. "Don't worry about anything. Which reminds me. For what it's worth, the meeting with Lauren was a success. She couldn't stop gushing. They've signed on the dotted line and we're to start production immediately."

"That's worth celebrating," Holly says, trying to rally. She clinks her empty glass against his.

"To Darling Skin Care," he says.

"To the fabulous lawyer who made it happen."

He shrugs modestly and takes a sip. "If you say so, it must be true."

"You know it is," she says. "I couldn't do it without you. You're a genius."

He bows, drains his drink. "Yeah," he admits. "I kind of am."

Holly puts her glass down. It's time to get to work. She stands, a little shaky still from the massive amount of adrenaline her body's been pumping out, and maybe a little woozy from the booze.

"A bunch of the team is going out to celebrate," Barry says. He's watching her as if he's afraid she might need rescuing again. "I know it's the last thing you must feel like doing, but why don't you come? It might take your mind off things, cheer you up, until you can get a flight."

Holly shakes her head. "I'm going to try and finish up some loose ends before I head home to Jack. Raise a glass for me, okay? I'll let you know what time I'm leaving, and we can figure out how to get Jack to you then."

"Of course," Barry says. She can read the pity in his face, and turns away to her desk. But he follows her there. Like he'd followed her to

16

Darling Skin Care. But the days of leaning on Barry, inviting him into her maelstrom of a life, have passed. He has a wonderful wife, a happy family. She won't jeopardize that.

"I'll leave you some notes," she says, opening her desk drawer and riffling through it. "The biggest thing will be feeding him. Jack eats more than even Minerva can cook."

She pulls out a piece of paper, starts scribbling random notes about Jack's schedule.

"Holly."

"Hmmm?" She doesn't look up.

"I really am so sorry. When was the last time you saw her? Eden, I mean."

She wants to say, *I see her every time I look in the mirror. Every night in my dreams. Every time I look at Jack.* But she doesn't.

"January," she says instead. "I saw Eden this past January."

And her face was still as beautiful as the stars.

Chapter Three

After Barry leaves, Holly calls her assistant about flights. There's nothing available until tomorrow morning, so she has the girl book it, then tells her to cancel all of her meetings for the next week.

"Should I reschedule them?"

"Say . . ." Holly hesitates. A vision of Eden the last time she visited comes to her, unbidden. The frail figure beneath the sheets, the pale skin, the unearthly stillness. She's seized with the certainty that it's all a mistake. A miscommunication. It has to be. She presses her palms into her eyes.

"Say I had a family emergency and you'll get back to them. Leave it at that." She hangs up, then calls the cottage again.

The same nurse answers. She's less hysterical, more firm in her answers: Yes, the staff has searched the whole house and property and Eden is not there. No one else has been spotted, either by the nursing staff or the gardener, who was outside working all morning. No one has contacted the house. Is Dr. Darling certain she does not want to call the police?

Dr. Darling is quite certain.

After she hangs up the phone, Holly stares at it. *Ring*, she thinks, but it doesn't.

If Eden is incapable of moving herself, then someone must have moved her. And if someone has taken her, Holly has to face the possibility that Eden herself is the prize, that someone has discovered her worth, despite the safeguards Holly has put in place. And the fact that no note has been left, that no one has called demanding money . . .

That thought alone almost sends her back into a panic attack.

But what if it's something more mundane? What if it *is* only because Eden's a Darling? A rich, easy target ripe for kidnapping? Is she being wildly foolish for not calling the authorities?

She has to move, do something, or she'll go crazy, so she leaves her office and heads to the far end of the hall. She swipes her key card at the locked door, and it opens with a sighing sound. There's a row of hooks with lab coats along the wall. She slips on a coat, pushes through the final door, and enters the lab.

Elliot Benton, her best scientist, is sitting on a stool in front of a computer. He looks up, startled.

"Everything all right?" she asks.

"Yes. Running one last quality control check on the latest samples. I saw you were here before me this morning, but I figured it never hurts to double-check," he says.

Holly nods. Elliot has been with her since the beginning, almost as long as Barry. His attention to detail and his desire to push the boundaries of what's possible are two of the reasons she appreciates him.

"Where is everyone?"

He looks around the room, as if surprised to find himself alone. "Um, I think they went out to celebrate. We closed a big deal?" he says, slightly baffled.

Despite the horribleness of today, she can't help but smile at him. "Right. We did, actually. With some thanks due to you. The Pixie Dust powder is officially a go."

He hops off the stool. "The masking pigments, right?"

She nods.

"I have an idea that could improve the product exponentially. I was taking my daughter to the aquarium the other day and noticed—"

Holly's loath to interrupt him, but she needs the lab. And privacy. "Elliot, I can't wait to hear all about it. But I'm heading out for a week or so. You're in charge of the lab until I get back. If you need anything and can't reach me, go to Barry."

Elliot's face falls. He and Barry do not always see eye to eye. Barry's more likely to spring for fancy product packaging than upgraded equipment or research.

"In the meantime, why don't you write up a short summation of the product changes you're suggesting. If you can get it done in the next few hours, I can read it on the plane."

His smile returns. "I'll get right on it," he says, which is what she was counting on when she made the offer.

She waits until she hears the lab door click shut behind him, until she sees him leave the secure area on the video monitor mounted on the wall. When she's certain she's alone, she heads to the back wall. A locked door there leads to her private lab. It's tiny, about a third the size of her office. There are no silk couches, no views of the New York skyline, only a metal desk and a lab bench and the smell of bleach. And Holly, alone. Which is the way she's always liked it.

At least, it used to be.

"You're making the rest of us look bad, you know."

Startled, Holly looks up from her workbench. She's been staring through the lens of her microscope for so long her vision is wonky and her eyes take a second to adjust. There's a man standing next to her. He has reddish-blond hair and a wide smile. He's about her age, but much better dressed than most of the male grad students she knows. Cuter too. And he's looking at her in a way that makes her heart speed up for no good reason she can explain.

"Excuse me?"

20

"Term ended hours ago. The building's closing. Or hadn't you noticed?"

She looks past him to the windows, now dark with evening.

"Shit." How could she have lost track of time today of all days? She grabs her books and papers and haphazardly shoves them into her carry-all. A handful of her notes flutter to the floor.

"Here. Let me." In one smooth motion he retrieves the fallen papers, takes the bag from her, and expertly packs it so everything fits.

"Thanks," she says. She retrieves her bag, blurts out a goodbye, and hurries toward the building's main entrance. The security guard behind the desk looks pointedly from her to the clock behind him. In desperation, Holly reads it. It confirms her lateness.

"I am so screwed," she says to no one in particular. Joanie had said she was leaving at five P.M. sharp. She'd meant it this time too, Holly could tell. It's after six, so there's no point rushing back to the dorm.

She slumps onto the bench just outside the building's entrance. As if on cue, snow begins to fall. Cold, wet flakes that stick to the trees and the ground, that slide down the back of her neck and make her shiver. Snow that will make getting home even more difficult. She groans. Even during the best of circumstances, Holly hates snow. "Shit," she says again.

And then that voice, amused. "Admiring the view?"

He's standing beneath the doorway's overhang, his own pile of books neatly stacked under his arm. Despite the weather, his overcoat is still slung across his shoulder. Now that she's no longer rushing, Holly can appreciate his blue eyes, the way they crinkle at the corners, and that same wide smile, which seems vaguely familiar. He radiates a calm confidence that is as foreign to Holly as it is attractive, and she finds herself saying more than she planned.

"Not exactly. I missed my ride to London. My mother's throwing her annual fancy dress party for the holidays and if I am not there, she may actually kill me."

He gives a low, sympathetic chuckle. "Well, it was nice knowing you, if only briefly. I'll look for your obituary in *The Times*," he says, walking away. He has a slim, athletic build, shown off in a snug pair of chinos and a button-down, and his hair is longer than she'd first thought, curling below his ears.

Holly slips lower on the bench. There's something wrong with her. She should be practicing her apology call to Jane, and instead she's admiring the body of a complete stranger. She'd like to call after him, tell him that in lieu of flowers he can make a contribution in her memory to the Society for Downtrodden Daughters, just to see that smile again. She's still debating what to say when he reaches the bend in the path. Too late.

"On the other hand . . . ," he says, pausing.

She looks up, hopeful.

"I'm heading to London myself. I'm happy to give you a lift."

"Yes. Yes, yes, yes," she says, leaping to her feet, for once not second-guessing herself. "Give me five minutes to get my things."

He cocks an eyebrow. "Just like that? No need for introductions? No worries I'm a serial killer?"

He has a point, but . . . "You haven't met my mother. Death at your hands will be infinitely preferable," she says. "Don't go anywhere. I'll be right back."

She sprints to her room, calculating the best possible time they can make. If they leave right now, they can avoid the worst of the holiday jam-ups and arrive late enough that her mother will be distracted greeting guests, but not late enough that she'll be angry. Luckily Holly packed most of her stuff the night before. Because she's not entirely crazy, she considers phoning from her room to tell her mother who she's traveling with, only to realize there's no point; she doesn't know the stranger's name, or what he does on campus, or even what kind of vehicle he drives.

He's in the parking lot scraping off the windshield of a sleek red car when she gets back. She stows her bag in the back, next to a small suitcase and a hanging garment bag. She hesitates, says a silent prayer to whatever saint has domain over bad decisions, and hops in. The car is already heating up, which she appreciates. She hadn't thought to wear gloves or a hat.

"You do travel light, don't you?" he says, glancing at the back seat as he slides in.

"I don't need much. Mostly my textbooks."

"I appreciate that in a woman," he says, "I'm Robert, by the way."

"I'm Holly. Holly Darling. Have we met?"

He gives a rueful laugh, and for an instant their eyes meet. There's a heat behind them so intense she has to look away.

Robert doesn't seem to notice, instead busying himself with his seat belt. "We were in the same practical ethics class—Ethics for the Modern World. You usually sat in front of me."

"Ah. Right." She glances at his face again, and again their eyes meet in a way that brings her suddenly and completely awake. "I was late for most of those classes. It was after my bio lab."

"Really? I hadn't noticed," he says. She can't tell if he's kidding or not.

The snow is falling more thickly, floating lazily down from the black sky to coat the landscape like a fleece blanket. In the darkness, it radiates light, swirling and eddying. Watching it makes Holly dizzy. She leans back and closes her eyes.

The auto is some type of sports car, luxurious and snug. The leather seats are soft, and she relaxes into hers, grateful for the coddling. She breathes deeply, catches the slightest hint of Robert's scent. It's warm and comfortable, a blend of spice and vanilla, a sharp contrast to the formaldehyde and bleach she's used to.

"You all right?"

She stretches, opens her eyes. "Yes. This is lovely. Thank you so much for the ride."

"Thank you, for the company. I really was going anyhow."

Before she can respond, he snaps on the radio. "Is music okay?" The station is playing a holiday medley at a volume loud enough to make conversation difficult.

But after a few minutes, he reaches to turn it down. His elbow brushes hers, and her heart goes careening against her ribs. How is it possible for someone she barely knows to affect her like this? She glances sideways at him, but his face is inscrutable and she can't tell if he feels the same connection. His next words make her doubt it.

"One more version of 'All I Want for Christmas Is You' and my head may explode. You?" he says. His arm is still touching hers.

"Charming the first three thousand times. But after listening to the a cappella version, the acoustic version, and the big band version, what's left?" The heat from his skin goes right through the fabric of her sleeve.

"Bagpipes?" He shifts, and his arm falls away.

"That would be worse," she agrees, ignoring the sudden cold where his arm once was.

"Now that we've got that sorted, there's a thermos of tea and some biscuits in the bag by your feet. There should be two cups, if you don't mind pouring."

She reaches down and opens the bag, then shoots him a sideways glance. The biscuits are chocolate-coated gingerbread, her favorite kind. Who is this man?

They munch for a bit in companionable silence. Normally at this point in the ride Holly's gnawing on whatever stale crackers she or Joanie have uncovered at the bottom of their bags, swigging cold tea from a petrol station, and running over their lab results. But now the knots in her neck and back are loosening. Warm and fed, a buzz of electricity just beneath her collarbone, she feels as if the night is magical, as if anything could happen.

"It's beautiful, isn't it?" Robert says, breaking the silence and nodding at the sky. "Like being in our own private snow globe."

"Lovely," she agrees. She has so many questions—who Robert is, how he appeared at the exact right moment—but the one at the top of her head comes spilling out before she can think. "How is it I've never seen you before?"

He laughs. "An excellent question. One I've asked myself regularly. But why don't you tell me what you *do* see? What's so compelling to make you brave the wrath of Lady Darling by being late?"

She eyes him. "You *have* met my mother."

"Let's say we've crossed paths," he says, shuddering. "I may or may not have attended a holiday luncheon at the Tate hosted by your mother at which the wrong vintage of champagne was served. Tears were shed. And not by her."

"That sounds like my mother." Holly sighs. "Her talents are wasted on charity work—she should have been a commander in the Royal Tank Regiment. Please accept my apologies."

"Not necessary. Unless you are in fact secretly Jane Darling, in which case I am terrified and will pull over immediately."

Holly laughs. For the first time in days, she feels light, as if she could float away. "You're safe with me."

"That's reassuring. But you never answered my question."

Holly could talk all night about the swirling, secret worlds she spies on through the lens of her microscope, but that doesn't mean most people want to listen.

Robert turns out to be the exception.

He is an excellent listener, one who plies her with intelligent questions at all the right moments. It seems as if he's interested in everything—her lab experiments, her studies, the professors she's had, her career goals. From there, the conversation winds its way to music, the bands they both like, and the friends they have in common. Robert, it turns out, knows a surprisingly large number of the same people she does, especially for someone studying for an MBA.

"Whatever were you doing in the science labs then?"

He shrugs. "Waiting on a friend."

Before she can follow up, the top of her street comes into view. She glances at the clock on the dash, shocked. How could two hours have passed so quickly?

"Here we are," Robert says, pulling over to the curb. The house is ablaze with lights. From the safety of the car, Holly watches her mother open the front door to greet a cluster of guests. Jane is dressed in her best finery—a beautiful silvery blue gown with a white fur stole around her shoulders. When she turns her head, Holly catches the cold sparkle of the diamonds adorning her neck and ears.

"Damn," Holly says. "Just a little too late. Would you mind turning onto the next street? I think I'd be better going in the back way."

Robert obliges, cruising down the street until Holly directs him to stop. "Thank you so much for doing this," she says, reaching for her bag. "I'd invite you in, but my mother is very . . ." She hesitates. "Very particular about changes to her guest list. She doesn't like last-minute additions," is what she settles upon.

"But there's nothing here," he protests. "I can't let you out."

"I'll be fine," she assures him. "Watch."

She slides out of the car, counts the wide boards in the fence that encloses the back garden. When she finds the right one, she pulls on the top with all of her might, causing it to swing up, revealing a space barely large enough for her to wriggle through. She pushes her bag through first, using it to fend off the thorns on the other side, then carefully squeezes behind it.

"Goodbye," she calls to Robert, who is watching from the car. "See you next term." At least she hopes so. Too late, she realizes she has no idea how to reach him. She doesn't even know his last name. She's tempted to go back, but he's already turning the car around and she won't make herself ridiculous by chasing after it. She lets the board swing shut.

The garden is a dark space, empty and cold, quite unlike its summer self, when she's usually escaping out, not sneaking in. There's a statue of Peter Pan in the center—her mother's latest tribute to their ridiculous family story—and as she reaches it, the wind picks up, sharp and cruel, a faint sound like laughter beneath. She shivers and Robert drifts from her mind as she rushes to the kitchen's back steps, and from there up the servants' stairs to her room. A new dress of white and silver silk is laid out on her bed, silver shoes on the floor.

There's no time to shower, so she strips off her clothes and shimmies into the dress, holding her breath as she yanks the zipper up. It pours over her skin like liquid. She steps into the shoes, grabs the first pair of earrings she finds in her jewelry box, and wraps her hair into a messy bun. A quick glance in the mirror, a swipe of lipstick, and she's done.

When her father was alive, these parties were, if not fun, bearable. His eyes would meet hers from across the room with a spark of mischief, and ten minutes later they'd be taking a clandestine hot chocolate break in the library, doing impressions of the guests. Her mother would roll her eyes at their disappearance. "Really, Alfred," she'd chide, when they'd been gone long enough for her to notice and come find them. "These are your guests as well." And then she would take his arm and sail from the room and back into the party, but not before whispering, "I do believe Lady Iveness looks rather like a parrot in that green silk. Unfortunate woman certainly sounds like one," just loud enough for Holly, trailing behind them, to hear.

But Jane's sense of humor died when Holly's father did, fourteen years ago. So Holly hurries down the hall to the main staircase. At the top, she takes a deep breath to steady herself. Three, maybe four hours to endure before she can escape. Not so bad. She rolls her head from side to side, trying to release the tension that's returned to her shoulders and neck. Robert's face pops into her brain. What would the party be like with him here? She'd have someone to make her smile, at least. Someone to remind her to breathe, to eat. Someone enjoyable to dance with.

But the idea is ludicrous. She barely knows him. And even if she did, bringing him home to meet her mother . . . Holly shudders. No man deserves that. She pushes the thought away and descends the stairs, one careful step at a time.

"Holly," her mother hisses from her place at the foot of the landing. "Where have you been?" Up close, Jane's dress is even more beautiful, glinting under the lights as if it's been spun from ice and snow. Her hair, shot through with silver, is pulled back into a sleek dancer's chignon, not a strand out of place, and her posture is as perfect and graceful as if she were still a prima donna onstage. She casts a withering look at Holly's own hair and opens her mouth to speak.

And then, impossibly, he *is* there. Standing between Holly and her mother like her own personal champion, blue eyes twinkling. He's so handsome in a tuxedo that Holly catches her breath.

"Lady Darling," he interjects before Jane can say a word. "As ravishing as ever." He gives a courtly bow.

"Why, thank you, Robert," Jane says. She turns to Holly, all traces of pique forgotten. "Holly, you do remember Robert Wightwick, don't you? Robert, this is my daughter, Holly. I believe you attend the same school?"

"Indeed we do. In fact, I must apologize for both our tardiness. I was your daughter's ride home and I lost track of time."

He reaches out a hand toward Holly but smiles so winningly at her mother Holly can't be sure who his next words are directed at. "Forgive me?"

The band is striking up a new number, and before Jane can say a word, Holly is in Robert's arms and he's whisking her away. This close, his cologne is the best thing she has ever smelled in her life.

"So do you?"

"Do I what?" she says, distracted by his scent and his closeness and those beautiful eyes.

"Forgive me." His hands are on her back, and he expertly steers her through the crowd until they reach a sheltered alcove by the library.

"Tell me your sins, my child," Holly says. She's drunk on the music, on the night and the snow and her heady escape from her mother, who is actually beaming at her from across the room. On the heat of Robert's hands. The way he's looking at her.

"The list is long and illustrious," he murmurs into her ear, and the feel of his breath makes her gasp. "Do you know that in all the years I've been coming to this party, you've never once given me a second glance? And you're terribly oblivious to everything that isn't a lab. I saved you a seat in front of me in that ethics class for a whole term, woman, without a single word of thanks."

"We're talking about your sins, not mine," she reminds him. And then she can't say anything else because he's laying a tiny trail of kisses along her jaw.

"Fine. Mark me down for dishonesty. You have a terrible issue with punctuality, have I mentioned that?" he says between kisses. "So tonight I took fate into my own hands. Your roommate was taking your name in vain in the parking lot, and I promised I'd be responsible for you. I wasn't waiting for a friend. I was waiting for you."

"Dishonesty isn't one of the seven deadly sins," Holly says, but it comes out as a sigh, because now he's kissing her collarbone. Her neck. The corner of her mouth.

He pulls away, looks her in the eye. "It's not?" he says, and the absence of his mouth leaves such a hole in her skin that her hands of their own accord twine their way to the back of his neck, pulling him closer. "Then what is?"

"Lust." The snow is falling like a thousand lost stars and the world outside the window gleams as if brand-new. Before he can say another word, she kisses him on the mouth and pulls the curtains of the alcove closed around them.

Holly stands quietly at her workbench, waiting for grief to release its hold on her. When the softness of vanilla finally fades enough to be replaced with the sharp odor of bleach, she moves to the far end of the room, where there is a refrigerated safe. She punches in her code and its door unseals. There are two drawers behind it. She reaches into the top one and extracts a bag of blood, still in its hazardous-materials packing. It came in yesterday from Cornwall, and with the Pixie Dust launch she hasn't had time to handle it until now.

She carefully deposits the contents of the bag in a serum-separation tube, then places the tube in the centrifuge. It takes fifteen minutes for the blood to separate. Holly watches the entire time, keeping her mind still, trying to lose herself in the work and not think of Robert or Eden or any of the memories clamoring for her attention. Trying to breathe.

When the machine comes to a stop, she unlocks the lid. The red blood cells have collected at the bottom of the tube, the plasma and serum at the top. She draws off the plasma and serum into an unused sterile jar. She labels and dates the jar, then puts it in the top drawer of the safe.

Next she opens the bottom drawer—the freezer. Inside is a test tube of frozen blood and a thermometer. Holly checks the temperature, then shuts the door.

She takes the test tube containing the red blood cells out of the centrifuge machine and places it in a specially designed padded chiller bag, then locks her lab. She studies the video monitor to make certain she is alone before she slips out into the corridor.

Back upstairs in her main office, she nestles the bag into an inside zippered pocket of her leather tote. She takes one last look around the room, running through a mental list of tasks. Satisfied she's not leaving anything undone, she pulls off her lab coat, tosses it into a hamper in the corner of her office, and leaves for home, shutting the door firmly behind her on any lingering ghosts.

Chapter Four

The apartment is silent when she lets herself in. There's a note from Manuela, the housekeeper, saying there's a roast chicken in the oven. Holly texts her that she can have the week off. She texts Barry too, telling him she's on tomorrow's flight out, that she'll have Jack dropped off after school. And then she takes a deep breath, soaking in the quiet of the sanctuary she's created.

With its clean-lined modern furniture and bright white walls, the apartment is about as far from her family's London home as can be. No dust-collecting antiques, no gloomy corners, just white leather couches and gleaming hardwood floors. The first time Holly's mother, Jane, visited, she'd taken one look and offered the loan of some family artwork. Not the Sargent oil, of course, which displayed Grandmother Wendy in all her luminous, adolescent glory, but perhaps the sketch he'd done of all three of the famous siblings? Holly thought of Great-Uncle Michael's vacant stare and shuddered before firmly declining. It might be beneficial to trade upon her name at work, but she wanted no ties to the Darling family and its pedigreed history here.

Instead she'd purchased a few pieces of modern art to add color to the walls. And while there's a bank of floor-to-ceiling windows at the far end of the living room, there are no curtains, no space for anyone to hide behind. Most importantly, only a handful of the windows open, and those only a few inches wide.

Her quiet is broken by the thud of feet in the hallway outside. Even the apartment's sound-dampening acoustics are no match for the energy of a teenage boy. She hears his key in the lock moments before the front door opens and tries to compose herself.

"Jack?" she calls from the kitchen, in the cheeriest voice she can muster. "I'm in here."

He slouches in, all long limbs and effortless grace. Seeing him, Holly has to fight the instinct to wrap him in her arms. It would annoy him or, worse, freak him out. Instead she conjures up a bright smile, pushing her panic down as hard as she can.

"Hi, honey. Did you . . ." She catches sight of a long, ugly scrape along his chin. Instantly her smile disappears. "You're bleeding!"

"It's a scratch," he says. "I took an elbow to the face going after the ball."

"Let me see." She crosses over to him, grabs his chin in her hand, angles it toward the light. "How much did you bleed? Did it get on anyone else?"

"No!" he says, twisting out of her grip. "Jeez, you germ-freak. I know the rules by heart. Some kid whacked me. I covered the cut with my sleeve until I stopped bleeding—not even a drop hit the floor. End of story. Relax."

"Fine," she says, feeling anything but. "Make sure you wash it really well, and put some antibacterial cream on it."

She'd keep him from all sports if she could, rues the day she allowed him to talk her into letting him go out for lacrosse. He'd caught her at a weak moment, a day when he'd been playing at the park and she'd marveled at how quick he was, how far he'd come from the days he could barely drag himself from bed to wheelchair. Jack thinks she freaks out when he gets hurt because she's worried about him, and she is. But that's not all she worries about.

He has no idea how precious each drop of his blood is. Or of the high cost that has been paid for it.

He sniffs the air, pulls open the oven. Takes the serving fork off the stove and tries to stab a potato.

"Jack!"

"What? I'm hungry."

"They're not done yet. You'll . . ."

"Get salmonella," he choruses in unison with her, his voice a perfect mimicry. He successfully captures a potato, slides it into his mouth, and grins at her. The same grin that gets him out of late assignments at school, overdue library books, and trouble Holly doesn't want to know about. She can't help but smile back.

"Aside from the elbow to the face, was it a good session?"

"Yeah. We wound up scrimmaging a team from New Jersey that's renting practice space for the weekend. We totally decimated them." He ransacks the cabinets, searching for more to eat.

"Chicken," she reminds him. "It's almost dinnertime. Go shower."

"'Kay." He grabs a fistful of pretzels before she can stop him and heads toward his room.

As soon as she hears water running, she carries her tote bag into her own bedroom and locks the door. Reaches into her closet and pulls out the box that contains her needles and vials. She selects a syringe, then uses it to draw the blood from the tube. When the syringe is full, she caps the needle, puts the syringe into the cooler bag, and puts everything else away.

She brings the syringe with her to the kitchen.

Jack's still in the bathroom, so after she pulls dinner together and pours herself a glass of wine, she checks her phone. Plenty of emails and texts, but nothing from Cornwall. She's about to ring the cottage again when Jack walks in. Swiftly she puts her phone down.

"How was school? Anything good happen?"

"It was okay." He's pulling the platter of chicken toward himself, more intent on filling his plate than on conversation.

"The meeting went well today—it's a done deal," she says. "This time next year Darling Skin Care will be in every premiere makeup counter and store in the nation."

"Great," Jack says around a mouthful of food. He gives her a thumbs-up.

"Oh, I almost forgot. I have something for you," she says. She gets up and goes to the bench in the hall, where she's left a package. She brings it back and hands it to Jack. "Here."

"What is it?"

"Open it and see."

She smiles as he tears open the box. It's the latest model of his favorite brand of sneakers. She'd sent her assistant out this afternoon to scour the city for them, a gift to soften her leaving.

But when he opens the box, his expression falls.

"What's the matter? Are they the wrong style?"

"No," he says, pulling a shoe out and holding it up. "Thanks."

"But?"

"It's just . . . none of the guys wear this brand anymore. They're kind of last year. But they're great," he says quickly. "Thanks for getting them."

"You're welcome," she says, deflated. She takes a sip of wine and a deep breath. "I wanted to tell you—I need to go away for a few days. To England." She keeps her tone light. "Nothing major. A little trouble with one of our suppliers. Sorry to spring it on you last-minute, but it came to a head today."

"When are you leaving?"

"First thing tomorrow morning. I'll drop you at school on my way to the airport."

He doesn't answer, keeps shoveling in his food. She takes another sip, watches Jack eat. When he looks up at her, his blue eyes are so like Eden's that she stops mid-swallow.

"I may have to go to Cornwall," she says abruptly. "Do you remember Cornwall? We lived there, for a little while."

That catches his attention.

"We did? When?"

"Oh, it was our summer place, before." She doesn't need to say before what. Jack's grown up with the shorthand, his life neatly divided into before and after the car crash. "And then for a little time while you were recovering."

Already Holly's regretting her slip into sentimentality. She makes it a point not to talk about the past. Her personal mantra has become something along the lines of "Face firmly forward." Any evidence of their previous life has been exorcised with surgical precision, neatly boxed, taped shut, and left stacked in the cavernous reaches of the Darling House attic, along with the previous generations' secrets. "There's no reason for you to remember."

"What was it like?"

It's her turn to shrug. "Typical England. Rainy, cold, damp. Windy too, because it's on the ocean. But beautiful," she can't help adding.

He shakes his head. "I remember London, a little bit. At least I think I do—it's all kind of blurred together with the trips we've taken to see Grandma. Was it just the two of us in Cornwall?"

She freezes. "Of course. Why do you ask?"

"I dunno. I thought maybe Grandma would have been with us. I remember living in her house, a little bit. Mostly the nursery upstairs."

"No," she says firmly. "Cornwall was just us."

"Huh." He frowns for a second, as if he's struggling to recall something. Cursing herself, Holly changes the subject.

"I've arranged for you to stay with Barry and his family while I'm gone. I'll have a car pick you up tomorrow after practice and bring you to his building."

"Why can't I stay here? Manuela will be here," he says. "Please?"

"No, she won't," she says, glad that she's already texted the house-keeper. "I've given her the week off. Besides, Barry and Minerva are so excited to have you. They love you, and you've spent hardly any time at all with them lately. Every time they ask, you're always busy."

He stabs at his chicken. "I'm not a little kid, okay? I don't need a babysitter. When Brett Pike's parents went away last month, they left him home for a whole week with the housekeeper and a driver. It was awesome."

"I can imagine." She drains her glass. "Do you want dessert? I think there's some ice cream. Black raspberry chip—your favorite."

"No," he says moodily. "I'm going to my room. Homework." He stands up.

"Before you disappear, there's one thing." She stands and clears their plates to the sink, so that her back is to him. "I need to give you an injection."

"I had one a few weeks ago!" he says. But it's a half-hearted protest, uttered only because he's already angry.

"It's been a month," she corrects. "You're due next week, but I may still be away. I don't want you to miss it. It's important for you to keep your iron levels up."

"Fine," he grumbles, rolling up his sleeve. Holly cleans the area and injects his arm with quick, practiced motions. Jack's so used to the sensation he doesn't even wince anymore.

Even before the needle is out, she can see the change in him. There's a slight flush to his cheeks; his skin and eyes are brighter. And she's sure she's not imagining it: The mark on his chin, which by itself would heal to a scar, has already begun to fade.

"You know," she says, capping the needle, "we may be able to start weaning you off these. You've done so well, and it's been a long time since you've had any problems."

"Do you think so? What about my iron levels?" He doesn't sound convinced. And why would he? Since her discovery, Jack has never gone more than a month without an injection, because after thirty days she can see him fade. His energy level sags, his coordination diminishes, the ghosts of old scars trace their way along his skin.

But it's more than that. There's a buzz that comes with the blood, a high of well-being. She's sure part of his reluctance to cut back comes from the threat of losing that brief high. Still, if Holly can't find Eden, she'll have to stretch out what she has until she can perfect the synthetic version of the blood. She's close, so close, but it's not enough. Not yet.

If she's careful and reduces the dosage, there's enough blood in that test tube in her lab for two months. Another six-month supply stockpiled at the Cornwall cottage. Beyond that . . .

"I think we should try cutting back to once every month and a half—see how it goes. If you don't feel well, we can always go back to the old schedule."

"I guess." He rolls his sleeve down. Still sulking, he won't meet her eyes. Fine. He can stay mad so long as he stays safe—that's all she cares about.

After she's done cleaning the kitchen, she tells Jack to pack a bag and takes her own suitcase out of the hall closet. Packing is something else to focus on besides the constant whispering worry that's taking up all the room in her head.

Once she's sorted what she needs, she slides her hand beneath the lining of the suitcase. Tucked into a slit in the fabric is a photograph, faded and creased. In the center, sitting on a low tree branch, is a small blonde girl. Even frozen in this fragment of time, she gives the impression of irrepressible energy. Caught in the act of turning toward the photographer, her heart-shaped face is a soft blur.

But Holly can remember every detail. She's never needed a photograph to recall her daughter. In order to function, she's just had to make the decision not to.

Holly's tried to think of the blood as an antibody, a way to help Jack fight the damage done during the crash. She's seen how the injections have changed him, erasing scars, healing his bones, giving him a chance to live a normal life, the life that was denied to his father and his twin. What mother wouldn't give her child that second chance?

She's always done everything she can for Eden too. After her fall, she made sure Eden was seen by the very best doctors. And they've all told her the same thing: There was no chance of recovery. Still, she's tried every cure she can think of—some legal, some not—to wake her up, to stop her accelerated aging. None of them have worked.

So who has she hurt? No one, she tells herself. She's saved everyone she can. It's just that "everyone" has turned out to be only Jack somehow.

And now, without Eden, he's at risk too.

Chapter Five

Holly's awake in the morning when her alarm goes off. She's barely slept, torn between worry over Eden and Jack. And there's a storm coming, a bad one. Now, even in the air-conditioned apartment, pressure builds behind her eyes. Her right leg aches so much she has to rub it before she can stand.

There's no sound from the other end of the apartment. Jack's room is dark. She has to shake him awake. He moans, pulls the covers over his head, and turns away from her.

"Jack! Get up *now*," she says, shaking him again. She hears the impatience in her voice, tries to soften it. "I won't be able to take you to school if you don't hurry. I'll miss my flight."

He mutters something, and she leaves him to dress and heads back to her bedroom. Her right leg is dragging, and the pressure in her head is relentless. She hesitates, then opens her bureau drawer and pulls out a nondescript plastic container, the type that might contain an inexpensive brand of cold cream. She dips a finger in and scoops out a minute amount of lotion, rubs it on her temples, across her forehead. Dips in again, rubs the lotion down her leg, from knee to ankle, where the faintest of white scars twists along the skin.

Relief isn't immediate, but the pressure in her head lessens, and her leg no longer aches as much. Even better, when she enters the kitchen a few minutes later wheeling her suitcase, Jack is there, eating a peanut butter sandwich. He takes the bag from her and brings it to the front hall. He's not wearing the new sneakers, but she lets it go.

"What about you?" she asks. "Are you packed?"

"Yeah," he mumbles.

"Well, bring out your bag. We need to go—the driver will be waiting for us."

"I'll pick it up after school," he says. "I don't want to have to carry it around all day, and it won't fit in my locker."

"Fine." She picks her purse up off the counter, slings it over her shoulder. "But I want you to run in and get it and then go directly to Barry's house, understood?"

He nods.

"All right then. Let's go."

They ride down the elevator in silence. The driver loads her bag into the trunk while Jack and Holly slip into the back seat.

"You'll be able to reach me on my mobile anytime," she says to Jack. "And I'll call you when I land."

"Okay."

"Anything you want me to bring you?"

He shakes his head. "Will you see Grandma?"

"I don't know," she says. Jane is hard to reach at the best of times. And the thought of explaining to her what's happened makes the constant pain in Holly's stomach even sharper. But . . . "I suppose so."

They're a block from school when Jack points to the window. "Look, there's Brett." Holly leans forward, but she can't find Jack's friend in the scrum of khaki- and polo-wearing teens milling toward the building.

"Could you let me out here? Please?"

Holly hesitates. "But I won't see you for a week. Maybe longer."

"Mom, it's one block. Please!" He looks at her beseechingly, his expression almost identical to when he was younger. But back then, he was always begging her not to go. Her pocket baby, she called him, because he always wanted to be in her lap, snuggled under her arm. When she traveled for business and couldn't take him, he cried every time she left. Once he'd even tried to pack himself in her suitcase as a surprise.

"Mom!"

"Sorry. I was thinking." She hesitates a second longer, but that little boy is long gone, so she relents and tells the driver to pull over. As soon as the car is stopped, Jack opens the door, but she pulls him back so she can kiss him. She inhales, trying to capture his scent. He squirms away.

"Bye," he says. He slides across the seat and swings his backpack up in one easy move. In three steps, he's caught up to the edge of the crowd. She watches, but he doesn't look back.

"The airport, Dr. Darling?"

"Yes, please," she says, leaning back against the seat. She debates calling the cottage again. Starts to punch in the numbers, hangs up. If there was news, they would have called. Tries Jane. The phone goes to voicemail. Holly doesn't leave a message.

To distract herself, she scrolls through her emails, finds the one from Elliot Benton, and scans it. It's hastily written, but shows promise. Like Holly, Benton came to the beauty industry from the outside. A biologist with an interest in mollusks, of all things, he can see the big picture and make connections most people can't—he'd caught her attention at a conference years ago when he told her a quahog clam could live up to five hundred years.

When Barry balks at Elliot's salary, she points out that Darling Skin Care is one of the few beauty companies to have a biologist. It's an advantage not many other companies have, and plays into the current trend for products heavy on natural elements. Already Elliot's work on the Pixie Dust line has paid for itself.

She emails Elliot back, telling him to pursue the modifications in trial form. She hesitates, her fingers poised over the screen. Elliot might know a way to stabilize the proteins in the blood she gives Jack. He could help her synthesize the serum. Could possibly even help her find a way to cure Eden. Slow her growth, wake her up. But bringing anybody in on that is too risky. As tempting as it might be to have someone to work with, to talk with, she has to go it alone.

She shakes her head to clear it. Her days of collaboration with scientists like Elliot are over. The handful of people she's kept in contact with from before the crash can't believe she's happy manufacturing lotions and creams that cheekily promise to defy time. But they're not in on the irony. And they never will be.

Time stopped for Holly the day of the car crash. She's been defying death, defying time, for all these years, and she's not going to stop now.

"We're here, Dr. Darling."

She looks up. She's been so caught in her thoughts she hadn't noticed they've arrived at the airport. And as if on cue, an alert dings on her phone. Her flight has been delayed. While she hesitates, trying to decide what to do, another ding—now it's canceled.

Shit.

"Give me a second," she tells the driver. She calls her travel agent. "What's the best you can do?" she asks. "I have to get to London today."

There's a pause as the woman reviews her itinerary. "Your flight was full, and so are the subsequent ones," she says. "There's a whole line of storm fronts with high winds coming in, so it's going to be a while. But there's a flight leaving . . . let's see . . . I can get you on a flight at eight."

"Tonight?" Holly bites her lip in frustration.

"I need to know right now, before it's gone."

"Fine. Yes, I'll take it," Holly says. "But keep trying for something earlier."

"I'll do my best, but I can tell you it's unlikely," the woman says.

After she disconnects the call, Holly considers her options and decides to go home. Her head is still sore and she's exhausted. This way she can rest, get some work done, then have the car service pick her up with Jack's bags. She'll surprise him after practice and drop him at Barry's herself before heading back to the airport. She's certain he's still upset that she won't let him stay home alone, and she hates leaving with tension between them. Maybe she'll even stop and pick up his favorite pizza as a peace offering along the way.

Traffic is snarled, and by the time she gets home, the rain is sheeting down. She's soaked in the few steps from the car to the door, and her leg is twinging again. She's glad she decided to go home instead of to the office—she'll take a hot bath before she picks up Jack. She'd like to reapply the cream too, but she knows from experience its potency lessens if she uses it too often.

As she reaches the door, a tall figure brushes past her, face obscured by a hoodie. The person is in such a hurry he bumps her shoulder as he passes. The doorman scowls at him before offering to take her luggage, but she waves him off, takes her bag to the elevator, and then it's blessedly quiet. Except, as she steps out onto her floor, it's not. There's a low heavy throb in the air, thumping through the walls so hard it reverberates in her chest. It takes her a second or so to realize it's actually music, another second to realize that the sound is coming from her apartment. She tests the doorknob—locked. Could she somehow have left the speakers on? Or perhaps Manuela came back for something, although Holly for the life of her cannot imagine her grandmotherly housekeeper listening to music with a bass line like this. She unlocks the door, cautiously opens it. And in a glance understands everything.

Two of Jack's friends are lounging on her couch, dirty sneakers draped across either end. Beer cans litter the coffee table in front, and there is the faint but unmistakable aroma of pot. Jack himself is leaning against the kitchen wall, holding a cloth to his nose. Blood is dripping down his shirt, puddling onto the floor.

Eden's blood.

One of the boys must have heard or sensed the door opening over the music. He raises his head and sees her. It's Brett Pike.

"Oh, shit," he says. "Dude. Your mom."

But Holly's already moving past him to Jack, fear propelling her forward. "What happened? Where are you hurt?" she says, taking the cloth from his face. His nose is grotesquely swollen.

"It's fine. I'm fine," he says, his voice nasally. He takes the cloth back. "I got punched in the nose, is all. It's no big deal."

She looks at him, at the blood on his shirt, and suddenly she's furious. At the waste. The price she's paid—the things she's done—and for this? And then it occurs to her that more is at stake.

"Did you bleed on them? On anyone else?" She doesn't wait for an answer. She crosses the room before he has a chance to speak, inspects Brett, the other boy. Their eyes are red, their breath smells like beer, but there's no blood and, more importantly, no visible cuts on their skin. Satisfied, she jerks her head at the door. "Out. Now."

Sending two high and drunk teens out onto the streets of New York may not be her finest moment, but Holly doesn't care. They're lucky she doesn't call their parents or, worse, the police. But she has no time for them. She grabs paper towels from the kitchen and uses them to clean off Jack's face. His nose is swollen, but she's pretty sure it's not broken. She gets another paper towel, wraps ice in it, and makes him sit at the kitchen table with the ice on his nose.

She scrubs the kitchen floor, mourning every single drop of blood she cleans up. She has no idea whether it's still potent. For a second, she considers trying to save it, but the scientist in her points out how unsterile it is, so she puts the paper towels in the sink and burns them, one at a time, so she doesn't set off the fire alarm. She wets down the remains until they're formless black sludge, then throws them in the trash. Only then, when she's expended some of her energy, is she ready to face Jack without killing him.

She takes off her cleaning gloves, snapping them away from her wrists, and tosses them in the garbage. She leans against the counter, arms crossed.

"Now talk."

"What?" Jack says, his voice muffled through the cloth. If he rolls his eyes at her, she swears to god, she'll undo all the years she's spent trying to keep him alive with one blow.

"Oh, I don't know, let's see. Let's start with why aren't you at school? Who punched you? Or, my personal favorite, where the hell did you get the pot?"

She sees him thinking about a way to deny all of it, can recognize the thoughts as they come and go behind his eyes. But his brain must be too muddled from the beer and the weed to lie. He shrugs his shoulders.

"Some guy. Brett knows him."

"Really, just some guy, huh? Does he have anything to do with the bloody nose?"

He starts to shrug again, but even in his inebriated state, he can recognize the warning signs. He's fast approaching her breaking point. "Yeah. He got here and tried to overcharge us, and then he tried to stiff us. So Brett and I took care of it."

"You had him *here*? And what do you mean, you took care of it?"

"We pushed him around a little bit, that's all. There were three of us, and he's some skinny dude from Brett's sister's college. And he . . . he didn't like it, and he tried to fight back. And he was flailing around and hit me in the nose, that's all," Jack says defensively. "He couldn't have hit me on purpose if he tried. It was a total accident."

"So what, he just left after that?" She knows Jack, and she thinks she knows Brett, that little piece of pond scum. There's no way they'd let the dealer just walk away.

"Well, not exactly. Brett hit him a few times first while Vince held him down. But the guy was fine. He totally got off easy."

Holly closes her eyes. She can imagine it.

"Did you bleed on him at all?"

"What?"

"When you got hit in the nose. Did you bleed on him? Or on anyone?"

"I don't think so. I mean, I wasn't exactly worried about it," he says. He looks affronted that she's not more concerned about his own injuries.

There's nothing she can do. It's not like she can go find this drug dealer—she can imagine how that conversation would go. Besides, Jack would have had to have dripped blood directly on a cut for there to have been any significant reaction, and even then, what are the odds a bunch of teenagers would notice? But she doesn't like it. Not one bit.

She leaves Jack sitting in the kitchen, goes to her bedroom, and takes the plastic jar out of her drawer. She catches sight of her face in the mirror and stops. Her eyes are wide with panic and anger, her face is flushed, and her normally perfect blowout is sticking up in clumps around her head. She looks wild. She takes a deep breath, counts to ten, then ten again, before going back into the kitchen.

Jack is still where she left him. She takes the ice pack off his nose and inspects him. He's stopped bleeding. She doesn't know if that's natural or the result of the infusion he got last night. Still, to be sure, she scoops out a tiny amount of the cream and rubs it all along the sides and bridge of his nose. She tries to be gentle, but even so he jerks away.

"Ow! What is that?"

"Something I've been working on at the lab," she says. "It will make the swelling go down." It won't work as fast or as well as an injection might, but she can't afford to use another one so soon, not until she finds Eden. She won't think about what might happen if she doesn't.

"There," she says, putting the lid back on. "Now where's the stuff?"

"What stuff?" he says, looking innocent. But she's not fooled.

"Hand it over," she says, extending her hand.

He pulls a small baggie out of his pants pocket.

"That's it?"

"Brett got most of it," he says sulkily. "He and Vince were going to split it."

She walks over to the sink, turns on the food disposal, and dumps the package down, baggie and all.

"I paid for that!" he says indignantly.

She doesn't answer. Instead she goes to the living room and picks up the remaining beer bottles. She opens each one over the sink and pours it down the drain, then puts the empties in the recycling bin under Jack's gaze.

When she's finished, she scrubs the sink out with bleach. Then she turns to Jack. His nose is still swollen, but the redness seems to be going down.

"Go pack your bag," she says. She's made her decision. What if this drug dealer comes looking for Jack? Or what if Brett talks him into another stupid stunt? There's only one way to keep Jack safe. She can't trust anyone else, even Barry. If Jack gets hurt again, she'll be too far away to save him.

"I did already," he says sullenly. "I was going to bring it to Barry's tonight."

"Pack a bigger one," she tells him. "Change of plans. You're not going to Barry's, pal. You're coming to England with me."

Chapter Six

Holly settles back into her seat with a deep sigh, the complimentary glass of champagne clutched in her hand. Jack is stuck back in economy, but Holly doesn't have the slightest pang of guilt. After what he's put her through today, he's lucky she didn't strap him to a wing.

His last-minute ticket cost a fortune, and they had to take a later flight with room for both of them. Then Holly had to call his school and explain his absence. Arrange for assignments to be emailed over. Placate the headmaster over pulling Jack out so close to the end of term—although she really shouldn't have to, given what she pays each year for Jack's tuition.

Finally she texted Barry. He wasn't surprised, which makes her wonder. Barry's always been good at spotting trouble almost before it happens. Maybe that's why Jack hasn't wanted to hang out at Barry's house lately.

It's too late for regrets, but she can't shake the disquieting feeling she's making a mistake by bringing him. On their infrequent visits to London in the past, she's had time to plan their trips with military precision, keeping him busy but also within arm's reach. But in Cornwall, she'll be searching for Eden. She won't be able to keep Jack close for that. She won't be able to protect him. She downs a large gulp of her drink.

At least his nose looks better, though still a bit swollen. She'd made him shower, shave, and change his clothes before they left for the airport. She'd been terrified one of the drug-sniffing dogs would pick up the scent of pot, and a search of their luggage was the last thing she needed. She's packed the unlabeled cream in her bag. It's all she has to protect him.

Jack sulked and raged all afternoon, right up until they got on the plane. But she has no doubt now that he's out of her direct line of sight, he'll charm any female flight attendants lucky enough to come his way. Too bad for him there aren't any open seats in first class.

When Holly deplanes, she waits for Jack so they can go through customs together. He comes out grinning, a nice change from the expression he was wearing when she showed him to his seat.

"What's up?"

"Nothing," he says. But he can't resist. "I think that flight attendant totally wanted my number. Did you see her? She was hot!"

"Lucky you," she says. In truth, he's a beautiful boy. Even while she's walking next to him, other women slide frequent glances his way. He's handsome, but there's something else. He radiates youth and health, a subtle golden glow that's almost irresistible.

Once they're through customs, she hands him back his phone, which she'd confiscated earlier. "I put you on my international plan—you have a limited amount of data, so don't use it all up today," she warns. She passes him some money and tells him to find breakfast and meet her at the car rental window.

By the time he returns, with a horrible pastry for each of them and a passable cup of tea for her, she's secured their car.

"Are we going to Grandma's?" he asks as he straps himself in.

"I wasn't able to reach her. You know your grandmother. She's probably off on another vacation," Holly says, careful to keep her own disappointment out of her voice. Jane's an inveterate traveler, incapable of staying put for more than a month at a time. She's always searching for the next new paradise, the newest adventure. "I'll try again later."

Jack falls asleep almost immediately. He misses the sunrise, the way the clouds turn a rose gold. He doesn't see the flock of birds wheeling darkly against the sky, and misses how the glass and steel of the city gives way to rolling expanses of green.

The air is different here, more liquid, expansive, the opposite of her climate-controlled life in New York. Holly breathes deeply, her shoulders unfurling for the first time in days.

But there's a reason she's chosen air-conditioning over soft breezes, a reason she insists on keeping the windows in New York closed at all times. She tells Jack it's his allergies and he complains she's overprotective, that a single gust of wind won't make him ill.

It's not the breeze. Holly is afraid he'll disappear. Just as Eden has. Just as Holly herself almost did, once.

When Jack finally wakes up, he's starving and back to being grumpy.

"Where are we?" he mutters, rubbing at his eyes.

"There's a pub not far," Holly says. "We'll stop and get something to eat before we press on to the hotel."

At the pub, she parks and sends Jack ahead, claiming that she needs to call the office. The time difference makes her lie unlikely, but he doesn't argue. Once he's out of sight, she calls the cottage and tells the day nurse what time to expect her. She wants everyone ready and assembled when she arrives. Then she hurries inside.

The pub is new to her but looks clean. She finds Jack in a corner booth puzzling over the menu.

"Can I get a Guinness?"

"What? No. Absolutely not."

50

"Why not? I looked it up before we got here. The drinking age is eighteen, but you can buy me a drink at almost any restaurant."

When he had the time to research that, Holly has no idea.

"Because I say you're not old enough, that's why. Not to mention it's not even noon. And this isn't a vacation for you. This is a punishment."

"Tell me about it," he mutters. He spends the rest of the meal alternately poking moodily at his eggs and bacon and glaring balefully at her. The waitress, an older, heavyset woman, smiles sympathetically at Holly and brings her a fresh pot of tea without being asked.

"I have one of my own," she says when Holly thanks her. "I know the signs."

Once they've settled the bill and are back in the car, he perks up a bit, looking at the rural landscape with interest. Flocks of sheep and stone houses have replaced the tidy, close-quartered villages they've been driving through.

"What type of supplier works way out here?" he asks once. "There's nothing but sheep. And cows."

"We have several in this area," she says. "We purchase a blue seaweed from one of them to use in our overnight cream." They do too, although the use of the seaweed is nothing but a cover for her trips to visit Eden—it contains no miracle ingredients that she couldn't find in seaweed back in the States.

By the time they pull into the inn's car park, Holly is exhausted and relieved to be done driving. She's booked a two-bedroom suite. The hotel has a pool and is close to a tiny sandy beach. There's a restaurant on-site as well, so there's no need for Jack to go into the village. The odds of someone recognizing him are absolutely nil, but Holly doesn't want to take a chance. The inn provides exactly what she needs—until she finds out the tutor she'd booked last-minute can't make it.

The front desk manager apologizes. "She woke up with a fever," he says. "We looked all about, but there's no one else qualified."

Holly doesn't need qualified—she needs a babysitter. But she grits her teeth and thanks the manager, telling him her son will be staying here while she's working. "Could you keep an eye on him?"

"I'll do my best," he says. The manager, who is clearly overworked, nods in an unconvincing manner.

It's not particularly reassuring. Nor is Jack, when Holly catches up to him inside their suite. He's brought in their bags, but now . . .

"What am I supposed to do here?" he complains. He's sitting on her bed, bouncing a little as he tests the springs, and the squeaking annoys Holly all the hell out of proportion, although she struggles not to show it. "There's just a stupid small TV. Not even a flat screen. And the WiFi is too slow." When he can't run or work out, Jack's fond of playing an ever-rotating list of games, although none, to Holly's relief, seem particularly violent.

"Study," she says, whisking her clothes into the closet. "As I said, this isn't a vacation."

She heads into the bathroom, takes a fast shower to wash off the travel grime and wake up. When she comes out, Jack is stretched out on the sofa in the living area, eyes closed.

"Hey," she says, shaking his arm. "Don't go to sleep."

He drowsily shakes her off. "One minute," he mumbles. "So tired."

"Jack." She nudges him again. Reflexively checks his forehead. He's cool. "You'll be up all night. Come on."

He opens one eye sleepily, notices that she's changed into slacks and a blazer, and sits up. "You're going out? Already?"

"I told you, this is work for me. I have to meet with the seaweed farmers. I won't be gone too long. A couple of hours at most." She crosses her fingers to cover the lies.

"If you get hungry, order something from room service or go down to the restaurant, but wait to have dinner with me, okay?" Holly's read that dinner with parents is one of the biggest factors in raising well-adjusted teenagers. No matter what crisis she's facing, she always tries to make it home to eat with him, even if it means going back into the office later. "Do some studying, hit the pool, but don't leave the hotel. I'll be back before you know it."

"Can I come with you?"

"No," she responds, too quickly. "Not today, at least. I have too much to do." She leans over and kisses his forehead. "I'll see you soon."

She leaves him glaring on the couch, but at least he's awake. He can't get into too much trouble at the isolated, half-empty hotel—as long as he stays there. Holly's only option at this point is to hope that he does.

The hotel is on the outskirts of the village, new in the years since she's left. But the village looks remarkably the same. There's a pub, a chemist's shop, a fishmonger, and a butcher, all with brightly painted wooden fronts. A small grocery store at the far end, followed by a handful of houses. Overlaid over it all, the sharp tang of the sea. And then she's through the village and into open country, driving toward the house. No more than fifteen minutes later and she's topping the grassy knoll that frames the view of Grace House. She pulls the car over to the side of the road.

As always, her heart catches in her throat, the way it has since the very first day she saw it. Somehow that makes it worse—with all that's happened, the house can still evoke a visceral response from her; it isn't simply a pile of stones. The house stands there unchanged—and she does not.

She'd been six months pregnant with the twins when she first saw this house.

"We need a break, before you melt," Robert had said, and bundled her into his wildly impractical red sports car and out of the hot city. It was unlike him—he'd just gotten started at the brokerage firm and was eager for everyone there to take him seriously. He had enough family money to live comfortably, if not well, but he wasn't ever the type to sit back—that was one of the things she'd loved about him ever since the night she'd gazed down from her mother's staircase and seen his blue eyes looking up at her.

"Where are we going?" she'd asked, her belly barely fitting into the car's passenger side.

"Never you mind," he'd said, revving the engine. They left London late Friday afternoon, and by the time they'd arrived, it was too dark to see the outside. She'd gotten a sense of age and mass, but was so exhausted she fell asleep as soon as she'd climbed into the bed. In the morning, she'd woken to boring white walls and heavy drapes, no art or color anywhere.

She'd poked Robert until he'd opened his eyes.

"Not your usual style," she'd said. Robert loved his flash. And he'd smiled and lumbered out of bed and drawn the curtain back and she'd caught her breath. The view was spectacular. Dark blue ocean contrasted with sloping green hills. Brightly colored boats bobbed and rocked in the water, all beneath a brilliant sky. With no other distractions on the walls, the window dominated the room.

"Like it?"

She couldn't speak, just nodded.

"If you like it, it's ours," he'd told her, then laughed, a bit ruefully. "It's ours even if you don't like it, actually. I put a payment down last week." He climbed back into bed and kissed her belly through her T-shirt. "It will be a great place to raise them in the summer. There's nothing around. They can get away from everything." Away from the Darling name, he'd meant. From the paparazzi and the tourists who drove by the London house to gawk, from the fans and the stalkers. His kisses trailed up, to her collarbone, her neck, her lips. "So can we."

She turns her thoughts away, won't let herself remember what they'd done next. They'd had two summers with the twins, a few stolen weekends during the rest of the year. One Christmas holiday, their last as a family. So cold in the morning she could see her breath, and even Robert, normally a furnace of warmth, had yelped when she'd pulled back the covers. She'd worried the twins would catch cold, so she'd warmed their beds with the ancient hot-water bottles she'd found in a cabinet and made them wear sweaters to bed.

What else had she worried about in those days? Simple things, probably. Whether the twins would ever sleep through the night. Croup—Isaac had it several times. Making sure Jack, who was always so hard to catch, so fast moving, didn't get too close to the water on cold afternoons, or plunge in over his head in the summer. Normal things, although they seemed like the end of the world at the time.

But now she knows she'd worried about the wrong things. She never sat up at night worrying about drunk lorry drivers, about how small Robert's beloved sports car was, how a collision could crush it like a tin can in a giant's fist. She'd never imagined the awful wheezing sounds Robert could make, and how even more terrible than the noise was the silence when he stopped. Most of all, she never thought to worry about how gut-emptying it would be to hear absolutely nothing from the back seat where the twins sat, no matter how many times she screamed their names.

She would give anything, would give her entire life, to go back in time for one more day when her husband's cold feet and her baby's croupy cough were the only things that kept her from sleeping. But she can't. So she puts the car in neutral and coasts the rest of the way down the hill, between the stone walls that mark the entrance to Grace House. She stops in a pool of shadow and gets out beneath the giant elm that saved her son but took her daughter in exchange.

Chapter Seven

The nurses are waiting, peering out the window of the front hall. By the time Holly reaches Grace House's door they've come out and cluster about her. They all begin to talk at once, a swirling cloud of words she can barely follow.

She raises a hand. "One at a time." She points to the woman closest to her. It's Maria, who has operated as charge nurse for the past year. "Walk me through what happened. And let's do it inside, so you can show me as you talk."

They go through the day step by step. Who was on duty, what procedures were followed, how it was discovered that Eden was missing. Everything, it seems, was done as Holly has wanted, right up until the moment the nurse opened the door and found Eden gone.

Everything, that is, but the window. But each nurse insists that she did not open it, that it always remained closed on her shift, as Dr. Darling had ordered. They have no explanation for how it could have been found ajar. They walk en masse down the hall to the former library, now converted to Eden's room. Holly opens the door, and the four women crowd around her in the doorway, anxious, she can tell, to show that they've searched every inch and that Eden cannot be found, that she will not magically appear from behind the curtains or inside the closet.

But Holly asks them to wait outside, closes the door firmly behind her. She takes a deep breath and looks around.

The room hasn't changed since her last visit. The hospital bed is still tucked in the far corner. An IV pole stands next to it, empty bag dangling. There's a heart monitor, electrodes slung around its top. A vase of daisies, lilies, and roses is tucked into the niche opposite, the flowers wilted and fading. The room is empty. What else had she expected?

Still, she looks. She slides her hand beneath the pillow, pulls down the sheets. Checks under the bed, which is spotlessly clean. Opens the closet, where dressing gowns and medical supplies are neatly stacked. She finds nothing unusual, nothing out of place. At last she crosses to the window. She'd asked Maria to leave it as it was when they'd discovered Eden was missing. It's open to its full height, something Holly has always expressly forbidden.

She examines the sill. A faint film of dust or pollen, but no thread, no bit of cloth, the way there always is in television thrillers. She leans out, holding one hand on the bottom of the raised sash to make sure it can't come crashing down on her neck. The grass below the window is muddy, but there's no sign of anything that resembles a footprint.

As she's pulling her head back in, a soft breeze caresses her face. She can see the tree from here, but its leaves aren't moving. And then she hears the strangest thing. A ringing, like tiny golden bells. She searches the tree for wind chimes but sees nothing.

The bells sound like laughter.

She pulls her head back in so violently she bangs it on the window before slamming the casement shut.

There's a knock on the door. "Dr. Darling?" The voice is soft. "Dr. Darling, the gardener is here." Holly sighs, kneads her neck. She's so bloody tired, and she has the sense she's forgetting something, but she has no idea what. She opens the door.

Maria is waiting on the other side, her face sorrowful. It occurs to

Holly that perhaps the nurses aren't solely worried about losing their jobs or their work cards. It is possible that they genuinely care about her daughter.

"Did you find anything?" Maria asks. Holly shakes her head. Maria gingerly touches her arm, as if she expects a rebuke. "We will keep looking. Are you sure no police?"

"Yes," Holly says sharply. "No police." At least not yet. Not until she's searched as much as she can on her own. She flounders for a plausible explanation. "Our family, we are . . . well-known. For the story, the one about the Darling children. Do you know it?"

Maria nods. She walks into the room, glancing back as if for permission, and crossing to the bookcase on the far wall, takes down an old illustrated volume. "*Peter Pan*," she says, holding it out to Holly.

Holly sucks in her breath. Right after Eden's accident, she'd searched for answers in that story, but she hadn't found a clue. She thought she'd gotten rid of all the copies, but here's proof she missed one. She doesn't take the book.

"One of the girls found it in an upstairs closet," Maria explains, flipping through the pages.

"Yes, that's the one," Holly says. "And Eden . . . well, she's not like other children. I don't want the press to make up some terrible story, you see. It would only make it worse."

Maria nods again. "No, she is not like others," she says, and Holly tenses, but Maria's next words let her relax. "She has the growing disease, as you explained. I have seen it for myself." She puts her hand on Holly's arm again, this time more confidently. "But you will find her, Dr. Darling, and you will fix her." She pulls a phone out from her uniform's pocket and passes it to Holly. "You have not seen this one yet."

Holly takes the phone. Maria sends her a photo every month, so that she can see Eden for herself. In this picture, her daughter's face looks like someone who is almost an adult. Holly pulls out her own phone and opens the album where she stores Eden's images, compares last month's photo with the one on Maria's phone. Eden has lost the roundness of middle school. Her cheekbones are sharp, her face elongated. Even with the softness that comes with sleep, she could easily pass for eighteen. Her disease is worsening.

Holly returns the phone. "Send it to me, please," she says, her voice unsteady. "And now, the gardener?"

"He is outside."

Even before Holly crosses behind the hedge wall, the scent of the garden calls to her, as familiar as a lover's skin. Rich, loamy earth. Sweetness and rot. Primrose and bluebells. Fat bees buzzing against spiky lavender blooms. She's dizzy suddenly, intoxicated, drunk on a wave of heat and memories. There's a rosemary plant near the entrance, and she crushes a sprig in her hands, brings the bruised stem to her face. The clean, astringent scent helps settle her.

The gardener is watching her, clearly concerned. A quiet, gawky man, he's eager to help but clueless. Holly runs through all her questions, but it's pointless.

"It was a regular spring day," he says. "Quiet. But really bright. I remember on account of my shadow."

Holly freezes. "Excuse me?"

He scratches the back of his neck, looks down at the ground. "It's balmy," he says apologetically. "But I remember thinking how big and black my shadow looked. The kind you get on the beach late in the day, where it just stretches for miles. I was working in the back garden, mowing, and every time I passed the house—"

"Yes?" she prompts, impatiently.

"It was like my shadow reached for it." He looks at her face. "You must think I'm daft."

"No," she says. But it's as much a response to his story as it is a plea. That kind of shadow can't be here. Not at Grace House. Not near Eden.

The gardener is walking down the drive to his truck when he stops and turns back to her. "The village will be real sorry about your girl," he says shyly. "We still remember you, from the summers. Your boys were some fast little ones. I tend the cemetery too, you know. There's speedwell growing about, and I always leave a bit on your little 'un's grave. You probably never seen it—it dries up and blows away after a day or so. But, well, he's not forgotten." He scuffs his shoe against the gravel, then walks away.

As his truck pulls out, Holly walks to the tree. She leans her forehead against its trunk, closes her eyes. The leaves rustle overhead and it's as if they're whispering secrets too low for her to understand. It's the time of day she used to love, a sleepy early evening when the sky is still unnaturally light. The rich smells of earth and cut grass fill the air, and beneath it all is the sharp scent of the sea. What time does it get dark in England in the spring? She's been away for so long she's forgotten. She's let herself forget so much.

Chapter Eight

The day of the accident, Holly forgot the cocoa.

It was a beautiful day. The first morning since the car crash that Holly had woken up and realized there was still color left in the world. She looked out the window and saw blue sky, saw green grass, and it shocked her. Everything had been a flat, monotonous gray since Isaac and Robert died.

The day demanded to be recognized. So she bundled the children up and took them outside, carrying Jack, letting Eden run ahead in her favorite blue party dress. At two, she was almost as big as her five-year-old brother. Holly spread a blanket under the tree, unpacked the hamper that she'd filled with sandwiches and fruit and a cake. A party, of sorts. A quiet celebration that they were still alive, even if the ones they loved were not.

While Holly set out the food, Eden took a book from behind her back and began reading it to Jack. It was *Peter Pan*. "Where did you get that?" Holly asked, trying to hide her loathing for it. Not, *How did you learn to read?* She'd almost ceased being surprised by what Eden could do. After all, she'd been a surprise since the beginning.

The doctors estimated Holly was four months along when they found the pregnancy. Their shock was obvious—how had they missed it, with all the tests and exams they'd performed during her hospital stay and recovery?

But Holly knew better. This baby came after the car crash, no matter what the growth charts and sonograms said. And she grew crazy fast, at a rate the doctors couldn't explain. They fiddled with Holly's medication, blaming the growth on the drugs she took after the wreck. Still, she went into labor almost two months early, delivering a perfect baby girl. Perfect, and by all appearances full term. Eden hadn't stopped amazing everyone since.

Now Eden paused her reading as Holly looked for the thermos, then realized she'd left it in the kitchen of Grace House.

"It's okay, Mama," Eden said. "I can watch him."

Holly hesitated. Since he'd come home from hospital, it was rare for her to let Jack out of her sight. She'd even put a bed for herself in his room those first few weeks. But how much trouble could he get into, in the short time she'd be gone?

So she left them and ran to the house, breathing in the sharp, sweet scents of spring. She'd grabbed the thermos off the counter and hurried out. She'd been gone for what, maybe five minutes? She's been over it so many times in her head, but the outcome never changes.

When she'd come back, they were both sitting on a branch of the elm, tucked into the crook, the book open between them. Ten, perhaps twelve feet off the ground. Sunlight dappled their faces, tiny bits of gold. There were no steps, no easy handholds, no ladder to explain how they'd gotten there. How had Jack, who could barely walk unsupported, managed to climb that high?

"Jack, Eden!" Holly called, not thinking. They looked down, startled, and Jack wobbled precariously before regaining his balance.

"Mummy, Eden says she can fly," he said, excitedly. "She can, can't she?"

"Don't move," Holly said, trying to keep the panic from her voice. "Stay there. How did you even get that high?" She searched the trunk for a foothold. Nothing.

"I have him, Mama. I have him," Eden said, stretching her hand toward her brother. The branch swayed.

"No, don't. Sit still, do you understand me? Both of you. Please, just sit still."

She could run to the house, find a chair or a ladder, but what if they fell while she was gone? She kicked off her shoes, wrapped her arms as far around the trunk as she could, and shimmied up. She managed to get a foot, then two, off the ground. She kept going, gritting her teeth, the rough bark ripping into the soft flesh on the underside of her arms, her bad leg cramping and burning. But she was reaching them. She was almost there. Jack turned to her, smiling, and as he did, his arm jarred the edge of the book. It fell, plummeting toward the ground.

"I'll get it," Eden said happily. The faintest sound beneath her voice, like laughter or tiny bells. She leaned forward, as if to push off, and Holly shouted. Fiercely. Terribly. And Eden looked down and saw her face.

All these years later, Holly can still see it, the way the smile, the happiness drained out of her. Her fingers not quite brushing Jack's as she fell. The horror of her scream. The sickening thud. Then silence, broken by Jack's cries.

In shock, Holly managed to snag the end of his jumper. She swung him to the ground before tumbling down herself. She left him on the grass and ran to Eden.

"Eden, can you hear me?" No response. Holly felt for a pulse. It was there, but faint and erratic, and there was a horrifying amount of blood. *Oh, God.*

"I'll be right back," she said to Jack, as calmly as she could. He nodded, crying. She raced into the house to call 999, her fingers trembling as she punched the numbers. "This is Grace House. My daughter's had a terrible fall. She's breathing, but not conscious," she told the voice on the other end, then let the receiver drop.

She grabbed a clean tea towel to stanch the blood, wrapped ice in another one, and pounded back, willing her damaged leg not to collapse. She sank onto the grass next to Eden.

"Eden, honey, it's Mummy. I'm going to put something on your head that will make it better, okay? Can you hear me, Eden?"

Still no response. Jack's breath was coming in hiccuping sobs. He'd left the edge of the blanket where she'd deposited him and crawled closer. He was stroking Eden's hand, kneeling in a puddle of blood. Holly tried to move him back, but he clung to Eden even tighter, so she gave up.

Carefully, she wiped the blood away from Eden's head, assessing the swelling and the source. The cut was so deep she could see bone. She placed the towel with ice on the large bump that was developing and held it there with one hand. With the index finger and thumb of her other hand, she carefully pried up Eden's eyelid. The pupil contracted. She did the same with the other eye, uttered a short, silent prayer of thanks when the same thing happened.

"Is Eden dead?"

"What? No, honey." She took a few precious seconds to reach out and wrap her free arm around Jack. "She's hurt, badly hurt, but she's alive," she said, hugging him and not letting herself think beyond that. "You know what I bet she'd like? If you talked to her. I need to try and find out where else she's hurt, so maybe you could tell her a story while I do that, okay?" She gave him a final squeeze, then let him go.

"Can she hear me?" he asked doubtfully.

"Of course she can," Holly said. She turned her attention back to Eden. She didn't want to move Eden's neck—she didn't have anything to brace it with—so she contented herself with feeling along the length of her limbs. Eden's left arm was twisted at an odd angle, clearly broken. Holly tickled her toes—Eden never would keep her shoes on—and at the reflexive curl away, relief flooded her so hard she gasped.

Jack had been whispering to Eden, but at Holly's exhalation he stopped, eyes wide and frightened.

"It's all right," she told him. "It's good—she can feel her feet, can move her toes. See?" She did it again, and again Eden's toes curled. "If . . . if everything else is okay, it means she'll most likely be able to walk."

"Not like me?" There was something in his voice, a pain that cut at her even now.

"You do walk, Jack, you know that."

He didn't reply.

There were sirens in the distance. It seemed as if she had called for help hours ago, although she knew it couldn't have been more than a few minutes. To Jack, she said, "The ambulance is almost here, love."

He leaned forward, his ear almost brushing Eden's lips. He stayed in that position for a minute, then straightened. "She doesn't want to go," he said.

"Go where?"

"To hospital. She doesn't want to. She wants to stay here with us. At Grace House."

"How do you know that?"

He looked at her as if she were crazy. "She told me."

"Well, she has to," she said, ignoring his last sentence. "I can't help her here—she needs doctors."

"You're a doctor."

"Yes, but not a people doctor. I can't do much more than this," she said, nodding at the ice she still held against Eden's head. "Eden, sweetheart," she said, leaning closer. "It's going to be okay. We're going to go with you and get you help." She brushed her lips over Eden's forehead.

The sirens were closer. In a moment, Holly could see them—an ambulance and, lumbering behind, a police car. Everything blurred after that—the way they took Eden's vital signs, looking somber, the way they carefully maneuvered her onto the stretcher, her face as white as the sheet beneath her.

There was no one to stay with Jack, and he wasn't allowed in the ambulance. Instead the responding officer offered to follow behind in his car. He turned to Jack. "Shall we use the sirens, then?" Jack had looked down at the ground. He hated sirens.

"Jack." Under the guise of a hug, Holly helped him to his feet. "I need to stay with Eden," she said as he clung to her. "I'll see you in a little bit. You'll be all right?"

He nodded.

"That's my boy." And then she was in the ambulance speeding away. She couldn't see Jack, couldn't watch his slow progress to the police car. Instead she grasped Eden's hand, felt it cold and limp in hers. Put every ounce of her being into willing the words *Don't die* into Eden's head.

She didn't realize she was speaking aloud until the EMT put a hand on her shoulder, making her jump. "She's stable. For now. We're about half an hour out."

"Right," she said grimly. She knew from experience that stable wasn't enough.

She stayed with Eden as they brought her through the emergency doors. She held her hand right up until they got her to the OR. And then they made her let go.

She filled out the forms they pushed at her. Hesitated a little too long at the line asking for Eden's father's information before firmly writing, *Deceased.* She called her mother, who didn't answer, so she left a message, asking Jane to come. She checked on Jack, made sure the officer could stay with him. And then she waited. A lifetime seemed to pass before anyone came to talk with her. The world had descended into gray again before the doctor called her name.

Eden was *stable.* That word again. There was swelling, but they wouldn't know more until some time had passed. Multiple stitches to close the scalp wound, some bruising, but nothing like they'd expected to see in an accident of this magnitude.

"Amazing, really," the doctor said, shaking his head. "She's still being examined. But you should be able to see her in an hour or so."

"What about her arm? The left one? It looked broken to me."

The doctor frowned. "There's evidence of a former fracture there, but nothing new. I take it she's an active child?"

"Former fracture?" she'd said, confused. She'd been about to ask more when the doctor's phone buzzed. Before she could speak, he was already turning away.

She found Jack in the cafeteria. The policeman who'd come to the house was next to him, drinking tea.

"Here she is," he said to Jack. "I told you she'd be back soon. How's the little girl?"

"She's stable," Holly said with a quick glance at Jack, who hadn't looked up. She sank onto the cafeteria seat. Now that the adrenaline was wearing off, she was exhausted.

"Brave laddie you have," the policeman said, nodding to Jack. "Although he doesn't care for sirens. He made that plain."

"No," Holly said. "Neither of us do."

"Not a good place for him to be then," the policeman said, jerking his chin toward the outside, where another ambulance wailed its arrival. "There's no one you can leave him with?"

Holly shook her head. "I put a call in to my mother, but . . ."

The policeman, it turned out, had a teenage niece who babysat. "I can ring her and see if she can fill in for a few hours, if you like. And run you home in the meantime to get your things."

"That would be amazing, thank you." She realized she didn't even know his name. "Officer . . ."

"Beale. Come along then." He pushed back his chair. "I'll fetch the car and meet you out front. I'll give Mallory a call along the way."

"Let me tell the nurses," Holly said. "Come on, Jack. We're going home."

She scooped him up in her arms. Holly appreciated that Officer Beale didn't comment on how big Jack was, or how he was too old to be carried. Then again, unless the policeman was a complete fool, he'd probably already grasped how laborious it was for Jack to move anywhere on his own.

She took the elevator to the nurses' station, still carrying Jack. She needed to see Eden before she left, to hold her, if she could. The same doctor who had spoken to her before was standing outside a patient's door. When he saw her, he frowned, and the bottom dropped out of her world.

"Eden," she said, her voice barely more than a whisper.

But no. "Ah, Mrs. Darling, good," he said. "I wanted to confirm— could you tell me how old your daughter is?"

"She's two," Holly said. She wouldn't let herself think about Eden's chubby arms, the cloud of curls that wreathed her face, her funny high-pitched voice. The way she'd looked on the ground under the tree.

The doctor raised an eyebrow. Slightly, but Holly saw it.

"My daughter has a rare disorder," she explained. "It causes her to grow faster than other children her age."

"Is she seeing someone for it?"

"She has a specialist in London." She tried to calm her breathing. She should have expected the doctor to notice—in the panic of Eden's fall, she hadn't been thinking clearly.

"Well. You may want to have them consult on this. Just in case."

Holly nodded. She didn't say that she'd stopped taking Eden, that the specialist hadn't been able to find anything to explain her rapid development. But Holly knew exactly what—and who—had caused it. And there was no one who could help, not now.

Officer Beale's niece was on the front steps of Grace House when they arrived. A tall girl with flaming-red hair, she waved when she spotted them. Beale made the introductions and left. Standing inside the house, Holly caught Mallory's horrified gaze at Jack and realized he was still covered in blood.

"Jack, let me wash you up, all right?"

"No."

"Come on, baby, you're all dirty. At least let's change your clothes." Holly moved to pull his jumper over his head, but he scooted away across the floor on his bottom. His lower lip was trembling.

"What's the matter?"

"Don't want to."

Holly hesitated. She couldn't leave him like this. She looked at his pants again. The knee was torn—he must have cut himself when he fell. Some of the blood was his.

"Does your leg hurt? Let me see."

He didn't answer. His cheeks were unnaturally flushed, his eyes bright. He looked as if he was running a fever.

"Jack." She took a step toward him.

"NO!" The force of it startled her—it wasn't like him to be so intractable. She backed away, spread her hands to show she wouldn't touch him. "All right," she said. "Stay like that, if you want."

She told Mallory not to worry, that she'd bathe Jack when she got home, whenever that might be. Luckily the girl was fine with spending the night. Holly packed a quick bag, kissed Jack, and left.

On the ride to hospital, she checked her voicemail messages. Nothing from the doctor, but there was a message from her mother, full of cool concern and a promise to arrive first thing in the morning. *Don't rush*, Holly thought bitterly, then immediately felt guilty. Jane had been a rock star after the car crash, moving Holly and Jack into her London house and helping them through the worst days. But things had changed between them since Eden's birth. And maybe it wasn't entirely fair to blame Jane for the distance that had grown between them.

At hospital, Holly checked in at the nurses' station first. There'd been no change, no sign of Eden awakening, which was unusual but not necessarily alarming. Another scan was scheduled for the morning, the nurse said, but at the moment Eden's vitals were good.

"Poor little angel," she said, her voice sympathetic.

And when Holly entered Eden's room, her daughter did look angelic. Someone had washed the blood from her scalp, and her blonde halo of curls spread across the pillow. Holly crawled into bed with her, careful not to dislodge the IV and monitors. It was a skill she'd perfected over the past two years, and one she almost could not stand to use again. She tried not to think of Isaac, not to think of Robert, but to be here, present, with Eden.

Instead she listened to Eden's breathing, reassured by the quiet regularity of it, by the warmth of her skin, by how, even in the antiseptic atmosphere of hospital, she smelled like fresh air, like cut grass and sunshine.

"Hey, sweet girl," she whispered. "Time to wake up now." She talked of Jack, who missed her, reminded Eden of the kittens they'd found playing in the hedge yesterday, of the cold ocean water and fresh air that waited for her at Grace House. She painted a story for her tiny girl to anchor her firmly to this world and keep her from leaving.

But Eden didn't respond. Holly slipped an arm under her, curled her body closer. Eden was so warm nestled against her. It was the first time Holly had stopped moving since Eden fell, and she was exhausted. The beeps and clicking of the monitors turned into the warning calls of the birds among the branches, the draft from the hallway into a cool breeze as Holly fell asleep.

Sunlight dapples the leaves as she and Eden and Jack climb the branches of the giant elm. The sky is so blue, and somewhere in the distance a rooster crows, making Holly uneasy. *Peter?* No. She hears the bells of a wind chime, like tiny musical laughter, but she can't see anyone but her children.

They're all going to jump, and this time Holly's going to fly with them. She takes a deep breath. The ground is so far away, and then she's plummeting through the air toward it. Eden's giggling, but Holly is holding her hand and she knows that she's dragging her daughter down. She wakes in panic, heart pounding, just before she hits the earth.

A thin gray light is coming through the window, and a nurse is checking Eden's IV bag.

"All right, love?" the nurse asks, and Holly nods, her mouth dry and sour. The dream is still with her. Eden must have been so terrified when she fell. She hit the ground so hard. Hard enough to knock herself unconscious.

Hard enough to break her arm.

Holly slides her hand out from beneath Eden, pulls down the sheet that's covering her, and stares at her daughter's left arm. Runs her fingers gently down it. There's no bump, no swelling, nothing to indicate it's injured at all. Holly thinks back to how it looked right after Eden fell. It was twisted at such an unnatural angle it must have been broken. So how is it fine now?

She tries to recall what the doctor said when she'd asked him— something about an old break at the spot. But Eden's never broken a bone before in her life. She's barely ever had a scratch. Aside from her precocious growth rate, she's always been a healthy child.

She stares at Eden's face, at the dimples in the corners of her cheeks, the long-lashed lids. She looks as if she could be five years old, easily. There's a whisper of unease in the back of Holly's mind, trying to break free, but Holly won't let it. She can't right now. If she does, it will drown out everything else, and she doesn't have the strength for that. She tells herself instead that whatever is causing Eden's growth, whatever is keeping her from waking up, cannot possibly be related to who her father is.

It can't.

✳

She spends the next few hours at Eden's bedside, talking and singing to her until her throat is hoarse. Holly's waiting for the nurses to take Eden for another scan when the phone rings. It's Jane, who is now at Grace House.

"Everything is fine, but if you can leave, I think you should come home," her mother says without preamble.

"Is Jack all right?" Holly can't bear to think anything else could have happened.

"Yes. But there's something you need to see."

Holly presses her, but Jane won't elaborate, only repeats that there's something Holly must see.

"All right," Holly says at last. She glances at Eden, who is resting motionless in the bed. "I'll be there as soon as I can."

She couldn't go with Eden for the scan anyhow. She kisses her cheek, asks the nurses to call her if anything changes, and hurries to the car.

On the ride home, she runs through the possibilities, her mind stuck on an endless, horrible loop. Jane isn't given to hyperbole, so whatever it is, it must be major. Despite Jane's reassurances, Holly's stomach cramps with fear. She presses down the accelerator until she's well above the speed limit.

And then she's pulling into the yard at Grace House. There's movement behind the front window, and before Holly can even get out of the car, Jane has opened the front door. She stands to the side, as if waiting for someone. Holly starts toward her mother, but Jane motions her to stay.

And then Jack is running out the door. Moving so fast he stumbles, almost falls, but rights himself and keeps on, laughing. Holly gasps. He's racing to her—he's *flying*—and he's doing it all on his own.

Chapter Nine

M a'am? Dr. Darling?"

Holly blinks, realizes her forehead is still resting against the tree, and judging by the crick in her neck, she's been there for some time. She straightens. It's Maria.

"Are you all right?" Maria asks. "May I get you tea?"

"I'm fine," Holly says. "There's no need. I was . . . thinking." Remembering. How Jack's crisscross of scars faded from his body. How she'd finally realized what caused this miracle. The beginning of it all—the research, the experiments, even Darling Skin Care.

She looks at her watch. It's well past dinnertime. "I'll be back first thing in the morning. Please ask the other nurses to think of anything that happened that day that seemed out of the ordinary, all right? And search the house and grounds one last time. Check every corner, behind every tree and shrub. I don't care how small."

Maria nods. "We will do that."

Holly knows it's futile. There's no sign of Eden anywhere in the house, no clue to her disappearance. Eventually she's going to have to call the police. She shudders. No one will believe that she's done everything she can to keep Eden safe. And Jack. That her life revolves around them both, a wobbling ellipse, always tilting back and forth, never quite in balance. But it's the best that she could do, for both of them.

✳

Back at the hotel, she unlocks the door to the suite. A soccer match is blaring on the television, but Jack is asleep. An empty plate rests on the table between the beds. Holly picks it up, and as she does, her foot strikes something. She leans down and discovers an empty pint glass under the bed. She sniffs it. Beer. Relatively fresh too, although she suspects her son will try to pass it off as belonging to the room's previous tenant.

"Jack?" She shakes him, but he groans and curls up tighter. She sighs. She doesn't have the energy to have this out with him right now. She puts the plate and glass into the hallway, locks the door, and falls into bed and a deep, dreamless sleep.

She awakens to a knock on the door. Weak morning light is streaming through the windows—she never drew the curtains last night. "One moment," she calls. She pulls a jumper over her nightshirt, then struggles to the door. When she looks out the peephole, no one is there, but there's a breakfast hamper and a tea tray on the ground.

She opens the door and brings the food inside, placing it on the table in the suite's dining area. Then she goes to check on Jack. He's still sleeping.

Not for long. She shakes him awake.

"What?" he mutters, digging his head deeper into the pillow.

"Hey. Wake up. We need to talk."

"No, we don't."

"Jack!" Reluctantly he turns over to face her.

"Where did you get the beer?"

"What beer?"

"Come off it, Jack. I found it when I came back last night." It's clear from the expression on his face that he'd hoped she might not notice.

"So I had one beer, what's the big deal? It's England, I told you—everyone drinks over here."

"Given that I actually grew up here, I beg to differ," she says. "But the point is that I told you not to, and you deliberately disobeyed."

"You didn't tell me not to—you told me you wouldn't buy me a drink at the pub yesterday," he says innocently.

"Fine. Let me make it clear. No drinking while you are here. Period. Or at any other time, since you are underage. Do you understand?"

He nods sullenly.

"Good." What she doesn't say is she has no idea how alcohol or drugs might affect the injections and how long they last. Given how little they have left, she doesn't want to chance it. But she can't tell Jack that. He'll freak out and ask questions she won't be able to answer. Or, rather, doesn't want to. "And to make sure, I'll be having a word with the inn too."

He glowers. "Is that all?"

"No. There's breakfast on the table. Get up and get dressed. Study while I'm gone."

She leaves to take a shower before he can mouth off to her. When she comes out, dressed in jeans, trainers, and a jumper, he's at the table, wolfing down the baked goods. She takes a scone, kisses him on the head, and tells him she'll check in with him at lunchtime. She's happy to see he has a chem book out.

"Study hard," she says, and closes the door behind her.

At Grace House, the nurses are clustered in the kitchen. Holly talks with them each individually before she searches the house and grounds again—there must be something she's missed.

Interviewing the first two nurses leads nowhere. But Tala, the nurse who was on duty the day Eden disappears, is fidgety and anxious. As soon as the door shuts behind her, she starts to talk. She tells Holly that the nurses keep a few personal items in one of the bedrooms, for when they spend the night. She checked yesterday, when Dr. Darling asked them to search everywhere. A pair of her jeans and a T-shirt are missing.

Holly takes a breath. It could be coincidence—Tala could have lost the items, or another nurse could have borrowed them—but Tala shakes her head.

"I have asked everyone. No one has seen them," she says. She starts to say something else, then stops. Tala is the youngest of the nurses, slender and petite. With her hair pulled back with a ribbon and her face scrubbed of makeup, she looks like a child.

"And?" Holly coaxes.

Tala shakes her head. She crosses her arms, looks down at the floor. "You'll think I'm crazy."

Holly waits. The silence builds. Tala shifts in her seat. "It's just . . . ," she says at last. "The bedroom we use—it's the blue one on the second floor. You know which one I mean?"

Holly nods. Of course she does. She painted that room herself, the perfect shade of blue for the twins. It has two dormer windows that face the back and window seats upholstered with a truck print. She hasn't been in it for years.

Tala leans forward, her voice dropping as if she's afraid she'll be overheard, although there's only the two of them in the room. "It's nothing really," she says. "Just . . . I don't like to stay there. Not by myself. It always feels like someone is watching. I've looked, and there's no one there. But I still feel it. And then last week . . ." She pauses, looks at her lap. Holly follows her gaze, notices her cuticles are chewed bloody and ragged. "Last week, when I turned around quickly, I'd swear I saw a shadow by the window. And then it was just gone. Which is impossible, because that window is on the second floor." She shakes her head. "Crazy, right?"

"Crazy," Holly agrees. Her voice is so steady no one could tell she's covered in goose bumps.

"That's what I thought." Tala shifts uncomfortably again. "That's why I didn't want to say anything."

Holly's struggling with what to say, how to sound calm when her insides are quaking, when through the window behind Tala she catches sight of a car bumping over the road. It pauses at the top of the hill, then starts the descent that leads to Grace House. Holly frowns, distracted. She isn't expecting anyone, but perhaps one of the nurses has ordered something from the village.

The car glides to a stop in the circular driveway. There are no logos on the outside of the vehicle. Tourists, maybe. Lost and looking for the village or the beach. But there's something familiar about the person in the passenger seat, despite the glare that makes it hard to see. And then Holly's heart lurches before she even knows why, before her brain has had time to process the way he opens the door, swings his legs gracefully to the ground.

It's Jack.

Shit.

For a moment she's frozen, her stomach doing flips. But she doesn't have the luxury of more than a few seconds of indecision. She races outside and stands in front of him.

"Jack?" she manages. He's looking at the house, studying it, as if he's trying to recall if he's seen it before. For a minute she thinks he's going to ignore her. But then he looks her right in the eyes.

"Why didn't you ever tell me?"

She can't breathe. To buy time, she turns to the driver of the car, who is standing with the door open, leaning across it. It's a woman, tall and thin, with a shock of flaming-red hair. At first Holly doesn't recognize her, but then the woman smiles, and Holly flinches.

"Mallory?" she says in disbelief. All her ghosts are coming back to haunt her, it seems.

But there's no mistake. It's the girl who babysat the day of Eden's fall. This woman has the same distinctive red hair, the same quick way of moving.

"Dr. Darling? I wasn't sure you'd remember me."

"Of course. How very nice to see you again," Holly says. She brushes past Jack and extends her hand, and all the while her mind is frantically racing. Mallory was gone by the time Jack woke up all those years ago, so she hadn't witnessed those miraculous steps. But if she'd told Jack why she was there that day, how she knows him . . .

"I'm so sorry," Mallory says. "I had no idea he didn't know about Grace House. When he came into the shop, he seemed so familiar, and then, when we started talking, I figured out who he was, and . . ." She shrugs apologetically.

"No, it's fine," Holly lies. "I'd planned on telling him this trip, it's just . . . it's a hard conversation. So many memories here. Not all of them good." She stares hard at Mallory, gives the subtlest shake of her head, wills her not to speak Eden's name. To her relief, the other woman nods.

"You've raised a lovely son," she says. "I simply told him how much the village enjoyed having you here, all those years ago."

"Thank you," Holly says. She forces herself to put warmth in her tone, even if her gaze is cool. There's a beat, where under normal circumstances she'd offer Mallory tea. Invite her in.

She doesn't.

"Well, I really should be getting back," Mallory says awkwardly. "It's just me, so when I ran Jack down, I had to close the shop. I'd love to have you stop by sometime, when you have a moment," she says. She fishes out a card case from her pocket, extracts one, and hands it to Holly.

"It's the little bakery on the corner," she says. "Right next to the pub. We provide the breakfast hampers for the inn where you're staying."

"How charming," Holly says. She doesn't ask about the bakery or inquire after Mallory's uncle. So after a short pause, Mallory makes her goodbyes and drives away, leaving Holly to deal with Jack.

"So," Holly says. So much for leaving him tucked up safely at the hotel. Round one to Jack. She can hear those wind chimes again, like musical laughter, and underneath them the rustle of the long grass in the meadow near the graveyard, as clear and distinct as a voice. She waits for him to say something, so she can gauge where to start, but he doesn't speak, so she presses on.

"This is Grace House. We bought it as a summer home before you were born, and we came for weekends and whatever other time we could. Until the crash."

She pauses, but there's still no response, so she continues. "And then after, while you were recuperating, we moved here. Remember, the other day I told you we lived in Cornwall? I thought it would be a better place than the city for you. But it was a mistake. So we moved back to London, and then my little chemistry project took off and we went to America, for a fresh start."

"I'm sorry I never told you," Holly says. Her words cover so many omissions, and even as she phrases her response to shield him from the past, she aches for all he doesn't remember. The house. The glorious summers here. His sister. Forgetting is best for him, she knows it, and yet her apology is true. "I thought it would stir up memories of the car crash, and before. I didn't want to make you sad."

He looks at her, considering. "If we own this house, why aren't we staying here, instead of at the hotel? And if you didn't want to live here, why didn't you sell it?" he asks finally. There's no anger in his voice, only curiosity, and relief courses through her so hard her knees wobble. It's proof he doesn't remember, doesn't know. Because if he did, he'd be furious.

She shakes her head. "I'm not sure," she says honestly. She's thought about selling Grace House a dozen times over the years, but what would she have done with Eden? Move her to London, to a nursing home that would ask too many questions? Take her to the States, where someone might make the connection between Jack's injections and his forever-sleeping sister? No, this was better.

"I guess I was holding on to it," Holly says, surprising herself.

"Holding on to those memories from before, even if I couldn't bear to actually think about them." Eden's never been the only reason she's kept Grace House. She's just been the only reason Holly could admit to.

The sound of the bells and the rustle of the grass in the graveyard are louder now, as if the ghosts from Holly's past have decided they've been silent far too long, that now is the time to speak. They're swirling around her; they're calling out to Jack; they're wanting to be heard.

But Holly won't let them. To talk about Eden here, to remind Jack that his father and brother are buried around the corner from where he's standing—it's too much. All she's ever wanted to do for Jack since the crash is to protect him, to take away the pain of those dark years and keep him safe. But the truth is, by not talking about them, she's been protecting herself too. And she's not ready to stop.

"Can I go inside?"

Holly's been lost, listening to those voices. But now, as if on cue, Maria comes out the front door carrying a cup of tea. Holly offers a brief prayer of thanksgiving that Maria's not in nursing scrubs today but regular street clothes. She holds up a hand to forestall her.

"I'm sorry, give me one moment," Holly says. She puts an arm around Jack's shoulders, physically moving him farther from the house so no one can overhear.

"I don't think so, sweetheart," she says quietly. "Not today. I've been renting to a family and . . . their daughter is quite sick." She hesitates, then piles on to the lie. "They're interested in purchasing it, actually. That's why I came by today. But listen. There's a beach around the corner where you used to play. That little path behind the house leads to it. Why don't you go check it out? I'll meet you there in a few minutes."

Jack doesn't move at first. But then he catches sight of Maria's expression. She's clearly miserable. He nods and starts down the path Holly points out. She steels herself, then crosses the lawn to the front steps and to Maria.

"What is it?"

"Ma'am," Maria begins, then licks her lips and starts again. "Dr. Darling. There is one place I had not looked. One place we did not check."

"Yes?" Holly wants to reach out and throttle Maria to make her hurry.

"The safe. I did not check it because we had no need, without Eden, to go into it. But while you were talking to Tala, I remembered. And went to check."

The safe is the same as the one Holly has in her lab at home. It's a refrigerated, secure container. Every two months—the same amount of time the Red Cross requires between donations—the nurse on duty is supposed to take 470 milliliters of blood from Eden. Maria then places the blood in the safe. She is the only person, aside from Holly, who has the code.

"And?" Holly asks, although she already knows the answer.

"The blood is gone. All of it."

This is what Holly forgot to check yesterday. The most important thing. Without these samples, all she has left for Jack is what's left in her New York lab. It's not enough. And it's too far away if there's an emergency.

"Are you sure?" she asks helplessly.

Maria nods. "There were three full bags when I opened it last. There are none there now."

Holly's stomach contracts as if she's been punched. For one wild moment, she thinks that Maria must have done it. She must have seen something, figured out how valuable Eden's blood is. But in her heart she knows. The fail-safes she's put in place make it almost impossible.

There's only one other person in this world who would know how to benefit from Eden's blood. One person who could move so lightly no one would notice, one person who could slip in and out of a window without being seen.

In the distance, she swears she can hear a rooster crow, and the hairs on the back of her neck stand up. It's ridiculous; it's only an animal. But as she leans against the front door to catch her breath, she sees, under the tree, a flash of something red. As if she's sleepwalking, she walks over.

Impossible, she thinks. Just like a summer shadow on a spring day. Or the feeling of being watched from a remote second-floor window. But she bends to pick it up anyhow. A red feather. She turns and looks around the space. There is nothing else. It's a message. And a threat— to her, to Eden, and to Jack.

She knows where she has to go. To London. To find Eden's father.

Impossible as it sounds, to find Peter Pan.

Chapter Ten

There's another, less-traveled path behind the house than the one Jack took to the beach. Holly uses it now. Despite her urgency, she can't help but brush her hands against the hedgerow that lines the way, can't help but stop at the top of the hill for a second and breathe in the scent of damp, of moist earth and oldness and new-mown grass that she associates only with this place.

One lazy summer day she and Robert found their way here. The twins, exhausted after a morning spent swimming in the ocean, nevertheless grumbled as the nanny shepherded them back to the house for naps. At the split in the path, Holly turned to follow them, but Robert tugged her away.

"Just for a little bit," he told her. "Let's walk." So they had, into a grassy hollow studded with age-grayed stones. They'd lain on the ground, listened to the sleepy buzzing of insects, watched the clouds pass overhead.

"'Lark song and sea sounds in the air and splendour, splendour everywhere,'" he'd murmured into her neck. Holly stands stock-still as she remembers and touches the hollow of her throat. When the time had come, she'd known where he and Isaac belonged.

On her trips to Cornwall she's never failed to visit them, to spend an hour in the quiet, her hands on cool stone, whispering love notes and a lullaby. Jack hasn't been here in years, not since they left England for the States. Those days are lost to him. The crash and subsequent surgeries blotted the early memories from his brain. Even if they hadn't, the thick fog of adolescent oblivion keeps everything but his immediate wants and needs from filtering through.

But she doesn't want him to recall, especially not today, when the air is heavy with their spirits and so much hangs in the balance. When the telling of one secret could lead to the accidental unveiling of another. So she makes her visit a quick one, before he gets restless and comes to find her. She closes her eyes at the large grave trimmed in white stones from the beach—a bit of flash—then at the small grave covered in grass, a handful of speedwell resting at its head. She whispers a prayer and an apology and turns away.

The path to the beach from the cemetery is a short one. As Holly catches sight of the water, the trees thin and Jack comes into view, skipping rocks into the gray Cornwall sea. For just that moment both her sons are there, two tall, lanky boys gazing into the sea, so identical that only someone who truly loved them could tell them apart.

She looks away, closes her eyes. For months after Isaac died, she thought she saw him. Jack would turn a corner, and she'd catch a glimpse of Isaac right behind him. Or she'd come into the bedroom to kiss Jack good night and see movement out of the corner of her eye, and for one heart-stopping second she'd be convinced it was her other son. She'd reach for him and find she was reaching for empty air.

Holly opens her eyes, and there is only Jack again. She has no time for sentimentality. No time for handsome dead husbands, for twins who never grew up. Not if she wants to save Jack, to keep him the way he is now, whole and vibrant, not the shell of a child he was after the wreck, unable to walk, to run, to live a day free of exhaustion and pain.

Not if she wants to save Eden.

"I'm all set," she calls, her voice brusquer than she'd intended. She tries to soften it. "Ready to go back to the hotel and check out?"

Jack looks out at the water. His shoes are off, his pants cuffed up. When he steps out of the surf line, she notices his feet. They're rough and calloused, and the smallest nail on the right foot is blackened and dead, a victim of his punishing training regimen. The feet of an athlete, of an almost-grown man. Not a child's high arches and ten perfect toes she'd somehow been expecting.

Jack stoops to pick up one last rock. He hefts it, smoothing its shape with his fingers, and she thinks he's going to throw it, but he slips it into his pocket instead.

"I thought we could take a few days and visit your grandmother," Holly says with forced cheerfulness. "We're this close, after all. And I have some other business in London."

"What about lacrosse? And school?"

"I wasn't sure how many days I'd be here, so I left it open-ended with your headmaster," she says, ignoring the question about lacrosse. "So long as you get your work done, we should be good. And in any case, it's nearly summer holiday."

He doesn't answer.

At the hotel, he packs up his things and carries the luggage down to the car with a lack of protest that's unusual for him. She probably should be worried, but it's a relief.

She calls Jane from the road. To Holly's surprise, her mother picks up. In careful terms, since the call is on the car's hands-free speaker, Holly tells her she's been in Cornwall dealing with a business crisis, Jack is with her, and they've decided to stop in London for a few days.

"That's wonderful," Jane says. The Darling women are nothing if not quick. "I hope the crisis wasn't too . . . severe."

"One of my vendors—my favorite, really, the main reason I come to Cornwall—has somehow decamped. We can talk about it when I get there," Holly says with a quick glance at Jack.

Jane, it turns out, has been visiting friends. She won't return until tomorrow night, but she tells Holly and Jack to make themselves at home. She'll call the housekeeper and make sure the rooms are ready.

"Can't wait to see you, my lovely," she says to Jack before hanging up.

Jack spends the rest of the drive staring out his window. At least he's not fighting with her, Holly tells herself. She tries not to think about past road trips, when they'd play the alphabet game, listen to audiobooks, or take turns singing made-up lyrics to favorite songs loudly and off-key. She tries to appreciate the silence.

"You're quiet," she says at last, glancing sideways. He's fingering the rock he picked up on the beach. "Everything all right?"

"Yeah," he says absently. "Hey, what kind of a kid was I?"

"What?"

"You know—when I was little. What was I like?"

"Well," she says cautiously, "you were serious. Even before, you were always the serious one. But you loved sports. You loved to run."

That had been one of the hardest things to watch, after the crash. Once she'd gotten over the immediate fear of his dying, of course. But his agonizingly slow movements, the dawning recognition in his eyes that it would always be like this, the way he'd eventually all but given up . . . that had been unbearable.

She clicks the radio on, searches till she finds a classical station. She waits. Sure enough, a few minutes later, he asks again.

"Was I . . . Did I have a good imagination?"

"I would say you were typical of your age." An inkling of unease pricks at her. "Why?"

"No reason." He looks down at the stone in his hand. "I don't remember a lot about when I was little."

"Well, a lot happened to you in a short time, so it makes sense you would block some of it out," she says. "Plus, you had a few surgeries, and being under anesthesia can impact memory."

"Yeah, I guess," he says. "But when we were at that house today—at

Grace House," he corrects himself, "I started to remember. Just a few things. Only they don't make sense."

"What type of things?" Dread pools in her body, heavy and cold. She was so very stupid to bring him here. "Skipping stones on the beach? You did a lot of that, you and Isaac." Maybe the name of his twin will distract him. But Jack only shakes his head.

"No. I don't really remember him. Except as a feeling, you know? Something that's always there . . ." He trails off. "Anyways, I kept seeing this girl. She's my age, maybe older? But she can't be real—the stuff I keep seeing . . ." He shakes his head. "That's why I asked what I was like as a kid. Was I the kind who would have an imaginary friend?"

This is the moment. This is when she tells him. Holly's heart is pounding and her hands are slick with sweat, but he's given her the perfect opening and she has to take it. She has to. She takes a breath, but the words don't come. How does she tell him? He'll freak out; he'll never speak to her again; he'll stop taking the injections that are keeping him whole. She can't do it.

She has to.

Jack, mistaking her silence, shakes his head again. "She had to have been imaginary. You know how I know?"

"How, honey?" Her voice sounds shaky even to her own ears. She knows, before the words are even out, what his answer will be.

"Because she could fly." He laughs, but it's forced. "At least in my head, I thought she could. Just saying it sounds crazy, right? Grandma must have read me *Peter Pan* one too many times."

"Crazy," Holly agrees. She thinks back to the day of the accident, the way she found them in the tree. *Mummy, Eden says she can fly!* Tiny tinkling bells. But she doesn't tell him, and in her silence the moment for truth passes.

"I must have been a weird little kid," he mutters. He goes back to staring out the window.

Only a very small part of Holly is sorry.

＊

Traffic picks up a few miles outside of London, and it takes all of Holly's concentration to navigate the city. When at last they pull into Jane's street, it's late. Darkness swirls outside the soft glow of the streetlights. A shadow slips from the topmost corner of the Darling house, raising the hair on the back of Holly's neck. She strains to follow the shape with her eyes, glad that Jack is still inside the car, unseen. Then the shadow vanishes in the blackness of the night sky.

Holly wishes Jack were ten years younger so that she could scoop him into her arms and carry him up the stairs, cradling his head against her shoulder, protecting him. But he's not. So she takes a deep breath, parallel parks with an aplomb she does not feel, finds the spare key Jane keeps buried in the planter, and unlocks the front door. She hustles Jack inside and sends him up the stairs to get ready for bed.

She finds milk in the refrigerator, heats a mug of it in the dented old saucepan her nanny once used. There's hardly any food, but she finds bread and cuts thick slices, toasts them, and spreads them with butter and honey. She carries everything upstairs to the guest room where she's put Jack. He's bundled under the covers, exhausted.

"Drink this," she says. "It will help you sleep. My nanny always said it would keep away bad dreams."

His eyes are closing before he's finished. She takes the mug from him, smooths out the coverlet, and kisses him on the forehead.

"Sleep tight," she says. "Don't let the bedbugs bite."

"Night, Mom," he says.

And then, even though he's almost sixteen, she clicks on the night-light. She makes sure the windows are closed and locked before she leaves the room and descends the stairs.

The Darling house is large. Kitchen, library, dining room, parlor, and drawing room on the first floor. An office and a handful of bedrooms, including Jane's, on the second. And on the third, a warren of storage space, servant quarters, and the nursery. It's a big house to be alone in on a black London night, and not for the first time, Holly glances at the windows and shivers. Still, when a floorboard creaks upstairs, she pays it no mind. As a teenager, Holly spent many evenings wandering the house alone, waiting for Jane to return from a gala or reception or dinner party. She knows its sounds intimately because she's explored every inch, from the butler's pantry to the attic, and found secrets everywhere. Sherry hidden behind the oatmeal tin by the cook. A packet of love letters, tied with pink ribbon, written in her mother's hand and forgotten in the bottom drawer of her father's desk. Jewelry and clothing and box after box of photos in the attic, including a curious leather album with photos of a very young Wendy in a white gown, a man standing stiffly behind her with his right arm on her shoulder.

In every picture, the man's face is cut out.

Holly's own secrets are in the attic too, caught in photographs that have been packed into boxes and sealed tightly shut. They add to the oppressive atmosphere of Darling House, although once they were a bright beam cutting through the dark. If she closes her eyes, she can still see them, her boys. Jack and Isaac running races on the long corridor of the second floor, baby legs churning. Robert's booming laugh as he taught them to slide down the grand banister into his waiting arms. His sheepish, guilty grin when Jane had caught him. And almost unbelievably, her mother's amused expression, followed by her ringing laughter. A sound that echoed through the house, warming it, bringing it alive again in a way Holly would never have thought possible in the days she'd skulked through its dark hallways as a forgotten teen.

Other memories are there as well. Some captured in pictures, others existing only in her mind. These are the ones she'd prefer to forget.

She opens her eyes. Even though the overhead chandelier in the hallway is on, it's as if she's lost in the dark. She turns and heads to the kitchen, where she selects the wickedest knife she can find, a long, serrated beauty so sharp she has no idea what Jane could possibly use it for. And then she climbs the steps again.

She climbs past the room rumored to be where mad Mr. Barrie stayed, feverishly observing the Darling family, especially beautiful, languorous Wendy. Beyond the room that once belonged to poor Michael, Wendy's youngest brother. Michael suffered an accident the family prefers not to think about. All of these rooms are now empty. Holly could sleep in any of them.

But she keeps climbing, to the top of the house where the servants' quarters and the nursery are. This last room is full of old toys, of shadows. A rocking horse with sightless glass eyes stands motionless in one corner. A dollhouse with broken furniture rests in another. The pink roses that paper the walls are from Wendy's time or even before, but the crisp cotton quilts that cover the row of beds are new. Memories, her own and those of the Darlings who came before her, are everywhere, reminders of what was and what might have been.

Holly ignores them all. A long corridor separates the nursery from the servants' quarters, with a small bathroom just outside the nursery door. She washes her face there, then finds her old white nightgown wrapped in lavender-scented tissue paper in the nursery dresser and changes into it. She ties her hair back with a blue ribbon. She does all of this in the dark, with only the moonlight filtering in through the window.

When she's finished, she goes to the door, takes the old-fashioned key from over the frame, and locks it from the inside.

She's not worried about someone coming in. She doesn't want anything to get out.

She lights the stub of a candle that is on the dresser and carries it with her to the windows. These are open, thanks to Jane, who insists they be kept ajar at least a crack, no matter what the weather. Holly runs a finger along the sill, finds the faintest trace of soot. Nothing at all that glitters. Still, when Holly looks out over the London sky, she shivers. She calls his name softly and listens. Not a sound, not even the rustle of the wind, only dark sky and the hard diamonds of the stars. She leaves the candle burning on the dresser, a signal beacon, and crawls into bed. She slides the knife under her pillow.

It's dangerous to be here, especially with Jack. Cornwall was bad enough, but London? It's like dousing the water with blood in front of a shark. In the dark, alone, she worries she's made a mistake, second-guesses her decision not to leave him in New York.

And yet she has to try, for the sake of both her children. It's been years, but there's a chance that he'll return.

A chance that he never really left.

She closes her eyes. Stills her mind. Pictures a small boy flying through the air. A little girl reaching up to take his hand. Starlight against the dark blue sky. What every London child, every Darling daughter especially, has imagined. A dream come to life.

And then, in Holly's memory, the boy turns to her and smiles. White glittering teeth. Soulless eyes. And it's no longer a dream.

It's a nightmare.

Chapter Eleven

In the morning, the candle is out. The windows are still open, and the room is cold. Holly rubs her eyes. She's alone in the locked room.

After closing the window, she pulls on a jumper and a pair of jeans. She makes the bed but leaves the knife where it is.

Downstairs, Jack is sleeping, so she makes a pot of oatmeal, then starts a grocery list. Jane doesn't eat much, and she has no idea how to feed a growing boy.

Holly looks up to see Jack shambling into the kitchen. He drops into the chair across from her, yawning.

"Morning!" she says brightly. He mumbles something incoherent in reply.

"I've made breakfast—hungry?" It's a rhetorical question. Jack is always hungry. She crosses to the stove, scoops out the oatmeal, serves it to him with lashings of brown sugar and the last of the milk.

"There's not much food here," she says, eyeing him as he shovels the oatmeal in. "You know how your grandma Jane is. I'm putting together a list—anything special you want?"

He shakes his head.

"Did you sleep well?"

"Fine," he mumbles.

"Sweet dreams?"

"Okay, I guess."

She doesn't like the way he looks—pale skin, dark circles under his eyes. Now is not the time for Jack to get sick. She reaches out to feel his forehead. He brushes her hand away.

"I should find a place to practice. Coach is going to get mad if I come back out of shape."

Jack playing a game that could get him injured is the absolute last thing she needs right now, but she smiles and pretends it's fine. "I'll keep my eyes open when I go out this morning," she says. "In the meantime, why don't you take a shower while I clean up."

When he's gone, she scrubs the oatmeal pot so hard the sponge disintegrates in her hands. She *has* to find Eden soon. Whatever Peter wants, however he discovered her, it's unlikely he's stepped up to play the role of father. He may be injured or ill and need her blood. Or perhaps he's finally decided to go home, and take Eden with him.

She can't let that happen. She won't.

She thinks of her sweet sunshine girl, the way Eden bubbled over with joy. The way she always tried so hard to please. Her bright curiosity. If she'd never fallen asleep, would she be like that today? Would she still come down the stairs singing each morning and throw herself into Holly's arms as if they'd been apart for years? Or would the hormones of adolescence take over, pushing them apart?

There's no way to know. And no way to guess, either, how Eden might feel toward her now. All Holly can do is focus on finding her.

So she cleans until she's mastered the panic, or can at least keep from showing it on her face. When she's ready, she goes looking for Jack.

She finds him in the library. Dust motes drift around him, the filtered light turning them into flecks of gold. He's found the Darling treasure, a signed first-edition illustrated volume of *Peter Pan* kept under a glass cloche. He's lifted the cover and is paging through it. In the dimly lit room he looks like someone underwater, murky and distant. Someone otherworldly.

✳

There's a vase of daffodils on the side table. Wendy's favorite. The soft yellow, the sweet scent, the dim light, all tug at Holly. They bring her back to childhood—she was six, no, seven—in this same room with Wendy and her mother.

Her tights had been so itchy, but Holly couldn't scratch. Her mother wouldn't like it, doesn't like the way that Holly lies across the chair, dangling her head over the armrest. Looking for a distraction, Holly sees a glass dome, tucked away into a corner. It's like the ones people use to cover delicate plants. But instead of greenery underneath this one, there's an old book. She points.

"What's that?"

"Don't point, Holly," her mother says. "And sit up. You do have a spine."

"What's that?" she repeats without pointing. But she doesn't sit up.

"An old book, dear," her grandmother says.

"An heirloom," her mother says, without looking at Grandma Wendy. "Something precious."

Holly slides into a sitting position. "Will you read it to me? Please?" She asks the question of the room, careful not to make eye contact. The air is always funny when her mother and Grandma Wendy spend too much time together—electric, like lightning between them. She never knows what will make it spark. But she likes books.

"Oh, my dear," her grandmother sighs, but Jane cuts her off. "Yes, Mother, why don't you? I've told her bits and pieces, but you're the one he came to see." The lightning crackles beneath her words. Holly straightens in her chair.

There's a long pause. "All right," Wendy says at last. Jane crosses the room to lift the glass dome, and Holly slips onto the sofa next to her grandmother. Wendy is very old but very beautiful. Her skin is glowy, as if she's eaten a candle and the light is still shining inside, and she smells good.

Jane brings the book to her mother, but she doesn't sit on the other side of the sofa. Instead she stands by the door, arms crossed. Waiting. For the story to start? Holly's waiting too. But Wendy doesn't open the old book.

"Perhaps this isn't such a good idea after all."

"Please," Holly says.

Wendy sighs again. "What has your mother told you? About our family and Peter Pan?"

That's one of those questions that can make the lightning come out, so Holly thinks carefully before answering. "He's a boy," she says. "And you had adventures together. People think he's just a story, but he's not."

Her grandmother looks out the window. "Yes, I suppose that's true enough."

"Will you tell me about them? Your adventures?" Holly isn't certain if she wants to have her own adventures with this boy when she's older. But she knows her mother does.

"It was all very long ago," Wendy says softly. She glances at Jane, still by the door. "But I'll try."

Grandmother is a very good storyteller. Not like Jane, who skips ahead and only talks about the exciting bits, like flying through the sky and fighting pirates. Grandmother Wendy starts at the proper beginning, which Holly hasn't heard before.

"Once upon a time, a very long time ago, when I was just a girl, I was in the nursery with my brothers, John and Michael. It was just after bedtime."

"What were you doing?" Holly has always wanted a brother or sister to play with.

"Oh, dreaming. Telling stories."

"Were you sad?"

Holly tells herself stories at night in the nursery when she's all alone and her parents have gone out and her nanny is sleeping. The stories keep the shadows away. Most of the time.

"Yes, I was," her grandmother says, a glimmer of surprise in her eyes. "Why?"

Wendy shakes her head. "That's not the story. And it was a very long time ago. It doesn't matter anymore." She smooths the fabric of her blue dress across her lap, though Holly can't see any wrinkles. And then she tells Holly about the boy who came to visit.

When Wendy gets to the part about Tinker Bell, Holly can't help it. Excitement wells in her. The yellow daffodils on the side table, the last of the day's sunlight streaming through the library's heavy curtains, all catch and reflect the dust motes, flaming them into gold. Into pixie dust.

"I see her! I see Tinker Bell!" she shrieks, pointing to the window where the gold specks are thickest.

Jane is there before either of them can move, pulling back the curtains, opening the window wide and peering outside. She shakes her head, disgusted. "It's only pollen. Only dust."

Jane doesn't notice the shadow that winds its way past the curtains and over the cornice, like a thick black snake. But snakes don't have the shape of a young boy, don't have arms and legs. Holly shivers, moves closer to her grandmother. Holly doesn't like shadows.

Grandma Wendy notices. Holly can't tell if she sees the shadow too, or if she just feels it, but she tells Jane to come away from the window. Holly's mother doesn't move, so Wendy says it again, this time with enough force that Jane obeys and slams the window down, then glares at Holly.

"I've told you a dozen times," Jane says brusquely, "Peter Pan only comes at night."

Holly thinks of the shadow. But her mother is already too angry to ask. So she whispers to her grandmother, "Is that true?"

Wendy doesn't answer right away. Instead she tells Jane to lock the window. And then, when Holly's mother is occupied, she whispers back.

"It used to be," she says. "It used to be that night was the only time he could escape."

"Mom?"

Holly blinks, lets Jack's voice pull her back to the present. "Sorry. I was woolgathering." She shivers, rubs her arms. "What did you say?"

"I asked if this was an original copy of *Peter Pan.* It must be worth a fortune."

"Yes, it is. It's signed as well. Don't let your grandmother catch you handling it, please. And speaking of your grandmother, would you ask her to call me when she arrives? I need to go out for a little while." Where *is* Jane? Holly would rather talk with her in person, but she can't wait anymore.

"I want to go with you." Jack closes the book and slides it back onto the stand, covering it with the cloche.

"No," Holly says sharply. He looks startled. She softens her tone. "Someone needs to be here for your grandmother," she says. "She'll be hurt if she comes back to an empty house—you know how she is. Besides, I have some preparation to do for a meeting later this week— boring stuff. You'd hate it."

He flops down on the couch. "I'm bored *now.*"

"Life will get much less boring when your grandmother arrives," Holly says unsympathetically. "She'll have something planned. She always does. She likes to show you off."

She gets her bag, makes him come out to the hall. "Lock the door behind me. And don't go out. You don't know this city well enough. Understood?"

He nods sulkily. "Don't forget to look for a lacrosse field."

"I won't," she lies, then pulls the door shut behind her. She waits to descend the stairs until she hears the snick of the lock.

She finally has an idea of where to start her search, though it's not one that she likes. Once, years ago, she was walking to the Tube in Soho when she got turned around into one of the seedier sections. The walls were papered with stickers advertising prostitutes and porn shows. It was getting dark, but the streetlamps weren't lit yet and the glances she was getting made her uneasy. She kept her head down and was trying to find her way back when she caught a glimpse of golden hair. A handsome young man with a wide-eyed innocent look—well muscled and very, very familiar. It had been a few years since he'd crept through her open window, but his face was older than it should have been, pockmarked and scarred. He was standing on the curb, talking to a man in a BMW.

Holly's breath caught, although she wasn't certain. She took a few steps closer. The man in the car handed over a roll of bills. As the streetlamps winked on, Peter smiled, and in that second his face changed from innocent to predatory.

She'd stopped, frozen, any thoughts of calling out forgotten, and in the next instant he'd gotten in the car and was being driven away.

She'd been stupid enough, in the beginning, that she'd gone back once or twice, half hoping to see him, telling herself the whole time that she was doing it for Eden. Not because she was curious. Not because she wanted to know what had happened to the strange boy her mother loved, the one determined to never grow up. The boy whose smile filled her with dread. In any case, she hadn't found him.

Still, Soho is the only link she has. So that's where she'll go. She's taken one of Jack's baseball caps, and now she pulls her hair into a ponytail and slips the cap over it. She's brought her sunglasses as well. It's a bit ridiculous, like she's playing at being a spy.

But when she gets to Soho, it's changed. It's been years since she visited, and it's not as disreputable as she remembers. There are still a few rock and roll clubs, some dodgy-looking pubs, and at least one shop with a window full of leather chaps, whips, and masks. But the streets are clean—no puddles of urine to dodge, no piles of trash. And the grottier pockets are surrounded by industrial-chic coffee shops selling fair-trade coffee, vintage record stores, and clothing boutiques where the T-shirt prices start at triple the minimum wage. The people she sees don't have that hungry, covert look, either.

Holly spends two hours walking around, looking for something, anything, that could lead to him. She asks after him at a few of the seamier-looking pubs. "Boyfriend done a runner, eh, love?" one of the bartenders says sympathetically. "Leave you with bills to pay or kids?"

"Both," she says honestly.

"Sounds like a real bastard. Not that most here won't answer to that description. Still, I'll keep my eye out. You want to leave your number?" She does not.

At last she concedes defeat. She could look again tonight, when the rougher side of London comes out to play, but she doesn't think she'll find him here.

As much as she hates to admit it, she needs help.

She's out of options, with no idea where to look or what to do next. So she finally does what she always does when she's in trouble. What she should have done from the beginning.

She calls Barry.

Chapter Twelve

The conversation is not an easy one. Holly doesn't actually tell him *everything* (she hasn't completely lost her mind), just what he needs to know. She says that there are complications keeping her in England. That long ago, when Jack was still recovering and she was in shock at the turn her life had taken, she fell into a short-lived affair with an old family friend. That when she conceived Eden so quickly, she panicked and let everyone assume it was Robert's baby. That the father made it clear he wasn't interested in sticking around, or providing any kind of support, and that she hasn't kept in touch.

"But I need to find him now," she says. "It's important. And I don't know where to start."

On the other side of the Atlantic, Barry is quiet. She can almost hear his brain whirring. A daughter she's never mentioned. An affair she never talked about. And now an old lover she urgently needs to find. What's next? To his credit, he doesn't ask.

"I'll see what I can do," he says at last, and that's all.

Barry has two personas: the shiny, public one he's constructed where he's everyone's favorite guy and a quieter, more authentic one. So far as Holly knows, she and Jack, along with Barry's wife and children, are the only ones who get to the latter. The price for getting behind the curtain is total trust on both sides, and now he's realized she's kept secrets all these years. That even when they first met, when they were at their most intimate, he had no idea who she really was. There's no easy way past that. But she has no choice. She needs his help, in a way she never has before. She needs him to find Peter.

She's pulling into the drive when the door opens and Jane flits down the steps. "Darling!" she cries. It's an old family joke, but one with an edge. Barrie, unhappy about Wendy's pending nuptials, added a clause to his will, stating only children with the Darling surname were eligible for future royalties from his works. Wendy kept her name, as have all her descendants. Holly would have chosen to be a Wightwick happily, but Robert—ever the practical one—persuaded her not to be foolish.

"Mother," Holly says. She steps out of the car and leans into Jane's embrace. Her mother smells like cold fresh air, clean and crisp. She draws her arm through Holly's and leads her into the house.

"Whatever are you wearing? Don't tell me you've finally succumbed to that dreadful American style?" Jane asks, eyeing the baseball cap Holly's forgotten to take off. Jane's own silver locks are neatly coiled into an elegant bun.

"No, I . . . I'm trying out a new product that makes your skin more sensitive to the sun. I didn't want to burn," she says lamely. She takes off the hat as they step into the cool darkness of the front hall. She pulls out the ponytail and runs her fingers through her hair.

"Goodness, much better." Her mother releases her with a final squeeze. "Let me see you. Still as lovely as ever."

"How was Surrey?" Holly says self-consciously.

"Beautiful. Bit boring though. We went to see the spring gardens, and the couple I was with had a horrid time keeping up. Quite disappointing, really. I met them through yoga, and I must say, you would think they'd be in better shape. But they did give me a remarkable bottle of whiskey. You must try it—I've put it in the library."

She breezes down the hall ahead of Holly with the easy, carefree grace that marks her as the dancer she once was. The same grace Holly used to have, and misses every single day. She follows behind her tiny mother, trying not to feel ungainly.

"Where's Jack?"

"I sent him out with the housekeeper. He's looking so pale—I thought the air would do him good." She catches Holly's frown. "Darling, don't worry—this isn't your New York. It's perfectly safe. And there are so many groceries on your list, poor Nan will never manage on her own."

"Nan?"

"The housekeeper."

At Holly's raised eyebrows, Jane nods. "I know. I would have hired her anyhow—she's really a wonder—but her name was quite the good omen, I thought."

"Quite the coincidence, rather. Is that her real name?"

Jane lifts an elegant shoulder and lets it fall. "I haven't the foggiest. Nancy, perhaps? But the original nanny—Wendy's—was a Mary, you know. A proper Irish nursemaid by all accounts, always popping in and whisking Wendy off for a bath or a walk or some such. Sir Barrie simply loathed her. Making her the dog in the story was his petty revenge. 'The nose of a bloodhound with the face to match,' he'd say. 'Whenever we'd get up to a spot of mischief, in she'd come.' Anyhow, when I heard her name, I simply had to have her. Besides, she's a marvelous cook, which turns out to be fortuitous. Do teenage boys truly eat that much?"

"You have no idea." Holly sinks into the leather armchair across from her mother, suddenly exhausted.

"Well then, we shall have to impose upon poor Nan to stock the refrigerator with casseroles and roasts. It's the only way he'll survive. I'm afraid my cooking skills have not improved over the years. Now do try this. It's not too early for you, is it?" Jane glances at the antique watch that adorns her slender wrist. "No, it's definitely cocktail time. No excuses." She hands Holly a cut-crystal glass and raises her own.

"To the Darling women, past, present, and future," she says, as the portrait of Wendy gazes down on them from its place of honor above the mantel.

Holly clinks her glass against Jane's and dutifully sips the whiskey. It's vaguely illicit, sipping spirits in a dim library in the afternoon. Not the type of example she wants to set for Jack. But the whiskey does help to wash the taste of her morning away. Her mother is right—it is remarkable. She takes another sip. It burns on the way down.

Jane watches her for a moment. "Good, isn't it?" she says, holding her glass up and turning it slowly in the light to admire the liquid's color.

"Very," Holly agrees. There's a pleasant warmth spreading throughout her center. It belatedly occurs to her that she's had nothing to eat all day. "I should get lunch," she says, gesturing with her glass in the direction of the kitchen.

"Well," her mother says, "I could fix some toast, I suppose. Or there might be a package of Hobnobs left in the pantry. But I'm afraid that's it until Nan returns."

Neither option appeals to Holly. Her mother pours more whiskey into her own glass, brings the bottle over to Holly.

"No, thank you," she says, but Jane pours her a splash anyhow.

"Oh, don't be such a prude," she says. "Sit back and relax. A little whiskey won't hurt you."

It's hard to argue with that, so Holly takes another sip. The whiskey is making it easier to forget that she's hungry, easier to not think about everything that's gone wrong in the last week. Easier not to worry.

Until Jane speaks again.

"Now tell me. Your phone call was absolutely cryptic. What's happened with Eden," she says. It's not a question. She's looking at Holly with her bird-bright eyes remarkably unclouded by drink. People who meet Holly's mother for the first time are lulled into being charmed by her airy, engaging social patter and graces. They see her as simply a very, very wealthy widow, devoted to preserving her family's history and lineage, finding pleasure where she can. Those who know her well or have the misfortune to cross her recognize she is the proverbial steel fist in a diamond-laden velvet glove. Now Holly can't help but wonder how much of the whiskey, of their time alone, was serendipity, and how much was shrewdly planned by Jane in advance.

Still, Holly has no choice. There's a chance, if only a small one, that Eden could show up in London, at this house. She spent time here as a very young child, an infant, really, and although most children could not recall that far back, Eden has always been precocious. If there's any possibility she could turn up here seeking help, whether on her own or escaping Peter, Jane needs to know.

She couches it carefully. "I'm not certain. It's possible she woke up, that she was confused and wandered off. But whatever the case, she's disappeared."

"My dear," Jane says. "How terrifying. You must be out of your mind with worry." A pause. And then, slowly, "But no police." Again it's not a question.

"No police," Holly echoes.

"You know what would happen." The Darlings have learned the hard way over the years that police inquiries and press coverage lead to unpleasant questions that often cannot be answered satisfactorily, starting with the disappearance—and then return—of Wendy and her siblings. In Eden's case, what would they make of the equipment at the Cornwall house? What might the nurses let slip? Holly could lose Jack if that happened. She could lose everything. So she nods.

"Her waking. It could be a miracle," Jane says lightly. The silver-framed charcoal sketch of Wendy, John, and poor Michael on the coffee table in front of her is slightly askew, and she reaches out a hand to adjust it.

"*If* she's woken up, yes, it could be."

"But you don't think so."

Here is where it becomes very, very dicey. Jane has never directly inquired into Jack's astonishing recovery. She's never visited Eden since she fell. And aside from those very early days, Jane has never commented on Eden's frighteningly premature birth, her rapid growth rate, her abnormally clever and advanced mind.

Because she knows. She has to. Even though they've never talked about it. She knows and she wants to forget. Because recognizing who Eden's father is destroys the narrative of Peter Pan, the unspoiled innocent.

Of course Holly can't be certain. But Jane spent her childhood and adolescence believing in the Darling story. She always slept with her own window open and probably does still—if she's not spending nights in the nursery when no one else is home. She'd told Holly, as she grew into a teenager and then a young woman, that she'd have to wait her turn, because Jane had never yet seen Peter, and it was only fair she got to see him first. The words may have been teasing. The look in Jane's eyes was not. Neither is the look today, when she makes it clear that she knows more than she has let on.

"If there's any chance that Peter is involved, that settles it. Imagine what a police investigation would do. He'd never forgive us. He'd never come back," she says.

If Holly's ever had any doubts about who her mother would choose if it came down to it, Jane's last comment is just the latest in a lifelong series that has made it abundantly obvious.

Which may be why, in hindsight, Holly didn't say a word when he finally came for her.

It was a cold winter night the first time she saw him. She was alone in the house, Jane gone to a party. "Just for a bit, darling. We must try and be brave."

For days and days, Holly had been nothing but brave. She'd put on a courageous front for Jack, who was still in hospital. She'd nodded and taken notes and struggled through her own operations and physical therapy. But tonight, unable to sleep, she'd gone to the nursery, and it was on her childhood bed that she gave into her grief, huge, wracking sobs that shook her whole body.

How was she going to get through this night, and the next, and all the long painful nights that stretched endlessly in front of her? Even if Jack lived, it would never be the same. *She* would never be the same.

She would have wished she were dead. But that would leave Jack. And she couldn't.

She remembers what happened next so clearly that shame flushes her cheeks. She'd thought of Jack dying, how it would free them both, how the struggle wasn't worth it anymore. At that moment the faintest whisper of a breeze caressed the back of her neck, a slight, icy hand. She'd raised her head, thought muzzily that the nursery window must be open. It was always open, no matter the weather, because Jane wanted it that way.

And then he spoke.

"Why are you crying, girl?"

She froze. It took a moment to find him, hidden against the curtains. He took a step forward and she gasped. He was the most beautiful thing she'd ever seen, and much older than he'd been described in the stories. He crossed the room to her. It was like having a hummingbird alight on her hand. She didn't move, not even when he reached out and his finger brushed her cheek, capturing a single tear. He studied it, clearly fascinated.

This close, she could feel how warm he was. His scent was like springtime, like new grass. Like that first cup of coffee on vacation somewhere magical, rich and full of promise. It was heady and redolent of everything she wanted back: youth and beauty and not happiness, exactly, but a wild exultant joy, a fierceness that knew nothing of loss or pain. She breathed it in. So sweet.

Intoxicating.

She leaned closer and brushed her lips against his.

He froze, then in a flash was at the window. She didn't move, just watched him go. The joy drained out of her, an unbearable sadness added to her existing grief, threatening to drown her. She closed her eyes and knew he'd be gone when she opened them.

But when she did, he was so close their lashes touched.

"Do it again," he said.

So she did.

So when Jane looks at her with those bright eyes, Holly knows what she's thinking. She's remembering the morning when, all those years ago, Holly stumbled downstairs with a glow that was quite inexplicable, given her physical and mental condition. When the scent of springtime clung to her, even though it was February. When she retired alone each night to the nursery bedroom on the third floor, but somehow became pregnant. A pregnancy that within a few weeks was so far along, the doctors were convinced they'd somehow missed it during all the tests and examinations they'd run after the crash.

Jane is remembering that she never got her turn. And how, because of Holly and what she did, she never will. Once the forbidden fruit has been tasted, there's no going back to paradise. For anyone. Even Peter Pan, it seems. Innocence, once lost, is impossible to regain.

All the stories say so.

Chapter Thirteen

Barry takes two full days to get back to her. If it were anyone else, the turnaround time would have been impressive. But pulling off the impossible is one of Barry's best traits. So Holly has to wonder, when his ID shows up on her phone, precisely how hard he's been looking.

"I may have somebody who can help," he says without preamble. "I've spent the last couple of days making calls and reaching out to my contacts. They all push the same guy. But I don't know him personally, so I can't recommend him."

"That's okay." She hates how detached he sounds. "Thanks for doing it."

"He's an ex-soldier who served in Afghanistan. He got shot up, came home, signed on with the police—the bobbies, as you people so quaintly say."

"I don't want to use the police," Holly protests. Police mean public records, and public records mean press.

"You don't have to. The guy had some conflicts and left the force. I'm not clear on whether it was voluntary or not, but my gut says no. He set up shop a year or so ago on his own and seems to be doing well. My contacts say he's the best private detective around. He's not cheap, and he's not pleasant, but he gets results."

"I don't care about his personality," Holly says. "I'm not planning on marrying him."

"Another thing." Barry pauses, and she can hear him deciding how much to say. "When he was in Afghanistan? He came home with some issues. My sources didn't say what. But the word on the street is he's a little . . . damaged."

Holly's taken the conversation in Jane's office for privacy. There's a picture of Holly and Jack on the desk, a photo from last Christmas. They're standing in front of the Rockefeller tree, arms around each other, laughing. To anyone watching them that day, they must have looked vibrantly healthy and normal. Holly has idly picked up the frame while Barry's been talking. Now she sets it down.

"Aren't we all," she says.

Barry's silent on the other end of the phone.

"You sure you want to do this?" he says at last.

"I am."

"Then let me call this guy first for you," he says. "At least let me do that. If he checks out, I'll give him your number. If not, I'll keep looking."

Holly thinks about it. A prescreening isn't a bad idea, especially since it's Barry, whose bullshit meter is off the charts—another one of his special talents.

"All right," she says. "And thank you. It means a lot."

"How's Jack doing?"

"He's fine," she lies. "Happy to be avoiding school, actually."

"Driving all the young English girls crazy?"

"The old ones too—he and his grandmother almost came to blows last night," she jokes, relieved at how natural he sounds. Barry's never met her mother, but he's heard the stories.

They spend a few more moments on the phone, running over the business. She's barely had time to think about the company, and getting up to speed on the latest product trials and consumer-feedback tests is a good distraction. With help finally in sight and Barry not as standoff-ish as she'd feared, she's slightly less anxious by the time they hang up. She spends the next few hours sending and answering emails and reviewing lab reports before going downstairs.

Jane has disappeared, but Nan, the housekeeper, is in the kitchen. She's younger than Holly expected—she looks as if she's in her early twenties—and she moves around the kitchen with an easy familiarity that comes from working under Jane's demanding eye for the past six months. Jack is sitting at the counter next to her, scarfing down an omelet. "Hey, Mom, guess what? Nan's brother Ed plays lax too. He's going to take me the next time they practice."

"Fabulous," Holly enthuses, when she means the opposite. She's becoming more and more like her mother.

"Do you think we could have him over? Please? He's out of school today," Jack says. "And I've already done most of my assignments for this week."

Holly looks at Nan, who is biting her lip. She gives Holly a subtle shake of her head.

"I don't know," Holly hedges. "Your grandmother might have something planned." Jack's protesting as her mobile goes off. She glances down at it. *Barry.* She holds up a hand. "Hold on a sec. I have to take this."

But Jack looks so pleadingly at her that she relents. "Ask your grandmother," she says, then steps out of the kitchen.

"That was fast."

"So I talked to him," Barry says. "And I don't like him much, but I think he's on the level. But there's one thing."

"Yes?"

"At first, he flat-out refused to help you. Said he wasn't interested, that it wasn't the kind of thing he did. But I kept talking. I told him who you are and what you do, and suddenly he became extremely enthusi-astic. In fact, he couldn't wait to speak with you. Any idea why?"

"What's his name?" Holly asks. There's always the possibility that she knows him, that he's the brother of a friend or a relative.

"Christopher Cooke."

"Doesn't sound familiar. Do you think he's a fame stalker?"

She still runs into these types, people obsessed with her family and story, who can quote entire chapters from the book and have scrapbooks and websites devoted to Wendy and John and poor little Michael. They're usually as odd as one would expect.

"I didn't get that impression. But something definitely piqued his interest. He's willing to meet you today at noon. There's a pub near Hyde Park. That's where he'll be."

"That's only an hour from now," Holly says, glancing at her watch.

"I got the distinct impression that he didn't care whether the timing was convenient for you. If you want this, you need to be there. I'll text you the address if that's what you decide."

"How will I recognize him?"

"I asked him that. He said he'd find you."

It's a public place, and likely to be crowded at lunchtime. And if Barry's contacts say he's good, there's a solid chance he can help her. She makes up her mind. "He sounds odd. But if he's as good as you say, I'll have to risk it. Text me the address. If I'm going to make it by noon, I need to run. And Barry? Thank you. I don't know what I'd do—"

"Let me know how it goes," he cuts in, preventing her from embarrassing them both. "And Holly?"

"Yes?"

"Be careful."

As soon as she disconnects the call, Holly dashes upstairs for a quick shower. She chooses a well-cut black dress that shows precisely the right amount of cleavage. She uses a light hand with her makeup, sticking with a spare palette of pale browns and pinks.

When she's finished, she double-checks her work in the mirror. Good, but . . . she hesitates, then reaches into her bag and pulls out a tiny sample of Pixie Dust. It's her own personal concoction, adapted from the recipe the company is using for the launch, and it has a single drop of plasma from Eden in it. She blows a minuscule amount into the air, closes her eyes, and holds her face up.

For these few seconds she lets herself think of her daughter, the way it felt to hold her in her arms, the warm squirmy weight of her as a child, the way she was never still. When the dust lands on her skin, it feels like a thousand tiny bubbles popping.

When she opens her eyes and looks at herself again, her face is glowing. Beauty can be wielded as a weapon, she's learned, and she's happy to add it to her arsenal if it will captivate Mr. Cooke and help her find Peter and her daughter.

She goes downstairs. Jack is still eating, a sandwich of some sort, and playing on his phone. He stands when he sees her and gives her a quick, casual hug, so fast she isn't sure it happened.

"What was that for?" she says. He's already eating again.

"Nothing. Grandma Jane said yes. But she wants to see you," he says between mouthfuls. "She's upstairs in her room."

"Ahhh," Holly says. Still, she'd brave the lion's den a hundred times if it meant getting that reaction from Jack. She steals a glance at her watch. It needs to be quick.

"Okay," she says. "And then I have to head out for work. Behave. Especially if you have this Ed kid over. Hang in the library and watch a movie or something."

"Of course," Jack says, giving her his best wide-eyed and innocent look.

"I mean it," she says. "And so will your grandmother."

Upstairs, Jane is sitting at her dressing table, brushing her hair. Long, slow strokes, as if she has all the time in the world.

"You wanted to see me?" Holly says. She strives to keep the impatience out of her voice.

"Such a strange day," Jane says, gazing out the window. Her voice is low, as if she's speaking to herself. "Sunny this morning and now such dark skies. And the paper said a flock of starlings flew through the city, so many that when they landed on the hour hand of Big Ben they stopped the clock. Stopped time, for a brief moment. A murmuration, they called it. Can you imagine that?"

This is unsettling. Jane isn't given to flights of fancy except for Peter. "Mother. I'm sure you didn't call me here to discuss birds with you."

Jane doesn't turn around, but she squares her shoulders. She meets Holly's eyes in the mirror. "You do realize what an awkward position you've placed Nan in, having this boy over? The poor girl works for me."

"You're the one who said yes."

"I refuse to play the role of bad policeman to my grandson," Jane says. "That's your job. And I have no problem with them socializing outside of the house. But I expect you not to make a habit of it here."

"Right," Holly says, biting back a smile at her mother's botched American expression. "Got it." She knows from past experience that agreeing is the fastest way out of the room.

"And don't expect me to supervise. It would be too awkward. Besides, I have a tour and lunch at the Tate scheduled."

"I need to run out for about an hour or so. Work," Holly adds in answer to her mother's raised eyebrows. She has no intention of telling Jane about the private detective until she's sussed out the situation herself. She leans forward and pecks her mother on the cheek Jane proffers. "I'll see you this afternoon."

Downstairs, Ed has arrived and is sitting in the kitchen with Jack and Nan. He's handsome, with dewy skin any of the Darling Skin Care models would die for, as if he has his own supply of Pixie Dust, and a wide build. He stands up when Holly enters the room, and it's impossible to miss the pride in Nan's face when she looks at him. A quick, sharp pang stabs Holly's heart. Jack would have been like this with Eden. With Isaac. He's been robbed twice over. Left with nothing but shadows of memories.

"Hey, Dr. Darling," Ed says. "Thanks for having me over."

"Our pleasure," Holly says, pulling herself back to the present. She eyes Ed again. Someone has certainly taught him good manners. "It's very kind of you to come." She turns to Nan. "I need to run out for a bit. I know the boys will probably be fine, but would you please keep an eye on them, just in case?" She ignores Jack's eye roll. "And here's some money for lunch. They can order takeaway from wherever they want."

She kisses Jack's forehead. "I'll be home as soon as I can," she says. Despite the eye roll, he doesn't duck away. She takes it as a good sign. With a little luck, this detective will be skilled enough to bring Eden home soon too. And maybe, just maybe, Jack will get a chance to be a brother—and Eden a sister—again after all.

Chapter Fourteen

Holly takes the Tube to her meeting. On the ride there, she checks her phone. Barry has texted the address, as promised, as well as another reminder to call him when she's done. Maybe he's forgiven her for her sins of omission after all. She hopes so. She can't imagine life without Barry. It's one of the reasons she'd slid them toward friendship after those few times together, away from the flaming disaster her love life inevitably becomes on the rare occasions she's tried dating since Robert. As her friend, he'd stay.

At her stop, her map app shows the pub is only two blocks away. Luckily she's brought her umbrella, as it's pouring.

The pub isn't the dark place she'd assumed a private detective would want to meet. Perhaps she's watched too many American television shows. Even so, it takes her eyes a moment to adjust. The room is crowded, and as she glances around, she sees she's easily the best dressed person in the room—in a sea of jeans and trainers, the black dress makes her stand out as she'd planned. Good. When you have to go begging, it's never wise to appear as a beggar.

A man in the far corner of the room is looking at her, his gaze lingering. He's the perfect image of an ex-military detective—close-cropped gray hair, white button-down, blue suit jacket—so she starts in his direction.

"Dr. Darling?" says a voice in her ear. She looks up, startled. There's a man standing next to her, but even as she nods, he's turning away.

"I'm over here," he calls over his shoulder. It's too fast for her to get a good look at his face. Without another word he walks to a booth in the back of the pub, leaving her no choice but to follow. He's tall, but slender, with longish black hair. He's wearing jeans and a thin black sweater with sleeves that fall past his wrists.

The man slides into the booth, leaving her to take the chair. She leans the umbrella on the wall beside him. He's pale, with full lips and blue eyes so dark they're almost black. A trace of stubble, not quite a beard, covers his jaw. His upper torso is heavily muscled, which surprises her because he moves as lithely as a dancer.

He tucks a stray lock of hair behind his right ear, and she sees that he wears a small silver hoop in it. She tries to guess his age. The way he's dressed, his grooming, makes her think he's a few years younger than she is, but there's something about his eyes and face, a world-weariness, that belies his appearance.

Either way, he's not at all what she was expecting.

She realizes she's being rude, but he doesn't seem uncomfortable with her scrutiny. He leans back in the booth and nods to her.

"I'm Christopher. Christopher Cooke."

"Holly Darling."

He doesn't offer to shake hands. Fine. Tall, strong, and handsome is a type she's encountered many times before, and she knows how to play this. She leans forward, aware that half the men in the room are gazing at her, and gives Mr. Christopher Cooke her best smile. But before she can utter a word, he speaks.

"Your lawyer friend said that you're trying to find an ex-lover?"

The way he says it, eyebrows raised, is slightly insulting. It catches her off guard, makes her flush. He's managed to somehow imply both that she's had too many lovers, and at the same time, that she's woefully naive, as if she has no idea how difficult finding even one such carelessly misplaced lover will be. She rocks back in her seat and loses the smile. This isn't going the way she'd planned.

"That's right," she says coolly. "We share a daughter, and she's disappeared."

"Your lawyer didn't mention a missing daughter in our telephone call. Does he know?"

She ignores this. "The person I'm trying to find—her father—I think he's involved in her disappearance. I'm sure of it."

He looks at her with considerably more interest.

"Your lawyer didn't mention that, either."

"It's not his job to know everything," she says, with a silent apology to Barry. "His job was to prescreen you. And frankly, based on the conversation so far, I'm not certain he was successful."

He's about to reply, but is interrupted by the appearance of the waitress, who smiles at him with a familiarity that implies he's a regular.

"Drinks, love? Or just food?" she says.

"Both, please. The usual to start. And my guest will have . . ." He turns to Holly.

"Tea for me, please," she says stiffly. The waitress's smile fades and she leaves.

"Drinking on the job?" Now it's Holly's turn to raise an eyebrow.

"Ah, but I'm not working yet, now am I?" He grins at her.

"Excuse me?"

"Right now I'm not working. I'm deciding whether I want to."

She bites back the words she wants to say, takes another deep breath. If Barry thinks this . . . this bounder . . . is the best, then he must be.

The waitress returns with their drinks—a pint for Christopher, and Holly's tea.

"Sure you don't want food? Shepherd's pie here is quite good."

"No, thank you."

"Suit yourself." He orders and the waitress leaves. He turns to Holly again, takes a sip of his beer, then puts it down.

"With a missing kid, why not go straight to the police? Why come to me?"

"My family is well-known," she says, happy to be back on comfortable ground. "The Darling family has been stalked by the media for years. The police would mean publicity—lots of it."

"You mean like with Mad Michael?" he says, humming a few bars of the ditty. Holly grimaces. Michael, Wendy's baby brother. Brilliant, quiet, and by all accounts kind in a way his siblings were not. Until the accident, which no one could explain—a sensible boy falling from the third-floor window of his house. After, he developed a penchant for misadventures large and public—disrobing in Hyde Park, waving wooden swords, claiming he could fly. It all culminated in a popular 1920s ditty, written when he tried to jump from his old nursery window naked, arms flapping as he crowed at the sky.

"I detest that song," Holly says through gritted teeth. "But yes. Great-Uncle Michael, and other, more recent events. I've experienced it first-hand, and it was miserable. I have a son as well as my daughter, and I'd like to spare them both that."

"Right," he says, all levity gone. He looks her up and down, as if it's his turn to assess her. "I read the newspaper coverage. The car crash was tragic. I'm very sorry for your loss."

She's startled and takes a sip of her tea to cover it. People never mention the crash to her. But there's something in his face. The semi-smirk he's worn since she sat down has disappeared, but it's more than that. It's as if he somehow understands what she's lost.

"It was a long time ago."

"Your daughter was born after, I take it? There's no talk of her in the newspapers."

Her hackles go up again, even though it's rational—expected, even, given his profession—that he would have researched her before their meeting.

"You've been busy," she says.

He shrugs. "It's my job. How old is your daughter?"

She hesitates, sees him notice. "Eden's biological age is thirteen, but she looks considerably older," she says. "She was born with a rare disorder that ages her prematurely. It's one of the reasons we've kept her life so private all these years."

The *we* is deliberate, as if someone else has sanctioned Holly's decisions. If Christopher catches it, he doesn't follow up on it.

"Has she been in contact with her father?"

"Not to my knowledge."

"Then why would he be interested now?"

Holly thinks of all the uses Peter could make of Eden and shivers. "We've kept her very sheltered because of her health problems," Holly says. "She's been . . . bedridden for the past few years. I don't think she'd be able to run away on her own. Her father is the logical person to facilitate something like this. And, to be honest, he might find it amusing to know I'm worried. Let's just say he's never really grown up."

He asks more questions. About Peter, about what he looks like and what he does for a living, and she tap-dances around both of those. She invents a fake name, says she doesn't know his occupation.

"He had a certain glow. Charisma. Like a movie star," is what she tells Christopher.

Christopher also asks about Eden. Again Holly skirts the truth. She can't simply say, *Actually, I haven't spoken to my daughter in years. She's been in a coma all this time, and now she's vanished, whether under her own power or someone else's I have no idea.* Nor can she share that for all of those years, she's been taking large vials of Eden's blood every month.

After a few moments he changes course. "Tell me about your business. Darling Skin Care?"

She looks at him, surprised. "You're interested in skin care?"

He gestures to his face. "Can't you tell?"

He's still far too handsome, but now she sees the dark circles under his eyes, the way his skin looks weather-beaten, as if he's spent too much time outside, the trace of a scar along one cheek. She looks at him uncertainly, and he laughs.

"Sorry. That was a joke," he says. "I never accept a client without knowing as much as I can about them. How long have you been in the business?"

"About ten years," she says. "I was a scientist before that. I started in London, then moved to New York for the market." What she doesn't say is that New York's other attraction was that Jack would be far, far away from Peter.

"Darling Skin Care didn't start to go big until a few years ago," she continues. "And now we're poised to go even bigger with a new cosmetics partnership. If it goes well, we're going to be a worldwide brand."

"I'd imagine you'd be that already, just based on your name," he says. "I mean, there's the book, the movies, the merchandise, and, yes, that unfortunate song. There can't be that many people left who haven't heard of you."

Holly takes a sip of her tea, lets it cool on her tongue before swallowing. "My name got me in the door," she says evenly. "But it's my effort—not the Darling name—that's put us on the map. And it's my product that will keep us there."

"Right then," he says, and the amusement in his voice makes her want to throttle him. Until she realizes he's provoking her just to see what she'll divulge.

After a pause, he seems to come to some sort of internal decision. "I'm happy to work with you to find your daughter and her father. Going forward, I'll need to get a picture of both of them, and hear as much as you can tell me about your ex. That may mean talking to others around you, including your son."

Holly shakes her head. "That's not possible. I told you, I want to spare him this." She also doesn't mention that photos of Peter don't exist.

"You told me you wanted to spare him the police," he corrects.

"Same thing."

"Not quite," he says, and there's something in those dark eyes that makes her shiver. She has a fleeting thought that hiring Christopher Cooke, no matter how highly he comes recommended, is a bad idea. But she needs him. She's had no luck finding Eden on her own.

"There's also the matter of my fee," he says. He names a retainer that is ridiculously high, even by Holly's standards.

"For that price, I expect results," she says coolly.

"For that price, you'll receive them. I hope they'll be what you want."

She looks sharply at him, but he's smiling, a wide-open, friendly smile. She lets the remark go and scribbles her mobile number on her napkin. She pushes it across the table to him.

"That's my private line. Text me your bank address, and I'll send you your first installment. I trust that's acceptable?"

He smiles again. "For now."

And once again, there's more meaning than she cares to parse behind those words. She prays she's not making a mistake. Either way, it's time to go. She stands, pushing in her chair. He starts to rise as well, but she gestures at him not to get up. "Please, don't bother," she says, slinging her purse over her shoulder.

Out of the corner of her eye she can see the waitress hurrying across the room, bearing a tray of food. "Enjoy your meal," Holly says, turning to go. At the last second, she remembers her umbrella. She steps back to retrieve it from its spot along the wall, then realizes the waitress will trap her in the corner if she isn't quick. She reaches for it, but in her haste knocks it toward the floor. Cooke sweeps out an arm to pin it against the wall.

Only then does she see that where his hand should be, there's a shining metal hook.

Her eyes widen. Her face, usually a cool mask, wears a look of shock. Perhaps horror. But she can't help it.

"Jesus bloody Christ," she mutters. But not for the reason he must think.

He holds it up, the umbrella neatly snagged in its curve. "Sorry. I didn't mention it, did I?" he says. There's a glee that borders on malice in his voice, although his expression is neutral. Unlike hers. "Roadside bomb. The fellow trying to defuse it ran out of time. Quite literally. Will it be a problem?"

"No," she says stiffly. She snatches the umbrella from him and works to force her expression back to something resembling calm. "Not for me."

"Good. For me, either. Luckily I've always been a lefty." He's flat-out grinning at her again. She tucks her purse more tightly against her side and slips past the waitress.

"I'll be in touch!" Christopher Cooke calls after her. Holly can hear the waitress chortling long after she flees out the door.

Chapter Fifteen

Holly's read the book a hundred times or more. First as a wide-eyed child, entranced by her mother's whispers that all of it was real. Her grandmother Wendy had flown to Neverland on an adventure that the world would not—did not—believe. Less often as a teenager, when she'd grown sick of Jane's obsession, when she'd decided the family stories were nothing more than wishful thinking, a fantastical escape. She'd almost forgotten it in college and graduate school. And then she'd fallen in love with Robert, the twins were born, and life itself seemed magical. For those few years, she'd seen the book as other people did. A harmless fairy tale. A breath of lightness.

The crash and everything that followed changed that. She went back to the story as a scientist and a mother, searching for the details that might awaken her daughter. By then Holly knew the story wasn't true—not in the way her mother thought it was. When Jack asked about the book—because of course there was no way to escape it—she told him it was pure fiction. She forbade Jane from saying otherwise. And that was that.

Until now. Because no matter how many times Holly read that damn book, she'd always known that her world and Neverland were separate entities. Only Peter, and those who traveled with him, crossed. But now? Now she's wondering if she's been wrong. Maybe the line between the real world and the magical one isn't quite as solid as she thinks. Maybe there are rules that Holly doesn't know—rules about who comes and goes, who stays. Who disappears. Maybe there's more than one way to come back from Neverland.

She stays out in the downpour until she's stopped shaking. Then she goes home to her mother's house. Nan has ordered a pizza, and crusts still litter the kitchen table.

"Sorry," Nan says. "I had a fair right time setting up the movie. Your mum's telly could be an antique. Did your meeting go well?"

"Fine," Holly says. "I'll be in the library if Jack needs me."

"Want some pizza? There's loads left."

"No, thanks." But her stomach is rumbling, and she realizes she hasn't eaten since this morning. And she's damp and cold.

"How about tea then?" Nan asks. "I'll bring up some biscuits as well."

"That would be lovely. Thanks."

She stops first to check on Jack. He and Ed are watching a football documentary and howling with outrage over the announcer's comments. They don't even notice her.

She spends the afternoon in an unsettled frame of mind, combing through all the Pan books once again, searching not so much for the boy himself as for his description. She writes down any characteristics she finds. When she's finished, she's amazed by how few there are, and how wildly unhelpful they will be in assisting Christopher. She adds all the details she can recall, but it's not much. No matter how hard she tries, Peter slips through her memories like a shadow. But then so much about those days and nights is lost to her. Grief, pain, and the lack of sleep engulfed her, cocooned her in a gray fog it was impossible to escape. She's still in the library when her mother returns.

"Hello, darling." Jane presses cool lips against Holly's temple. "Locked in here away from the boys? Lovely day for it. The rain is sheeting down. Of course we were inside all afternoon. The exhibit was fabulous—some newcomer from Ethiopia, I don't recall his name, but brilliant use of color."

"Sounds it," Holly says.

"Did you have a good afternoon? Was your work thing successful?"

"It was okay."

Jane unwinds the silk scarf from around her neck. "I can see you're not paying a bit of attention. Out with it, then. What's on your mind?"

"Nothing," Holly says, then hesitates. Jane will kill her if she knows she's hired a private detective. But . . . "Do you ever wonder about Nan? How odd it is, your hiring someone with that name?"

"Is that still troubling you? I'm sure it's just coincidence, darling. It's a wide world, after all, and a common name. No different from your Mr. Barry, I assume."

"I suppose." And it's true, when she'd first befriended Barry, they'd laughed about it. A fluke, nothing more, she'd thought. "It's just . . . how much do you really know about what happened to Grandma Wendy?"

Jane gives her a sharp look. "Something's certainly disturbed you." When Holly doesn't answer, she sinks gracefully into an overstuffed leather chair. "Over the years I've told you whatever I know. Whether you've listened is a completely different story. But ask away."

Holly lets the barb pass her by. She's had a long and complicated relationship with her family's history. But now Jane is right here. And Jane has studied Peter, studied Wendy, more than anyone she knows. It can't hurt to ask again, now that she has a different reason for her questions. She tries to think.

"How did our family meet Sir James?"

"In the park." Jane twines the silk scarf through her fingers. "He spotted the children—Wendy, John, and Michael—when they were on an outing, playing about. He found them fascinating, but then he was a drab little sparrow and couldn't believe his luck, falling in with such a bevy of swans. Especially Wendy. He was dazzled by her, drawn to her glamour and more than a little jealous of her imagination. He was a writer, after all, but couldn't match her stories. Or her life. So he stole them.

"And she tolerated it, in part because she was so young. But also, I think, because she could tell, even then, that he could help her. She wasn't particularly happy at home, although she never talked about why, and Barrie's story and the fame it brought, as well as the money he left her from the books and the movies, gave her a freedom not many women possessed at that time. He changed her life."

The scarf has gone slack in Jane's lap, but now she picks it up again. "I met him once, you know," she says, and her voice has gone dreamy, the way it used to when she told Holly bedtimes stories about Peter Pan.

"After he was knighted? Yes, you've told me that," Holly says, trying to keep the impatience out of her voice.

Jane shakes her head. "No, before. The first time. I was a little girl, very young. He'd come to the house, and my mother said we were to have a special visitor, and I looked at this tiny man in a brown plaid jacket that was too big and thought, 'There's nothing special about *him*.' He smelled of liniment and tobacco smoke, and I couldn't understand why my beautiful mother would have anything to do with him, or why she introduced him as one of her dearest friends."

She's silent a moment, lost in her memories. "We were here, in the library. Mother's face was strained. She was waiting for the tea things to be brought. I had the distinct impression she was watching me, which was unusual, because she almost never paid attention to anything I did, so long as I was clean and polite and quiet. But she turned away to speak to the maid, and as soon as she did, he beckoned me over.

"'Hello,' he said, leaning forward. He was sitting and I was standing, and we were almost exactly the same height. He took a peppermint stick out of his pocket and offered it to me. We both checked that Wendy wasn't watching before I took it.

126

"'Seen that Peter fellow about?' he whispered.

"'Mother won't talk about it. Father says he's just a story.'

"'Don't let *him* hear you say that. I have it on excellent authority he's a real live boy,' he said with a nod toward Mother. 'I made her famous, you know. I can do the same for you, if you tell me any tales.' A distant look came over his face. 'I always wanted to meet him. He seemed like such a nice chap.'"

The scarf has fallen to the floor. Jane makes no move to pick it up. "It was the first I'd heard that, that Peter was real," she says, and her voice is still far away. "Mother had never told me before—she'd always treated it as a story."

"What happened?"

"Oh, she came back to the conversation and that was the end of our little tête-à-tête," Jane says. She picks up the scarf. "Mother must have overheard, because she was quite cool to both of us, but I badgered and badgered her from that day forward until she broke down and admitted what he said was true. We owe him quite the debt, Mr. Barrie. If it weren't for him, if it were up to my mother, we might never have learned the truth of Peter at all."

"Indeed," Holly murmurs. There are no answers in Jane's story, only more questions after all.

Holly set her phone to silent while she was working. At the end of Jane's tale, she glances down and sees a string of texts across the screen. One is from Christopher Cooke with his banking information, and the rest are from an increasingly worried-sounding Barry. They break the spell Jane's had her under.

She holds up the phone. "I'm sorry, would you mind? I have a work call I have to make."

"At this hour?" Jane glances at her watch. "Surely those Americans don't expect you to work twenty-four hours a day?" She sees Holly's face

127

and relents. "Oh, all right. I'll cajole the boy into helping me set the table, and then we can have a cocktail. Don't be long."

As soon as the door closes, Holly wires the money to Cooke's account. The amount makes her wince, but she's out of options. Besides, she'd pay anything to bring Eden home. She also texts him a list of places to start looking, including Soho, nursing homes, and hospitals. Then she calls Barry. He answers on the first ring.

"Are you all right?" he asks immediately.

"Yes. I'm sorry to have worried you. After the meeting, I was . . . working on ideas for a new product and I lost track of time." The lie stings. Work has always been Holly's refuge, but now there's no room for anything else but Eden and Jack.

"I got a bad feeling when I didn't hear from you. I thought you'd been kidnapped or something," Barry says. He sounds serious. "I have to tell you, I called my contacts back and pushed them, hard. Not sure this guy is such a good idea after all."

"Too late," Holly says, trying for cheerful. "I've already sent the money." She taps her fingers against the laptop's case. She supposes it's still possible to stop the transfer. "Please, tell me I won't regret this."

"He has serious anger issues. He got bumped off the force after a series of conflicts, the last one of which culminated in him grabbing a dealer by the neck. Almost crushed his windpipe. But guess what . . ."

"He used his hook," she says.

"Yeah. You saw it?"

"Hard to miss."

"He seems to think it's hilarious. But it's a strange coincidence. The guys on the force? They refer to him as Captain Hook. Any chance he could be a Darling fame stalker after all?"

There's an uncomfortable silence. Barry knows she doesn't like to talk about the novel or her family's link to it. Even as her panic rises, she knows there's little she can tell him—or nothing he'd believe—so she tries for a light tone.

"The press would have a field day, wouldn't they?" she says. "'Captain Hook Searches for Darling Girl's Lost Lover.' But no, I don't think he's a stalker. Even the craziest ones wouldn't go to that length."

She hopes he buys it and is relieved when he shifts focus.

"Either way he's a bit of a black sheep. My contacts weren't big on the details, even when I pushed, but they implied that his usual clients are the parents of teen addicts. He hunts down the dealers and convinces them to stay away. Sometimes the convincing gets physical, and the rumor is he often does that part for free. A part-time vigilante."

"So why help me?"

"He uses expensive clients like you to finance the cost of the addict work. That's what my source says."

"The expensive part is right. You should hear what his retainer was. Is he really that good?"

"He's supposed to be the best. But Holly, he sounds volatile. I'm not sure it's worth it."

"I have to try, Barry. I've got nothing else."

He's quiet for a bit. She can almost hear his thoughts, and she bites her lip, hoping he won't push. Keeping secrets from Barry by omission is hard enough. A direct question could be her undoing. But:

"I'm not going to pry. But you know I'm always here if you need me."

She hopes that's true. She doesn't know if he would say the same if he knew how many secrets she still had.

Holly spends the next day working. She signs off on the final Pixie Dust marketing campaign, approves a list of Instagram influencers tapped to receive free samples, and reviews ideas from Elliot and the rest of the science team on everything from an eye cream with yeast and caffeine (green light) to a serum containing sea cucumbers (she sets a reminder on her phone to call Elliot for more details). In between emails she paces. Anxiety about Eden is never far away, and she's bleary-eyed from another sleepless night spent with the nursery window open to the sky.

Jane has set up a dinner with some of her friends and their grand-children. When Holly finally makes it downstairs, showered and dressed for the evening, she overhears Nan offering to take Jack to Ed's lacrosse practice the next day.

"Thanks so much, Nan, but that won't be necessary," Holly says, stepping into the kitchen. "I'll take him." She can see the disappoint-ment on Jack's face and feels a twinge of guilt.

"But you don't know where it is!" he protests.

"It's no trouble, really," Nan says. "I have to run my brother over as well."

Holly smiles at them both. "I'm not sure what Jack's grandmother has planned for tomorrow. But if we can fit it in, we will. Thanks."

"Let me give you the address," Nan says, scribbling it and her phone number on a piece of paper. Jack snatches it from her before Holly can.

Damn. Lacrosse is not what Jack needs right now. Holly has to shut this down. "I didn't realize how late it was—I'm so sorry to have kept you," she says brightly. "Have a good night. And Jack, you should prob-ably go clean up. We'd better leave if we don't want to be late. You know how your grandmother is about punctuality."

He scowls at her but leaves the room. Holly sees Nan out. She'd like to tell her not to come tomorrow, but she can't do that, not without angering Jane. So she settles for locking the door behind her.

Chapter Sixteen

Jane's chosen a trendy Middle Eastern restaurant for dinner. There are a handful of teens present, and they sit at a separate table from the adults. Holly glances over at Jack a few times. He seems to be happily engaged. Good. Maybe she'll get lucky and they'll all make plans for tomorrow and lacrosse will naturally fall off his radar.

The evening passes quickly. Jane's friends are interesting and entertaining, and despite herself, Holly enjoys their company. Several of the women use Darling Skin Care products, and they exclaim about them to Jane, who gives Holly an approving look. An unexpected warmth floods Holly, and it's not from the wine she's drinking.

At the end of the meal, the teens decide to see a late-night movie. The show is within walking distance, and one of the older boys offers to drive Jack home after. Holly hesitates. She'd like to say no. Thinking of Jack walking the same streets as Peter gives her chills. It's why she left London for Cornwall, then fled to New York when Cornwall turned out to be not far enough. But she can't come up with a plausible excuse. So she gives him some money and reminds him to stay with the group and to call if he's going to be later than midnight.

"Let him enjoy himself," Jane says. "You can't keep him a baby forever."

Oh, but I can, Holly thinks. *Or at least I can keep him safe.* She banishes that last day in New York, Jack's bloody nose, from her mind. The cut from lacrosse the day before that. What will happen to him if she can't find Eden. Or if Peter finds him first.

No.

Instead she concentrates on the nursery, on the knife under her pillow there.

I can.

"I'd like to go for a little drive, see what's changed in the city," she says instead to her mother. "Any chance you can get a ride home?"

Jane gives her a sharp-eyed look. "Should I be worried?"

"Of course not," Holly says innocently. She feels a sudden, surprising solidarity with Jack. Who, if he were still in the room, would surely be laughing at her.

Holly heads back to the same section of town she'd explored on her first day. At night, the shadows make it more ominous. Bits of broken glass shine under the streetlights, and every stranger on a corner seems suspicious.

She doesn't get out of the car, just cruises the streets. Couples stroll through the night, holding hands. A few homeless men sleep in doorways or sit on the sidewalk, cardboard boxes and knapsacks by their sides. None of these people look anything like Peter. None look like Eden.

She parks and waits under an old bridge. It's darker here, and trash blows into the corners of the supports. She glances at her watch. She'll give it another twenty minutes before she heads home. She turns off her headlights, lets her eyes adjust to the night.

Shadowy figures come and go, but it's hard to see. Everyone is beautiful in the dark. Once, she's certain she's found him—there's a flash of golden hair, and a boy with easy grace walks out of the darkness toward a waiting car. Her heart lurches, but when he stops under the streetlight, he's too young. Jack's age. Holly's stomach roils with disgust, then anger as she watches the car drive away. If Christopher Cooke is protecting children like this, she has more understanding of his windpipe-crushing rage.

A few minutes after eleven, she calls it. She wants to be home when Jack comes in. She starts the car, puts it in gear, and is pulling away when something catches her eye. She brakes, watches the figure striding along the sidewalk on the opposite side of the street. It's lithe and boyish, in a dark jacket and cap. Familiar somehow. She holds her breath, studying, trying to parse out where she knows it from. Could it be . . . and then a beam from the streetlight catches an errant lock of hair. Silver, not gold. Not Jack. Not Peter.

Jane.

She's nowhere near the restaurant where they ate dinner. Nowhere near home.

What the bloody hell?

Before Holly can do more than gawp, Jane disappears down the Tube entrance.

Holly guns through several yellow lights and breaks the speed limit, but she makes it to the Tube stop closest to home in record time. Traffic is light, so she double parks. She doesn't have long to wait. Less than ten minutes after Holly pulls up, Jane hurries out of the station. She doesn't even look around—that's how confident she is. She heads straight for home.

Not so fast, Holly thinks.

She lowers the passenger window and calls out. Jane doesn't hear her, so Holly beeps her horn, a shocking breach of the neighborhood's etiquette. Jane's head whips around. To her credit, her eyes widen only fractionally when she sees Holly.

"Hey," Holly calls. Two can play it cool. "Want a ride?"

Holly expects her mother to say no, but Jane doesn't. She slides right into the front passenger seat. She doesn't make excuses about where she's been. She doesn't lie. She doesn't talk at all, not until they're pulling into the driveway.

"You know," she finally says, looking down at her hands, "in the stories, it's always the children who fly off and have adventures. The mothers have to stay home and wait for them to return." She looks up. "I'm tired of waiting."

And with that, she goes inside, leaving Holly to put the car away herself.

When Holly comes in, the house is quiet. Jane must have gone upstairs. Holly, waiting for Jack, finds herself turning her mother's words over in her mind. Holly's spent her own fair share of time waiting, of putting her wants and needs on hold to put those of her children first. Hasn't she? The move to Cornwall, that was all about waiting for Jack to recover. And before that, the time she took off from her research position at the university when the twins were born. She was waiting then too.

But what about New York? an insidious little voice whispers inside her head. *You weren't waiting then, were you? Not for Eden to get better. And not for Jack, either, not really. New York is all about you. Your laboratory. Your work.*

It's not true, she tells herself. She'd fled over the ocean so that Peter couldn't follow, not for a job opportunity. If she found success there, that was an added benefit, one she couldn't have predicted. And Darling Skin Care has given her the money to take care of Eden and Jack, the contacts and the equipment and the research to save them, if saving is possible. Staying home and caring for them herself wouldn't have accomplished anything.

Even so, she's glad when Jack comes home at the stroke of midnight and she can ask him about his night before he climbs the stairs for bed. It shuts the voice up, for now.

The memories are harder to silence.

On Eden's fifth birthday, the library at Grace House looks like a party scene right before the guests arrive. Brightly colored streamers and balloons cover every surface of the room. A *Happy Birthday* banner hangs over the window. Flowers stand in vases. Music plays from the radio. She's given the nurses the afternoon off, so it's just the two of them. She'd wanted to create some sense of normalcy, wanted for one day to pretend her daughter isn't sick, only sleeping. One day to weigh the decision facing her.

Eden is wearing the blue party gown Holly sent from London last week, and her golden hair has been curled into ringlets. If you didn't know better, if you could overlook the tubes and IVs and monitors, you might think she was asleep. Pink cheeks, long dark lashes, glowing skin. The picture of health.

Except she won't wake up. And she can't stop growing.

Holly sets her packages down at the foot of the bed, brushes her lips across Eden's forehead. She smooths a lock of hair off Eden's face, then pulls a chair over and sits beside her daughter.

"Happy birthday!" she croons. There's no response. Holly hadn't expected one, not really, but three years later it's still a gut punch to see her spirited daughter so still. Holly's tried everything the doctors have given her as well as whatever she could find on her own—steroids, antibiotics, fish oil, animal hormones imported from South America, chemical compounds she'd go to jail for if anyone found out. But nothing wakes Eden. And nothing stops the growing.

Holly reaches out and holds Eden's hand, massaging it between her own. "You're five, big girl!" Her voice cracks, and she clears her throat before continuing.

"Jack sends his love. He's getting to be so big and strong. You wouldn't recognize him."

Jack asked after his sister for the longest time. He cried during every visit when it came time to go, was depressed and lethargic for days after. Holly stopped bringing him.

The doctors Jack sees, the physical therapists he needs, are in the city. They're all amazed at his physical recovery.

Holly glances at the IV bag and then away.

Eden, on the other hand, did not thrive in London. She grew thinner and thinner in her hospital bed on the second floor of Darling House, no matter what nutritional supplements the nurses put in her feeding tube. She broke out in angry bedsores no matter how often they turned her.

And at night, when shadows fell across the room, her blood pressure spiked to dangerous levels.

No matter how often Holly checked to make sure the windows were shut and locked, no matter how many times she argued with Jane about the importance of keeping them that way, she couldn't shake the feeling that Eden was being watched. Couldn't help but wonder what Peter would do with a damaged daughter.

A damaged daughter with special qualities.

So in a last-gasp effort based more on instinct than science, Holly moved her back to Grace House, a place Eden had always loved. Where miraculously the shadows didn't seem to follow. Slowly the color returned to her face. She put on weight. Holly still holds out hope that someday the sea air and the surroundings Eden loved will bring her back.

Because nothing Holly's tried so far has.

"I have some news," she says, squeezing Eden's hand. Her words echo in the room. "I've been offered a job. Well, not a job, exactly. More like a company. The compounds I've been working on to help you and Jack—it turns out they might have other uses. Isn't that exciting?"

When the investors had first come to her, lured by a paper she'd published, she'd turned them down. She was a serious scientist. Not a bored rich housewife looking to start a skin care line for vanity's sake. But they'd been insistent. And with the money and terms they offered, she could create a top-notch lab that just might help her save both her children. If that meant making skin cream during the day so she could research at night, it was an easy trade-off.

Other choices weren't so simple.

"The only drawback is . . ." She hesitates, straightening Eden's blanket. "They want me to come to New York.

"It's a long ways away. Maybe too far. And I haven't decided yet. But no matter what, I'll still come to see you. And when you wake up, you'll join us no matter where we are. And we'll be a family again just like we were. All right?"

Jack is starting to forget. Not just Isaac and Robert, but Eden too. Hard as that is to witness, it's made his life easier. New York would bring a new school with new friends, people who don't know about his missing twin, his dead father, and his comatose sister. People who can't remind him of his tragic past.

A fresh start.

"Eden?" Holly says softly. "Can you hear me?"

She waits, searches Eden's face for some sign that she's heard, some indication she's listening. But the only answer is the steady sound of Eden's breathing.

She won't cry in front of her daughter. She won't.

She takes a deep breath, blows it out, lets go of Eden's hand and turns away. When she faces back, her smile is in place.

"Let's look at your presents," she says cheerily.

Ridiculous now, the pile of shiny gifts at the foot of the bed. Books for the nurses to read aloud to Eden. Soft cotton dresses in bright colors. Plush stuffed animals. Holly unwraps each one, holds it up, and exclaims over it in the empty room.

When she's finished with the last one, she is so very tired. She puts her head down next to her daughter's and closes her eyes. Beneath the scent of antiseptic, she still smells like Eden, fresh and clean.

Like spring.

"Eden," she whispers. "Please wake up. Please."

Nothing.

Holly sits up. "Right. Cake time," she says unsteadily. "I'll just fetch the candles."

The corridor is dark and cool after the warmth and brightness of Eden's room, and Holly is glad for it. She finds the candles and matches in the kitchen drawer, grabs them, and starts back down the hall when it hits her. The candles are blue and green. The twins' favorite colors.

The last time she'd used them was for their third birthday.

She stops where she is. Takes deep, calming breaths the way her therapist taught her. Leans against the wall to steady herself. When she looks up, it's to see Isaac gazing back at her from a black-and-white photo. He's on the staircase, caught in the moment before he leapt into her arms, rosebud mouth open in a shriek of glee. His delighted gaze goes straight through the glass and into Holly's heart. Instinctively she finds herself reaching out to catch him. To feel the warm weight of him nestled safely into her body. Instead she stretches out a finger and touches the frame.

And then pulls it from the wall and smashes it to the floor.

The next photo is of the twins. They're on the beach in Irish knit sweaters, arms wrapped around each other, chubby faces beaming. Holly looks at it for the longest time. She's never noticed before, but together their two bodies form the shape of a heart.

She lifts the frame high and smashes it down. It breaks, glass shattering across the floor.

The hallway wall is lined with pictures, moments she'd once wanted to remember forever: Robert, his shirt off, chasing the twins on the beach. Jack, Isaac, and Robert cuddled together on the couch, sound asleep. She and Robert captured in candlelight, leaning in, about to kiss. She remembers that night with crystal clarity: the heat of the flame on her face, the warmth of Robert's knee pressing into hers. The pictures stretch on and on.

Holly smashes them all.

Dimly, she knows she's out of control, but she can't stop. She's tired of deep breaths, of holding on, of being strong. She can't do it anymore.

When she reaches Eden's room, she leans her forehead against the door. The wood is damp, and it's not until she touches her face that she realizes she's crying.

She's still clutching the birthday candles in her hand.

She stays there a long time, alone in the dark corridor. There's no sound other than her ragged breathing. At last she rubs her eyes, swipes her sleeve across her face. Glances at the trail of destruction behind her. She'll have to clean it up. But for now she turns her back on it and pushes open the door.

"I found them," Holly says. "Let's light them up, shall we?"

There are ten candles left in the package. Her daughter is only five, but Holly lights them all. She doesn't blow them out, just watches them burn. It takes longer than she'd thought, and when they've extinguished themselves and dripped wax all over the frosting, she throws out the ruined cake that her daughter was never going to eat. She sweeps up the glass and piles the broken frames in the trash. She can't bear to throw the photos out, so she shoves them in the bottom drawer of a dresser. Later, she'll have them boxed up and sent to her mother's house for safekeeping. And then she sits in silence beside Eden, staring at the floor.

When she hears the nurses return, she kisses her daughter's forehead, trying to store up the scent of her hair, the warmth of her skin. As she stands, she notices one last photo on the bureau. It's of Eden.

She's sitting on a low tree branch in the garden, and her face is alive with mischief and energy. Holly picks it up. Hesitates. Looks at it for a long time. Glances at her daughter.

"Goodbye," she whispers.

She slips the photo into her purse. Then tugs her jacket straight, opens the door, and steps across the threshold, toward New York.

Chapter Seventeen

Holly's still sitting at the kitchen table, lost in her thoughts, when her mother appears at the door.

"Did Jack come in?"

Holly nods. "About half an hour ago. Linda Neil's grandson dropped him," she says. "He sounded as if he had quite the time."

"Lovely. Who knows, they might become fast friends."

"I hope so," Holly says. Plans with the group from dinner means less time for lacrosse, and all the better if he skips it with no urging from her. It's one less thing for him to resent her for.

"Come have a cup of tea with me in the library."

"I need a shower," Holly demurs.

"I'll put the kettle on," Jane says, as if she hasn't heard. Holly debates with herself for a moment, but she already knows who will win this battle of wills. She sighs. Whatever her mother has to say, she hopes it will be quick.

It's not, of course. Jane takes her time, setting the table in the library as if they're settling in for a full repast instead of a cup and a few biscuits. And Holly can't help herself. It's after midnight and she's exhausted. She's the one who breaks the silence first. Two points to Jane.

"Mother."

"I've been thinking," Jane says, as if she's been waiting for Holly to speak. "Perhaps we are going about this all wrong. Perhaps we could help each other." She pours tea into Holly's cup. The mint-scented steam rises toward her face, and Holly breathes it in gratefully.

"How?"

"It has occurred to me that we both want the same thing. We both want to find him," Jane says. She says *him* with an emphasis that makes it perfectly clear who she means.

"Yes . . . ," Holly says cautiously.

"You want to find him to save Eden. I do too, of course," Jane says. "There's nothing I want more than to see her safe in your arms. When I think of what that poor child has already been through, think of that whirlwind of a child so still all these years . . ." She shakes her head. "I'll do anything I can to help bring her home, and that includes using all my knowledge to search for Peter. But there's another reason."

The only thing that gives Holly the self-control not to roll her eyes at her mother is the image of Jack doing the same thing to her. She bites her tongue, takes a too-big sip of tea, and manages to stay silent.

But her efforts aren't lost on Jane. "Oh, I know what you're thinking," she says. "That I've been obsessed with Peter from the time you were a little girl. But that's not the truth. Not entirely." There are silver tongs and a sugar bowl on the table, and she takes a single lump and drops it into her cup, watching it dissolve as she swirls it with her spoon. Silence stretches between them.

"Do you remember your grandmother?" Jane finally asks. Her voice is wistful.

"Of course."

"By the time you met her, she was quite old, and worn from taking care of Uncle Michael for so many years," she says. Jane, of course, makes no reference to the song. "Caretaking wasn't really in her nature, at least not by the time I was born, no matter how Mr. Barrie portrayed her. She found children, especially her own, quite dull. But she did tell the most wonderful stories sometimes, especially when her guard was down."

142

Jane sees the look on Holly's face and frowns. "About Peter, certainly. But also about traveling as a young girl and seeing the world, rebelling against her parents by working during the war, finding your grandfather and having adventures with him. About *living*."

"But you—" Holly starts to say, but Jane cuts her off.

"I never did any of that. Oh, yes, I danced for a few years," she says, waving a hand dismissively. "And I was good. Just not good enough to be one of the greats, the ones whose names go down in history. So I waited and waited for Peter to come, for it to be my turn. I thought that's when my life would start, like it had for Wendy. But he never did. And then I met your father and had you, and my chance to meet him was over. I kept house and I raised you and I joined all the organizations that a rich, titled lawyer's wife should. But it's only since your father died that I've really begun to live, to discover what I want. And now I find, as I reach old age, that I don't care to stop."

For one heart-stopping moment Holly thinks Jane has guessed her secret, that she wants the youth and vitality that comes from Eden's blood. To buy herself time, she reaches for the charcoal sketch of Wendy, John, and Michael that rests on the table, pretending to study it. But her mother sees her face and shakes her head.

"I don't know for certain what you were up to with Eden, and I don't want to know. I see what you've done for Jack—it's a miracle. But I don't want eternal life—how terrible would that be? I want to *experience* life, really live it, before I die. I want strange new countries and whatever comes with them, whether it be late-night flying lessons, pirates, or fairies. I want the moon and the silver stars and the midnight sky all to myself, when everyone else is asleep. I have no husband now, no small children, so perhaps it is my turn at last."

She looks away for a moment, then turns back to Holly and smiles. "When I say it aloud, it sounds crazy. But finally seeing Peter would count as an awfully big adventure, wouldn't it?"

"He's not who you think he is," Holly says. "He's dangerous." She makes her voice forceful, her tone certain. If she told her mother the truth, would Jane believe her? She hesitates. It's not a chance she wants to take right now. But at least Holly can try to disabuse her of the idea that Peter is still some kind of hero.

But even before she's finished speaking, Jane is leaning forward, intent on her point. "But even that's an adventure, don't you see? He's not like the storybook. In a sense, he's become someone completely new, someone Wendy never met." Jane smiles again. "I think that sounds terrifically exciting."

Holly shakes her head. Jane will never believe her. "What do you want from me?"

"I want to help," Jane says promptly. "Surely you must see you'll never find him the way you're looking. It's too random. And driving through all the seedy neighborhoods of London at night—no, don't deny it, I know that was you—it's too dangerous."

Holly exhales hard. "What about you?"

"I'm perfectly safe, my darling. I'm a woman over a certain age. I might as well be invisible."

Holly starts to protest. Her mother is still beautiful, and even if she weren't, she'd still be vulnerable, especially in that neighborhood. But Jane puts a hand up. "You can't understand what I mean. Not yet. You're too young. But if you'll let me help you, I promise to curtail my . . . nocturnal adventures. For now. How's that?" She sips her tea.

"What do you propose?"

"I've been searching for him for years. No one alive has studied Peter more than I have, and I swear, I've been within a hairsbreadth of him more times than I could count. He's been at the window—I could *feel* him there—but he didn't want me. Once, he must have wanted you. If we work together—if we go to the places I've found, together—perhaps he'll show himself."

"And what do you want in return?" Holly asks. With Jane, there is almost always a quid pro quo.

"To see him. Talk with him." Jane looks out the window, although it is so dark out there's nothing to see. "Perhaps to ask him why he never came back. Not for me."

There's such longing on Jane's face that Holly can barely look. She has to wrap her own arms around herself for comfort. Has her mother ever wanted anything else as much in her life? Did she ever feel that way about Holly, about her father? And what would Jane do if she knew the real reason Peter has stayed away all these years?

Holly doesn't want to think about it.

"I suppose," she says. If her mother is going to look for Peter anyhow, it would be safer for everyone if Holly can keep an eye on her. But she won't tell Jane about Christopher. There's a strict line the Darlings aren't supposed to cross when it comes to talking about their problems with outsiders, particularly those affiliated with the police or the papers. And Christopher skates perilously close to it. And then there's the oddity of his name, of his arm. It makes her uneasy, and Jane would demand answers Holly can't give. So she'll keep him to herself. For now. "We can try it."

"Do you really think he has Eden?"

Holly nods. "There's no way Eden could have left Cornwall on her own. Even if she did wake up on her own, why wouldn't she stay? Why wouldn't the nurses notice? And she has no money, no way of getting around. She had to have assistance. Peter is the logical choice."

"It might help," Jane says slowly, "if I knew why he came for you. It might help us find Eden. Or draw Peter out."

They've never talked about it directly. And Holly can't tell Jane the whole truth, but she can tell her pieces. "It's not like the stories. It's not innocence that draws him. When Peter came to me, it was after . . . after Robert and Isaac." It hurts to say their names. "I was at the end. I wasn't sure I could go on." Something occurs to her. "The night he came to Grandma Wendy, wasn't she upset as well?"

"Yes. She'd been banished from the nursery, remember? Condemned to grow up. It was to be her last night there. She'd sleep in her own room after that."

Holly thinks of the leather album she'd found in the attic, all those pictures of Wendy and a man with his face cut out. She's sure now that there was more to Wendy's story, secrets that her grandmother kept. Reasons Peter came for her that had nothing to do with a last night in the nursery, but with moving to a room where she'd be alone. "Maybe it's not the innocence, it's the loss of it."

Jane leans forward, clearly intrigued. "You think he's drawn to emotions?"

Holly hesitates. "I think he's drawn to pain. That could be what happened in Cornwall. If Eden woke up after all these years and found herself alone, even if it was only for a short time, she might have despaired. She might have thought she'd lost everything, and that's what drew him in. And he's connected to our family, to the Darlings. Maybe he can somehow sense our feelings, the way sharks sense blood."

"Not a very flattering interpretation. He must have changed terribly from what by all accounts was an enchanting child. But then again, I had no idea he could grow older."

"The story never says he can't grow older," Holly says. "Only that he can't grow up."

"Fascinating," Jane muses. "I'd never thought of that."

"And as for changing, I don't think what I saw was innocence," Holly says slowly. "More . . . willful ignorance. A deliberate decision not to know."

She pauses, trying to put it into words. "When he came in through the window that first night, he was like . . . like everything you can imagine. Christmas and springtime both. If there's truly magic in this world, that was the closest I'll ever come to experiencing it."

"Goodness. It sounds terrible," Jane says. Her voice is entirely without sympathy.

"I was so broken that night, so close to giving up," Holly says, ignoring her. "And it was as if he healed everything that was wrong with me." She thinks back, shivers. *And then deliberately broke me all over again.* "For a bit, anyways."

There's no way Holly can explain, not in words. But that doesn't mean she doesn't remember.

Chapter Eighteen

She's never spoken of that night to anyone, let alone Jane, but it haunts her dreams. The way Peter had reached out, curious, and traced a finger across her shoulders, along her collarbone, then down her side to her exposed knee, his touch as delicate as a butterfly, but curious too, as if he'd never touched anyone before. She'd stood motionless, barely breathing, afraid a single careless movement would drive him away. As if he were a wild creature visiting her room.

The breeze from the window moved through her thin nightgown, but she already had goose bumps. He kissed her in odd places: The crook of her elbow. The back of her wrist. The nape of her neck. Each kiss accompanied by the warmth of his breath, the heat of his lips, so that the contrast with the cold air from outside made her dizzy. She closed her eyes, shivered. When he kissed her lips, she wouldn't let herself think at all. But her body, starved for touch since the crash, had a mind of its own. When at last she wrapped an arm around Peter's neck and slowly, gently, drew him down to the bed, she'd almost forgotten who he was. Or, rather, who he wasn't.

She kept her eyes closed, concentrated only on sensation: Hands spread like starfish over her breasts, cupping them through the fabric. Warm lips along her collarbone. Fingers running along her legs, up the inside of her thighs, rucking her nightgown to her waist. Weight, surprisingly solid, pinning her to the bed, pressing her hips down. A long hesitation, during which she remained perfectly still. When she felt him enter her, she gasped, willed herself to stay where she was, someplace between awake and dreaming. Someplace she'd been only with Robert.

He moved deliberately, long slow strokes that made her arch against him. His rhythm carried her, drove her along like a swimmer caught in a current. If she didn't move, she would drown. Faster and faster, until a shower of stars exploded through her body, filling every inch of her with warmth and light. She cried out, bit her lip to stifle the name she'd almost called. Kept her eyes closed.

She felt him collapse onto the bed next to her. He hadn't said a word, and he didn't touch her. When at last she could pretend no longer, she turned on her side to look at him. His face was pale, his eyes huge, and she felt a sudden wave of sympathy that pierced through the darkness cloaking her. Perhaps he was more of a boy than a man after all.

"Are you all right?" she asked, reaching out her hand to touch him. It was as if she'd broken a spell. In the blink of an eye, he was at the window and then gone, the tiniest flicker of a light at his heels.

She'd slept then, her body sated but still worn by grief and pain. In the morning, it had seemed no more than a feverish dream, the type she'd had almost nightly since the wreck. Only for the first time, she hadn't dreamed of Robert. Not really.

The next night, she bathed with lavender oil and plaited her hair. She sat by the window, watching the stars wink against the darkness, and told herself she'd imagined it all. Even so, when she shivered, it wasn't entirely because of the cool night breeze. At last she made her way to bed, sliding under the crisp white sheets and closing her eyes.

"Does it hurt?" A voice said in her ear. She opened her eyes and sat bolt upright. He was there, to the right of the bedpost, so still he could almost be a shadow.

"What?"

"What we did. Does it hurt?"

"No." She didn't elaborate, just watched him, not moving as he came closer. He knelt on the bed, staring at her. He'd shut the window, and a small golden light fluttered against the glass. She closed her eyes again, tilted her face. Waited.

The kiss, when it came, was like a butterfly landing against her lips, so light she could have imagined it. He kissed her again, moving down her jaw, to her neck. A flock of butterflies, moving in the breeze. She leaned toward him and—

"Ow!" Her eyes flew open.

He was studying her, head cocked, an expression of almost clinical interest on his face.

"Did that hurt?"

"Yes," she said, struggling to stay calm, putting a hand to her neck to make sure she wasn't bleeding. The fugue state she'd been moving through for what felt like months receded, leaving her completely and shockingly wide-awake. "Yes. It did hurt when you bit me. Very much."

"Oh." He reached out and she flinched, but he simply traced the mark on her neck with his finger. "Did you like it?"

"No," she said firmly. "Not at all." And then, as the thought occurred to her: "Did you?"

"I'm not sure," he said. He kissed her again, but this time she kept her eyes open.

The third and final time Peter visited, Holly almost shut the window. She was bruised from the night before, which was how she knew it was not a dream. That and the startling clarity she had, as if she were awake for the first time in ages. He'd made it impossible for her to be any-where but present. Each time she tried to slip off in her head to Robert, she'd found herself yanked back by a pinch, a too-hard squeeze, a kiss that took all her oxygen, and not in the good way. Nothing lasted more than a second, and nothing left a lasting scar. It was as if he was testing, pushing her limits, trying to see how far he could go.

It was disturbing, and at the same time oddly thrilling: To have a secret, something that was hers alone, that pulled her from the edge of the abyss she'd been teetering on and kept her centered here. To have something to think about besides the past, the painful present, the terrifying future. All the same, she'd made up her mind that if he visited this evening, there would be ground rules.

But he came through the window so suddenly there was no time to speak. He'd barely latched it closed before he was grabbing her and swinging her onto the bed, bending her over it. She tried to say something, to call his name, to tell him stop, but he pushed her face firmly into the pillow and held her there. He was so much stronger than she'd thought. Her bad leg wouldn't bear her weight, was collapsing beneath her. She couldn't push off enough to claw at him without falling deeper into the bed. He was biting her neck, as if to hold her in place while he finished. She couldn't breathe. The blackness behind her eyelids was darker than the room, and tiny crackles of light shot across her vision.

And then the pressure was gone. She turned her head, took in a gasping breath. And another. A third. Pushed herself up.

He'd thrown himself next to her on the bed and was watching.

"We've been doing it wrong," he said conversationally, as if nothing had happened. "I watched the animals today at the zoo. It's not supposed to be face-to-face."

"Get out," Holly whispered. Even though she hadn't screamed, her throat felt bruised. She tried to stand, but couldn't get her leg to hold her. She moved as far away from him on the bed as she could. "Get out now."

"We're married now, aren't we? That's what all the married ones do. That's what it takes. I've seen them, looking in the windows. Most of them did it wrong too."

"Get out," she said again, louder. She wanted to shout, to throw things at him, but she had no breath, no way to stand. And there was no one to hear her if she did. Her mother was not home. And Holly hadn't told her about Peter. She hadn't wanted to share him.

She had wanted him all to herself.

"We're married now," he repeated cheerfully. "You have to come with me." His tone reminded her of the twins, before the car crash, when they'd done something wrong and were pretending they hadn't. A determined, studied innocence. He looked at her leg, nudged it with his foot. She recoiled.

"I can fix that for you," he said temptingly. "If you come with me. There's no pain in Neverland. Nobody's broken there."

She looked around the room for a weapon. There was a silver frame on the bedside table, a charcoal sketch of Wendy, John, and Michael. She grabbed for it, afraid he'd stop her. And then thought: *Jack*.

I can fix that, he'd said. Could he fix Jack too? She took a deep breath, tried to steady her shaking hands. He was watching her carefully, those too-bright blue eyes taking in her every move.

"You could run again," he said. "You could even fly."

"How?" Her voice came but was wobbly, and she cleared her throat, tried again. "How could you fix my leg?"

He shrugged. "Don't know, do I? It's in the air, maybe. Or the water." He grinned, showing bright white teeth. "Or maybe it's just me. You'll have to come and see."

If she went with him, if she brought Jack, there was a chance he could have a normal life. That he could come back healed. Not in a wheelchair, body broken. A chance he could run. She weighed the chance against what had just happened. It didn't take long for her to make a decision.

"I'll come," she said, and Peter's face lit up. She made her voice honey sweet, put all thought of what he'd done out of her mind. "But I want to bring someone."

Would it matter to Peter that she was a mother? Would it make him more likely to take her, or to change his mind? "Another boy for you," she said at last. She thought about how he'd sounded when he'd talked about the zoo, his idea of marriage. A child's view. "Someone to play with, to be a friend."

"No more boys," he said immediately. "I've got enough boys. What I want is a girl. What I want is you."

She took a breath. "But you see, it's *my* boy. I can't come without him. I can't leave him."

"Why not?" he scoffed. He stood up, paced away from her. "I've seen that one. He spends all his time lying in hospital. He's too broken to make the journey. Besides, I told you. I'm tired of boys."

She didn't let herself think about the fact that he knew where her son was, that he'd been watching. "But you could fix him," she cajoled. "Couldn't you?"

He laughed, a crowing sound. "I'm Peter Pan. I can do anything."

"Well then, won't you show me? Won't you fix Jack? Then we could all go together."

He scuffed at the carpet. "It's work," he said darkly. "Too much of it."

The picture frame was still in her lap, and he pointed to it. "I tried it once, for her."

"For Wendy?"

"She wouldn't stay. So I took her home. But she missed Neverland. Found out she liked it better there after all." He shrugged. "I heard her calling me, so I came back. But that one made a fuss. He didn't want her to go." He glowered at the Michael of the portrait, round-cheeked and innocent.

"Great-Uncle Michael?" Holly felt a prickling at the back of her neck, a warning. She wanted to know, but didn't. The question left her before she could stop herself. "What do you mean?"

"He clung to her skirt as she was climbing out the window, bawling like a baby. Stupid git." That shrug again. "He was dragging her down.

153

So I made him let go. I sliced through her skirt and . . ." He made a tumbling motion with his hand.

"He fell? From the nursery window?" Holly shuddered, glanced at the window. A three-story drop.

"Wasn't my fault," Peter said defensively. "He should have let go when I told him to. And Wendy was crying and carrying on. So I tried. I did my best. But it was no use. His head was too staved in, you see. I could heal the wounds, but his brain was still scrambled."

The family story had always been that Michael had an accident, unexpected and unfortunate, and was never the same. Grandmother Wendy never spoke of it, and now Holly knew why.

"Wendy wouldn't leave, after. She stayed with him," Peter said, jealousy in his voice. "I told her I could fix it. One quick blow and he'd have been out of his misery. No more suffering, and she could have come back with me." He shook his head. "But she wouldn't. No one ever does. Not for good."

Holly thought of her grandmother, the way she spent hours watching cartoons and reading stories to Michael, as if they were both children again. The way she never passed a bakery without bringing back his favorite treat. The way she insisted Michael have pride of place under the tree Christmas morning, that he open his stocking first. As a child, Holly hadn't understood. But now . . .

"I could fix it for you too," Peter wheedled. "Not much of a life, is it, strapped to machines? Your boy loves to run—I've seen him. How do you think he feels, knowing he'll never race again? It would be a kindness, really. It wouldn't take much. And then you'd be free."

Her own words, back at her. Isn't that what she'd been thinking the night Peter had first come through her window? Without Jack, she'd be able to let go. To give up. Isn't that what she had wished for? Her face burned.

But not like this.

"Get out," she said. Somehow she found the strength to stand. Her leg was shaking and so was her voice, but she was on her feet, the picture frame clutched firmly in her hand.

Peter looked at her the way she'd seen predators on television look at prey, as if she was something weak and defenseless, something that would go down with one blow. But he didn't know Holly, not really. He hadn't learned anything from watching her after all.

She, on the other hand, had learned a great deal.

"Get out," she said again, more strongly this time. "And stay out. Stay away from me, from my family. From all of us. Forever."

Peter looked hurt for a moment, and then he closed off, became the same cocky boy as before. "Wasn't expecting you to say yes," he said. "But you don't make the rules."

Yes, I do, she thought, and placed one hand protectively across her stomach, as if she'd known even then.

"Stay away," she said clearly. "From all of us, forever. Or I'll tell the world what you've done. I'll tell them you're a monster. That book you're so fond of, the one where you're the hero? It will become a joke when I tell everyone about the real Peter Pan. I won't keep your secret."

He hesitated mid-step. "No one would believe you. And if they did, they'd see my side. I'd just be doing what you wanted, after all."

"Let's try, shall we?" she said. "I'll tell Jane. Let's see what she thinks." She hobbled to the door, hoping he'd been so intent on her he hadn't noticed that Jane wasn't home. "She's always been your biggest fan. Let's see if we can change that."

She was half afraid he would grab her, drag her back before she could open the door. But she guessed right about how powerful his belief was in his own narrative. It wasn't Tinker Bell who couldn't survive without the faith of others in her existence. That had been Peter's part of the story all along.

"Fine," he said slowly. He backed toward the window, his eyes never leaving her. "But you won't live forever. You can't. It's not in your nature. And then . . ." He turned his palms up. "There'll be a new generation for me to play with."

"Try me," Holly said aloud. But it was too late. She was speaking to empty air.

She moved across the room to the window. He'd left it open behind him, and the night sky was dark. There was no trace of him, not even a whisper. It didn't occur to her until years later to wonder where the little light that normally flickered at his heels had gone.

"Holly?"

Jane's voice pulls Holly back to the library, reminds her that she's years away from that night, no matter how intense her memories are. She takes a deep breath, pulls herself together. She's kept her promise, such as it was, and kept Peter's secret, superstitiously afraid that some-how he would know if she spoke ill of him and return. She doesn't tell now, either. She hedges, sharing half-truths that don't begin to touch on what really happened on that night so long ago. Not just what Peter did, but her own guilt, rational or not, at letting him in, at kissing him first, at using him to escape her anguish, if only for a little while. At being foolish and stupid and young.

"Peter . . . he's not like others. It was lovely and then . . . He knew exactly how much pain to inflict before you'd say stop. And he did it all with this . . . this smile. This beautiful golden smile."

"Like those horrible boys who torment kittens," Jane says thought-fully. "Or put insects in jars and pull off their wings, then set them on fire to see what happens. But surely he wouldn't hurt Eden. He's her father, for goodness' sake."

Those words fall into the room and sink into a pool of silence be-tween the two women. Holly blinks, hearing Jane acknowledge this for the first time. But it's not enough.

"You don't understand. It's all a game to him. You want an *adventure*," Holly says, throwing Jane's words back at her, "but I don't think he cares who he hurts."

"Well then," Jane says, "if he's as terrible as you say, we'll have to work quickly to find her, the poor child." She leans over to adjust the silver frame that holds the sketch of Wendy, John, and Michael, the one that used to be in the nursery. Looks at it thoughtfully. "And then, once we've found her, we can see what happens. That should be very interesting, don't you think?"

Chapter Nineteen

Over the next few days, Holly and Jane reach an uneasy agreement. Each night on her own, Holly lights the nursery candle and places it in the window, a "Come home, all is forgiven" message, of a sort. She whispers the same thing to the dark night sky, trying to let Peter sense her desperation, to lure him back with it. During the day, she follows Jane's lead, traipsing to the places her mother suggests they look—a park that's mentioned in the book, a house where the author once lived, a famous statue in Peter's likeness. Once or twice Holly could swear she detects the faintest hint of that springtime scent. Jane does too. Holly can tell by the way she pivots her head this way and that, trying to locate the source. In those moments, Holly's certain that when she turns around she'll see him. She shivers, some animal response of dread and anticipation mixed. But he's never there, and she's running out of time.

So when Christopher Cooke calls her, she's hoping for good news. He offers to meet with her at the house, but there's no way in hell Holly's going to do that. She still doesn't know exactly who Christopher is. She hasn't ruled out anything. His name and hook could be a wild coincidence. Or he could be a very motivated Darling stalker. But Holly's leaning toward a third, more complex possibility, one that's been developing since she and Christopher first met: that Neverland has more than one way to reach inside her world, that there are parts of the story that Wendy didn't share with anyone. Peter can move back and forth; is it any more outlandish to meet a reincarnation of his nemesis who has crossed not just space but time?

Of course Christopher might be no more than a very attractive private detective. She still doesn't want him in her home, near Jack. She suggests his office instead. They schedule it for later that afternoon, as soon as he is free.

While she waits, she distracts herself with an email from Elliot, who wants more funding to study the sea cucumbers. Over the past few weeks Holly has done plenty of bedtime reading on sea cucumbers, thanks to detailed and frequent reports from Elliot. She's learned that not only do the creatures vomit up their intestines when threatened (Elliot used the more technical term *expel*), they're able to regrow entire parts of their bodies as well. Elliot believes that the proteins that cause the elasticity and regeneration could be used in a new line of skin care aimed at what he tactfully calls the "mature population." His initial findings look extremely promising.

Could this be the breakthrough she needs for her own research? Holly shoots a quick reply, saying she'll approve the funding but wants to be part of the test group. It will give her access to the product, and possibly the raw materials, without arousing suspicion. She couches it as a joke. "I'm a reluctant member of the target audience, after all," she writes.

But Elliot's response is a quick and unequivocal refusal: "Sorry. Including you could be seen as biased by outsiders at best—at worst, it might raise questions of data manipulation."

She reads his answer and frowns. She respects Elliot's ethics, she really does, but this isn't the NIH. She debates on whether to insist, but decides to let it go. She'll gain access some other way.

She spends the next hour brooding over the lab results on the last synthetic sample of Eden's blood. It's like a Rubik's Cube—she gets one aspect of the sample to work, and the others fall apart. If she could just discover how the protein ages Eden, she might be able to figure out how to stop it and wake her up—and find the key to a synthesized version for Jack. She pores over her notes, looking for the solution. But she's too close to the data, has been working on it for too long. Whatever the answer is, she's not seeing it. Frustrated, she puts it away and heads downstairs to say goodbye to Jack.

"What's on for your afternoon?" she asks.

"I dunno. I may try to go for a run when I finish," he says, drumming his pencil on the library table. "And at some point I need to talk with my geometry teacher to go over this crap."

"All right," Holly says. "Let me know how it goes, okay? And if you run, take it easy."

"Whatever," he mutters, shifting restlessly away from her.

She lets the comment go. Keeping him on this short of a leash is tough on both of them, but it's the best she can do right now. If she's honest, it's all she can do, at least until she figures out how to replicate the proteins in Eden's blood. Or finds Eden.

And when she does—she tries hard not to think otherwise—what then? What if Eden is awake? For years, Holly has longed to hold Eden, to hear her voice and see her smile. But there's a very real possibility hugging won't be what Eden has in mind. Not after serving as a human science experiment for so many years. Even though at least half of the science was done for her benefit.

And what about Jack? Eden was always a generous child, and she loved her brother. But a niggling voice in the back of Holly's brain worries Eden may feel differently about being a human pincushion now that she's awake. *One step at a time*, Holly tells herself.

First they have to find her.

Christopher Cooke's office is located at the far end of a quiet, leafy street. It's a comfortable brick cottage with a grassy yard and a few fat rosebushes climbing a trellis in the front. Like Christopher himself, the house isn't what Holly expected. She drives past twice before she's certain she has the correct address.

When she parks and gets out, she sees a side door with an *Office* sign discreetly lettered in green and gold. She makes her way along the path to the side door and rings the bell.

He must have been waiting for her because he opens the door almost immediately. He's dressed in a pressed white shirt and dark-wash jeans, and his long black hair is damp, as if he's stepped out of the shower. He's not handsome, not exactly—the scars on his face and the world-weariness with which he carries himself take care of that—but there's a magnetism to him that's impossible to ignore. He reminds her of a sleek panther she saw once at the zoo. It's hard to look away.

"Come in," he says, standing back to let her pass. She's careful not to stare at his right hand, but when he leads her to the office she can't help but sneak a glance. He turns around in time to catch her.

"Ah," he says, with that amused grin she finds so infuriating. He holds his arm up, rotating it from side to side. He's wearing a prosthetic today, one that ends in an articulated hand. He extends, then curls the fingers, waggling them at her. "No hook today. I tend to save that for first impressions and occasional practical jokes."

He's standing in front of a large window, and with the sun behind him, Holly can see through the thin fabric of his shirt. The artificial arm, a sleek metallic black, joins his own at the elbow. In the soft afternoon light, it's oddly beautiful.

"How does it work?" Holly asks, fascinated.

"Osseointegration," he says. "A fancy way of saying that it's grafted onto my nerves and bones." He rolls back his sleeve to show her the implant site. She's conscious of how closely he's watching her, but if he's hoping for a reaction, he won't get it from Holly. She has too many of her own scars.

"Does it hurt?"

He shakes his head. "Not much. Not anymore. My arm gets tired sometimes, after a long day. But not often."

He rolls the sleeve down, then stretches out his hand to her, palm upright. She hesitates, then meets it with her own. The artificial hand is cool, not humanlike at all, yet touching it is uncomfortably intimate, as if he's showing her the truest part of himself. It's so quiet she can hear her own breathing, and maybe his too. His gaze is steady, but she struggles to meet his eyes. She wonders if he can detect the pressure of her skin against his hand, and the thought makes her breath come more quickly.

Ridiculous.

She steps back and breaks their contact.

"The best titanium and plastic you can buy," he says, dropping the hand to his side. If he's noticed her agitation, he doesn't show it. "It even comes with a silicon sleeve that makes it more realistic. Lets me blend in better at fancy parties and whatnot. But I don't get invited to many of those, and I've never been a fan of artifice, so I go with the black."

Holly can't tell if that's an insult or not. It sounds like one, and she leaps at the chance to take offense and put that moment of connection behind her.

"Since that hefty retainer I paid came from the profits of artifice, I'd think you'd be more of a fan," she says.

He shrugs. "No disrespect meant. There's no way to hide this, so why try?" he says, waving the hand at her again. "On the other hand, when the robot revolution comes, I'll be on the winning side. Do you see what I did there?"

Holly tries not to smile, but it's such an awful joke she can't help herself. "Do you have something for me?"

He sighs theatrically. "To business, then. Please, take a seat." He gestures at a desk and chair across the room. She walks toward it and he follows, and she tries not to be conscious of his eyes on her back. She focuses on his office to distract herself. It's different from what she'd expected. White, filled with light and a few simple pieces of furniture, it's understated in a style not that different from her own. There's no clutter, only a single plant on a side table by the window.

She sits in the chair, and he settles himself behind the desk. A laptop is on its center, and Cooke opens it. He types for a moment, then swivels its screen toward her, and Holly braces herself for what she'll see.

Except she's looking at a blank screen. A single white page with nothing on it. She looks at him inquiringly.

"This is what I've found so far," he says.

"Is this some sort of a joke?" She takes a deep breath, trying to calm the anger that flares through her. Her children have no time for this.

"Not at all," he says. He pushes the computer out of the way and leans forward. "At least not on my end."

"Excuse me?"

"Holly—may I call you Holly?"

"I prefer Dr. Darling," she says coolly.

"Dr. Darling, I am very, very good at my job. Good enough to command—and deserve—that retainer you mentioned. Good enough to be in high demand, which lets me pick my clients. And although I picked you, I think your story is a bunch of bollocks." He smiles winningly.

"What exactly are you saying?" Christopher Cooke is far more intelligent—and charming—than she'd originally given him credit for. She bets he enjoys being underestimated, just like she does.

"I'm saying that I've done everything I'd normally do in a situation like this, and more. I've searched property records, I've checked arrest records, I've even had a look at the driving licenses database. If there's a record and you can think of it, I've checked it. And of the many, many Peter Smiths I've found—and there are a multitude, I assure you— none of them come within a whisper of meeting the description you've given me. So either this Peter person is very good at hiding—better than I am at finding, which is difficult to believe." He pauses. "Or . . ."

"Yes?"

"He doesn't exist. Which begs the question, why would someone such as yourself pay me a great deal of money to search for a phantom person?"

"Perhaps he's living under an assumed name," she says, desperately trying to keep the panic from entering her voice. Why did she ever think this would work?

He looks at her, that same intense gaze, and she has to work to keep herself from squirming like a teenager in the principal's office. *He works for you*, she reminds herself.

"When I knew him," she blurts, "he used to like to call himself Pan."

"As in Peter Pan?" Cooke asks, his brow furrowing.

Holly nods miserably.

"That would have been helpful information to have. He sounds like quite the rabid fan, another useful bit." After a long pause, he adds, "You're never too far from that story, are you?"

Holly bites back a hysterical laugh. He has no idea.

"Also helpful? A photo of your daughter with her eyes open."

"Eden spends most of her time sleeping, due to her medical condition," she says. "I believe I mentioned that."

"And I believe you're keeping things from me," he says with a hint of that mocking grin. "That's what makes this case so fun."

"I'm glad you find my missing daughter entertaining," she says coldly. She stands. "I'll see if I can locate another picture of Eden. Is there anything else?"

He shakes his head and comes around the side of the desk to see her out. "I'll search again using that alias and be in touch about what I find," he says. "And I apologize. You're right—my comment was insensitive."

She looks at him in surprise. "Thank you."

He shrugs. "Needed to be said." He's standing close to her, and his eyes are such a dark, magnetic blue it's hard to look away. She can feel the heat coming off him. She takes a step backward to put distance between them, and as she does so, her hip bumps the side table holding the plant.

She looks down. The leaves are shiny and green, with tiny blue flowers, a picture of health.

"Beautiful plant. Rosemary, is it?" she says inanely. Anything to break the silence.

He nods. "For remembrance."

She looks at him with confusion and he shrugs. "A friend gave it to me. I don't sleep much since . . ." He waves the fingers on his mechanical hand. "I never did, not really. I've always had crazy, intense dreams, like memories of another life. And they've gotten worse since the accident. Between the lack of sleep and the dreams, it can be hard to tell what's real sometimes. To remember." A shadow passes across those brilliant eyes. "I figured I've tried everything else, I might as well try this."

"I'm sorry," she says, and she is. It's hazy, but she remembers what it was like after the crash. It felt as if it were years before she slept soundly, before she stopped dreaming of it. There are still nights when she finds herself in Robert's sporty red car, the twins strapped in the back, and she knows what's coming and can't stop it. She sees the lorry veer across its lane and feels their car suspended in the air for a moment that holds all of eternity.

She wonders what it is that Christopher sees.

"Not your problem," he says. "Besides, my therapist approves. Of the plant, that is. She's not a fan of herbal mumbo jumbo, but she's happy to see me invested. She seems to think I have some kind of subliminal death wish, that I can't keep anything around me alive."

His eyes are still serious, but he's grinning again, and Holly's heart gives an inexplicable skip.

"If I keep the plant going for a full year, she said I might be ready for a fish. I'm angling for a dog though. What do you think?"

He's reaching for the door, to open it for her, but Holly beats him to it. With her hand on the knob, she turns back to him. She's still thinking of the car, of the twins, of Jack and Eden and Robert, of the way her heart has suddenly stopped being under her control. The words tumble out before she can stop them.

"I think," she says, "your therapist would have a field day with me."

And then she flees, leaving him in the doorway staring after her.

Chapter Twenty

The house is empty when Holly gets home, which is just as well, since her meeting with Christopher has her rattled. Jane has left a note saying that Jack's gone to dinner and then to a movie with the teens he met through her friends. Jane will also be out for dinner, and the note informs Holly not to wait up. There's a covered casserole dish in the fridge, but Holly ignores it and makes herself some toast. All she wants for the rest of the night is to shower and crawl into bed, with that damn nursery window shut and locked for a change. But Jack's still out. So after she bathes, she waits up for him. Around ten P.M. she retires to her room and tries to read, but she leaves her door open. She hears Jane come in around eleven but doesn't go out to greet her. Jack's curfew comes and goes. Holly tells herself not to worry, that it's nothing more nefarious than a teenage boy pushing boundaries, that he's in a group and perfectly safe. And at least it's a movie, not something more physical like lacrosse or a gym session.

At 12:30 she tries his phone. It goes straight to voicemail. She goes downstairs to the kitchen to brew herself a cup of tea, and that's where she's sitting when at one A.M. she hears his key in the lock.

He startles at seeing her, then recovers, his stance in the doorway turning truculent.

"Hey," he says. "Hope you didn't stay up because of me."

"I did, actually," Holly says. She takes a sip of tea and forces herself to ignore his tone.

"Yeah, well, sorry. You weren't here when I went out. And I'm not really in school, am I." It's not a question and he doesn't sound sorry at all.

He starts to leave, but she's not done. "Sit down for a moment," she tells him, and hears echoes of Jane in her voice. Well, too bad. This is different.

He comes back into the room reluctantly, slides into the seat farthest away from her. She takes a deep breath, tries to hold on to her patience. "Look, I know this is hard, being away. But I have some important work I need to finish here," she says. "I'm hoping we can go home soon, but I really need you to stay on track in the meantime. That means getting your work done and keeping to the plan. Do you understand?"

"Yeah, I get it," he says sullenly.

"Good," she says. "Next time, if you want to stay out past curfew, you need to check with me." She stands up and walks around the table, thinking she'll kiss him good night. But when she gets to him, she smells beer.

"Have you been drinking?" she says in disbelief.

"No."

"Jack, I can smell it on you."

"Somebody spilled their drink. Some of it must have landed on me."

"Don't lie to me."

She leans in to smell his breath, but he turns his head away. "Jesus, Mom. You're like the police!" He stands and backs out of her reach.

"Jack, listen to me," she says. Anger mixes with fear, and the fear is winning. "The cells you're injected with—they're very sensitive. I don't know if alcohol affects them, but if you're drinking, you could be damaging them."

"Big deal. You can always inject me with more."

"No, I can't." She tries to sound calm. "The supply, the ones that match . . . you have a rare blood type and the source isn't—I can't get more of it right now."

He stands still and looks at her. "What does that mean?"

"I don't know," she says. "I'm trying to figure it out. But you need to be careful for the next few weeks, okay? Only until I find a way to get more."

"Can you?" For a moment, he looks less like a young man and more like the child she remembers, wide-eyed and scared. It tugs at her, and the last of her anger slides away. Unthinkingly, she reaches out to tousle his hair. He doesn't move away.

"Of course," she says, instilling her words with a confidence she does not come close to owning. "It may take some time, but of course."

She's relieved when he doesn't ask anything else.

She decides to keep the windows open after all, just in case, and wakes at every little sound. She finally falls into a fitful sleep as dawn is stretching over the horizon, and stays in bed past her normal time. When she comes downstairs, Nan is in the kitchen.

"Good morning," Nan says. "Can I pour you some tea?"

"That would be lovely, thanks." Holly sits down and takes the tea gratefully. Her head feels as if it's stuffed with cotton wool. "Where is everyone?"

"Your mother is in the library. She got a call about a charity dinner she's helping to plan."

"And Jack?"

Nan grins broadly. "Ed picked him up. He's taking him to lacrosse practice. Jack was totally chuffed."

Holly sits completely still. The anger that disappeared last night roars back, white hot, and every word, every thought, is acid. What is the matter with him that he can't listen? Even after their talk last night.

She tries to tell herself that it's not all his fault, that she's never explicitly forbidden him from playing, but then she thinks of Eden in that hospital bed in Cornwall and her stomach twists. Jack has so much, and he's throwing it away. And for what? A stupid game.

"Dr. Darling?" Nan is hovering over her. "Are you all right? You've gone pale."

"Where did they go?"

"The boys? The field is about fifteen minutes away. It's walkable, but Ed drove them there." She rolls her eyes. "Don't worry—he's an excellent driver. His dad taught him when Ed was ten, mostly to upset our mother. They'll be fine."

"No, they won't." Dimly, Holly realizes her hands are clenching. She makes an enormous effort to unfold them.

"Excuse me?"

"Jack has a . . . a condition. He's not supposed to be playing sports right now."

"I'm so sorry," Nan says, looking horrified. "He said nothing to me."

"I want you to give me the address of that field, and then I want you to leave." Part of her knows she's being unreasonable, that it's not Nan's fault, that she's overreacting because she hasn't had a solid night's sleep in weeks and she's holding on to hope for Eden by a thread, but the other part doesn't care. She wants Nan gone.

"Are you . . . are you firing me?"

"Luckily it's not up to her," Jane says, coming into the kitchen. She still has her reading glasses on. "Nan, you've done nothing wrong. But why don't you go home for the day all the same, with salary. Consider it"—she eyes Holly—"hazard pay."

Nan nods. "I'm so sorry, Dr. Darling. I didn't mean to cause problems."

Holly doesn't reply. Nan scribbles a note on the pad by the kitchen phone, rips it off, and leaves it on the table. "Here's the address of the lacrosse field."

"I'll see you tomorrow," Jane says. "Enjoy yourself today."

170

Nan scoops up her sweater from the back of the chair and hurries away. Holly waits until she hears the door shut before she rounds on her mother.

"How dare you," she seethes. "Do you know what she did?"

"Of course I do. I could hear you all the way in the library," Jane says calmly. "Be that as it may, the girl has done nothing wrong."

"She's been after Jack to go to lacrosse, and this morning, her brother took him. Without telling me." Holly knows, even as she says it, how ridiculous it sounds, how overprotective to Jane's ears. But she doesn't care.

"She's not Jack's babysitter, Holly. Nor is she your personal assistant, to be fired at will." Holly starts to speak, but Jane holds up her hand. "Please. I'm well aware of the fact that every time I call your office, someone new answers the phone. Keeping help has never been your strong suit. But Nan does not work for you. She works for me, and she's the best housekeeper I've had in quite some time."

"And that's more important than your grandson's health?" Holly snaps.

Jane takes off her glasses and polishes them with the hem of her silk shirt. "How bad is it, really?" she asks.

Holly slumps down into her seat, her anger draining away. "It's bad," she admits. "Very, very bad."

She takes a breath, decides to tell Jane the truth. At least some of it. "After the crash, Jack never really . . . He didn't recover. Not like you think. He made some progress, of course, but . . . and then, by accident, I found . . . not a cure, exactly, more a temporary reversal. From Eden."

"The fall," Jane guesses. "That day he walked. I thought it must be something like that. Because of . . . who Eden's father is?"

"Yes." Holly nods. She skates to safer ground, to the science of it. "So far as I've discovered, a protein in Eden's blood works like an antibody, binding to damaged cells and repairing them. But the reversal is short-lasting—a month, maybe two, without the protein and Jack will return to the way he was, like he did that first time. And I haven't been able to duplicate the results with a synthetic version. Not yet. I've made a portable cream that combines the leftover plasma and serum, but it doesn't work nearly as well as Eden's blood. If I don't find Eden soon . . ." She lifts a hand, lets it fall. Hearing the words aloud, what she's done, makes her sound like a monster to her own ears, as if she's sacrificed one child for the health of the other. *It wasn't like that*, she wants to say. *I did everything I could for both of them!* But she won't defend her choices, won't waste time or energy that could go toward finding her daughter and keeping her son safe.

"If Jack gets hurt or sick, I can't fix it," she says instead.

Jane puts her glasses back on, looks at Holly over their rims. "I imagine that's true for most parents," she says quietly.

She leaves Holly sitting in front of her cooling tea.

Chapter Twenty-One

After her dustup with Nan, Holly had planned to drive to the lacrosse field to retrieve Jack. But her mother's words keep ringing in her head. She can't protect Jack, not really. If it's not lacrosse, not drinking, it will be something else. He's pushing the envelope of the perfectly safe world she's created, testing all the time for gaps. And someday soon he's going to discover one.

Still, she can't do nothing. Maybe she can reason with him. At the least, she can watch the game and be there if he needs her. But as she grabs her keys from the nursery bureau, she finds herself captivated by the crib in the corner of the room. She can see the twins in sleep, pink and plump and so curled about each other it was impossible to see where Isaac ended and Jack began. She sees Eden too, but never sleeping. In those days, Eden was like a chrysalis on fast-forward. Every morning when Holly walked into the room and saw Eden's toothy grin, she knew there'd be some new miracle, some new skill her daughter had impossibly mastered. Back then, Holly could barely bring herself to close her own eyes, she was so afraid she'd miss something.

She's been watching her children so closely all these years. So how is it possible that they've changed so much without her realizing?

She's still standing there when she hears footsteps pounding up the landing. Her heart jackrabbits. Something's wrong. She's on her feet when Jack bursts through the door, his face white.

She rushes across the room to him, already scanning for signs of damage.

"What's happened?" she asks, grasping his arm. "Are you hurt?"

He shakes her off. "Ed got a call when we were on the field. From Nan. She was in tears. She said you'd tried to *fire* her."

"That's an exaggeration. But she shouldn't have sent you off with Ed to play lacrosse. What if you got hurt? I talked to you about this last night, Jack."

"You told me not to drink. You didn't tell me I couldn't play lacrosse. What am I supposed to do, live in some kind of bubble for the rest of my life?"

Yes, Holly wants to say. It's so close to what she's been thinking. But she doesn't.

"God, Mom. You should have heard Ed trying to calm Nan down."

He's pacing about the room like a caged animal.

"I'm doing what I think is right for you," Holly says sharply. This conversation isn't going the way she wants it to.

"When do I get to start making my own decisions? When do I get to start living my life?" He's moving back and forth, back and forth, closer and closer to the open nursery window. The window Michael fell from. The same window Peter came through. It's irrational, Holly knows, but she doesn't want him near it.

"Come away from there, please," Holly says, striving for calm.

"That's another thing. What is your crazy fear of . . ." His voice dies off.

"Jack?"

He doesn't answer. There's a small round table to the left of the window. There's a lamp on it and a tableau of silver frames. Jane has pictures everywhere, and Holly hasn't paid attention to these, not in years, not since she insisted her mother move the sketch of Wendy and her brothers from the nursery. But one of the pictures has caught Jack's eye. He picks it up, his back to the window, his body leaning against the sill.

"Come away from there," she says again. "Please." But Jack isn't listening. He's staring at the photograph with the strangest expression on his face.

"Jack, what is it?"

He turns to her, still holding the picture. She moves closer. The photo is of a very young Eden, holding onto a wheelchair. In the chair is Jack.

"This is the girl I told you about. The one I thought was imaginary. Who is she? And why am I in a *wheelchair?*"

All the air leaves Holly. She's trying to speak, struggling for the right words, for a story that will work, but her mouth keeps opening and closing with no sound. So when Jack hears the truth, it's not from her.

"That would be your sister." Jane, standing in the open doorway, delivers the news in a matter-of-fact voice.

"Stop," Holly hisses, fear and anger cutting through her paralysis. But it is too late.

"My sister?" Jack repeats, bewildered.

"Yes," Jane says with a glance at Holly. "Her name is Eden."

Holly has boxed up or destroyed all of her own photos of Eden, all except the one hidden in her suitcase. She hasn't wanted to take the chance Jack might stumble across them. It had never occurred to her that Jane, of all people, would not only keep but display one.

Jane reads her face, shrugs. "Despite what you may think, she is my granddaughter."

"You hid that I had a sister from me?" Jack says incredulously. "Why?"

"I was trying to protect you," Holly says. "You were so young, you'd already suffered so much loss, and your sister had been sick for such a long time." She pauses. She's tempted, so tempted, to add that Eden is dead. But it feels like bad luck, as if saying it might make it come true.

Besides, Jane is right here, and Holly isn't certain she'd let the lie stand. But Jack's mind gets there all on its own.

"Where is she?" His eyes widen. "The house, right? The one in Cornwall. With all the medical equipment. I saw it through the window. When you told me someone who lived there was sick, she's who you meant. Did she die? Is that why you're selling it? I had a sister you never even told me about, and now she's dead?"

Jane opens her mouth to speak. "Don't," Holly says. "You've done enough." She takes a step toward Jack, but he backs away, clutching the photo to his chest. She reaches for him. "Jack," she says, coaxingly. "Listen."

"Don't touch me." He pushes her hands away. "Leave me alone." He bolts across the room and is out the door before she can even try to stop him.

Jane grabs Holly by the shoulder. "Let him go."

"Are you joking?" Holly shakes her off. "He's all alone!"

"You've tried everything else. Give him some time and see what happens."

"And if Peter finds him first?" She turns on her heel, intending to go after Jack, but she's too late. She's just reaching the stairs when she hears the front door bang shut. By the time she gets there and opens the door, he's gone.

A part of her—a small part—knows Jane is right. She should give him time to cool off. But she can't leave it alone. She's afraid of what he'll do, of the chances he'll take. And despite everything, she still knows her son. She knows where he'll go when he's upset. She finds the scrap of paper Nan scribbled on in the kitchen. Bingo.

Chapter Twenty-Two

At the lacrosse field, Holly spots Jack at once. He's racing down the field in a scrum of players and wears an exhilarated look she hasn't seen since . . . she can't remember when. She's always been nervous about his playing, about seeing him surrounded by players both larger and heavier than he. It was Barry who suggested she give Jack some space, let him have one area of his life she wasn't involved in. He'd teased her about micromanaging her son the way she did the office and she'd backed off, a little hurt but also secretly relieved. Watching Jack play was always nail-bitingly intense for her. But her fear has made her forget how much he loves the sport.

She gets out of the car and crosses over to the field. Nan is sitting alone on the sidelines. She's spread out a blanket and arranged what looks like a small feast: oranges, cheese, crackers, and bottles of water. When she sees Holly, she visibly flinches.

"Hi," Holly says. "Mind if I sit down?"

"Suit yourself," Nan says. But she moves over slightly.

"Which one is your brother?" Holly asks. It's hard to tell with the helmets. Nan points without comment. Ed is taller and broader than Jack, but he doesn't have Jack's speed or agility. Still, Holly tries to be generous. "Nice shot," she says when he tries to score from the left side of the crease.

"He loves it," Nan says. "Your son does too."

Holly is quiet for a moment. She's going to need allies with Jack; she can see that. He's pulling away from her, more and more every day, his face eagerly turned toward a future that doesn't include her. Rationally, she knows this was bound to happen, that to some degree it's normal, even good, but still it leaves her stunned that hormones and adolescence can separate her from this child she's built her life around. Stunned, and a little hurt. "I'm sorry about this morning," she says finally. "I was upset and worried. I shouldn't have taken it out on you."

"It's all right," Nan says. "Jack told my brother you had another son, a twin to Jack, and he died?"

A frisson of surprise sparks through Holly. She and Jack never talk about Isaac or Robert with strangers. She turns her head to look at Nan, who is silhouetted against the sky, and the undercurrent of loss that always rests below her surface widens, becomes fresh and overpowering, until suddenly she's falling into it, drowning in a sea of blue the exact shade of Eden's eyes. She misses her daughter so fiercely she can't breathe. She imagines walking this lacrosse field with a teenage Eden, their shoulders bumping, their faces close together as they share secrets and wait for Jack to finish. Eden's smile at the end of the game. Her voice at the dinner table.

"Dr. Darling?" Nan's face is concerned.

"Yes," Holly manages. "That's right."

"I can see how that might make someone protective," Nan says. She pauses, as if weighing what to say. "Our mother died as well. A few years ago. Maybe the boys are good for each other."

"Maybe." Holly's gotten her breathing under control. She wonders what, if anything, Jack let slip about Eden today. And then she realizes what Nan has said. The girl can't be much more than twenty-one herself. "I'm sorry. Truly."

"Yeah, well . . ." Nan looks away, at the field. "Me too."

A player runs down the field near them and Nan cups her hands to her mouth. "Go, Ed! Move your blooming feet!" Ed bodychecks the ball carrier on the other team, knocking the ball to the ground. Jack swoops in to scoop it up, and Ed waggles his stick at his sister, who is still shouting at him, before the play moves to the other end of the field.

"He's not the fastest, but he recovers the ball more than almost anybody," Nan says proudly.

"He certainly got the height gene in your family," Holly observes. Nan's lucky if she comes up to Ed's shoulders.

Nan laughs. "Different fathers. Ed takes after his dad, height-wise. Got his good looks too. And his charm." She doesn't sound as pleased with that last bit. "Even before our mum died, I practically raised him. She was always working and Ed's dad . . . he's a bit of a tosser. Comes around when it suits him. He's got a short attention span, that one, and he's not the greatest influence in the world, you know? When he's here, he puts a spell on Ed. But Mum always did have crap taste in men." She picks at a corner of the blanket. "I used to worry Ed would take after him, but Mum used to say Ed was born sweet, he grew sweet, and he'd die sweet, and nothing would change that. I think that's true." She looks out on the field toward her brother. "So far, anyways."

"Well, it's clear you've taken excellent care of him." The boy radiates good health. Even from here, Holly can see how his skin glows.

"Thanks." Nan shrugs. "Somebody had to make sure Ed got fed and got his homework done. Turned out to be me."

"Impressive," Holly says, and it is. Nan's raised a healthy teenager who acknowledges her in public. That puts her ahead of most parents—including Holly. The image of Eden returns, only this time her face is closed off, and she's stalking ten paces ahead as they walk. Holly closes her eyes.

When the scrimmage is over, there's fist-bumping and a little friendly shoving between the two sides. Jack and Ed bang shoulders, grinning.

They sling their sticks over their shoulders, grab their helmets, and head toward Nan. But when Jack sees Holly, his smile disappears.

"Jack," she says, but he walks past her without a word. Ed, brown eyes wide, gives an apologetic shrug to Nan.

"Hey, Dr. Darling," he says, then grabs an orange and hurries after Jack.

"I'll see what I can do," Nan says. She bends to pick up the blanket. "Maybe give him some space."

Holly bites back a reply. She should be grateful, but she isn't. Still, she swallows her pride, smiles, and thanks her.

"I'll try and get him home by dinnertime," Nan tells her.

"Perfect," Holly says, as if they are talking about a recalcitrant toddler who won't go down for a nap. She walks with Nan to the car. Jack is sitting in the back seat, staring straight ahead. He won't look at her. She wants to check his breathing, make sure he's recovering from the game, but she doesn't. She gets into her own car and drives away.

She winds up cruising some of the seedier side streets of London, driving for hours on the pretext of looking for Peter. She doesn't want to go home, where she'll only pace and wait for Jack to return. She's too antsy to focus on work right now, on mailing campaigns and brochures. She misses her lab, the peace she finds looking through a microscope, the way she can lose herself in the tiny worlds pinned to a specimen slide.

Right now, she's chasing fireflies through the dark, telling herself she has a chance at snaring the sun.

If Christopher Cooke can't find Peter, what chance does Holly honestly have? She tries to picture what he'd look like now. How quickly did he age? In her memory, Peter is older than when her grandmother Wendy first described seeing him over a century ago, but not by much. Does time work differently for him somehow? Holly thinks back to what he'd said about Neverland when he'd spoken of how it could heal her. *It's in the air, maybe. Or the water.* Maybe his visits there—wherever or whatever *there* is—are how he's managed to stay young. And perhaps that's why Eden ages so rapidly, because she's never been.

But she's guessing again. Peter could be any age at all. He could be hiding in plain sight, but Holly doesn't see anyone who looks remotely like him.

Still, if he's in London, he'd need a way to support himself. With his sharp, clever mind and charisma, he could work in almost any field. She lets her imagination run wild. A businessman. A lawyer. A salesman or CEO.

Yet instinctively she knows Peter wouldn't have been drawn to any profession quite so clean. There's an edge to him, a seam of dirtiness. She thinks of a boy pulling wings off a fly and shivers. No. If Peter is still in London, he's not helping anyone.

Finally she turns the car toward home, the knots in her shoulders no looser. On a whim she picks up an Indian takeaway, buys extra naan because she knows Jack likes it. There's no car parked in front of the house when she arrives, but when she opens the front door, she hears her mother talking and Jack's low voice in answer. She sags with relief against the wall, then straightens her spine and walks into the kitchen.

"There you are," Jane says cheerfully. She has a hand on the phone. "I was about to requisition provisions. Weren't you clever to bring dinner home. Is that a curry?"

Holly nods. She'll play pax with Jane—for now. She fishes the package of Indian bread out of the bag. "And extra naan," she says, waving it temptingly toward Jack, who is leaning against the far corner of the counter.

"Wonderful!" Jane exclaims. "Jack, be a dear and set the table. Use the good china from the living room—curry calls for a celebration." She speaks firmly, and after a moment, Jack leaves to retrieve the dishes.

"He came home a half hour ago," Jane says sotto voce. "Nan brought him—I received the distinct impression that it had been quite the challenge to get him in the car."

"That was kind of her," Holly says sarcastically before she can stop herself.

Jane looks at her. "You'll have to do better than that when she shows up to work here tomorrow." She pauses to deliver her final blow. "Jack seems quite fond of her."

Holly takes a breath. None of this is Nan's fault. Jane, on the other hand . . .

"Don't look at me like that," her mother says firmly, correctly interpreting Holly's face. "The boy needs to know about his past. You can't hide it from him forever."

"I'll keep that in mind." This time, she sounds like a surly teenager.

Dinner is a largely silent affair, despite Jane's attempts at chatter. Jack sits in the middle of the table, sulking, with Jane at one end and Holly at the other. He's showered and changed, but he's pale. She tries to stealthily inspect him, but he glares at her, so she stops, afraid she'll drive him away from the table. Although he physically stays in the room with her, it's clear he'd rather be almost anywhere else. He responds monosyllabically to every attempt to draw him out, and by the end of the meal Holly is perversely pleased to see Jane as frustrated as she is. Her satisfaction is short-lived.

"For goodness' sake," Jane says, standing up from the table and folding her napkin. "I've forgotten what a misery it is to have a teenager in the house. Holly, he certainly reminds me of you at that age. The two of you can do the dishes tonight—I don't want them left for poor Nan in the morning. I'm going out. The McHales have asked me to a dessert bar this evening, and as boring as they may be, their company has to be an improvement over yours." She drops her napkin on the table and sails from the room.

Jack and Holly are left looking at each other.

"I'll wash," Holly says after a moment.

"Can't we put them in the dishwasher?" It's the longest sentence she's heard out of him since this morning.

182

Holly snorts. "Your grandmother's Stafford china? Do that and you'd better start swimming home."

He gives a small smile, one that lasts barely a second. But he does help carry the plates out to the kitchen. Since dinner was only the three of them, cleanup is relatively quick. Holly is sudsing the last plate when he finally speaks.

"What was she like?"

She knows immediately what he means, and extends him the courtesy of not pretending.

"Eden? Brilliant. Mercurial. Quick as a hummingbird," Holly says. She rinses the plate, careful to keep her eyes on it, as if all her energy must go toward not dropping it. "Devoted to you."

"What happened to her?" He reaches for the plate, but she shakes her head and takes the cloth from him. She needs something to do.

"Eden was born with a rare condition. It caused her to grow rapidly, probably more rapidly than her body could sustain," she says. "And then she had an accident. She hit her head. The doctors think her body, which was already stressed, couldn't handle the damage. She's spent the last decade in a coma. Her brain couldn't wake up."

She's surprised by how easily the truth rolls off her tongue. Almost as easily as all her lies have lately.

"What type of accident?"

"She fell. She was climbing a tree and lost her balance."

"I remember that." He screws up his face. "Ever since we left the house in Cornwall, I've been having bits and pieces of memories. I thought I was going crazy."

She wants, so badly, to ask what he remembers. But she doesn't. That line of questioning could lead to other memories, and she's not ready for them. Not now. Maybe not ever. She doesn't think Jack is ready, either, although she's not certain. But he's blocked them for years, leaving his twin brother no more than a shadow at his heels—what good will remembering do now?

"It was a long time ago," she says instead. She takes her time drying the dish.

"I was in the tree. She reached out to me. I think I'd lost my balance and she was trying to save me."

"It's not your fault," Holly says. "It was an accident. Eden fell. That's all."

"I think we were trying to fly," he says, as if she hasn't spoken. "That's crazy, right? Little-kid stuff. Like the stories Grandma used to tell. But I don't remember what happened after."

Holly polishes the dish, concentrating on the gold rim. She doesn't look up. "There's really nothing else. After she fell, Eden went to hospital. She never recovered. She never woke up."

"She was smart. I remember how smart she was," Jack says. "And her laugh. I remember it was like bubbles. It would rise and rise and rise until it exploded."

She turns to him, surprised. "Exactly." She can hear the pleasure in her own voice. It's been such a long time since she's had the chance to talk about Eden with someone who knew her before. She longs to recall aloud the stubborn curl that always stood up on the back of Eden's head. Her funny little baby voice, unexpectedly raspy. The greedy way she ate raspberries straight from the box, popping them in her mouth so quickly the berries were gone before they got home from market. Holly's heart aches with the weight of all the memories she's locked away.

She sets the plate down carefully. It's so fragile it could shatter in her hands. Jack will think she's a monster if he knows the truth—that she pursued a job that took them away from Eden, all the while using Eden's blood, experimenting with it. He might freak out, and that's the last thing he needs. So it's easier not to encourage the conversation, not to tell the truth.

Unless he asks. She won't lie directly to him. Not anymore. The risk that he won't forgive her again is too great.

She crosses the kitchen. Tentatively hugs him. His heartbeat through his shirt is so rapid it frightens her. She wants to ask how he feels, what he's thinking, but she knows if she does he'll close down.

"I'm sorry," she says instead. *For everything*, she thinks but does not say.

He doesn't respond. Instead he yawns so widely she almost believes it's real as he shrugs out of her embrace. "I'm tired. I'm going to bed."

His face is still pale. She decides it's because he's upset, because he's exhausted. There's nothing wrong.

"What are your plans for tomorrow? It's supposed to rain. Typical weekend."

He shrugs. "I dunno. I might hang with Ed. If the weather's good, we're going back to the park."

The bloody hell you are, she thinks but does not say. Instead she kisses him on the cheek. "Sleep well."

She wipes down the table and the counters. Checks the clock, surprises herself when she thinks of calling Christopher. She tells herself it's to see if he has anything to report, but she knows his silence is its own answer and resolves against it. Hands off—in every sense of the word—is the smart path there.

At last she settles by the edge of the nursery window. If Peter truly is an emotional vampire, he'll sense the uproar in the house and come now. But there's nothing: no rush of movement through the air, no tiny light that signifies his presence.

The first two nights Peter had visited, he'd shut the window behind him, locking that light out. It has taken Holly years to wonder why. Perhaps his motives had been less than pure from the beginning. The last night, he hadn't bothered to close the window, but no light had followed him, beating against the glass.

She wonders too if his absence signifies more than a reluctance to return. Perhaps he can no longer fly? That would be ironic. Although it's true she never actually saw him take to the air—when he arrived, he was suddenly just there. And she never saw him leave. For a time she'd tried to convince herself she'd dreamed the entire thing. A hallucination, brought on by grief and lack of sleep.

Aside from Eden, of course.

One other detail has haunted her—why Peter never came for Jane, why he picked her instead. Now she thinks she knows: It's because something in Holly was damaged after the crash. Not only her body. Something inside.

She leaves the nursery to check on Jack. He's asleep, or faking it well, his arm stretched over his head as if to ward off a blow. She doesn't like his color; it's too pale. She tells herself it's because of the dim light from the hall, ignores the finger of fear on her heart, the little voice that whispers it's all starting again—the endless vigils by his bedside, the midnight checks to make sure he's still breathing. He's just tired. He's just asleep.

She takes a deep breath, puts her hand on the bedside table to steady herself. Her fingers brush something hard. It's the picture Jane had left in the nursery—Jack must have kept it. She picks up the frame, moves to the light by the window so she can examine it. She'd seen it for only a few seconds this morning. Now, as she studies it, she can see Eden's sparkle, her joy.

And then Holly looks at Jack in the photo and her heart squeezes tight. The whiteness of his face, the pain-dulled eyes. The smile that looks more like a grimace. She lived those days with him once, and she won't let him go back.

But perhaps that smile, pained though it is, is why Peter has never come for her son, why he will never come. Why Jack could sleep in the nursery every night and be perfectly safe. Maybe, Holly decides, her mother was wrong. It's not emotions Peter is drawn to after all.

Jack might have lost his innocence with the car wreck, but he still has one thing to protect him from Peter, that usurper of childhood. One thing that Holly lacks.

He still has hope.

Even so, Holly checks to make sure his windows are closed tight and locked. Tomorrow, no matter what Jane might say, she'll nail them shut.

Chapter Twenty-Three

In the morning, the rain is sheeting down. In her time away, Holly's forgotten how gray London can be. It matches her mood.

She's not hungry, and she's not interested in sparring with Jane at this hour, so she delays going downstairs. She does some work on her laptop, takes her time showering, secure in the knowledge that there will be no lacrosse today. When she finally descends to the kitchen, she expects to be greeted by a mopey Jack, so she's surprised when Nan says she hasn't seen him.

"He hasn't been downstairs, at least not since I've been here," Nan says. "But it's a good day for a bit of a lie-in."

"It is," Holly agrees. They're both practicing diplomacy with each other, being perfectly polite, as if yesterday never happened. But Jack's absence makes Holly uneasy. It's not like him to sleep this late, especially when there's food to be had. "I think I'll go and check on him. It's getting close to lunch."

She heads upstairs, knocks at the door. "Jack?"

No answer. She pushes it open. Inside, the room is still dark. She crosses to the window, pulls back the shades. The dim light filters in to show Jack curled in a ball under the covers. His face is a pasty white, paler than it was last evening.

"Jack!" She shakes his shoulder, gently at first, then with increasing urgency. He doesn't respond for a heart-stopping length of time. At last he mutters something and pushes her hand away.

"Jack. I want you to get up," she says. She tugs him into a seated position. "Do you feel all right?"

"Tired," he mumbles. But she's seen him tired. This is something else.

She touches his forehead. It's cool, almost clammy. "Why don't you try and eat something," she says, forcing herself to sound calm. "Your blood sugar is probably low."

She calls downstairs and tells Nan to put the kettle on. As soon as she hears it shriek, she hurries to the kitchen and makes him a cup of tea laced with milk and sugar. In the time it takes her to run back up the stairs with it, he's fallen asleep again. She pulls at him, trying to wake him and get him upright.

"Jack," she says. "You need to drink this. Now."

She presses the mug into his hands. After he's taken a few sips, she opens the curtains more widely so she can get a better look at him. He's far too pale.

"Maybe you overdid it yesterday," she says. "Why don't you take it easy for a bit." She keeps her voice calm, phrases it less like an order and more like a suggestion.

"Yeah," he mutters. "But I don't understand. I was in decent shape before we left. It hasn't been *that* long."

"It could be the weather. Or maybe you have allergies or a touch of the flu," she offers. Right now isn't the time to point out the truth, that she'd warned him about this exact reaction. She needs to keep him as relaxed as possible—if he's agitated, it could make him even worse. She counts backward in her head. It's been almost three weeks to the day since his last injection. "Just rest."

He doesn't argue, which is the biggest tip-off that he isn't well. She leaves him to hurry to the nursery, where she's hidden the jar of cream made from the byproducts of Eden's blood in her top dresser drawer.

When she returns, Jane is standing by his bed.

"Is he well?" she asks. Her long silver hair is piled loosely atop her head, and she brushes aside a stray strand as she peers in concern at her grandson.

"I think he overdid it yesterday," Holly answers. She tries to keep any note of *I told you so* out of her voice. Even if it is true, it won't help Jack.

Instead she rubs the cream sparingly along his temples and then his chest as Jane looks on with interest.

"What's that?"

"The cream I've been working on," Holly says. "The one I told you about. It can't hurt." That's true, but she's not certain it will help. Jack has no visible injuries or actual pain. But she has nothing else to try. And after a few moments he does appear better. His cheeks, although still pale, have lost that sickly whiteness, his forehead isn't as clammy, and he's sitting up unaided. Holly tells him to stay in bed, then runs back downstairs and asks Nan to make up a plate of toast and eggs.

It's Jane herself who takes the plate from Holly at the door and sits with Jack while he eats, who regales him with stories of how Holly once spent an entire week in the nursery with chicken pox, refusing to eat anything but strawberry-lemonade sorbet, which her then-housekeeper normally made once a year, on St. Swithin's Day, and how Jane had to pay her extra to get her to stay. By the time she's finished the tale, Jack has recovered enough to talk about calling some of the kids he met during dinner the other night and going out. Holly suspects a good part of it is bravado.

"Well, I'll let you two decide the wisdom of that," Jane says, standing up from the bed and taking the plate. "But if you stay home, I'll see if we can find the recipe and let Nan try her hand at it. No promises though. And now I really must finish my calls for the charity auction." She looks at Holly. "Perhaps you'll consider donating a collection of skin care products."

And with that she glides from the room before Holly can even mouth a silent *Thank you*. She shakes her head. Only her mother. She turns her attention back to Jack.

"I think you should chill today," she tells him. "Maybe tomorrow, okay?"

He bunches the sheet through his fingers. Looks down at his hands, avoids her eye.

"Do you ever wonder why we're alive?" he asks quietly.

After the lightness of the last few moments, Holly wasn't expecting this. Not now. She sits down on the bed.

"What do you mean?" she says, buying time. She knows exactly what he means.

"After the crash. Why we lived and Dad and Isaac didn't. You never wonder?"

"No," Holly lies. "I don't. You can't think like that."

"I see him sometimes. I'll be passing by a window or turning a corner and I'll catch a glimpse of him. And then I realize it's just me."

"You never told me that."

He ignores her. "And then the accident with Eden. I fell too. But she's the one who died. And I look at that picture of me in the wheelchair and I try to remember . . ." He trails off. "It's like I'm bad luck to everyone around me."

"Jack. There is nothing bad luck about you. If I hadn't had you after the car crash . . ." She can't tell him her real thoughts in those days, so she amends it. "I don't know what I would have done without you."

And it's true.

The only thing Holly had in her life besides her family before the crash was her work at the lab, and she doubts that alone would have been enough to sustain her after losing them, to get her out of bed in the mornings the way her drive to care for Jack did. She imagines a version of that self living with Jane in London postcrash and shudders.

"But Dad and Isaac," Jack says. "And Eden."

Holly takes his hands, starts again. "Jack, look at me," she tells him, forcing his eyes up from the comforter. "Cars crash. Accidents happen. It's not your fault. None of it is your fault."

"But Eden," he says again.

Now is the time. Holly starts to tell him, starts to say the words. "Eden . . . ," she begins. And stops. What can she say? She doesn't know if Eden is alive or dead. She doesn't know if they'll ever find her. And if they do, if Christopher Cooke somehow manages to bring her home, what if she's awake? That's the question that's been keeping Holly up at night with both anticipation and terror. Will she see what Holly's done and understand, or will she decide that ten years of being a living science project is too much to forgive? Holly doesn't know. And it's not fair to put that burden on Jack.

"Eden," she says, "Eden loved you so very much. She would have done anything for you, Jack."

And as she leans over to kiss his forehead, she prays that it's still true.

Chapter Twenty-Four

The next day dawns bright and clear. When Jack straggles downstairs, he's rubbing his eyes, but his color is good and he has no trouble downing the plate of eggs and bacon Nan puts in front of him. He takes one look out the window and perks up.

"Think there will be practice today?" he asks hopefully.

Nan shakes her head.

"Ed told me he's bunking off today. Some new movie came out and he can't wait till the weekend to see it. I think he'll be giving you a call after school," she says conspiratorially. She looks at Holly. "That is, if it's okay with your mum."

"If you get your assignments done," Holly says. She can't make it look too easy. "And only if it's the early showing."

When Jack leaves to go shower, Holly shoots Nan a sidelong glance. "Thanks," she says.

Nan shrugs. "No worries. Ed could use the break anyhow. He's turning into a total lax-head." She looks down at the kitchen table she's scrubbing. "Was yesterday . . . did Jack feel like that because he played? Because of that condition he has?"

It's Holly's turn to look away. "Probably," she admits. "Jack is prone to overdoing it, and he hasn't been at his best since he's been here." She doesn't go into details. There's no point.

＊

Holly spends the morning in the office. She has a huge stack of marketing items to sign off on, and she's getting serious pressure from Barry to fly home. She knows she needs to consider it. But she's afraid to leave Jack. It's clear that he's struggling, between his discovery about Eden and the news of his own health.

She could take him back to the States with her, but she wouldn't be able to watch him if she's in meetings all day. And she's worried about how air travel would affect him. The normal hormonal changes of adolescence may be behind some of what he's experiencing in terms of the injection wearing off so quickly, but it's also possible that flying, or the time change, or jet lag contributed to his current weakened state. And if she takes him home with her, what happens when she needs to fly back? She could force him to stay with Barry, but what if he gets worse? Or starts hanging out with his friends again and makes another stupid decision?

Christopher Cooke had better earn that enormous retainer soon.

She works through the rest of the day, signing documents, writing emails, packaging her thoughts into crisp sound bites for her PR team. And all the while, the germ of an idea is growing. It's a bad idea, she knows, but she doesn't have any others. And so, when she's finished for the day, before she heads downstairs, she calls the lab and asks for Elliot Benton.

There's a long wait. She sits on the edge of the desk, twining the phone cord through her fingers and imagining the scene on the other end—Elliot deep in research, shaking off the first call, then the second, looking up when someone finally tromps all the way to his office. It makes her smile, on a day when very little else has. If things had turned out differently, she imagines, she would have been quite like Elliot.

At last he comes to the phone. He's flustered, she can tell, but that

194

doesn't stop him from launching into an excited monologue about his current projects. She listens patiently. Finally he draws a breath.

"Elliot," she says before he can continue, "that's all fascinating. Especially the latest bit about the sea cucumbers. But I may be in London for longer than I'd planned, and I'd like to keep working on something I'm researching myself. I'm calling you because I know you'll understand. Would you do me a favor?"

There's no reason for him to be suspicious, but still she holds her breath.

"Of course," he says jovially. "We scientists have to stick together." He's flattered, as she'd counted on him to be.

She walks him through the procedures, her private lab, the secret vault. She's toyed with the idea of bringing Elliot in on her research, but it's too much to explain, too complicated. Plus, he's a stickler for protocol, and what she's done violates almost every rule available.

Once Elliot understands what she wants, she has to explain how to get it to her. "Because it's human blood, you can't just have the lab send it out," she says. For that reason, and because it is the last of what she has from Eden, she's considered paying someone to hand-deliver the vial. But it's too risky—too many people would have to know about the transaction.

She describes to Elliot how to package it, promises to send him a link to a checklist he can use.

"It's . . . human blood?" he says, as if he's just realizing this.

She wonders again if she's making a mistake. "Yes. It's . . . it's a type of genetic study I'm working on. A personal one. And Elliot?"

"Yes?"

"I'd really appreciate if you'd take care of the whole thing yourself. It's a private situation, and I'd prefer not to let anyone else know."

"Of course," he says again. She has to trust that he means it.

When they hang up, she calculates how long it will take him. She's told him not to start the process until the morning, when he can mail it out promptly. A day to process and package, another two days in transit . . . She figures it will be here by the end of the week, if she's lucky. Which lately she is not.

In the meantime, she needs to keep Jack healthy. She spends the next few days alternately working and mother-henning him. She feeds him all the iron-rich foods she can, requesting steamed spinach, liver and onions, even kidney pie, on the theory that it can't hurt. Nan looks at her as if she's crazy and Jane declares herself revolted, but Holly doesn't care. She practically forces Jack to eat, until she catches Jane smuggling in fish and chips one day after lunch.

"You're not helping," Holly growls when she discovers the subterfuge.

"Believe me, I am," Jane says, snagging an errant chip that's dropped onto the counter. Despite her alabaster skin, chips have always been her weakness. "You want him to eat, don't you? The poor boy is going to waste away on whatever foolish diet you've concocted. And Nan is truly going to quit if you keep making her cook these revolting messes."

"There are other housekeepers in London, you know," Holly says. But it's half-hearted.

"I do know," Jane says, dousing the errant chip in vinegar. "I've tried most of them. And I'm not losing this one."

Holly is settling into the office when her mobile rings. She glances at it and does a quick time calculation, expecting Barry or perhaps Elliot. But it's Christopher.

"Please tell me you have good news," she says.

"That depends," he answers. "I haven't found your Peter yet. So I decided to approach it from a different angle. I talked with Maria."

It takes Holly a moment to process what he's saying. And then it hits her. She has to sit down.

"You went to Cornwall? But how did you . . ." She trails off.

"I told you. I like to know as much as I can about my clients. Turns out, I learned a lot."

"You have no business investigating me," Holly snaps. "You took my money and you're supposed to be doing what I say, and that's helping me find my daughter. What about looking for Peter? That's what you said you were going to do." She can hear the hysteria in her voice. She fights to control it, to stay calm and discover what he knows. She was stupid not to have expected this.

"Peter wasn't panning out, if you'll excuse the pun," Christopher says, and Holly feels that familiar urge to throttle him. "I don't have enough to go on. So I decided to pull on the other end—to see why, rather than how, your daughter might leave. And that took me to Cornwall. Now I know what you were doing. But what I don't understand is why."

"I don't know what you're talking about," she stalls.

He sighs. "We can play that game if you want. But it won't work. Before my accident, people used to say I was typical Irish, a mix of charm and temper both. Well, these days I'm down an arm and short on charm. But I've picked up plenty of rage, especially when it comes to the safety of children. I need to know what you were doing with that kid. And trust me, you won't like what happens if you stonewall."

"If you must know, I was trying to cure my daughter." It's the truth. Part of it, at least.

"It might have been useful to mention she'd been in a coma for years," he says. "Somehow you happened to omit that tiny detail in our conversations. It certainly explains why you have no photos of her with her eyes open."

Holly struggles to think, decides that the best way to get information is to give some. "Fine. As I mentioned when we met, Eden has a rare genetic disease—it causes her to grow too fast. When she was young, she had an accident. She fell and hit her head. The doctors think her body couldn't heal *and* sustain that rate of growth, so she essentially went into a type of hibernation. Over the years I've tried everything to wake her up."

"That's why all the medical equipment? The IVs and everything else?"

"Yes." She swallows hard. "I have a PhD in immunology and microbial pathogenesis, and my postdoctoral training is in stem cell biology. I've been studying Eden's blood, hoping to find the answers to curing her."

Now it's his turn to pause. "It's a good story," he says at last. But his next words are a blow. "But I'm not convinced it's true. Or at least not *all* of the truth."

"Excuse me?" Holly's gotten her voice under control. She's cool and crisp, the way she would talk to an assistant, especially one she's about to fire. There's absolutely no reason at all for him to doubt her.

"Do you know what they call your daughter? Those women who cared for her?" he asks. He doesn't wait for a reply. "They call her *anghel ng mga himala*—the angel of miracles."

"What?"

"The angel of miracles," he repeats. "They think her blood will heal them—heal almost anyone—no matter what's wrong with them."

Holly's gripping the phone so tightly her fingers are numb. "That's ridiculous," she scoffs, putting as much scorn into her voice as she can without letting it shake. "You must have misunderstood. English isn't their first language. I'll talk to them myself and clear this up."

"Funny, they thought you'd say that. So they decided to head home, back to the Philippines. All of them," he says. "They made me promise not to talk to you until they'd already left. Now why would they worry about a thing like that?"

She pictures it. A drop of blood falling onto a nurse with a cut or a scar. She'd insisted they wear gloves, be fully gowned, every time they came in contact with Eden, but someone must have been sloppy. She can see the blood, ruby red, a single drop suspended when they cleaned around the port or gathered up the vials.

One drop would be all it took.

Her stomach churns. If they'd discovered Eden's secret, would they have taken her? And the missing bags of blood . . . Perhaps Peter was never involved. But no. Maria's grief and concern had been real. That feather Holly had found the day she went to Grace House had been real too. It was Peter. It had to be.

Christopher has said something, but she's missed it.

"What?"

"I said, they even suggested I try it, when we find her. On my stump." He sounds amused. "They actually thought it might work."

He doesn't believe them. Of course he doesn't believe them. It's too crazy-sounding to be true.

"Holly? You still there?"

She pulls herself together. "This isn't funny," she snaps. "My daughter is out there somewhere and you—"

"I never said it was."

"You let them *leave*."

"They were terrified after talking to me. Apparently you had some hell of a nondisclosure agreement in place. But I'll tell you this: they broke it because they truly want to help. They're worried because more people—like the police—aren't looking for her. And they don't have your daughter."

"How can you be so sure?" she cries, as much to herself as to him. She can't tell him about the missing blood, not now.

"I just am. I have a knack for these things," he says, and his voice has lost that amused tone. Instead she hears something else. Compassion. It tugs her back from the brink like a lifeline. "They love your kid, especially Maria. They're genuinely worried about her." He pauses. "Also, I had them followed. Your kid isn't with them."

More proof he's not as easily put off as she once thought. "I assume I'm paying for that, even though I didn't authorize it?"

"You are," he says cheerfully. "It will be in my next bill."

"Well, what's your next step?"

"Figuring out what else you're lying about," he says without hesitation. "I'll be in touch."

He hangs up.

Holly stares at the phone. She should have listened to Barry—she never should have hired Christopher Cooke. He's too independent, too hard to control. The best she can hope for now is that he doesn't find anything else he can use against her. She thanks god that there are no old pictures of Jack immediately after the crash, that she'd managed to keep the paparazzi away from the hospital and his rehab. If Christopher saw those and started putting two and two together . . .

No chance, she assures herself. He's already decided it's too implausible to be believed.

But a little voice inside Holly's head whispers that Christopher Cooke seems like the type who's more than willing to believe the impossible once he's found the proof.

Chapter Twenty-Five

At least the package from Elliot arrives in one piece. Holly's working in the office a few days later when it comes, so Nan signs for it. When Holly walks into the kitchen, the housekeeper is holding the cooler box and looking curiously at the bright biohazard warnings taped across it.

"Thank you, Nan, I'll take that," Holly says. She expects the housekeeper to get the hint, but she doesn't.

"Is this something from the States?" Nan asks.

"Yes," Holly says, trying to keep the impatience from her voice. Nan has been a huge help with Jack this week, keeping Ed's schedule busy enough so that including Jack in practice has been a nonstarter. Holly can tell Jack's frustrated, but he's not blaming her, which is a refreshing change.

"Is it safe to have in the kitchen? Around the food, I mean?" Nan asks dubiously. "It has all those warnings on it."

Holly had been planning on injecting Jack in two days. Superstitiously, she's wants to wait a full month from his last injection in the hopes she'll catch a break before then and Eden will be found. But it's clear Nan won't be comfortable storing the blood in the refrigerator next to the Brussels sprouts for tonight's dinner. And really, Jack's been so up and down lately she can't afford to wait until his next crash. Holly sighs.

"I'll take it up to the office." She takes the box from Nan and carries it up the stairs. On the landing, she bumps into Jane, who is exiting her room.

"Hmmm. That looks quite terrifying. What is it?" Jane asks. Her long hair is pulled back today, and a shaft of sunlight from the window on the landing catches it and turns it to molten silver.

"Just something I'm working on," Holly says, trying to slide past, but Jane is too sharp.

"For the boy? Let me see." She follows to the office, where Holly reluctantly opens the box. She unwraps the vial of blood and holds it up to the light, checking to ensure it isn't cracked or broken.

Jane shakes her head. "It looks ordinary enough. What do you plan to do with it?"

"It's the last one I have," Holly says. "But there's no sense holding on to it for too long. It won't be viable. I'll inject Jack with it today. All of it. He needs it."

Jane reaches out and gently takes the vial from Holly, turning it this way and that. "That cream of yours the other day was quite the miracle-worker," she says. "I might not have believed it if I hadn't seen it with my own eyes, the difference it made in Jack."

Against the office's subdued walls, Eden's blood takes on a rich, mesmerizing red. Holly can't take her eyes from it. "And this is the source, so it must be even more powerful," Jane muses. "Tell me. Have you ever tried it on yourself?"

She doesn't so much as glance at Holly's leg, but her scrutiny stings anyhow. *No*, Holly wants to say. *Of course not.*

And yet. In the aftermath of the car crash, it was Jane who canceled her vacations and charity dinners to sit with Holly in the hospital, to take her to physical therapy and to be fitted for a brace. Jane knows exactly how badly Holly's leg was damaged and how hard Holly worked to recover the use of it, because she was there. She knows no amount of rehab could have made it as fit as it is now.

Holly doesn't make a defense. She doesn't explain that she didn't dare test Eden's blood directly on Jack until she knew whether it was safe, until she understood what it would do. She doesn't talk about the hours she spent terrified that the tingling sensation that coursed through her body with the first injection meant she'd done something wrong, that she'd die when Eden and Jack needed her most. That she hasn't taken it since those early days, although regular usage would cure the limp that plagues her when she's tired or cold. That she'll never use it again. And that for every hour she's spent researching a cure for Jack, she's spent that and more on Eden.

And she doesn't say a word about how hard she cried the first time she took blood from her daughter.

"Yes. In the beginning," is all she says. She reaches over and takes the vial from Jane, wraps it back in its protective casing. When it's covered, the light in the room seems to dim a little bit.

"Well then," Jane says, "I suppose I should leave you to it."

"I suppose so." Holly turns away and busies herself tidying the desk.

"Holly," Jane says. She's lingered by the door.

"Yes?"

"It's quite all right to feel badly. Just not *too* badly." This time, those bright blue eyes look directly at Holly. "No matter how much you used, most people—myself included—would have used more."

And with that she is gone.

After Jane leaves, Holly finishes a few emails, checks over the marketing plan for Pixie Dust one last time. There's a problem with the vendor for the glass bottles—they're struggling to keep up with the advance orders—and Holly could leave it to Barry but drafts a letter anyhow. She's stalling, she knows, but the conversation with her mother has left her unsettled. She's done the right thing—anyone who has seen Jack run across the lacrosse field will attest to that—but she can't help but feel the wrong of it anyhow.

The work helps steady her, as it almost always does, and when she's calm again, she pulls the vial back out of its refrigerated box. She's readied the needle so often over the years she could do it in her sleep, but this time she's hyperaware of the sharp metal point beneath its cap, of the rich red color of the blood as she draws it out of the vial. It's as if she's under some sort of spell.

She gives herself a mental shake. She doesn't have the time for this. She needs to find Jack and get on with it. She carries the needle in its casing with her down the hall and to his room. But when she taps on the door, he's not there. Nor is he in the library or game room.

She hurries to the kitchen, where she asks Nan if she's seen him. "Ed's out of school for the summer, so I think they'd planned lunch and then maybe hitting some of the shops. Ed's dad might meet up with them, if he's bored enough with this week's chippie. He's a teacher, so he's done as well. But they should be back early."

Holly bites her lip in frustration. Jack's out as well, his school having finished two days ago. He'd been elated, a mood change she would have welcomed were it not for the fear his increasingly free schedule struck in her. "Why can't I go now?" he'd raged at her when she'd forbidden him from taking off on the Tube to explore London by himself. "There's absolutely no reason. You just don't want me to have any fun." He'd stomped up the stairs in a fury, slamming the door to his room behind him, and she'd counted herself grateful that he hadn't walked out the front door. She doesn't know how she could have stopped him.

She hates the idea of him wandering the streets. The shadowy figure of Peter is never far from her mind. *I can fix that for you . . .* But today Jack is with Ed, and possibly Ed's father. He'll be fine.

"He said he'd already talked with you," Nan offers. "That might be why he didn't come up to the office." She looks at the wrapped needle in Holly's hand with undisguised curiosity, but before she can ask about it, the doorbell rings.

The two women look at each other. "I don't think your mother is expecting anyone," Nan says. "Jack probably forgot his key again." She moves toward the hall, but Holly beats her to it.

"I'll get it," she says. She has a few things to say to her son. She doesn't want to leave the syringe in the kitchen with Nan, so she takes it with her as she hurries to the door. She'll pull Jack into the hall bathroom and inject him there.

She opens the door. "Where have you . . . ," she starts to say, but the words die on her lips. It's not Jack at all, but Christopher Cooke, dressed in a biker kit, his helmet tucked under his arm, his prosthesis hidden by leather gloves.

"Been all your life?" He finishes her sentence for her with a cheeky grin. "I've asked myself that same question."

"I wasn't expecting you," Holly says, unable to think of a snappy comeback. He's caught her off guard—again. Even worse, she hears footsteps behind her. She prays fervently for Nan but knows her luck's not that good.

"Holly? Is that Jack?" her mother calls before coming into view. "I'm heading out for a late lunch and wanted to make sure you'd found him before . . . Oh, hello." Christopher gives her his most winning smile. Jane, no slouch in her ability to recognize an attractive male, returns it.

"I'm sorry. I didn't mean to interrupt. I was wondering if you'd need the car to look for Jack," she says smoothly.

"You seem to have a distressing habit of losing people," Christopher observes sotto voce to Holly.

Holly glares at him but bites her tongue. Around Christopher, silence is a virtue. She does, however, answer Jane.

"Jack is out with Ed," she says. "He should be home soon, so I don't need the car. Enjoy your lunch."

"Well then, please tell me you aren't going to keep your . . . friend . . . standing on the steps," Jane says. She makes no move to leave.

"He's not my friend," Holly snaps back, as sullen as any teenager. She catches herself, in part because Christopher's smile is so wide it threatens to split his face. "Mother, this is Mr. Cooke. He's . . . he's working on a project. A special one. For me."

"Lovely to meet you," Jane says, extending her hand, and for a moment Holly thinks Christopher is going to kiss it to annoy her further. But he shakes it gently. There's no sign on Jane's face that she notices anything unusual about his grip. "Christopher, please. The pleasure's mine," he says. Truly, he's insufferable.

Jane turns to Holly. "Surely you don't wish to discuss business out here," she says. "Why don't you bring Mr. Cooke . . . Christopher . . . into the library? I'll have Nan make tea."

Holly hesitates. She doesn't want Christopher in the house. There's too much that can go wrong. Including, she now realizes, the fact that she still has Jack's injection clutched in her left hand. For now, it's partially hidden behind the door, but once Christopher steps into the hall, it will be in plain sight. She doesn't particularly want to leave him alone with Jane, either, but that seems the lesser of two evils.

"I'll tell Nan," she says quickly. "Would you mind showing him in?" And without waiting for her mother to respond, she dashes down the hall toward the kitchen.

"Please tell me you're not leaving that in here," Nan says as Holly stows the syringe in the back of the refrigerator.

"I need tea in the library," Holly says, ignoring her. "Something quick." She pauses to reflect. "And not too delicious. For two."

And then she dashes out again.

Just before the library door, she slows her pace, brushes back her hair, and takes a deep breath. No matter what Christopher has said—or not said—to her mother, or what Jane may have revealed, there's no advantage in looking worried. She makes herself count to ten, then ten again, and then she opens the door.

The scene that greets her is far too cozy for her liking. Jane and Christopher are bent over Jane's prized first edition of *Peter Pan*, Jane pointing to an illustration.

". . . utter nonsense," she's saying, frowning for emphasis. "Mr. Barrie—Sir James Barrie, of course, is the proper way to refer to him—certainly took his fair share of liberties, particularly with the descriptions of the Darling family."

Before Jane can elaborate on what those liberties might be, or anything else, Holly interrupts.

"Mr. Cooke and I have quite a bit of business to discuss," she says firmly. "Thank you for entertaining him, Mother, but I'd hate to keep you from your luncheon."

"Oh, no trouble at all," Jane says breezily. "It's with the Worths, and you know how boring they can be. Mr. Cooke is much more interesting."

"I'm sure. Well, I've asked Nan to bring tea. Perhaps you could see what's keeping her?" Jane and Holly both know that Nan's barely had enough time to put the kettle on, but still, Jane is gracious. She flashes a smile at Christopher. "Of course," she says, and sails from the room.

As soon as the door is shut behind her, Holly rounds on Christopher.

"What are you doing here?" she demands. But she can guess. He's discovered something and wants to see her face, gauge her reaction, when he tells her.

"I told you I like to know more about my clients."

He moves about the room, picking up books and setting them down, flipping through pages, asking her random questions about photos and mementos on the walls as she tries to bring him to his point, whatever it may be. When he picks up the sketch of the Darling siblings, he's thoughtful, turning it over in his hands.

"The famous Darling children," he murmurs, a perplexed look in his eyes. "Amazing how familiar they seem." He looks as if he's going to say more, but there's a knock at the door. Holly turns away, grateful for the interruption, as Jane enters with the tea tray.

"I'll put this down and you can serve yourselves," Jane says, setting it on the table. Holly breathes a sigh of relief. It's possible she'll escape this unscathed.

"Thank you," Christopher says. He raises a hand—the right one, still clothed in the glove—in mock salute. "Not all my clients' mothers are so accommodating to a private detective," he says.

"Client?" Jane raises an eyebrow. Clearly Holly's hopes are about to be dashed. "Whatever are you working on?"

"Later," Holly hisses. But it's too late. Jane has already turned to Christopher, who is helping himself to a biscuit. "Are you searching for Eden?" She pauses. "Or . . . her father?"

There's a sound outside the door, which Holly realizes has been left ajar. She looks at her mother.

"Don't look at me," Jane says defensively. "I was carrying the tea tray. If you wanted it closed for privacy, you should have checked."

Holly crosses the room, pushes the door open the rest of the way. She knows what she's going to find, but she's hoping with all her heart she's mistaken.

She's not. It's Jack, and he's ashen.

"Jack, sweetheart," she says, reaching out for him. He ignores her, looks straight at Christopher.

"You're a private detective? You're looking for Eden?"

Christopher shoots a quick glance at Holly, who is paralyzed. "That's right, mate. Any thoughts as to where she could be?"

Jack doesn't answer. Holly holds her breath, waiting for the explosion. Yet she's still stunned by its ferocity when it comes.

"You mean she's *alive*? All this time, she's been *alive*?"

"Jack . . . ," she tries. But he's having none of it.

"Why didn't you tell me she's alive?" he demands. "What else haven't you told me?"

All the secrets she's been keeping come crashing down on her. They pin her to the spot, make it impossible to breathe. Her mind is racing, looking for solutions, but she can't get any words out. Meanwhile Christopher is looking on avidly. If he'd wanted a reaction, Holly thinks grimly, this must exceed his wildest dreams. At least Jack seems to have missed the whole different-father bit.

"Christopher, you need to leave," she manages. "We'll discuss whether you're still employed later. Right now, just go."

"I need a word with you first," he says.

But Jack won't be put off. "You told me she was dead! I thought she died in Cornwall!"

Holly doesn't refute him, doesn't say that she never said those exact words. It's not going to help. Jack won't stop. He's shouting at her: questions about where Eden is and what's happened, and the more agitated he gets, the worse he looks. His lips are developing a bluish tint, and that pale, unhealthy color is returning to his skin.

"Jack," she says, "we'll talk about it, all right? I promise. But please, let's go upstairs."

She moves toward him, and he recoils. "Don't touch me!"

He looks like he's verging on collapse, but still he won't let her near him. Finally she turns to Jane for help. It's her mother who is able to wrangle him up the stairs with a practiced ease, as if she moves recalcitrant teens every day. Holly starts to follow, but Jane shakes her head.

"Best if I do it for now," she says, and Holly is left behind.

Christopher moves closer to her. "Is he okay?" The worry in his voice sounds real, but it's too little, too late.

"No, thanks to you. My son . . . I told you. He's not well. You need to leave. Now."

209

"Not until I talk to you."

She sees now why Barry warned her that Christopher was dangerous. For all his slenderness, there's something inherently menacing
about the way he's standing. The tension in his muscles, the intensity
of his gaze . . . he reminds her of a television special she once saw on
super-predators. Something fast, and ruthless, that would strike before
you even saw it coming. She thinks of the drug dealer in Barry's story
and swallows.

"Fine. But outside." She can't bear for Jack to overhear anything else.

She walks him to the door. She wants to shut it and lock it behind
him, but the way he looks at her, it's as if he's read her thoughts. He
waves her through ahead of him. "Ladies first."

They stand on the front steps, and Holly pulls the door shut behind
them. A slight breeze ruffles the hairs along the back of her neck, making
her shiver and setting her even more on edge. Christopher watches her.

"I have a hunch," he says quietly.

"About damn time," Holly snaps.

"There's a drug being released onto the streets," he continues, as if
she hadn't spoken. "It's been around for a bit, but the quality is getting
stronger. The dealer seems to target young boys. Teenagers. The drug
makes them euphoric, as if they're flying, but then they crash hard. The
highs get higher and the lows get lower until they can't get enough to
sustain the good part and the cycle puts them over the edge. We have
three comatose boys right now," he says, then corrects himself. "Three
that we know about, I should say. All about your son's age."

"Do they . . . do they wake up?"

He shakes his head. "Not in this world."

Holly shivers again, and this time it has nothing to do with the
breeze.

"Want to know what the police are calling them?"

"No," Holly says, but he tells her anyway.

"The lost boys."

"Why are you telling me this?" She struggles to keep her tone even.

He answers with another question. "This morning, I got another call, from a friend on the force. Another boy overdosed. This one had a paper packet in his bag with a name on it. Want to guess what it was?"

This time, he doesn't wait for her response. "Pixie dust. Sound familiar?"

Impossible. Too late, she tries to control her expression, to keep the horror from showing.

"Descriptions of the dealer have been vague," he continues, watching her closely. "At one time, the kids say, he must have been quite handsome. Like a movie star. Sometimes he appears to be a young man. Other witnesses describe him as middle-aged. But no matter what he looks like, the police can't seem to find him. Every time they think they're close, it's as if he flies away."

They stare at each other in silence.

"I think we're looking for the same man," he says finally. "And I think there's a connection between your cosmetics and his drug. I know why I'm looking for him. Why are you?"

"I told you. I think he has my daughter."

"The daughter you share," he corrects. "But why now, after all these years? Why is he interested in her now, when you said he hadn't been in contact her entire life?"

"I don't know." And she doesn't, not really. But if she had to guess, it has to do with the miraculous qualities of Eden's blood.

He studies her a moment. "We could work together on this. Or . . . I can work alone. I'm good at alone."

Holly thinks of Eden, what Peter might be doing to her. She thinks of Jack, his gray face. "No," she says at last. But then she adds the same condition that her mother did. For a completely different reason. It's possible Peter's creating drugs for the sheer pleasure of it. But if he's gone to the trouble to kidnap Eden, it's unlikely whatever he's doing is just for fun. So there's a chance this drug, whatever it is, has a purpose—youth, maybe, or health. It might help Jack and Eden. "I'll work with you, so long as when we find him, I get to talk with him first."

Christopher Cooke doesn't say yes. But he doesn't say no, either.

"I'll be in touch," is what he does say.

Holly waits until he's ridden off before she goes into the house. And then, far too late, she locks the door behind her.

Chapter Twenty-Six

J ane's face is grim when Holly returns.

"Whoever that man is, he has a talent for disruption," she says. She's pouring whiskey from the bar in the library and hands Holly a glass without asking.

"Well, you certainly gave him the opening," Holly says, taking a long sip.

"Don't blame me," Jane retorts. "How was I to know why he was here? Or that Jack would be eavesdropping? The next time you choose to seek help outside the family, I'd appreciate being informed."

"I didn't tell him anything he wouldn't believe," Holly says. "Only the bare bones. We weren't getting anywhere on our own, and Jack's getting worse. You can see that." She takes a deep breath, another sip of her drink. Lashing out at her mother right now won't solve anything. Instead she asks where Jack is.

"He's upstairs, almost asleep. I gave him a sleeping pill. Oh, don't look at me like that," she says, catching Holly's horrified glance. "It's perfectly safe. Dr. Shepherd prescribed them for me years ago, and I've been taking one every night. Just to take the edge off."

There's so much in this statement for Holly to unpack, she doesn't know where to start. But something else is weighing on her. "There's more," she says.

Jane cocks an eyebrow. "It seems there always is these days. Well? Out with it."

Holly takes a deep breath. "That man—Christopher Cooke. He has a prosthesis under his glove. A fake hand," she adds when Jane stares at her.

"Yes, thank you, I'm well aware of what the term means," Jane snaps.

"The day I met him, he was wearing . . ." Holly shifts uncomfortably in her seat. "He had a hook in place of the prosthesis."

Jane opens her mouth and utters a word Holly until this point didn't realize her mother knew. "You're just telling me this now?"

"I thought it was coincidence," Holly says defensively. "But now I think it has to be something more." She fills her mother in on what Christopher told her about the drug. The lost boys. Pixie dust.

Jane doesn't speak at first. She swirls the liquid in her drink. Then, "I've wondered . . . there have been times in my life, not many, when . . ."

It's not like Jane to hesitate, to search for words. Holly holds her breath.

"I knew a dancer, a striking woman. Her name was Lily, but no one called her that."

Holly already knows what Jane will say next.

"She fought hard for every role, but she also protected the younger dancers. Kept an eye on them. Helped them out." Jane looks up at Holly. "We all called her the Tiger."

Holly closes her eyes, but Jane's not done.

"Then your father had a cousin, bit of an eccentric, from an old Cornwall family. Roger Smee."

"How much do we really know about Neverland?" Holly asks quietly. "How much do we know about its rules—if it has any—and its connection to our world? About all the ways from here to there?"

"Not enough, it seems. Mother never liked to talk about it."

Holly thinks back to what Jane has told her about meeting Barrie.

How he'd called Peter a "nice chap." She wonders if it's how Wendy described him. It's certainly not how she would.

"How accurate do you think Sir James was, when he recorded her stories?"

Jane shrugs again. "I have no idea. And at this point, there's no way to find out. Mother, her siblings, and Barrie are the only ones who knew, and they're all gone."

There is one other person who knows, Holly thinks. But she's not willing to say his name right now, and apparently neither is her mother. So they sit in silence in the slowly darkening room, nursing their drinks and staring at each other, each thinking the same thought.

Peter knows.

That night, Holly dreams she is on top of the roof, looking at the stars. She used to climb on the roof when she was younger—pull herself out the window, balance on the railing, then swing herself up. To find herself there again is pleasant. In the dream, she's stretched out on her back looking at a thousand golden stars, and they are as familiar and welcoming as family. When she comes back inside, one of the stars follows her through the window. It's upset or worried, Holly can tell. It's trying to warn her about something, but Holly is too tired to open her eyes. Besides, everything it says sounds like tiny bells and she can't understand it. The star stands beside her bed for a long time, and then it disappears.

Holly wakes with a start. In the dark, there's the faintest scattering of golden glitter about the room. It leads from the window to her bed, from her bed to the door. She could almost be imagining it because even as she sees it, it starts to fade. At first she thinks she's still dreaming. But then she realizes where the trail must lead.

Jack.

She's on her feet before she's fully awake, and then she's running down the hall and to the steps, following the faint iridescent glow. The glow leads to his room, is brightest next to his bed. She panics, ripping at the covers, pulling them back.

"Jack?"

He's asleep. His skin is flushed, but when she puts her lips against his forehead, there's no fever. She checks his face, checks everywhere she can see. There's a new scar on his left wrist. Even as she notices it, it's healing, vanishing in front of her eyes.

"Jack?" She shakes his shoulder.

"I had the strangest dream," he murmurs. He opens his eyes, closes them again, snuggles deeper into the sheets. "A beautiful girl was standing over me." He frowns, opens his eyes again.

"She was telling me about a pirate ship. And she called me the funniest thing. An insect, I think. A bee?" He looks up at Holly. "That's not right."

"A flea," she says without thinking. "Because you were always underfoot, always attached to her. She used to call you Flea."

They stare at each other in the dark. The golden light is fading. In another second it will be gone.

"Go to sleep," she says unsteadily. She can't tell either of them it was only a dream. "Do you want me to stay here with you tonight?"

He shakes his head. She's about to tell him it's okay, to reach out and caress his head, when she catches sight of his eyes. Just before the last bit of golden light winks out, she realizes that he *is* afraid.

But not of Eden. Of her.

She can't go back to sleep. She turns the dream over and over in her mind. The sound of bells. The eerie glow. The impression of someone standing over her. She doesn't know whether to nail the nursery window shut or throw it wide open in welcome. If it was truly Eden, how did she get here? What did she want? And why didn't she stay? Holly thinks of that new scar on Jack's wrist and shivers.

She's the first one in the kitchen in the morning, ahead of even Jane. She makes tea, then decides there is no point in postponing the inevitable. She takes the syringe from the back of the fridge, prepares the injection, heads upstairs. She knocks on Jack's door. There's no answer, so she pushes open the door and steps inside, expecting to find him still asleep.

But his eyes are wide open and he's staring at the ceiling. When she crosses the room to him, he sits up.

"Hello," she says cautiously. So much has happened in the past twenty-four hours that she's not even sure where to start.

He doesn't answer, simply looks at her.

"Jack? Are you well?" She reaches for his forehead, but he turns his head away. "Jack?"

"I can't remember what she said," he says. "But I know that she was here."

Holly doesn't answer.

"It doesn't matter," he says, but it's as if he's talking to himself. "It doesn't matter what you say. I know what I saw." He rubs his wrist absently, although whatever mark was there is gone. "She was here. She called me Flea. She talked about riding a boat. A pirate ship."

Those last words stir something in Holly, a scrap of memory. She wants to chase it down, but all her focus is on Jack. She sits down on the bed beside him. "Jack," she says, "I'm really worried about you." She shows him the needle in her hand.

"I thought it was all gone," he says flatly.

"I had a last supply, and had someone send it over. I think we should use it now. All of it."

She waits, but he doesn't speak.

"Jack . . . ," she begins.

"It's Eden, isn't it?"

He's looking at her the same way he looked last night, a mixture of fear and . . . something else. Repugnance? Her stomach clenches.

"What do you mean?"

"I'm not stupid. When you have low iron, you take pills," he says. He turns away. "I worked it out. That's why there was all that medical equipment in Cornwall. Not because she was sick. But because she was some kind of perfect donor for me. And when she disappeared, so did the blood supply."

"Jack, she *was* sick."

"And all these years, you kept her that way for me?"

"No! Jack, listen. I—"

"You're the one who's sick. Not Eden. Not me."

"Please, Jack, you need to listen. And you need to stay calm." She tries to keep her voice steady.

"You kept my sister chained to a bed, and you're telling me not to get worked up?"

"It's not like that." She reaches out to him, but he recoils, and it's as if he's slapped her. Too late, she realizes her mistake. By not telling him the truth from the beginning, she's allowed him to imagine it now as so much worse.

"Listen." She tells him again about the accident, how Eden never woke up. "I did everything I could. I took Eden to every doctor I could find. You have to believe me." She blinks back tears.

"Right. If you loved her so much, why did you use her like that?"

"After the car crash, your right leg was destroyed, and your left wasn't much better. You had so many injuries, had broken so many bones—you fatigued so easily," she says. She looks at him and realizes some part of her still sees him, will always see him, as the frail child he once was. "You spent all your time trying to follow her, but you couldn't. And then I came home from the hospital, from being with her, and you ran to me."

"So?"

"You hadn't been able to run—hadn't even been able to walk, not really—since the car crash."

He looks at her uncomprehendingly.

"When Eden fell, she hit her head—that's why she couldn't wake up. There was a lot of blood. And somehow it got on you, on your injuries, and it . . . healed you."

"I don't understand."

"There's something special about Eden's blood," she says. She leaves out any mention of magic, of Peter Pan. Jack is a child of New York, not London. He has no interest in fairy tales, and Holly's always insisted this particular story wasn't true. "But the help it gives wears off. It doesn't last forever—only a month or so. You need another infusion of it or you start to fade."

With a teenager's self-absorption, he skips over the question of why Eden is different. "What happens if I stop taking it?"

"I don't know. I swear." There's a long pause while Holly weighs what to say. She decides that in this case the truth can only help. "Worst case? There's a chance you could die. You were injured so badly, the doctors were never certain you would recover."

She sees it on his face, the knowledge that what she's been doing has been keeping him alive all these years. And then she sees it harden into something she doesn't recognize.

"There has to be another choice," he says. "Something else that would work. A drug. Or therapy. Or maybe I'm really healed after all this time. You don't know for sure."

"I don't think so," she says gently. "Not the way you've been feeling. This is the longest you've gone without an injection, and every time you exert yourself, or do something like drink, you get worse. I don't know what's going on—maybe, because you're hitting puberty, your body and how it responds is changing. But the injections aren't working the way they used to."

"But I'm fine right now!" And then it's his turn to pause, and she sees him remember something. He looks at his wrist, rubs it. She follows his glance. There's nothing there.

"What is it?"

"Nothing." He shakes his head. "I don't care. I won't take it again."

"Jack . . ."

"You can't make me. You'll have to tie me down, keep me in a coma. Then I'd be the way you want. I can't talk back, I can't get into trouble." He looks her right in the eye. "I can't get hurt. I can't grow up."

"Jack!" she says, horrified. "That's not what I want."

"Isn't it?" he says. He lies back down on the bed, turns to face the wall. "Go away. Just go away." She can't be sure, but it sounds like he's crying.

She reaches out a tentative hand. "Jack?"

"LEAVE!"

So she does. She's barely to the steps when she hears the snick of the lock behind her.

At least she knows where he is, she thinks.

And then it occurs to her—thanks to Jack, she may finally know where her daughter is too.

Chapter Twenty-Seven

Holly stands in a dim corner of the open atrium, beneath the soaring glass ceiling. A cool breeze blows off the river, carrying with it the slightest scent of decay. On either side of her are immense sand-colored buildings; in the center is an enormous statue. Holly stares at it and tries to block out all the afternoons she spent here. But as with all of her recent attempts to suppress the past, the task is proving impossible.

Eden told Jack about riding a boat. A pirate ship. Another Neverland echo, like Christopher's lost boys and pixie dust, but this one might help her find her daughter.

Sheltered enough to be comfortable for Jack, large enough to keep Eden entertained, Holly often brought the children to Hay's Galleria. As far as a young Eden was concerned, the highlight was always a trip to see *The Navigators*, the grotesque statue with blank staring eyes. Steampunk sailor, fish, and boat captured in one metal form, stranded in a pool of dark water, dreaming of other voyages as its gears and oars slowly churn. Eden even developed a very American habit of bringing coins to toss into the pool that surrounded it, wishing for something she refused to share.

Holly remembers one trip in particular. She'd parked Jack's wheelchair in the shade and turned away from Eden for a moment to fuss over him. When she'd turned round, Eden had hopped over the rail and was standing on the statue's long broad skull, trying to clamber upward, giving Holly and several other bystanders a heart attack.

"It's a pirate ship," she'd said when Holly scolded her. "Not a statue at all. Someone's trapped it in bronze so it can't sail, someone's lulled it to sleep. But it wants to be freed. Can't you hear it crying?"

From the distance of all these years, Holly sees the parallel and shudders.

She tears her gaze from the statue, searches the crowd of people milling about—tourists come to gawp, businesspeople looking for a quick lunch, couples out for afternoon drinks. She doesn't spot her daughter.

She walks around the statue. A few feet from her starting point, she catches the faintest trace of the scent she associated first with Peter and, later, Eden—cut grass, spring, an effervescence she can't quite articulate. But the scent is off. It's heavy, decomposing. Rotten.

She turns in a slow circle, trying to locate its origins. A small woman is balancing on the concrete edge around the statue, ignoring the signs asking visitors to keep off. Sticking her tongue out toward the topmost fountain as if she's a child, reaching for the water that's spraying down. The tourists give her a wide berth, and as Holly gets closer, she can see why. The woman is wearing a stained white tank top and jeans that are too big, tied around her waist with what looks like rope. Her feet are bare and dirty.

And the scent is coming from her.

This close, although her frame is gamine, her face and body look bloated, stretched beyond their normal limit, like a tick that's fed and is now engorged. The water from the fountain slows to a trickle, then shuts off, and the woman jumps down. She lands directly in front of Holly and smiles, displaying a mouthful of blackened teeth.

Holly flinches. "Excuse me," she says, backing away. But then she catches sight of the tattoos along the woman's shoulders. Small feathers, golden and lovely, so realistic they seem to move in the river's breeze. Holly can't help staring. The woman stumbles forward, and as she moves, the feathers take on a shimmering radiance.

The woman looks up, sees Holly's gaze, and smiles again. She says something in a surprisingly musical voice, but it's too quick, too high-pitched, for Holly to catch.

"Pardon?"

Before the woman can repeat what she said, a stranger intervenes. "That's enough. Why don't you take a nap?" she says, pointing to a bench on the other side of the atrium.

The small woman mutters again, looks at Holly dourly, but shuffles off, her too-large pants flapping around her legs.

"You could understand her? What did she say?" Holly asks, distracted.

"She said, 'Hello, Darling. You like these? They don't hardly work and I wouldn't waste them on you if they did.'" the stranger says quietly.

Holly looks up. The woman speaking has a pixie face with rosebud lips and eyebrows arched like butterfly wings. Her blue eyes are arresting under her short crop of white-gold hair. She looks as if she's twenty at least, but . . .

"Eden?" Holly breathes. It's her daughter. She's found her, she's finally found her, and she's alive and whole and healthy. Joy and relief flood her as she reaches out to hold her darling girl.

But her daughter moves away.

Anguished, Holly follows. "Wait!"

Eden stops in front of the statue and roots through her pockets. She takes out a coin, tosses it into the pool of water, and closes her eyes, perfect dusky lashes dark against her pale face. Everything in Holly screams to hold this changeling child, to wrap her in her arms and never let her go. The need to touch Eden is so deep and visceral her arms ache.

But her daughter's frame is rigid, her jaw set, her arms held close to her body. And when she finally opens her eyes, her expression is wary. So Holly keeps her distance. She takes a deep breath, grips her hands together so she won't be tempted. Bites back the questions that tumble through her mind—*Are you okay? What happened? Where have you been?* Instead she tries to make a connection.

"You loved this place," she says. "We came here often, the three of us. Do you remember?"

"A little." Eden shrugs. "The water used to be murky. You could never tell what was really down there." They gaze at the water, now the bright blue of a swimming pool. The statue too has been refurbished since those days, scrubbed clean, the green-gray patina replaced by shining bronze. "I liked it better before. That's what it really was. Gritty and sad." Her voice wavers. "But my wishes never came true then, either."

Holly's about to ask what she means when there's a commotion at the other end of the atrium. The strange little woman is lying on the cement bench in the corner, blowing bubbles into the sky with a wand. Both it and the container of soap are a bright fluorescent pink, a child's toy. Nearby a mother has her arms around a small girl, hustling her toward the exit and throwing furious glances over her shoulder at the woman.

Eden sighs. "Bell's all appetite," she says. "She always has been. She used to crave adventure, but what she's hungry for has changed. She's bored, causing trouble. We'll have to leave soon."

"Wait!" Panic claws through Holly as she focuses only on the last thing Eden said. "I've only just found you—what do you mean, leave? Where have you been? How did you get away? And what woke you up?" Her voice cracks. "Eden, I've been looking for you for so long."

At first she thinks her daughter won't answer. Eden keeps her eyes trained on the woman. "Bell woke me," she says at last. "I heard her talking for a long time in my dreams, but I couldn't understand. Her words were so soft, so pretty. Like tiny golden bells. And then something changed. Her voice got louder, more urgent. She told me I was in danger. That Peter was coming, and she couldn't hold him off much longer. He was going to find me. And if I didn't wake up soon, if I didn't make the leap to consciousness, I wouldn't be able to."

Bell . . . Holly looks from her daughter to the woman, who is now turning in slow circles, watching the bubbles rise into the sky. Beneath the grime and dirt she seems familiar, but it takes a moment to make the connection.

"Tinker Bell?" she says, horrified. "*That's* Tinker Bell?"

"She can't help what she is," Eden says coldly, "Peter made her that way. She's bound to him, to his emotions. And still she went behind his back to rescue me. She risked everything to save me from him. And from you."

Eden's words hit Holly like a blow. She can't breathe, can't get air. She sags against the railing that surrounds the statue. It's too much. First Jack, now Eden. Everything she's done, everything she's tried to do, has twisted, broken. There's a cold, heavy stone of dread in her chest where her heart should be.

"Eden," she manages to say.

But her daughter looks at her with dispassionate eyes. "Did you know I could hear everything? The entire time? And I was scared. When you told me you were leaving, I begged you not to go. But you stopped bringing Jack, and then you moved and left me with strangers. And no one could hear me but Bell."

"Eden, I'm sorry. I'm so, so sorry. I never meant to hurt you. If I'd known you could hear me, if I thought my staying would have made a difference . . . But I left to try and save you. You and Jack."

"Jack, maybe," Eden allows. Her lower lip is trembling. "But me?"

Holly looks at her face. Eden is so beautiful. So grown-up and poised. In her face Holly sees Wendy, sees Jane, sees herself. But appearances are deceiving—no one knows that better than Holly. Just because Eden looks as if she's an adult doesn't mean she is. Inside, she's still just a thirteen-year-old girl who thinks she lost her mother.

"You too. Always," Holly says firmly. Eden's hand rests on the railing surrounding the statue, and Holly moves her own so that their pinkie fingers barely touch. "Especially you."

"You took Jack to New York," Eden whispers. "Not me." But she doesn't move her hand.

"You and Jack are different people. You suffered when I brought you to London. New York would have been even worse for you." Holly takes a deep breath. "I came back as often as I could. I promise. And I never stopped trying to find a cure. Never stopped hoping I could save you."

"There might be a chance." Eden looks across the atrium, and Holly follows her gaze. Tinker Bell has abandoned the bubbles. She's walking behind a stout businessman in a suit, imitating his strut, doffing an imaginary hat to the crowd that is gathering and egging her on. A few people toss coins, and she picks them up, miming exaggerated thanks.

"There's a place that might fix me. But Bell won't tell me how to get there. Not yet."

"Neverland," Holly whispers.

Eden nods, then gestures to herself, encompassing all of it—the long limbs, the height, the face that even as Holly watches seems to age. "I'm growing too fast. Another six months, a year—who knows how old I'll be?" Tears fill her eyes. "I don't want to die before I've had a chance to live. I've never made a friend, never fallen in love, never even been to school. There's so much I want to do."

"There must be another way," Holly says, and the desperation in her voice echoes Jack's from a few hours ago. "A drug, a hormone. Something that will slow the aging." But even as she's saying the words, she knows they're not true. She's already tried everything.

"What about . . ." Holly doesn't want to say his name. "Peter. Is he aging the same as you?"

Eden looks away. "Bell hasn't told me. She won't say much, other than he's changed. He's dangerous now. All avarice, greed. So she is too."

They watch Bell stuff her pockets with the coins and bills tourists are throwing to her.

"But she doesn't want to be. I think that's why she's helping me. One reason, anyhow. I'm her chance to escape too." Eden shivers, and Holly reaches out and lightly wraps an arm around her shoulder. Eden lets it stay. "I haven't *seen* him, not exactly. But there was . . . a shadow at the edges of my dreams in Cornwall. Something dark that wanted me. Was reaching for me. I could sense it."

Holly holds back her own shudder. "It's possible he was there," she allows. "The staff saw . . . things. And I'd been saving your blood, using it to treat Jack and to try and find a way to cure you. I think Peter stole it."

Eden's quiet a moment. "That wasn't Peter," she admits. "It was me."

"You took the blood? But why? And how?"

"I'd heard the safe combination a million times. And I knew what my blood did for Jack. I thought it might help me. That it would slow everything down. Give me a chance."

She looks down at her hands. "I didn't mean to hurt Jack by taking it. That's one reason why I came to the house—to help him." She smiles, the first one Holly has seen, but it's a sad smile. "He's so grown-up. Not my little flea anymore."

Holly remembers the scar on Jack's wrist, the way it healed so quickly. But she can't think about Jack right now or she'll tumble back into an abyss of panic and loss and never find her way out. Instead she concentrates on Eden, on the spark of hope her words offer. For all her scientific background, Holly's never thought of injecting the whole blood directly back into her daughter. "That was clever thinking," she says. "Did it work?"

Eden shakes her head. "No. It had the opposite effect. I think it speeded up my growth." She looks sideways at her mother. "What you did—taking my blood—may have helped me after all."

It's a small concession, but Holly clings to it. The stone in her chest lightens, lets her breathe again in a way that hasn't been possible in years. She's carried the guilt of using Eden to save Jack for so long. To know her efforts may have helped Eden too . . . She can't help herself. She pulls her daughter close, into a full embrace. For a heartbeat, then two, Eden relaxes into her arms. Holly holds her, inhales that delicious scent of springtime and warmth.

But even this moment isn't enough to turn off Holly's brain. The question nudges at her, won't leave her alone, until she asks it aloud. "But if it isn't your blood, what does Peter want with you?" It doesn't make sense.

"It might still work on him," Eden says. She pushes away from Holly, just enough to see her face. "That's what Bell thinks. It's different for him, the aging. I don't know why. Maybe because he's been to Neverland? Or maybe because I'm only half like him. I'm only half his daughter, Bell says. I'm half like you too."

"Eden," Holly says. She pulls her daughter close again. "Eden, I'm sorry. I'm so, so sorry. For everything. There's so many things I should have done differently."

Eden doesn't answer. But she doesn't pull away, either.

"Do you think Peter knows how to get back?" Holly asks. "To Neverland?"

"If he could, don't you think he would?"

Holly thinks of her last conversation with Jane. Of how little any of them know about this place called Neverland. She thinks of Barrie and all the ways he might have changed Wendy's story. And she remembers Peter that last night, when he'd looked at her like prey. She has no idea what he would do.

A disturbance at the far end of the atrium breaks her train of thought. Bell is hurrying toward them. She pauses every few seconds to blow kisses to the crowd behind her, but when she looks at Eden, her eyes are wide with urgency. The mother from earlier stands in the far entrance to the atrium. There are security guards with her and she's pointing to Bell.

"I have to go," Eden says.

"No," Holly says. "Come with me. We can figure this out."

But Eden is surprisingly strong. She pulls out of Holly's grasp. Bell motions to an alley between two of the sand-colored buildings and Eden runs toward it.

"Eden, wait!"

"No. I need Bell, and she needs me. I trust her," Eden calls over her shoulder.

"Eden!" Holly hurries to catch her. Bell sees Holly and frowns. She holds her arms up and begins turning in a circle, spinning faster and faster. The feathers on her shoulder are so bright they seem to glow. Bits of gold shed from them, dancing through the air.

"Take care of Jack," Eden says. "Don't let him . . ."

But her words are lost as a flock of starlings swoops into the atrium. They circle around and around, matching Tinker Bell's rhythm. Faster and faster, lower and lower, until they are a diving, churning curtain blocking Eden and the alley from view. Beneath the rushing of the wings Holly hears the faintest sound, like tiny golden bells.

"Eden!" Holly calls, frantic. For a split second the birds part and Holly can see her. She's leaning into Tinker Bell's embrace, their heads touching. Jealousy and fear flare in Holly, white hot. And then the birds close in and rise. A cyclone of feathers darkens the sky. She covers her head with her hands. The tourists closest to her do the same, while the security guards stand openmouthed. And then the air is still. Holly lowers her arms.

Tiny bits of golden dust, already fading, speckle the floor. All around her tourists whisper and point, but the birds are gone.

And Eden and Tinker Bell have vanished.

Chapter Twenty-Eight

Holly searches the atrium for hours. She knows they must be gone, but still she enters every store, every restaurant. She runs through the adjacent streets and alleys, calling for Eden until her throat is raw, until the security guards stop and ask if she's lost her child.

"Yes," she says. "Yes."

They ask for a description so they can help her look.

"She's thirteen," she says, then corrects herself. "She's twenty-five. She's . . ."

Gone.

They back away from her. One of them mimes drinking. Another, more compassionate, quietly mentions calling the police for help, pulls out her phone.

"Yes," Holly murmurs. "Thank you. The police. I'll do that."

She leaves. Goes home. Crawls into her bed without even taking off her shoes and stares up at the ceiling. Her leg is throbbing. She needs to regroup. To rest for a minute. To stay here for the next century.

She keeps seeing the way Eden looked at her at the end, just before she ran to Tinker Bell. The way she'd said, "I trust *her*." As if Holly were a stranger.

All this time, Holly has been picturing her sweet little girl, but it turns out she really doesn't know her daughter at all. The baby in her memory is unchanging, static. Just like the toddler in her photograph. Neither have kept pace with her actual daughter. Eden has been maturing, learning, *listening* this whole time.

No matter what Holly does next, whether she gets up or stays right here, Eden is gone. She'll either die a wrinkled old lady in a matter of months—at best, a year or two—or she'll disappear forever, to a place Holly has never been and cannot follow. Either way, Jack's death is inevitable.

Holly has fought and clawed and done unspeakable things for her children. And none of it matters. Not one thing she's done has changed either of their lives, has saved either one of them. She might as well have died with Jack after the car crash. She closes her eyes and sobs.

When she opens her eyes, Jane is standing over her.

"Jesus." Holly sits up, pushing her hair out of her face, dragging her sleeve across her nose. "What? Jack? Is he okay?" And then she remembers. No matter what she does, Jack is doomed. Both her children are. How could she have forgotten, even for a second?

Jane purses her lips, looks at Holly's sleeve with distaste. "Jack is fine. Isn't it time you got up?"

Holly lies back down. "Close the door on your way out."

Jane ignores this. "I wanted to tell you I'm going out. And that man is here again."

"What man?"

"That detective. Cooke. With the . . ." Jane waves her right hand in the air. "He's most persistent. He's been calling the house—I have no idea how you've managed to sleep through it. When I wouldn't wake you, he just showed up. Quite nervy if you ask me."

"Where is he?"

"I left him sitting on the front steps. I refused to let him in. Not after what happened last time. Not after hearing"—she lowers her voice—"who he's like."

Holly turns onto her side, away from her mother. "Good. Tell him to go away."

"I have. I have also threatened to call the police, and do you know what he did? He laughed." Jane's voice quivers in outrage.

"I can't deal with this right now." Holly doesn't have the strength to tell Jane about her meeting with Eden, about Jack's fate.

Jane pokes her. "Well, I certainly am not going to be responsible for him. I have dinner plans."

"Leave him there then." Holly pulls a pillow over her face and hopes Jane will get the hint.

"Absolutely not. What would the neighbors think?"

Holly wants to sleep, wants to cocoon herself in dreams for a thousand years, wants to wake and sleep, then wake again so she can have those precious few seconds of not remembering. But she knows how relentless Jane can be.

"Fine." She rolls to the edge of the bed, stands up. She doesn't bother to change, to wash her face or comb her hair. Jane follows her out of the room.

"You're going out like that?" her mother asks. "What is your plan? To frighten him away?"

Holly ignores the gibe. "Where's Jack?" she asks. She wants him as far away from this potential dumpster fire as he can get.

"Nan took the boys out for dinner," Jane says. "They left about an hour ago."

Holly stumbles down the stairs, unlocks and opens the front door. Christopher Cooke is sitting on the top step, dressed in his bike kit, leaning against the railing.

"Evening," he says. He looks her up and down. "Or is that 'Good morning' for you?"

"Go away," she says blearily. Her message delivered, she starts to shut the door. But before she can, he sticks his hand in it. She stops, then realizes he's actually put his prosthetic out. She draws back, ready to slam the door shut.

"I wouldn't," he says. "It won't hurt me, but it will leave a nasty dent in the wood."

"Move."

"It looks like you've had a rough evening already," he continues, as if she hasn't spoken. He glances at his watch. "And it's only seven."

"You need to leave."

A Mercedes barrels out of the driveway. They both turn to watch it go. Jane has apparently decided to go out the back way. She comes within mere centimeters of knocking down Christopher's bike, and the thought of that, as well as the way Christopher swears when he thinks that's what's going to happen, is the only thing in this miserable evening that has the power to make Holly smile. At the last second, Jane swerves and the bike remains standing.

Christopher shakes his head, returns his attention to Holly.

"I have some news," he says. "And you're not going to like it."

"I don't care."

He studies her. She has no idea what he sees, but he looks so long, so deeply at her that it is as if he's looking inside her. No, not exactly inside, but through, as if there's something on the other side of her he's seeking, as if she's transparent.

"What?" she asks, more to stop him from staring than anything else.

"I need to talk with you."

"You're not coming in," she informs him. "You've done enough damage."

"All right." He thinks for a moment. "Then come out with me."

She gestures at the doorway, the steps on which she's now standing.

"No, I mean really come out. With me. I promise it won't take much time."

Holly has the sense that if she refuses, he's not going to go away anytime soon. She could try to wait him out. Or she could call the police, but that threat—at least from what Jane said—doesn't seem to bother him. The path of least resistance is to do what he wants.

"Fine," she says. She steps all the way outside, closes the door behind her. "Satisfied?"

"Not yet." He walks down the steps to his bike, takes something off the back. Brings it up to her. It's a helmet. "Put this on."

"What? You're crazy." There's no way she's getting on the back of that bike. Not with him.

"Come on. You know you want to." He smiles at her. It's an entirely charming smile, the first real one she's seen from him. She bets that smile gets him a lot. "And you know I'm not going away unless you do."

"God, has anyone ever told you that you're impossible?"

His smile gets wider. "I'm Irish. It has been mentioned."

She sighs and accepts the helmet. If she's lucky, they'll wreck and she'll be put out of her misery.

She puts the helmet on but struggles with the snap under her chin. Christopher comes closer, so close they're almost touching. Then he reaches over and deftly fastens it with one hand.

Holly doesn't like being this near to him. It makes her aware of things other than how miserable she is, and she doesn't want to be aware of anything else. But Christopher doesn't seem to care. He shrugs off his jacket, slides it over her shoulders. The jacket is heavy and smells of leather, of gasoline. It hangs on her, but its weight and warmth are comforting.

She doesn't want to be comforted.

"Where are you taking me?" she asks abruptly.

"Consider it a kidnapping. Go with it." He swings a leg over the bike, puts on his own helmet, pats the seat behind him. "Don't think. Just do it."

So she does. It's a relief, for once, to be told what to do, to shut her brain off and let someone else take the lead. She sits as straight as she can on the bike. But the evening is growing cool, and she's so tired. At last she succumbs and rests her head against his back. He's a very good driver. She watches the street through half-closed eyes as he weaves in and out of traffic. She wonders, briefly, what he did in the war, what it was like for him coming back. And then she realizes with a start that, for a moment, she's forgotten to feel afraid or despondent. Oddly enough, she feels safe.

They wind up near the Thames. He stops the bike so they have a view of the river. They don't talk, simply watch the boats go past. It's one of those quintessential English summer nights that seem to go on and on. The sun is starting its descent, but the sky is still bright, the air heavy and liquid. She's taken her helmet off, but her head is still on his shoulder. She doesn't move. She's surprised to find that she doesn't want to.

For years after Robert died, she couldn't bear to look at couples in love. A woman leaning her head against a man's shoulder, a husband leaning in for a kiss, was enough to make her incandescent with rage. Why them and not her? Eventually the rage turned to sadness. Now she finds she can watch couples without envy. Leaning against Christopher, she can almost imagine being a part of one again.

It's Christopher who breaks the spell.

"A boy died today," he says. He doesn't turn around to look at her.

She sits up stiffly, leans away, but Christopher keeps talking, easily, conversationally, as if he hasn't noticed.

"If we catch him, the dealer will go away for a very long time. Maybe forever."

Forever is a very long time, Holly thinks, and has to bite her lip to keep the hysterical laughter in.

"I couldn't find the connection," Christopher muses. "I know there's a link between this drug and your company. I know we are looking for the same man. But what I couldn't figure out is how your daughter fits into all of this. And then I remembered Maria and what she called her: the angel of miracles. So tell me, Holly Darling, what's so special about your daughter's blood? And before you lie to me again, understand I'm going to find this Peter. And I don't really care at this point how I do it."

He looks at her. "The kid who died? He was your son's age. He played football, had a right good foot. Not good enough to go pro, probably, but enough to play through university. His mother hasn't gotten out of bed since it happened. His father punched a hole through the wall so hard he broke his hand."

Holly shivers. She thinks of Eden, her face at the atrium, the terror in her eyes. And Jack. An hour ago, she herself couldn't get out of bed, the fear of losing them weighing her down so heavily. But both of her children are, at this exact moment, still breathing. Unlike the child of this other poor mother.

She'd like to lay her head back down and weep. She'd like to steal Christopher's bike, to ride off somewhere where every decision, every word she says, doesn't decide who lives and who dies. Someplace far away. Or maybe someplace long ago, back when it was easier to tell truth. Instead she calculates, deciding what she can keep safe and what she has to give up. It's like entering the cage with a panther—so long as there's something else to eat, you may be safe. But eventually the food supply is going to run out and then he's looking at you. She thinks of all the things she's done wrong, all the things she could answer for.

"Tell me what you know. Last chance," he says.

"It sounds crazy."

"I've seen some crazy things," he says. "The trick is, once you realize you don't know anything, the crazy is easier to accept. Just tell me. Everything."

And surprisingly, Holly does. Because she's exhausted, worn out by grief, by the fear she saw in her children's faces when she reached for them. Because she's tired of carrying this story alone. And because, when she looks at Christopher, she sees something in his eyes that tells her he also knows what it's like when all your choices are terrible ones but you still have to choose.

She keeps her arms folded, her gaze on the water ahead. She starts on that long-ago day when everything changed, the day when she lost it all. The day of the crash. Every other loss since then has merely been fallout.

She begins in cool, measured language—the road was slick, the treads on the tires worn—but Christopher is good at asking questions. Soon she's recounting details she's kept locked away for years. She tells him of being trapped in the front seat, her legs pinned, of hearing the twins screaming. She tells how she could hear Isaac's breaths grow slower and slower, further and further apart, until at last she couldn't hear him anymore. Jack was still crying, sobbing, but she couldn't reach him, and finally he went quiet too. She must have passed out, and when she woke up, it was in the hospital. She knew they were all dead. When they told her Jack had survived, she climbed out of her hospital bed to go to him. Since she couldn't stand, she tried to crawl. After that they sedated her. When she woke, she tried again and again, until finally they wheeled her bed next to his. She tells Christopher of the agonizingly slow hours that turned into slow days, waiting to see if her son would live, not daring to wonder what type of life he would have if he did.

She doesn't say Robert's name once. The sounds he made before he died are what she wakes to on her darkest mornings. Robert is stored so tightly in her heart that if she mentions him, it will split and crack her in half. She'll never be able to go on.

When her story reaches Peter, she leaves out anything that sounds too insane, like the tinkle of tiny bells, the flickering golden light outside the window, or how Peter got up to that window in the first place. She leaves out any mention of magic. She focuses instead on what he already knows—Peter's charm, his magnetism.

"I thought he was a hallucination," she tells Christopher. "A hallucination brought on by despair."

She glosses over Eden's childhood, simply says she has a genetic disease that aged her, that Holly hasn't been able to find a cure. She ends with the other accident, the bookend to the first, where what had been taken from Jack was miraculously returned. She describes how he ran to her when she came home from her hospital vigil.

"The best I've been able to discover, Eden's blood has a protein that promotes healing," she finishes. "It works like an antibody, binding to damaged cells and repairing them. But it couldn't heal her. Only other people." She stares down at her hands. "And there's one last thing. I've seen Eden. Just today—this morning," she says to forestall the angry comment she can tell he's about to make. "She wouldn't come home with me, and I don't know where she's staying. But it's not with Peter. She's terrified of him."

"Is she okay?"

Holly starts to speak, stops, waits for the pool of tears that is always just behind her eyes these days to settle into stillness. "I think so," she says.

"Good," he says. "That's good. And it makes it even more important to find Peter before he finds her. Could he have found a way to use this . . . this protein, to create a drug?"

"It's possible." She thinks of the euphoria she's experienced the times she's tested Eden's blood on herself, the flush of well-being she sees in Jack each time she administers it to him. "But he must be using it in conjunction with something else. The protein on its own couldn't hurt anyone." Holly doesn't mention that Peter must have another source besides Eden for the protein. She's sure Christopher has thought of that.

There's nothing else she can say. They sit in silence for a long time, both of them looking out over the water in the twilight.

At last Christopher kick-starts the bike, wheels it into traffic. Holly doesn't say a word. She sits erect the whole way back, touching him as little as possible. He drops her at the door.

"What will you do next?" she asks, but it's a detached interest, as if she's watching someone else's life play out on a screen.

"I don't know, exactly, beyond the fact that I'm going to find this Peter. There's something about him that nags at me . . ." He trails off. "About all of this, even you. It's too familiar. Like we've met. Like we've all done this before." He shakes his head as if to clear it. "I told you I have crazy dreams. Maybe it was there. But dream or not, this Peter is real. And somehow he has access to these boys. He could be a coach. A therapist. A teacher. I'm going to figure it out, and then he's going to pay. That's as far as I've gotten."

"It's a good start," she says. "You'll find him." He stares at her. "I mean it." There's nothing she can say that will change his mind, so why bother? She's negotiated enough deals to know when she has a chance and when she doesn't, and right now she has nothing to offer that he wants. Nothing that she can tell him that will help.

She takes off her helmet, hands it back.

"Thanks for the ride."

He nods but doesn't answer. Still, he waits while she walks up the steps. At the top, it occurs to her that there is one last thing she wants to know.

"Christopher," she calls. When he looks up, she asks, "What did you do in the war?"

He looks surprised, then smiles grimly. "Interrogator. I wasn't even supposed to be on the road that day. I was filling in for a mate. Officer in charge told me to shag off, but the rules said one was supposed to be present, so off I went."

"That's awful. I'm so sorry."

He shrugs. "When my mate came to visit me in hospital, he was gutted. Turned out he hadn't even been sick after all. He'd been off having fun and games with some of the local women. But I told him it could have been worse. The way I see it, the ones who feel sorry for themselves don't survive. Not with any kind of life to speak of. So I could whinge, or I could get on and make the most of what I still had." He raises his right hand—the one with the prosthetic—in a mock salute. "So that's what I did."

"Me too," Holly says quietly, but Christopher doesn't hear. He's already riding away.

Chapter Twenty-Nine

And because it wouldn't be Holly's life if everything didn't go to shit at the same time, within days of her ride with Christopher, Barry is demanding that she come back to work. He hints at first, texting about how much the office misses her. When Holly doesn't bite, he follows up with a call to her cell, which she ignores.

At last he calls her on her mother's home phone—a number that's unlisted, although it might as well not be, given how many people seem able to find it. When Jane, with an eye roll, passes the phone to Holly, Barry doesn't mince words.

"You need to come back," he says. "You're the head of Darling Skin Care—you need to show your face. People are starting to talk, and I can't hold the questions off much longer."

"This is why I never wanted to be the face of the brand in the first place," Holly snaps.

"But you are, whether you want to be or not," he says. "The Landers are saying that they signed the deal based on you being at the helm. They could pull out, Holly. And they're questioning your commitment to the brand, which puts future deals in jeopardy."

"Too bad for them. We'll find someone else."

Barry is quiet. "Look, I don't understand," he says at last. "You built this company. It's been your baby from the beginning. I know it's been a

241

rough time for you, with your daughter, but you need to think about Jack, about his future. Darling Skin Care guarantees that. We need you here for the launch next week. You don't have to stay. But you have to come."

With a start, Holly realizes Barry still thinks Eden is dead. Of course he does. So much has happened these last few weeks that she's somehow lost track of the lies she's told him, and now there's no way for her to explain what's happened, no way to walk it back. She said those words—*my daughter is dead*—and now they are coming true, one way or another. When she mourns again, she'll never be able to tell him why. Until it's for Jack.

She's still reeling when Barry speaks again.

"Holly?" he says, his voice gentle. "I hate to say this, but you're not the only one with a family."

The comment wrecks her. In all the years she's worked with Barry, he's never asked her for anything. She thinks of all the nights she's seen Barry rush home to Minerva and their kids, a jaunt in his step even after a fourteen-hour day, all the times she'd felt . . . not envy, not quite, but a wistfulness at what might have been if she'd trusted him from the beginning. But she'd kept him out, kept him at a distance. And even so, he's been her most loyal friend. Now he's putting it all out on the line. And for once, after everything he's done, he's asking her to do the same. What choice does she have? She hesitates, but there's no other answer she can give.

"I need a few days," she tells him. "And I can't stay long. But I'll be there as soon as I can."

"Thank you," he says simply.

She books a flight for three days out, then spends those days making a last-ditch effort to find her daughter. She stalks the atrium, following flocks of birds, diving down back alleys at the glimpse of a blonde head. When the atrium turns up nothing, she works outward in an ever-widening spiral, searching streets over a two-mile radius. Something jogs at the back of her memory, something Jane once said. *The starlings landed on Big Ben. A murmuration. They stopped time.*

Tinker Bell had summoned starlings. Why would they congregate there?

She stands beneath the giant clock tower at noon, but there are no starlings, just a handful of pigeons cooing on the sidewalk. Despite the heat, the air around the tower smells fresh and clean. Like springtime. Like Eden. The website said there's a tour, but the guard at the door tells her it's been canceled for the foreseeable future. "Maintenance," he says. "They'll be doing a big restoration project soon."

She walks around the clock tower searching for another way in. She doesn't find it. So instead does the only thing she can—she calls her daughter's name, screams it over and over again until the guard tells her to stop, that she's being a nuisance, that if she doesn't quit he'll call the police and have her arrested for being a disturbance to the peace.

She's no good to her children in jail, so she stops.

She doesn't find Eden.

Her leg is aching—a sure sign of stress—but Holly doesn't use the cream, can't bring herself to even look at it. She tries not to smother Jack, but it's so hard. Every time she looks at him, she sees his face the way it was in the hospital, so still and white he could have been carved of marble. There's a clock ticking in her brain, moving relentlessly toward the time the last infusion from Eden will wear off completely.

And what then? Will he gradually weaken, his legs shriveling, his lungs contracting, the scars on his skin rising to the surface, forgotten monsters pushing up to show they'd been here all along? Or will it be a sudden, horrifying end, his body overtaxed by one of the activities—lacrosse, running for the bus, roughhousing with his friends—once made possible by Eden's blood?

Even as she's trying to hold on to him, he's slipping through her fingers. He spends whatever time he can away from the house, leaving while she's out and not coming home until she insists. When she asks where he's going, he mutters and looks away. He won't talk to her about anything—about Eden, about the injections, about how he feels. He's flat-out refused to come to New York with her as well, a decision that surprises her and that he won't explain. She spends every minute from the time she wakes up until the time she falls into a brief, restless sleep absolutely terrified.

She knows he's spending time with Ed. Ed at least has the decency to look embarrassed when she stumbles across him on the front stairs or in the kitchen, where he's most often waiting for Jack. He'll unfold his long legs from whatever perch he's found and stand to greet her. "Hey, Dr. Darling," he'll say, towering over her. "Thanks for having me." Jack may snort and roll his eyes, but Holly can't detect any sarcasm in Ed's brown ones, just a bashful politeness.

She doesn't like them together, not one bit. She worries that Ed, with his glowing good health, is a bad influence, always talking about lacrosse. She can tell by the tightness of her face that Nan's worried too, that the boys will push it too far and something bad will happen and Holly will hold her responsible. She's always shooing them out of the kitchen when Holly walks in, always suggesting movies and shopping or other low-key activities. And her squeamishness about storing the syringe of blood in the crisper bin has forced Holly to buy a small refrigerator she keeps padlocked in her room.

"If she quits," Jane says once, after a particularly stressful breakfast where Holly discovered Jack had left the house at the light of dawn to meet Ed for a game, "I'll blame you."

"Add it to the list," Holly says, pushing back her chair and taking her tea with her. It's a banner start to her day.

Christopher too keeps his distance, and Holly is curiously disappointed by this. She tells herself it's because she's anxious. She wants to know what he's going to do with the information he's found. It has nothing to do with Christopher himself, his long black hair, the easy way he moves.

It has nothing to do with his dreams. Or his sense—and hers—that there's some other link between them.

He sends her the occasional text, each one a single question. The information he asks for is esoteric, details about Peter that have long since slipped her memory, or that she never knew in the first place. He asks about Jack as well—whether the injections give him an immediate sense of euphoria, whether they wear off in a gentle decline or sudden crash.

He hasn't asked her point-blank if she uses Eden's blood herself. She doesn't volunteer the information, either.

The night before she leaves, Holly does two things. She waits until Jack is asleep, then sneaks into his room and activates the GPS-location function on his mobile. Even at the worst of times in New York, she's always respected his privacy. Now? At least this way she'll be able to keep tabs on him, if she has to.

And then, even though it is late, she goes in search of her mother. She finds her propped up in bed, reading a book. Holly can see the title—*Sexual Politics and Peter Pan: How to be a Tinker Bell in a Wendy World*. She tries hard not to roll her eyes, she really does, but given Jane's terse "Yes?" she clearly failed.

"I wanted to remind you I'm leaving first thing in the morning," she says. Her mother's hair is pinned in loose waves about her head, and if it weren't for its color and the fine lines that cross her face, she could have been Holly's age or younger.

"So you've told me. Multiple times." Jane places her finger in the book to mark her place but doesn't shut it. "Surely at sixteen Jack can survive without you for a few days." Jane seems to think this is a good idea, a chance for Jack to grow. Holly tries to explain that in actuality, there's a chance he could die.

"You need to watch him every minute," Holly insists. Between the phantom of Peter, never far from her mind, and Jack's willingness to compromise his own health, she's almost canceled her trip a dozen times. But she owes Barry too much to let him down. And she's come to the realization that there's nothing else she can do in London for Eden or Jack. Plus, Elliot is in New York. If she can meet with him alone, if she has him face-to-face, she may be able to persuade him to help.

Jane peers at Holly over her reading glasses and may or may not give her own version of an eye roll.

"I raised you, didn't I?" she says.

Holly thinks of all the days she spent alone in the Darling house while Jane was at a fundraiser or dinner. The way she scaled the roof at night or slipped easily in and out after curfew.

"That," Holly says, "is exactly my point."

Chapter Thirty

Holly goes directly to the office after landing. Her assistant has scheduled almost every minute. She attends the launch kickoff, held at a swanky restaurant and packed with fashion editors and beauty bloggers. The entire space has been dusted with gold glitter, and models dressed as fairies with oversized wings circulate, holding trays of champagne. Huge faux flowers line the walls, and in the corners are fountains with chocolate and punch. In the center of the room a girl dressed in green and silver dangles from the ceiling, delicate battery-operated sparkly wings flapping slowly up and down. The wires holding her are so fine they are almost invisible, and every now and then she performs a lazy somersault or low swoop, drawing oohs and aahs from the guests.

"Don't you just love it? Isn't it divine?" Lauren Lander gushes, wrapping an arm through Holly's.

Holly grits her teeth. The party has all the elegance and sophistication of a sixteen-year-old girl with little taste and an unlimited budget, a far cry from Jane's exquisite affairs. Still, she smiles and lets Lauren show her off as if she's some rare species trapped under glass. Lauren seems to take special pleasure in dropping Holly's last name into every possible conversation, cooing and holding on to her arm as if they were best friends. But it's almost—almost—worth putting up with to see Barry smile. When Lauren's not looking, he winks at Holly and rolls his eyes.

Over the next two days, Holly also meets with board members, sits in on strategy sessions, even drops by a few photo shoots. Pixie Dust is everywhere—on billboards, in magazines, plastered across the front of every cosmetic store. Barry has left her a folder filled with celebrities sighted with the product, along with a chart detailing current marketing efforts and future expansion. Sales are crazy good, and Holly has to admit, being back in this part of her life is a wonderful escape. Still, she makes sure to text Jack between meetings, getting monosyllabic responses for her troubles. When she asks how he's doing, he sends a single thumbs-up emoji.

She doesn't bother texting or calling Jane, who is notorious for being impossible to reach. If there's a problem, her mother will call. She hopes.

Meanwhile Barry is pushing her to consider a full line of makeup. When she reminds him that this means more money into R&D, he laughs.

"We've finally made it. This is the big time, kid. You'll have all the R&D you can handle, if that's what you want." He looks as if he wants to say something else, but settles for "Enjoy it."

It's not until the middle of the second day that Holly finally makes it back to her lab. Even now, she's supposed to be at a lunch, glad-handing a few CEOs who weren't interested in Darling Skin Care two years ago but now can't wait to develop a line with her. Barry is the one who hooked them, but it's her they want to meet. Normally she'd take this moment to gloat, to celebrate that her little company has come this far. But she's desperate to see Elliot alone. All she thought about on the plane ride to New York was how to persuade him to help her, how the two of them working together might be able to solve the roadblocks keeping her from developing a fully functional synthetic version of the proteins in Eden's blood. If the sheer excitement of the science won't do it, then she'll have to appeal to his human side, assuming he has one.

She'll say anything, take any risk. Even if it means losing everything. Because everything is worth nothing without Jack and Eden.

But Elliot isn't in the general lab. She hasn't seen him at any of the launch events, either. Not that that's unusual for him. Elliot often skips the high-profile events, even though as lead developer he's invited to them all. But she'd thought even Elliot would want to take a moment to bask in how far he's helped bring the company.

Then again, Barry has been keeping her so busy it's quite possible she's missed spotting him. With all the excitement surrounding the launch, he's probably holed up in his office. She hurries down the corridor.

She takes a second to compose herself in front of his door, then knocks. There's no response. She frowns. He must be engrossed in his work. She knocks again before pushing the door open.

But Elliot isn't there.

The room feels off. It's too neat. The stacks of papers, the empty soda cans, the fast food wrappers that usually litter his work surfaces are gone. There are a few charts, a sample of Pixie Dust, and a handful of slides, but nothing else.

"Can I help you?"

Holly whirls around. A young woman is standing in the doorway. She's dressed in a lab coat, and she's scowling at Holly, as if she's the intruder.

"Excuse me?" Holly says, drawing herself up.

The woman's eyes widen. "Oh, Mrs. . . . Dr. . . . Darling! I didn't recognize you."

"Who are you?"

The woman extends her hand. "Pat Harper. I'll be heading up the research division. You were away when I was hired. I'm so excited to finally meet you."

Holly ignores the woman's hand. Dr. Pat Harper doesn't look old enough to be out of college, let alone in charge of a lab. Someone has clearly made a mistake. Or is joking with her.

"Where's Elliot?"

"Who?"

"Elliot Benton," Holly snaps. "Dr. Benton—the head of R&D?"

"Oh, I'm sorry," the woman says, clearly terrified she's said something wrong. "I think Dr. Benton was here before me? But we never actually met." She looks guiltily around the office as if Elliot might materialize out of thin air. "I don't know what happened to him."

She's still talking, but Holly isn't listening. She turns on her heel and walks, as quickly as she can, to her own lab. Fumbles her way through her security protocols and pushes open the door.

The safe is open. And it's empty.

She stands for a moment, trying to think. There should have been at least one bag of plasma and serum in the safe. She hadn't asked Elliot to send it when he sent the vial of blood. There's no reason for him to have taken it. But the only person besides herself who had access to this room was Elliot. And now that she looks around, none of her prototype samples are here, either. It doesn't make sense. Why would he take them?

And then she realizes that there's one other person besides herself at Darling Skin Care who has access to everything. One other person who has been here since the very beginning. Slowly she walks out of the lab. She doesn't bother locking it this time.

When she gets to Barry's office, there's a new receptionist she doesn't recognize who tries to stop her at the desk. "I'm sorry, but there's a meeting going on," she says. Holly isn't having it.

"I am Holly Darling," she snarls, pushing her way past and opening the door. A bevy of blank faces turn to her. The company has always been small, so why can't she recognize a third of the people looking at her?

She swallows, tries not to let her unease turn to fear. Instead she holds tightly to the anger that's fueling her. *Who does he think he is?*

"I need to talk to you," she says to Barry, who is sitting at the head of the table. "Now."

"Sure," he says easily. He turns to the people around the conference table. "Take a break, okay?" He glances at his watch. "We'll pick up after lunch."

Holly waits until the room clears.

"Where's Elliot?"

Barry leans back in his chair. "Why don't you sit down?" He gestures to the phone. "I could get us a drink, or order up a late lunch if you like."

Holly doesn't move.

He sighs, swivels the chair to face her. "Or we can do it the hard way."

"Where's Elliot?" she repeats.

"Look, I've wanted to tell you, but I thought I should do it face-to-face, and with you away . . . And then I wanted you to enjoy the launch. I needed you to focus on that." He makes an appeasing motion with his hand. "Holly, I fired him."

"You fired my lead scientist without telling me?" She thinks of Jack and Eden, and any hope she'd had of working with Elliot crumbles. The unease she's been choking back washes over her, extinguishing her anger, turning to full-fledged fear. "Why, Barry? What would make you do that?"

"I figured you had enough on your plate," Barry says. "And to be honest, you haven't seemed that interested in the company lately."

She doesn't take the bait. She doesn't mention all the new faces, either. "If you fired him, you can hire him again," she says. "Now. I want him back."

Barry shakes his head. "That's not possible."

"What the fuck, Barry!" She takes a breath, lowers her voice, tries to match his impossibly reasonable tone. "Look. Elliot's the best at what he does. I need him. *We* need him."

Jack and Eden need him.

"I'm sure that's true, but there are other people out there who are almost as good," Barry says placatingly. "Dr. Harper is one of them, and she could take this company in a new direction. Why don't you give her a chance, see if she works out?"

"Barry, I—"

"Look, I know you two were close," he interrupts. "But you have to trust me. Elliot was becoming a liability."

"I don't care what he was becoming," she says, glaring. "You had no right."

Barry sighs again. When he resumes speaking, his voice is barely a whisper, so soft Holly has to lean in to hear him.

"Elliot came to me and said you were using untested, unapproved human components in some of the samples. He found them in your lab. He raised the possibility of contamination in the actual products. He said you were . . . I believe his word was *sloppy*."

The blood drains from Holly's face. For Elliot, sloppy is the worst insult. Code for not following protocol. For working outside of ethical guidelines. For manipulating data.

In short, for everything she's been doing.

"He must have misunderstood," she says desperately. "He didn't realize what . . ."

Barry raises his hand. When he speaks, his voice is so calm he might as well be discussing the weather. "He showed me the samples, Holly. I don't know what you've been doing, and I don't want to know. Dr. Harper is in charge for now, and she's been warned to watch out for any irregularities. I sent Elliot away with a fat settlement, a strict nondisclosure, and a noncompete clause." He shrugs. "If you prefer, you can think of it as an early retirement—that's how I spun it. He can spend the rest of his life researching the life cycle of the purple sea slug or whatever the hell he's into, sitting on a beach in Tahiti. I hear it's a magical place."

"Elliot's a scientist," Holly protests, but the fight has gone out of her. She can't look at Barry. "He won't be quiet for long."

"He just has to be quiet for now, that's all that matters. If he opens his mouth, if he reaches out to anyone, I'll find a way to discredit him. It's his choice. He can fund his own lab or he can lose it all. And Holly, keep in mind he came to me. Not you. He was all set to throw you under the bus. I saved you."

"But why . . ." She trails off. It's not the magnitude of Elliot's betrayal that stops her, as terrible as it is. It's the look in Barry's eyes. It's one she's seen a hundred times before, an expression he wears when he's facing down a particularly knotty problem and thinks he's discovered how to make it go away. Always before, seeing that look has been a relief—it means whatever obstacle she's facing is about to disappear. Now it scares her because it's clear the problem he's trying to solve *is* her.

"Why did he come to me? Whatever you were working on, it shocked him. He told me he didn't know who you were anymore." He passes a hand over his bald head, briefly closes his eyes. "And I have to say, there's a lot of that going around."

Not for the first time, she wonders what would have happened if she'd told Barry the truth from the beginning, when they'd first met.

If she'd told him, even if he'd thought she was crazy, her life might have been so different. To have her secrets out in the open would have meant having someone in her life besides Jack, besides Eden. Someone she could lean on. But the secrets she carried had become so much a part of her by then they had formed a hard exoskeleton, a barrier between herself and the rest of the world. She'd never thought anyone could believe her.

If anyone could have, it would have been Barry.

"I'm sorry," she says at last. "You'll never know how sorry I am."

He looks at her for a long moment, his eyes probing hers. But the exoskeleton holds. He doesn't see beneath it. Or maybe there's nothing left to see.

"Look, Holly, I can't imagine what you've been through," he says, softening. "But right from the beginning, we were a team. What happened to that? If you were having trouble, why didn't you come to me? Why jeopardize everything we've worked so hard for? And if you don't want the company anymore, if it's all too much, why not talk about selling it?"

Holly thinks of the new faces around the table, the new receptionist. Is that what Barry's preparing for? A Darling Skin Care without her? "But I don't want to sell," she says.

He exhales and swivels his chair away, then back again. "You could have fooled me. Look, let's take some time and think about it, okay? We used to run this place like it was a family and Darling Skin Care was our child. But maybe it should just be business from now on. I handle the day-to-day operations and you supply the famous last name, that beautiful, mysterious Darling cachet at launches and special events."

Barry settles behind the table again, shuffles the papers in front of him. "Let me know if you run into any problems with the launch this week and I'll do the same. I'll have my assistant schedule a meeting before you leave to debrief. And Holly?" He glances up. "Don't dismiss the idea of selling out of hand. The company could be worth millions in another year or two. It might turn out to be what you want after all." He pauses, gives her a level look. "Besides, if you keep on this way, we might not have a choice."

Holly doesn't answer. What else is there to say? And suddenly the rage that fueled her march to Barry's office is back. Barry's secretary, the people waiting to see him in the outer room, keep their heads down. Some have seen her storm before. But what they don't know is that she isn't furious with Barry or Elliot.

She's angry at herself.

Chapter Thirty-One

Grief, Holly knows from experience, doesn't begin the day a person dies. The loss can start when the person is still alive, when the time is taken up with doctors' appointments and tests and treatments and plans. The busyness helps hide the fact that you've already begun grieving.

Right now, Darling Skin Care is still the company she built with Barry, and she's still busy. She does the afternoon meet and greet with another round of celebrities and beauty editors, then sits on a magazine panel with other skin care experts. Work has always been her escape, and right now it's no different. But it's a double-edged sword. What's keeping her so engaged is also what she could lose. It's a strange kind of torture, seeing the company as something that might go on without her. As just a business, as Barry put it, instead of the almost living entity the two of them coaxed into being.

But being tortured is better than going home to her empty apartment. Ever since her conversation with Barry, she's been keenly aware of what she's missing. She's never had a personal life, not really. Not since the car crash. She's had Jack, and then Eden, and a career she loved. And soon she'll have none of the above.

She finds herself thinking of Christopher, the warmth of his back when she leaned against him on the bike, the ridiculous way he sparks something inside of her whenever he's around, and it makes her blush. She shakes her head at herself. What's inside her chest beats like it's supposed to, but it's just muscle memory. It's not a real heart, and it hasn't been for years.

When the building is quiet and most of the employees have gone for the day, she heads to her lab. Knowing Elliot was there, that he went through her notes and experiments, makes her feel violated. Still, she pores over them with a critical eye, trying to see the information the way he might have. Perhaps she'll find something she's missed before.

She works until late into the night, meticulously going over line after line of data. At some point, she falls asleep at her desk. She must, because she dreams that the entire building is filled with pixie dust, a shimmering golden blanket that carpets the floors, a thousand times more beautiful than the product she designed in the lab. And then the sun comes up and the soft dawn light touches the room, turning it from clinical white to rose gold. It's lovely, and she reaches out a hand to capture it on her skin. But someone is calling her, and at the sound the sunbeams and dust scatter.

"Holly?" Barry's shaking her awake. The light is ordinary fluorescent light, harsh and cold.

She blinks blearily, trying to make sense of his words, to shake off the loveliness of the dream and clear her head.

". . . been trying to reach you. When you weren't at the apartment and I couldn't get you on your phone, I figured you must be here."

She glances at the wall clock, sees that it's close to four in the morning, and comes instantly awake.

"What's wrong?"

Barry's face is too pale. He licks his lips.

"Barry?" Her heart is pounding.

"Your mother's been trying to reach you. When she couldn't get you, she called me." He's still talking, but Holly isn't listening. She's picking up her phone, which is facedown on her desk. She turned the ringer to silent when she did the last meet and greet, and now she sees a string of missed calls from Jane snaking their way across the screen. Her hands are shaking so badly she can barely hit the number to call her mother back.

Jane answers on the first ring. She doesn't even wait for Holly to speak.

"Jack hasn't come home in two days," she blurts. "I don't know where he is. I can't find him, Holly."

Holly sags against the desk. From the corner of her eye she sees Barry start to reach out a hand to steady her, then stop. But he doesn't leave.

"I've been all over the streets, searching for him. At first I didn't even realize he was gone. I had a dinner party, and when I came home there was a note saying he'd be home late. In the morning, I assumed he was up before me."

"A teenage boy up before you? Jesus, Mother."

"He left another note, this one upstairs, saying he needed space and not to worry. I found it when I searched his room after he didn't come home last night. What do you want me to do?"

Holly tries to think, presses her palm to her forehead, tries to stop her mind from leaping to horrible images so that she can concentrate. As if she had the power to summon him, she cuts off any thought of Peter, but the shadow of him runs beneath every word she says. "Have you talked to Nan? Ed might know something."

"She asked for this week off. She's been so miserable lately I thought it wouldn't be a bad idea."

That gives Holly pause. She'd assumed Nan's recent angst was simply Holly's own presence getting under her skin, but perhaps there's more to it. Perhaps whatever is going on with Jack, Ed is involved as well.

"Call her," she says. "Find out if she knows anything and text me. I'll be home as soon as I can. And let me know right away if you find him."

Jane's still talking, but Holly's already moved on. She disconnects the call, then opens her messages. She texted Jack yesterday, after the meet and greet, and he never responded. She texts him again, a quick, *Where are you?* As she does, she remembers the GPS app she activated on his phone the night before she left London. She opens it on her own phone, where it spins and spins before telling her Jack's device is inactive. Does she want to be alerted when it comes back online? She sure as hell does.

Finally she calls him. It goes to voicemail, so she leaves a message. "Jack! It's me. Wherever you are, whatever you are doing, it's okay. Call me back. Let me know you're all right. Please." Her voice breaks on the last word.

"What can I do?" She'd forgotten Barry, but his quiet voice is a lifeline in the storm that's battering her. This time, she takes it. She doesn't lie or dissemble, just tells him exactly what she needs.

"I have to get home, Barry. I need to find Jack before it's too late. There's so much going on . . . It's too much to explain right now," she says, hurrying on before he can reject her, before he can turn away. "But I will, I promise. The bottom line is Jack is in danger. Either from himself or . . . or someone else."

That look is in his eyes again, but this time it's not directed at her. Right now, he's the old Barry, all the magnificent wheels of his brain turning on her behalf.

"What about that private detective you hired?" he says. "I'll bet he could help."

Christopher. Of course. If anyone can find Jack and bring him home, she's certain it's him. She's already fumbling with her phone when Barry speaks again.

"And as for getting you back to London," he says with a gleam in his eye, "let me make a call."

Chapter Thirty-Two

A scant two hours later Holly is winging her way across the Atlantic in a private plane, courtesy of Barry's call to their new BFF Lauren Lander. Holly knows there's a price for this speed, knows that Lauren will extract every last penny's worth, but right now she'd sell her soul to the devil and throw in Jane's for good measure if it meant finding her kids.

She uses the plane time to list locations Jack might have gone. It's pointless, but it keeps her mind occupied, keeps it from rushing to places she can't handle right now. Besides, it's what Christopher told her to do. She knows she must have sounded unhinged when she called him. It's like some terrible joke. *How many children can one person lose?* she'd half expected him to say in his coolly amused way. *All of them,* seemed to be the universe's reply, and there's nothing funny about it.

But Christopher hadn't said anything close to that.

"He's probably run off," he'd assured her. She couldn't tell from his voice whether he truly believed those words or whether he was trying to calm her down. Either way, he'd pointed out that without much money and with so few contacts, Jack wouldn't be too difficult to find.

But that was hours ago and she hasn't heard back. She knows in her heart that it's more than her son being sulky, more than his taking advantage of her absence to go wild. Jack might worry her to death, but he'd never do that to Jane. And if Holly has to guess, she'd bet Christopher knows it too.

Holly takes a car to her mother's house from the airport. Jane, grim-faced, is putting takeaway cartons directly on the table rather than transferring the contents into serving bowls, a sure sign of distress.

"Anything?" Holly asks. She gulps tea heavily doctored with cream and sugar and burns her tongue.

Jane shakes her head. "I've called everyone I can think of who has a child or grandchild his age. No one has seen him."

"Any luck reaching Nan?"

"Not a bit."

Holly's not hungry, but she realizes she hasn't eaten since yesterday, so she forces herself to spoon a few morsels of food onto her plate and eat. As soon as she's finished, she grabs her purse.

"What are you doing?"

"I'm going out. We need to find him."

"Don't be ridiculous," her mother says. "You're not charging out into the dark with no idea of where to go. You're exhausted. The best thing you can do is be here if he comes home and wait for Christopher to call."

But Holly can't wait. She's on the verge of a breakdown. If she doesn't keep moving, if she doesn't do something to find Jack and Eden, she'll die.

"Fine," Jane says when she sees the look on Holly's face. "Then I'm driving."

In the car, Holly shares the list she made on the plane. Jane has already checked most of the same places, but they drive past them again just in case. Jane has her own list of spots her friends say their grandkids go, so they try those as well—the local chippy shop, a dessert café, a coffee shop that is open late. They see plenty of teen boys, but none of them are Jack.

Holly's not ready to go home, so Jane, with a sideways look, suggests some of the back-alley streets where they searched for Peter. Holly agrees, the dread of finding him there among the lost far surpassed by the dread of not finding him at all. She tries Jack's phone again, first calling and then, when it goes straight to voicemail, using the GPS app. Still nothing.

At last Jane insists that they go home, and Holly is so tired she can't argue. She wants to call Christopher, call the police, but Jane points out that it's a scant few hours before dawn. Christopher would surely call if he had news. As for the police, Jane agrees contacting them may be wise. But she persuades Holly to wait till the morning.

"Whatever will you tell them? You'll need a decent story, particularly once they figure out who you are, to avoid getting bogged down in foolish questions and tied up with the press. Christopher can help with that. There's very little the police can do that he can't, and he's not bound by their rules and laws. He can look in ways the police simply cannot. Plus, it's likely there's only a skeletal staff on right now. There's nothing they can do tonight, and neither can we," she says. "Get some rest. You'll need it for whatever tomorrow brings."

But sleep won't come. Holly's awake, staring at the ceiling, when there's a knock at the door and her mother comes in.

"Take this," Jane says, handing her a mug of warm milk and a sleeping pill.

It's a mark of how exhausted Holly is, how desperate for sleep and the oblivion it will bring, that she takes both without a word of protest. Sleep follows, deep and dreamless, as if she'd been cocooned in black velvet.

She wakes feeling hungover, her tongue thick in her mouth. Even before she's fully conscious, images of Jack and Eden flood in, pressing against the insides of her eyelids. But when she tries to hold on to them, they disappear like shooting stars.

She opens her eyes. It's still early enough that the sky is laced through with silver. She blinks, staggers to her feet, throws on her clothes, and stumbles to the kitchen for a cup of tea to clear the cobwebs away. She doesn't even check the time before calling Christopher.

He answers on the first ring. He doesn't sound at all groggy. It's as if he's been expecting her call.

"Hello?"

A beeping interrupts her response. It's coming not from Christopher but from her own phone. She holds it away from her ear and studies the screen. The GPS app that tracks Jack's phone is suddenly working. The little green circle that's been churning every time she's checked it has disappeared, replaced by a map of London with a pin-drop over one street.

"Holly?" Christopher says. "You there?"

For a moment she can't talk.

"I've found him," she manages to choke out.

"Where?"

Unsteadily, she reads off the address.

"Okay, sit tight. Don't do anything until I get there," Christopher says. "We'll go together." But Holly doesn't even let him finish talking before she's disconnected the call. With shaking hands, she dials Jack's number. It goes straight to voicemail. Holly runs to her mother's room and bursts in without knocking.

Jane is awake, sitting in a dressing gown on the edge of her bed, brushing her long silver hair. She takes one look at Holly and drops the brush. "What is it?"

"I've found him," Holly says. She reads the address off her phone. "Does that mean anything to you?"

"No," Jane says. "But give me a moment." She pulls up the map function on her own phone. "Hmmm," she says, looking at it. "It's in East London—rather a seedy area, I should think. Give me a moment to get dressed and I'll come with you. And call Christopher. He can meet us there."

But Holly can't wait, not for Jane to dress, not to explain she's already called, not for Christopher to arrive. She's on fire, and if she doesn't move, she'll combust. She runs back to her room to find her container of serum. She grabs the first-aid kit her mother keeps in the kitchen, and at the last second throws a bottle of water and a granola bar in her bag. Jane is calling to her, is hurrying down the stairs still in her dressing gown, but Holly shouts that she'll be taking the car and leaves without waiting for a response.

The address is about a half hour away. She follows the directions on her map app, and as she drives, the houses get more and more run down. At last the app announces that she's arrived. She looks dubiously at the house in front of her. It's a council flat. Red-bricked with a bit of a garden, it might have been quite cozy at one point. But now there's a smashed window in the front, taped up with cardboard. The gate at the beginning of the walk is broken, hanging crazily askew, and instead of flowers in the yard, there are empty cans of lager.

She's sliding out of the car when her phone rings. She glances at it, hesitates. It's Christopher.

"I told you to wait," he says as soon as she answers.

"It's my son!"

"Look, I'm five minutes away. Wait for me to go in at least."

But the idea is unbearable. "Then I should be safe—you'll be here soon if anything goes wrong," she says. She disconnects the call. When she reaches the flat's door, she knocks once and waits.

No answer.

"Hello?" she calls. "Jack?"

She knocks again, more forcefully, and realizes that the door is ever so slightly ajar. Hesitantly, she pushes it open and calls inside.

"Jack?"

She waits a moment, then fumbles with her phone and dials Jack's number. When she hears ringing, she follows the sound inside.

The first room is the kitchen. There's a sink full of dirty dishes and a wooden table with water stains. A fly lazily buzzes near the ceiling. The room smells of stale beer, of old food and rot. An empty crisp bag is balled up on the floor.

"Jack?" Holly's voice is no more than a whisper. Where *is* Christopher, damn him? Perhaps she should have waited after all. But she pushes on.

Beyond the kitchen is a tiny den, darkened by shades, and past that is where the ringing is coming from. With a deepening sense of dread, Holly steps into what must be the bedroom. Aside from a stained mattress on the floor and a dresser scarred with cigarette burns, the room is empty. There's a bundle of blue-striped sheets piled in a corner. She pokes them with her foot, and a sour smell reaches her nostrils.

The phone rests on the corner of the mattress farthest from her. It's Jack's for sure—same blue case, same chip on the edge where he dropped it after practice last year. As she's reaching for it, she notices something beneath it. It's a photo, the type that comes from an instant camera. Gingerly, she picks it up.

It's a picture of a boy. He's wearing a gray sweatshirt and blue jeans, and his face is turned away from the camera. It looks as if he's asleep, asleep on blue-striped sheets, on a bed pushed against a wall like this one. She stares at the photo, her heart pounding. The photo is ever so slightly out of focus, but it's Jack, she's certain.

The phone has stopped ringing, but a message appears on the lock screen. It's a new address. Below it are the words *Tell no one.*

Holly stares at the phone. The message disappears as the screen goes blank. She enters Jack's passcode, but the screen doesn't unlock and she gets an error message. Her hands are shaking—she must have entered the code wrong. She tries again and the same thing happens.

Has Jack changed it? And how many chances does she have before she's locked out?

Before she can try again, the phone rings, and Holly jumps. A message appears, asking for permission to video call. Holly accepts, and the screen fills with the image of a boy in jeans and sweatshirt, just like the photo. He's sleeping, and once again his face is averted. But the shape of his head and the hunch of his shoulders . . . Jack.

She scans the video, looking for clues. The room has cream-colored walls. There's a window over the bed, but Holly can't see anything framed in it, only sky. The light is early morning, the same as it is where Holly is standing.

"Jack?" she calls. "Jack? Can you hear me? Wake up!"

Immediately the connection ends. Holly tries to call back, but the phone's screen fades to black. She pushes the home key, tries to restart it, but a message pops up, telling her the phone is being remotely wiped.

"No," she says, shaking it. "No, no, no."

Within moments, the message is gone, as is Jack's screen saver. It's as if she's just taken the phone out of the box.

"Shit," she says. "Bloody, sodding shit."

She scrabbles in her bag for a pen and piece of paper, afraid that she'll forget the address. She's finishing scribbling it when she hears tires squeal outside, followed by footsteps on the front steps.

"Holly?" Christopher calls through the door, his voice guarded. "Holly, are you in here?"

Tell no one.

Slowly she looks at the paper with the address, the photo she found on the mattress. She doesn't want to do this alone. Not again. She can't.

"Holly?" Christopher calls again. He's in the kitchen now, coming along the hallway. His footsteps are careful, deliberate, but quick. He'll be in the room in a second. As she turns to answer him, a spot of color near the door catches her eye. A red feather. She freezes.

Tell no one.

"Holly?"

There's a split second left, and Holly chooses.

"I'm in here," she calls. "I'm okay." She leaves the feather where it is. She doesn't want to touch it. But she puts the address and the photo in her pocket as Christopher rushes into the room.

"I'm fine," she says again. "I think it was . . . a prank. Jack trying to get back at me."

Somewhere outside, a rooster crows.

Chapter Thirty-Three

Tell me again," Christopher says for the umpteenth time, his voice unnaturally patient. Holly has to take a deep breath, has to will her body to be still, so she can match his tone. She exhales as forcefully as she dares.

"A prank," she says. "A stupid prank. Jack's been pushing for more independence for months, and he decided to take the chance while I was away to seize it."

Even to her own ears, it sounds pathetic. How much worse must it sound to Christopher? It's a terrible story, but the best she was able to come up with in the seconds she had. Even so, Christopher insisted on searching every corner of the dismal flat, and the only thing Holly can thank her stars for at the moment is how very small the place is. She needs to get to that address as fast as she can. But when the inside turned up nothing, Christopher moved on to the yard, where he found enough rusty cans and bottles to start his own junkyard but nothing else.

And still he wouldn't leave. He insisted they look through the bedroom again, that she show him exactly where she found the phone, as if knowing would somehow miraculously make Jack appear. Now he stands, arms crossed, blocking the bedroom door. With his black motorcycle boots, leather jacket, and smudge of dirt under his eye from crawling about in the yard, he looks like a modern pirate. An angry, obstinate pirate. It reminds her of how little she knows him, how trust-ing him could be dangerous. Of who he could be, and not just in his dreams.

"And you're sticking to that?"

Holly thinks of the way Peter used to slide into her room, the way he moved almost invisibly at night.

Tell no one.

He could be right outside eavesdropping and they'd never know.

"Yes," she says.

Christopher studies her. "And the phone?" he demands.

"Jack knew I had his GPS feature turned on, that I'd use it to keep an eye on him. He wiped it to make a point."

Christopher has confiscated the phone, but Holly doubts it will do him any good. Her own phone rings at that moment and she glances down, startled. It's Jane. Holly ignores it.

"You're hiding something," Christopher says. "We both know that."

Holly fidgets, the picture of the sleeping Jack and the scrap of paper with the address scribbled on it like hot stones in her pocket. She con-centrates on making eye contact with Christopher, on keeping her breathing slow and even.

"There's nothing to hide," she says, spreading her empty hands.

He snorts. "Please. You call me up in a panic, you cut short an im-portant trip, and this morning it's barely dawn before you're calling me again," he says. "And now suddenly everything is all right? I don't be-lieve it for a minute."

Holly shrugs. She keeps her voice calm, unhurried, as if she has all the time in the world, while in the back of her head she hears a clock ticking away the seconds. *Tick. Tock.* "It's a family matter now. I don't need your help."

A muscle twitches over his eye. Good. Perhaps her words have hit home and he'll wash his hands of her. Still, she's surprised to recognize that it bothers her, this idea of Christopher walking away. She tries to shake the feeling off. He's not even a friend, not really. How can she miss something that doesn't exist?

Her phone buzzes again. Jane. Holly knows her mother will keep calling until she answers. But perhaps she can use this to her advantage.

"Pardon me a moment," Holly says. "It's my mother." When Christopher doesn't move, she pointedly turns her back and steps as far into the corner of the little bedroom as she can.

"I can't stand it anymore. Have you found him?" Jane asks. "Is he safe? Holly, what is happening?"

Holly takes a deep breath. Then, "He did?" she says. "That's wonderful news. I'll tell Christopher. He's here now."

For a brief moment, Jane is silent. "You've found something," she says. "Something you don't want that private detective to know. What is it? Good or bad?"

"Yes, of course he should have told you. And I will talk with him when he gets home," Holly says, thinking hard. "But you have to admit, it was an awfully big adventure."

There's no way Christopher will understand, but even so, she utters those last words as casually as she can, without the slightest hint of emphasis, and prays Jane will make the connection.

There's a sharp intake of breath on the other end of the line. "Peter," Jane whispers. "Are you sure?"

"Without a doubt."

"Lucky boy," Jane says in wonder. "Lucky, lucky boy. I must hear all about it."

"Absolutely," Holly says, her own voice grim. This isn't the time or the place to dispel Jane's fangirl crush. "I'll be home as soon as I can. But it may be a while."

She says the last with a glare over her shoulder at Christopher.

"Great news," she announces, disconnecting the call. "Jack's been in touch. It's exactly what I thought—a stupid teenage prank."

"Really," Christopher says. He doesn't move from the doorway, doesn't uncross his arms. "Did he say where he was?"

"A friend of my mother's. She has a castle in the countryside, and she spirited off her grandson and a bunch of his friends, including Jack."

Christopher's eyes narrow as he studies her. "Did you happen to catch the friend's name?"

Holly shakes her head. "I was too relieved."

"How convenient," he observes. "And I suppose you have no idea where this castle is located, either."

"Not a clue. I'm just happy to know he's with someone my mother trusts." The irony of that statement overwhelms her, and she swallows a hysterical laugh. "Now, if you'll excuse me, I need to get back." She crosses the room and stands directly in front of him.

Christopher looks at her for a long moment. His face isn't angry, not anymore, but she can't read it. He reaches out and touches her shoulder, rests his gloved hand there. The weight is heavy and warm, and suddenly her breath is coming so quickly it muddles her thinking. She can't remember which hand is real and which is not.

"Holly," he says, and his voice is gentle. "You can trust me."

He means it, she thinks, and her earlier doubts vanish. Now is the time to tell him the whole truth, her opportunity to come clean. Her chance to explain what's happening to Eden, who Peter really is. What he's capable of.

Tell no one.

She can't risk it. No matter how much she wants it to be different, she still has to do this alone.

So she takes a step back. Looks Christopher in the eye. Resists the urge to thumb away the smudge of dirt on his face. "I need to call the office," she repeats.

He doesn't move, but when she squeezes past him, he doesn't stop her, either. He lets his hand fall to his side. She finds it doesn't matter whether it is the hand with the hook or not. The empty spot on her shoulder still feels bereft and cold.

The loss of his touch stays with her all the way through the little house, and she knows it's a bad sign. For Jack's sake, she can't let herself be tempted. Can't let down her guard and tell Christopher the truth in a weak moment. So when she reaches the safety of the front door, she doesn't let herself hesitate, doesn't let herself turn back.

No matter how much she wants to.

She knows, of course, that giving the slip to Christopher Cooke won't be that easy. As much as she wants to speed back to the house, she forces herself to drive slowly, to stop at every light, to signal her innocence with every turn.

It takes six blocks before she spots the sleek black motorcycle weaving in and out of traffic. He hangs back, at the edge of her sight in the mirror. He wants her to know he's following. Or he thinks she's too arrogant, too foolish to look.

Either way, her plan remains the same.

She holds a steady speed until she's home. Although Jane prefers to have the Mercedes parked in the drive, Holly leaves it in plain sight on the street. She walks to the front door, ignoring the whispers in her head that say time is slipping away, that she's taking too long, that she should run.

Tick. Tock.

Holly doesn't turn around, doesn't linger to see if he's pulled in behind her and is watching. She unlocks the door and goes inside, shuts it behind her as quietly as she can. Footsteps click along the second-floor landing, so she hurries down the hall to the kitchen and the back entrance. Unlocks the dead bolt.

"Holly?" Jane calls. "Is that you?"

But it's too late. Holly's already outside.

Standing on the back porch, she draws a deep breath, filling her lungs with air that seems different from the rest of London. The tiny yard that spills at her feet is a riot of color. It's Jane's own version of the fantasyland she's never been invited to visit. And in the summer, it's glorious.

Here tropical-colored flowers as wide as dinner plates engulf one wall. Half are real, brought into the conservatory every winter, the other half glass-blown. They shimmer iridescently and grow warm from the sun, fooling even the bees. Pots of lemons, of limes and figs, rim the patio, where once or twice a summer Jane holds candlelit dinners for a select handful of friends. In the far corner, white clematis twines about a wire figure. Viewed from the side, it resembles a swooping white bird. From the front, it's a young girl in a billowing white nightgown. Behind the clematis, pansies and lavender spill from the brim of a giant top hat. Between the two forms, a tiny teddy bear topiary rests as if discarded on the ground, Jane's nod to Great-Uncle Michael.

And in the center of it all is the statue of Peter, cast in bronze by the protégé Jane found years ago. The artist has portrayed him as young, no more than a boy, and through the clever positioning of filaments and wires, he appears to be flying. At night, tiny fairy lights flicker from a canopy of branches overhead, casting shadows so entrancing one might imagine the figure was alive.

There's a small fountain in the shape of Neverland, based upon a map Jane drew from Barrie's description in the original book. It burbles beneath the frozen image of Peter, water spouting from a volcano and creating tiny rainbows in the sunshine. The statue's hand is outstretched, as if beckoning.

And it's pointing straight at Jane's bedroom window.

As a child Holly spent years watching Jane work in this garden. She studied how her mother added elements and stripped others away, and struggled to decode the messages embedded in the landscape. She wondered where her place was in it, if there was a place for her at all.

Today she strides past the statue with scarcely a second glance. Thyme and mint bruise under her feet, releasing their scent, as she lines herself up with the bronze Peter's foot and counts off thirteen steps. There, directly in front of her, is the back wall of the garden. Old-fashioned climbing roses, their thorns as large and wicked as a small knife, have devoured all but the fence's outline.

Carefully, Holly slips past the guard of thorns, sliding her hand beneath the flowers, searching for the right board. At first all the wood feels the same, and a bubble of panic rises in her chest. It's been years since she's used this particular exit strategy—has Jane replaced the fence? But then her fingers find what they are seeking: a board with a series of knots at its center.

Holly reaches up to the top of the board and pulls. Nothing happens. She tries again, hanging on the board with all of her weight, and it gives a bit. She looks down, and sees that a rose cane has twined about the board, holding it in place. Holly wrestles with it and gets scratched for her trouble, but manages to slide it off. Then she pulls again, putting every ounce of her energy behind it, and the board swings up. A very thin, very limber person could wriggle through the opening.

Holly is no longer fifteen, the age she was when she created this escape. Nor is she twenty-three, as she was the night she first danced with Robert. But years of Pilates have ensured that her body is almost as slender as it was then. She slides through the hole with less grace but much more determination than her teenage self. As soon as she's through, she pulls the board back into place. If Jane comes to see if she's really home, it will seem as if she's vanished from the yard. More importantly, from Christopher's point of view, should he be watching—and Holly would bet a great deal that he is—she's never left the house.

She takes a moment to orient herself. She's in the narrow alley that runs behind her street. Even after such a short time in her mother's garden, the outside world, with its dustbins and honking cars, is jarring, and she wonders, as she always did as a teenager, if this was what it was like for Wendy and her brothers when they returned from the real Neverland. As a child, Holly couldn't understand how they gave it up. Now she wonders how they managed to escape.

Chapter Thirty-Four

Once she's gotten her bearings, Holly cuts through yards and alleys at random, until she's far enough away to be reasonably certain Christopher hasn't spotted her. Only then does she take out her phone and call for a ride. The driver is quick—he's there in less than five minutes. She checks the license to make sure it matches what she has on her phone, then slides into the back seat. Finally she's on her way.

"Heading to the school, right?" the driver asks.

Holly repeats the address she'd punched into the app, and he nods.

"That's it. You got a kid there? I didn't realize they were open over summer hols."

"Um, yes," Holly says. She doesn't want to talk to the driver, doesn't want to be remembered. She wishes she'd thought to grab a hat on her way out of the house. Instead she bends her head over her phone and googles the address, since she's had no time up until now to research. Pictures of an ivy-covered campus with brick buildings and mature trees pop up. Christopher was right. Peter could find an endless supply of boys here. And then the car turns, slows, and comes to a stop.

"Here it is," the driver says. "You want me to take you inside?"

"This is fine, thanks," Holly murmurs. She slides across the seat and out the door.

A short brick path leads to wrought iron gates. A sign on top proclaims *Saint Ormond's School for Boys.* As Holly walks up the path, trying to calm her racing heart, she wishes she'd paid the driver to wait.

But stalling won't help Jack or Eden, so Holly peers through the gates and sees a small brick structure smothered in climbing roses. A caretaker's cottage. Farther back, a huge estate looms over playing fields and grassy lawns. But there are no boys in sight. The driver must have been right.

The gates are chained shut, so Holly squeezes through a side door. On the other side of the gate, almost hidden in the shrubbery, is a brilliantly red Range Rover. Its vanity plates spell out *WYNDRDR.* A chill races up her spine. If she were choosing a car for Peter, this would be it.

She rings the buzzer at the cottage door. There's a low hum of voices from inside, one deep, one high, but no one answers. When Holly knocks, the cottage door swings open, but no one is there.

She peers inside, hesitates, then steps over the threshold. In the dim light she sees wooden beams and plastered walls. Someone is laughing farther in. The sound is bright and golden. Like bells.

She follows the voice. As she turns the corner of the hall, she's assaulted by the scent of rot. Sweet and cloying, as it was at Hay's Galleria. Her eyes water and she covers her nose, gasping.

And there, in the next room, is the childlike woman from the atrium. She's stretched out on a stained floral couch, her head hanging off the armrest, feet dangling off the back. She looks at Holly from her upside-down vantage point. Takes a crisp out of an opened package and licks it, then eats it so lasciviously watching her seems obscene.

Tinker Bell.

"Where is he?" Holly demands. She doesn't need to spell it out. "And where's Jack? Where's Eden?"

At Eden's name, the woman sits up in alarm. She puts her fingers to her lips, miming for silence.

Holly looks at her, considers. Tinker Bell's skin is still stretched and bloated, her dainty features distorted. But her concern seems real.

276

"Fine," Holly says, clenching her fists. "Just tell me where *he* is then."

Tinker Bell, maddening creature that she is, lies back down, languorously pointing to a door on the far side of the room. Holly jerks it open and stalks through.

She finds herself in the kitchen, a disaster almost as bad as the council flat this morning, a million years ago. The air is clearer here, and she realizes it's because there's an open door. Outside there's a garden and a man sitting in a chair, smoking. His hair is shoulder length, wavy and golden. For one single second Holly hesitates, and then she steps outside.

The man turns as if expecting her, his gelid eyes a brilliant blue.

"Hello, Holly. It's been some time."

She can barely speak, but she manages to get the words out.

"Hello, Peter."

He gestures for her to sit, pointing with the cigarette toward the plastic chair next to him. He still has a catlike grace, but his face is ravaged, pitted with scars and lined with wrinkles. He looks decades older than she does. She represses a shiver and remains standing.

"Where's my son?" she asks abruptly. "Is he here?"

Peter shakes his head, and his hair, which is still beautiful, covers his eyes. He languidly pushes it away from his face. "Manners," he drawls. "The Darlings have always been known for their manners, of course. But where are mine? Surely you can stay for a cuppa with an old friend? After all, it's been such a very long time since you sent me away."

This time she can't help it—she does shiver. Peter sees it and smiles, then rings a little bell that sits on the table between them. Nothing happens. He rings again, then cocks an apologetic eyebrow.

"Tink's gotten sloppy over the years. My apologies," he says. "I'll see to it myself. That's the best way, after all. Don't go away now, promise?" He smiles that same wicked smile.

"Where's Jack?" she says again.

Peter rolls his eyes. "Not here. But must we really jump right into it?" He looks at her face and sighs. "Fine. Have a look, if you like. I'll fetch the tea."

Holly doesn't hesitate.

As she searches the cottage though, she hears a clattering, followed by the sound of crying. When she runs into the living room to look for Jack, Tinker Bell is seated as she was before, only now a black-and-blue mark is blossoming on her arm. "Where are Jack and Eden?" Holly hisses in a low voice. But Tink closes her eyes and feigns sleep.

A scream of frustration rises in Holly's throat, but she bites it back. She doesn't have the time. Peter has such a short attention span—she can't take the risk that he'll grow bored and disappear. She hurtles through each room, searching under beds, in cabinets and closets, but there's no sign. She even runs outside to the red Range Rover, but it's empty.

Defeated, she returns to the garden. Peter is stacking sugar cubes and flicking them into his teacup one by one.

"Give me my son," she demands. "Or I'll call the police."

"You could," Peter agrees. He pours cream into his cup, stirs it. It's a thick, sugary sludge. "Or that private detective you seem so fond of. The one with the missing hand." At her start of surprise, he smiles. "I'll bet he could help. Bet he thinks he's a hero. Sanctimonious ass. Of course, while he's searching, sleepy Jack might doze off again. He's having such pleasant dreams too—this time, he might not want to wake up. Tea?"

He holds up the teapot and gestures to the seat next to him. Holly slumps into it. Peter pats her hand and she wills herself not to flinch. He pours a cup of tea and puts it in front of her. "Cheers," he says. He takes a sip, then puts the cup down with exaggerated care on the table.

"What do you want?" Her voice is surprisingly steady.

He answers with a question. "Don't you love youth? How fresh and innocent it is. How sweet it smells. Like springtime. Of course the young have no idea what this world is like." He tilts his head back, blows a stream of cigarette smoke across the table and into her face. "I do though. I've been scrabbling out here for years."

She's certain now that he blames her for his fall from grace. "I'm sorry," she tries to say. But the words stick, come out forced.

Peter shakes his head. "Don't be. If it hadn't been you, it would have been someone else." He leans forward, runs a finger down her arm. "But you were so delicious."

Her skin crawls and she pulls away, bile rising to the back of her throat. He's watching her so intently, the same way she remembers from those nights in the nursery. *Does it hurt?*

He's playing with her, poking at her wounds to see how much she bleeds. If she wants to find Jack, she has to stay in control, has to get him talking and hope he'll let something slip. So she blurts out the question that's been at the forefront of her mind all these years.

"Why me, that night in the nursery? Why not my mother? Or Wendy?"

Peter casts that still-magnetic gaze on her again, studies her face as if weighing what to say. Then he shrugs.

"Wendy had too many daddy issues. You should look into that particular bit of family history sometime." He pitches his voice high, mimicking a teenage girl. "'Have a thimble, Peter.'" He takes a sip of tea. "Stupid twat. Besides, she always had her brothers with her. Until she didn't. That's when she called me."

Holly thinks of Wendy's photos in the attic, of the man with his face cut out. "And my mother?"

"Jane?" he says, surprised. He starts to say more, then looks at her the way a cat looks at a canary and shakes his head instead. "Why did I choose you? Because you thought you had no one. Not really. And so you were just like me."

His words hit like a blow. Despite her resolve to stay in control, to not let him hurt her, Holly has to catch her breath. She is nothing like him. Nothing. She has Jack, she has Eden, she has the company. She's built a life.

But beneath the anger that's sustaining her is an icy wash of fear. Barry's voice rings in her ears. *How could you not tell me you had a daughter? I mean, Jesus, we're like family.* And Christopher. *You can trust me.* And even further, before that, the night Peter came through her window. She'd had Jack, but she'd wished she hadn't—had wished he would die so she could die too.

Not only was she alone, she'd wanted it that way.

She looks at Peter with a flash of insight. The stories she grew up on—the fearless boy in search of adventure—were wrong. When he flew through Wendy's window for the first time, he wasn't looking for adventure. He was looking for a home.

Holly will never forgive him—not just for taking Jack, but also for what he's done to her, to Uncle Michael, to Wendy, and even to Jane—but she understands him better now. And if she's lucky, she can use that understanding to save Jack.

Peter waves a lazy arm around the yard, encompassing the cottage and the school. "Now I have all this," he says, his voice heavy with sarcasm. "And as you may remember, I've always had a way with the boys—I've always been able to lead them astray. Now I get paid for the privilege to do so."

Peter's smile over the top of his teacup is predatory, but Holly refuses to react. "If you're not happy here, why not go back?"

His grin twists, becomes a snarl. "Like this?" He gestures to himself, taking in the wrinkles on his face, his tea-stained teeth, the age spots on his hands. "You really don't know, do you? Good old Wendy never shared the whole story, and that Barrie fellow? He was an ugly blighter. Stupid too. Followed precious Wendy all about, writing down her words like they were pearls and then changing them to suit himself. I listened outside the window more than once. Fairies and dancing lights and happily-ever-afters." He spits on the ground.

"No. If I went back now like this, they'd eat me alive."

Holy god, there's more like him? Perhaps Neverland wouldn't be a safe haven for Eden after all. But before Holly can follow up, he's speaking again.

"Barrie got a few things right. Made me the hero, which I am. The beautiful sodding hero, understand? Me. Not who she said. I hated her for that. Who put *him* in charge, gave *him* the right to decide the rules? Which games were fun and which ones went too far? We was mates, we was, till he set himself up so high and mighty. *I* found her. *I* brought her there, even when that self-righteous ass fought to stop me. *I* gave her a taste of magic and she loved it, until her idiot brother got his head smashed in."

Holly nods, afraid to interrupt him, though she doesn't understand half of what he's saying.

Peter's grin is back, and it's not pretty. "Barrie got the name right too. Came up with it all by himself, so maybe he wasn't as dumb as he looked."

"What do you mean?"

"Think about it. He listens to Wendy's tales and names it *Neverland*. Not Wonderland, like that other twit. Or Fairyland or Magicland or anything else. Neverland. The place in-between. The place of shadows and shades. Where people slip in and out."

He suddenly leans in close and Holly braces herself. "I saw him at the end," he says confidingly. "He'd always wanted to meet me, told anyone he could. Told the Darlings and the blooming flowers and the statues in the park. The night he died, I swooped in. Figured I'd give the old bugger his wish.

"He was in his bed, staring at the shadows, until suddenly I was one of them. I told him who I was. I told him some of the things he'd gotten wrong.

"'I don't believe it,' he said, his voice all quavery. 'She said you were beautiful. She said Neverland was magic. I made you the hero because you brought her there. You fought to keep the door open. Even later, I stood by you when she sang the praises of that dirty old pirate. But now, well, *look* at you.'" Peter sighs, rubs his neck. "He hurt my feelings, he did. But he apologized before he died," he says, his voice chilling. "Besides, like I told him, you can't be a hero with a big blooming hook."

Holly freezes. She starts to speak, swallows, starts again. But Peter doesn't notice. He's already moved on.

"And as for going back. Even if I wanted to, I'm not sure I can. There are ways out, you see, plenty of them. Or at least enough. Neverland's a crafty old girl. If she likes you, if she thinks you deserve it, she'll slide you out a back door when things get grim." His face turns dark. "She doesn't like me. Not anymore. So I've got to be on my toes when I'm there. No second chances for old Peter. But I've been around long enough to have learned all her secrets. And when it comes to getting in, there's only one way. It turns out, there's something to those 'happy thoughts' after all," he says, making quote marks with his fingers. "Too bad for me, it's been a long time since my thoughts have been light enough to carry me home."

He doesn't say it regretfully.

"Even Tinker Bell can't always manage it. Her wings have become sodding useless. Shriveled up. She's tattooed herself with the last of the pixie dust instead. The original, of course. The mother source. I've been using a bit myself in my refreshments for the boys. But it's losing power."

There's so much information Holly struggles to take it all in. But one detail jumps out at her, as she remembers the swoop of starlings in the atrium—Tink's found a way to boost her power, and she hasn't shared it with Peter. *Interesting,* Holly thinks, but she keeps it to herself. "I can't help you with the happy thoughts, but I've been working on—"

"Yes, your little potions and lotions," he interrupts, grinning at her surprise. "I've been following you. Keeping an eye, at least. Paid a few visits to Cornwall, but couldn't get too close. Windows always shut. Nurses always hovering about. That one"—he jerks a thumb toward the cottage and Tink—"persuaded me to give it up as a bad business. 'Nothing to see, move it along. Boring place, Peter, all cows and sheep.'" He looks at her speculatively. "But you've got something new, maybe? And whatever it is, you think it can un-age me well enough that if I can figure out how to get there, I can go back."

Holly nods, holding her breath.

"But what makes you think I'd want to leave?" He looks her up and down, his stare so blatant it's clear what he's remembering. Holly clenches her hands in her lap, and he throws back his head and laughs. "Thanks, but no thanks. I'm staying. The toys here are so much better."

"Then what do you want?" she asks, fighting to keep the frustration from her voice.

"What do you think I want?" he snarls. "I used to be beautiful. I used to be desired. I used to be young. Now look at me. Will your lotion fix all that? I don't think so." He slams his hand down on the table, and the teacup trembles, sloshing its contents over the sides. He picks it up, and for a moment Holly thinks he's going to chuck it across the garden. But then he takes a sip, and when he speaks again, his voice is composed.

"So I have a trade for you," he says, eyes glinting. He picks up the tray and proffers it to her. "Biscuit?"

Chapter Thirty-Five

Holly's exhausted, strung out on fear and jet lag, and her brain is numb. And Peter, being Peter, won't come to the point. Instead he waxes on about how brilliant he is, how very, very clever. How once he realized what Holly was up to, that her recipe could not only bind with cells injured through trauma but also those damaged by aging, he devised a formula of his own.

"It took a while to figure out the special ingredient. The secret sauce. But once I got Tink to contribute . . ." He shrugs, spreading his hands wide. "Of course you know Tink. She's mercurial, that one. Every batch came out different. And that's not safe, is it? Not safe for me at all."

He lights another cigarette. The shadows have lengthened, and they've moved into the living room. The cloud of smoke fills the space between them, eddies about his head, making his eyes hard to see. "So I found that using a bit of young blood smooths out the edges. All those rich virgin platelets."

Holly looks out the window, at the school grounds. "You take it from the boys here, don't you," she says flatly.

"Don't look at me like that. They give it willingly, they do," he says with mock indignation.

"In exchange for what?"

"Depends on the boy, doesn't it?" He shrugs. "Sometimes it's a boost in grades. Parents put so much store in the pesky things. And a nice, friendly teacher can make a difference in a struggling student's life. For a price.

"But there are other boys as well, ones who lurk the same streets I used to. They want simpler things. A pair of new trainers. A hot meal. A place to sleep and a bit of—fatherly attention, shall we say?" He smirks.

"Those types of boys—they're the easy ones. Bit boring, but they have what I want, so I play nice, I do. It's another group of wayward youth I find more . . . interesting. Imagine a young boy growing up in a posh house without a father for guidance. With a mum always working. He might run wild. Might start drinking. Smoking pot. Might start pushing boundaries. Taking risks. For them, I add a few special ingredients. Give it a bit of a kick, keep them coming back for more. Keeps me in pocket change."

Jack. He's talking about Jack. Holly goes cold. The tea does nothing to warm her. But Peter's leering, dangling information in front of her like a worm on a hook. And if she takes the bait, he'll have her. So she doesn't bite.

"Are those the boys who won't wake up?" she asks instead.

He shrugs again. "They're the ones who are looking for the next high. I simply help them find it. 'Product testers' is what you'd call them. I can't very well test it on myself, can I? If something went wrong, then where would I be? I have to make sure it's safe first. And then again, sometimes it's not. Sometimes the first dose is the last one they take. Sometimes those special ingredients are hard to source. Expensive too. Never know what they might be cut with."

As Peter talks, a humming fills the room. At first Holly thinks it must be the refrigerator in the kitchen, but the sound is too close. She realizes it is coming from Tinker Bell, who is still stretched across the sofa. She's finished another package of crisps and is licking the bag.

"Quiet, you." Peter stretches out a foot from his place in an overstuffed chair and kicks her. She moans but doesn't stop humming, doesn't stop licking the bag.

"She's getting rusty," he explains. "She's not what she once was. Well, none of us are. Except for maybe you. You're as lovely as ever." He looks at her, considering. "And why might that be, eh?"

Holly waits, looking back at him. When Peter doesn't speak, she prompts him.

"Jack," she says for the umpteenth time. "Where is Jack?"

"I'm getting to that," he says irritably. "Where was I?" He snaps his fingers. "Present day, right? This school seemed to be the trick. There's plenty of young blood, plenty of experiences to dine on. But none of the new formulas I come up with slow the aging anymore. It's accelerating instead. It's Tink, I think. With no more pixie dust, I've been using her blood, and it's no good. She's changed somehow."

Tink flops her arms out wide, as if she's being crucified, and Holly sees that the inner skin is cross-stitched with thousands of little scars that interlace.

"She's sodding useless. Oh, I can still combine a few drops with this and that, give the boys a bit of a buzz when I test it on them. But it does naught for me. If she weren't so stupid, I'd swear she was doing it on purpose," he says glumly.

Holly looks at Tink, but the little woman won't meet her gaze.

"But then you come back to town," Peter continues. "Details start knocking around in the old noggin, and I remember that present company"—he sweeps her an ironic bow—"had a boy child. There's something about the Darlings, always has been. Something that attracted me, drew me to you above all others. Whatever it is, we're linked. My troubles started when you kicked me out. So, if the Darlings had something to do with my aging, they might have something to do with turning it back."

"What do you mean?" Holly's careful to look Peter in the eye so he won't realize how terrified she is.

"Your boy," Peter says, his exasperation plain. "He's the new generation, isn't he? All that fresh Darling enthusiasm. All that young Darling blood. What better kind? After all, if it's good with a stranger's blood, how much better will it be with his? Besides, it's not a matter of want anymore. It's a matter of need. Without a tweak to the formula, without something to boost what I take from Tink, I age. And what's at the end of age? Death. Which, it transpires, is not such an appealing adventure after all."

"Not appealing for you," Holly points out. "You have no qualms about sending other people on it."

Peter grins at her. "Not such a great loss, those boys. They got greedy, all on their own. No discipline."

"Greedy for what you gave them."

He shrugs. "It's not like I put the needle in their arms. I only showed them the possibility. They're the ones who took it too far. Besides, I've been a little too busy to supervise lately. Something new's caught my attention, something I first caught a whiff of at your Cornwall house. Nothing panned out there. The scent went cold. Then, one night a few weeks ago, when we're sniffing around the Darling house, this one perks up."

He kicks Tink again, savagely. She makes no move to avoid the blow, just keeps humming. "She tries to hide it, but I notice. And then what do we see, eh? We see a glimmer, a glow, a bit of a slip of a thing buzzing about our old stomping grounds, the nursery. It visits another bedroom on a lower floor, one where the windows are locked. With your Jack inside. The glimmer causes a terrible kerfuffle. And then it's gone. But where it's been, the air smells . . ." He throws his head back, his tea-stained teeth bared in a smile that's positively crocodilian. "It smells like springtime. Fresh and new. Like the old place. Like Tink and I used to, once upon a time. And we think to ourselves that there's hope after all."

Holly's stomach twists. She sets down her teacup to mask how hard her hands are shaking. It's not just Peter's matter-of-fact cruelty, the way he casually hurts Tinker Bell. It's the idea that he's been this close to Holly, to her family, and she never knew. He's been in her house. In her bedroom.

"Unfortunately, the slip of a thing is gone before we can catch it. But I start to think again of Cornwall, of that vanished scent. Then one night, not long after that first visit, I catch her staring at you while you sleep. She doesn't come in, just peeks through the windows. She's gone in a flash, but I get a better look and she reminds me of someone, someone I couldn't place. My memory's notoriously bad. But then I get it. Finally." He's still speaking, but she can't hear him, not over the rushing in her ears. The room is spinning, she's sliding on the chair, her legs too weak to hold her in place. She imagines herself on the floor, the boards cool and comforting beneath her cheek.

But he's watching her. Like a cat playing with a mouse. Every time she thinks she's escaped, there's the razor-sharp flash of claw. She thinks of Jack, of Eden, and forces her mind back into her body, forces herself to take in air, to let it out, until she can speak.

"What? What do you get?"

"Who our little bit is, of course—and what she can do for me. Young Jack's blood helped some. But this one, she's the best of two worlds—Darling blood and me. Now, she's shy of her proud papa. She won't come. But for you . . ."

"Eden," Holly whispers, the name slipping out before she can stop it. "You want Eden."

"Exactly." He smiles winningly at her. "I like the name, by the way. Good choice. Paradise lost and all that. And I find it has a certain . . . symmetry." He looks away, as if remembering something, then back at her. "She's a canny girl, our Eden. I've been close, once or twice. But she's too quick for me."

He looks over at Tink, who feigns sleep, closing her eyes and breathing heavily.

"I think this one knows where she is," he confides, motioning to Tink. "She's getting a bit uppity lately, not so willing to help out, even after everything I've done for her. Creatures like her, they can have loyalty to only one, but I think Tink's loyalty to me is slipping. She's merely a vessel, you know. She holds emotions, experiences—the overflow, as it were—and I don't think she likes what she's holding lately."

Lightning fast, he reaches over and pinches Tinker Bell's arm. She opens her eyes and squeals. Peter laughs, but Tink stares at Holly, and her look is full of warning. *Tell him nothing.*

Holly tries to parse what's happening. Peter doesn't know that Tink's been in contact with Eden. That much is clear. For the first time, Holly thinks that Tink could truly be an ally. That she's gotten so tired of carrying Peter's malevolence, his greed, that she's switched her allegiance.

But Peter is studying her intently. If he figures out that Tinker Bell knows something, who knows what he'll do—how he'll hurt her to ensure that she tells him.

"If you've been watching, you must know that Eden hasn't chosen to stay with me," she says as calmly as she can. "What makes you think she'll come back? I don't even know where she is."

He flips a hand dismissively. "Mothers and daughters fight, don't they? It's what they do. 'Course she's bound to come back. Isn't that the way the story goes? Children always go back to their mothers. They choose them over Peter every single time. And mothers always choose their children." He pauses, and his voice turns bitter. "'Cept, of course, for mine."

The way he's talking . . . his speech is slowing, a tiny bit slurred, as if he's struggling to find the words. And the cadence is off. Something's wrong, but what? Holly studies him. That strand of gray in his blond locks—she'd swear it wasn't there earlier. And the wrinkles on his face seem more pronounced. She can't be certain, but it's as if he's aging in front of her eyes. She sneaks a glance at Tink for confirmation, but quick as a snake, Peter grabs her wrist.

"Even you. Quite sure I invited you. But you chose the boy." He sneers. "You could have stayed young forever. You could have stayed with me."

The urge to writhe, to pull her arm away, is overpowering. She forces herself to relax her muscles. "You said it yourself, Peter. Mothers always choose their children. Jack was hurt. He almost died. I couldn't leave."

Peter runs his free hand through his hair, tugs at the gray lock. His eyes are huge and wild. For a split second, something akin to pity stirs in Holly. It must be terrifying to feel life slipping away not minute by minute, like most people, but in great gulps of time. And it will be the same for Eden. Unless Holly finds a solution.

Her emotions must show on her face. Behind Peter, Tink shakes her head no, a warning, but it's too late. Peter twists Holly's wrist hard, and she gasps in pain. He grins.

"That's right. Don't go thinking you know what's in my head. Don't you dare feel bad for me. Wouldn't have wanted you anyhow. You're useless. All tosh. Like the others." His eyes are calm again and he lets her go. "Just find the girl. Our Eden."

"And if I do?" She won't give him the satisfaction of seeing her rub her wrist.

"What, no tears? Good. I've seen tears before. They were interesting once, but they bore me now."

"What do you want with her?"

Peter leans back in his chair. "A nice chin-wag over a cuppa. A chance to give her a bit of daddy-daughter advice. What do you think? Just hold her there. I'll know. And I'll come."

"And if I don't?"

He steeples his fingers, gazes at the ceiling. "He's comfortable now, your boy," he says, his voice serious. "He's in that sweet spot between waking and dreaming, the golden place. But it won't last. After a while, the dreams turn to nightmares. And you can't wake up."

There's a noise like a dry rattle as Tinker Bell stands. In the shadows of the room, her golden wing tattoos peek from beneath her halter top, appear to flutter. She leaves the room without a word, but behind Peter's back she gives Holly a long look.

"Where do you think you're going?" Peter calls. "If you're up, the least you can do is fetch me a pint." Tinker Bell doesn't reply. And she doesn't return.

Peter turns back to Holly. "Stupid cow. But it's time for you to go as well. I have things to do. People to see." He smiles, and she knows he means Jack.

"You're telling me to choose, aren't you? To choose between the two of them, Jack and Eden. But Peter, I can't," she says, desperate. She's shaking again, and this time she can't control it. "I won't."

"You have to," he says. He crosses to the door and opens it, then stands there waiting for her to leave. "That's what mothers do. They choose, remember? So choose. Or I will."

Chapter Thirty-Six

The ride home passes in a blur. Somehow Holly finds herself standing in the alley in front of the fence, slipping through the hidden spot. The roses on the other side tug at her clothes, slice her skin, but she doesn't care. She doesn't even notice the thorns.

In the twilight the garden is no longer a flower-covered fairyland. The white topiary form of Wendy is a ghost, fleeing unknown terrors, and Peter's statue leers malevolently. Fear-fueled rage bubbles through Holly. She'd destroy it if she could, but she needs this energy to fight the real Peter. Instead she shoves the statue as hard as she can as she passes it. It sways on its wires, creating dark shadows that reach for the house.

Inside, the warmth and light of the kitchen chase the shadows away. Jane is pacing, a teapot on the table. Her normally perfectly coiffed hair is scooped up in a messy bun, silver strands escaping in all directions. When she sees Holly, her face lights up. "I was beginning to think you might have gone with Jack and Peter and left me behind," she says.

It's the hopefulness, the naivete in Jane's voice, that destroys Holly. It's as if she's come back from a different world. She can't speak any of the terrible words burning under her tongue. Instead she pushes past her mother to the library, where she checks to make sure the windows are firmly shut behind the drawn curtains, then pours herself a healthy slug of whiskey, neat, to douse her internal flames. She drains her drink in silence as Jane trails into the room, the relief on her face changing to concern.

"You're bleeding! Whatever happened? I called you a half dozen times, but you never picked up. I assumed after we spoke this morning that you'd found Peter and Jack. Where is he?"

Holly looks down at herself. Scratches from the thorns mar her arms, and tiny beads of blood glisten along her skin. The abandoned council house from this morning feels years ago, not hours. She ignores Jane's question and refills her glass.

Jane frowns, gives a careful sideways glance, as if Holly is a wild animal she's gotten too close to, as if she's worried about the damage Holly will cause when she bolts.

"Do tell me what happened," she says again.

Holly wants to smash Jane's eagerness the same way she wants to smash the statue, wants to destroy it to make herself feel better. She reaches into her pocket, pulls out the photograph of Jack asleep, and tosses it onto the table in front of her mother.

"Maybe you should look at this first. That's your grandson," she says savagely. "Take a good long look because it may be the last photo of him you ever see."

Jane picks the picture up. "I don't understand," she says, turning it this way and that. "Why do you have a photo of Jack asleep?"

"Why don't you ask Peter?" Holly spits. "Since he's the one holding Jack hostage."

"Nonsense," Jane scoffs, but her voice lacks its normal conviction. "Why would Peter hurt Jack?"

"He still wants Eden. He's figured out she's our child. But now he's using Jack as bait. We should have seen this coming—I should have seen it," Holly corrects. "Because I knew what he was all along."

"There must be some mistake," Jane repeats. Her hand holding the photo trembles.

"The only mistake was not telling you the truth from the beginning." The whiskey is burning through Holly, making her light-headed. The anger that fueled her is deserting her, taking her strength with it. She's exhausted and weak and suddenly unable to stand. She sinks onto the couch, almost dropping the whiskey glass, and closes her eyes. She can't bear to look at her mother. But after all these years, after being this close to Peter again, she can't hold what's inside of her a moment longer.

"He raped me, that last night. He held me down and . . ." She can't finish. "He threatened to kill Jack if I wouldn't go with him."

She waits, curled into herself. The clock on the mantel ticks, the only sound. Seconds pass, minutes, an eternity. When Holly can't endure it anymore, she opens her eyes. She still can't bring herself to look at Jane, so she trains her gaze on the floor, on her mother's feet, encased in rose silk slippers and still as stones.

Finally Holly risks a glance upward. Jane is staring at her. But her face isn't angry or challenging. It's stricken.

"All those years . . . Why didn't you tell me?"

"Would you have believed me?" Holly asks, a flicker of anger still alight. "You spent years waiting for him, years building a monument to him in the backyard. My word against that, against a century of family legend? It didn't seem like the best bet. I did tell you he was dangerous."

"Dangerous is one thing," Jane says. "Dangerous can be appealing. What you describe—what he did to you—is a completely different matter."

"Would you have? Believed me?" The words spill out before she can bite them back. She doesn't ask if Jane believes her now.

But she doesn't have to. Her mother is already at her side, tucking a finger under Holly's chin and raising it up so their eyes meet.

"Listen to me," Jane says, and her look is unflinching. "You're my daughter. Of course I would have believed you then. It goes without saying I believe you now."

Something very hard and sharp shatters in Holly, puncturing the soft places it once protected. Tears prickle behind her lashes. She wants to curl up in her mother's arms, wants to place her head in Jane's lap and cry. But she can't. If she starts crying, she may never stop. And time is a luxury they do not have.

Instead she lets Jane wrap an arm around her shoulder, and they sit together in front of the fireplace. Above the mantel, Wendy's portrait gazes down at them, as mysterious, as secretive as ever.

Jane gazes back. "One thing I don't understand," she says slowly. "I believe you, of course, but why wouldn't my mother have warned us? Perhaps she didn't see that side of him? Perhaps he wasn't always evil."

Holly shakes her head. "I think she blamed herself." At Jane's questioning look, she realizes all that her mother still doesn't know. "Peter told me that he caused Great-Uncle Michael's fall."

"Surely not," Jane protests.

"It's true," Holly says. "Grandma Wendy was going away with him and Michael didn't want her to leave. He was clinging to her skirts and Peter cut him loose. That's why he fell."

Jane's face is white. "But why would she lie to me—to everyone—for so many years? Why not tell the truth?"

"You told me yourself how Barrie's story changed her life. The money and the fame, they made her independent. Maybe, in her own way, she was trying to protect you. Give you the same things," Holly offers.

Jane gives a short, bitter laugh. "Perhaps. But that wasn't Mother's style. More likely she was afraid the true story would get out and she'd be blamed, despised by all her wealthy friends. Either way, it explains quite a bit regarding her terror of the press."

For the first time, Holly sees Jane not as her own glamorous, sophisticated mother, but as she must have been years ago. A lonely, neglected child, jealous of the uncle who required so much attention, needy for the notice of the beautiful, always preoccupied Wendy. No wonder she'd been so hungry for the romantic stories Wendy spun.

"She probably did the best she could," Holly says, and she means it. After all, according to Peter, Wendy had had her problems too. Problems large enough that Peter and his home seemed like paradise in comparison.

"Perhaps," Jane murmurs again. And then her posture becomes even more ramrod straight. She withdraws her arm from Holly's shoulder and turns to face her. It's as if, at last, she's let the stories go. As if she's seeing the real world for the first time.

"I've been foolish," she says. "So very, very foolish. That's not an excuse. It's an apology. What can I do to make it right?"

Holly wants her mother's arm back around her shoulder, wants to lean into her warmth. Instead she shakes her head. "I don't know how anyone can help."

"I still want to hear everything. Every last detail about Peter," Jane says. She smiles grimly at Holly's surprised expression. "No, darling, not for the old reasons. There's nothing Peter could do or say now that would entice me to spend a second in his company."

She gets up from the couch and pours herself a small drink. Then she turns back to Holly. "But of all the people in the world, I may still be the one who knows the most about him. I've certainly studied him enough. I want every detail of what you saw so I can help you take the bastard down, as they say. Which reminds me." She glances at the window. "That man—Christopher—was on his motorbike in front of the house all afternoon. He's called as well. I didn't answer. I assume you gave him the slip out the back garden for a reason?"

At Holly's expression Jane arches an eyebrow. "You underestimate me. I learned long ago that if you wish to keep your loved ones close, you need to let them leave."

Holly doesn't know what to say to this. Instead she pulls out her phone. Six missed calls from Jane and three from Christopher. She crosses to the window and peers around the heavy curtain.

"Wherever he is, he's not there now," Jane says, joining her. "Why not enlist his aid?"

Holly tells her about the message on Jack's phone. How Peter has moved him somewhere else, and what will happen if Holly tells Christopher or the police. She tries to keep her voice from trembling, but fails.

"Could Peter be reasoned with? Bribed somehow?" Jane asks, leading Holly back to the couch.

"Maybe once. Not anymore. Something's happened to him. He looks like a man, but . . ." Holly hesitates, trying to find the right words. "It's as if he's a three-year-old, a giant toddler bashing about. And his memory is going, even worse than the stories. He may be more ancient than we can guess. He's terrified and angry and desperate enough, I think, to do anything."

"And what he really wants is Eden?"

"What he really wants is Eden's blood. I don't think he cares much how he gets it."

"Did you offer him . . ." Jane hesitates.

"I only have the one vial. It would transform him for a time, certainly, but it's not enough to last," Holly says. "Still, I thought of it. But if Jack is hurt or sick, it could mean the difference between life and death."

"What about the cream?"

"He knew all about my 'potions and lotions,' as he called them," Holly says grimly. "Apparently he's been making his own concoction for years, mixing the blood of teenage boys with Tink's own pixie dust. In Jack, the serum repairs damage from the crash. Peter's using it to repair deterioration at the cellular level—to make himself younger. But it's failing now, and I don't see how my formula would be any different. For a full transformation, he needs Eden's blood itself. And given the dreadful shape he's in, lots of it."

"If you did find something that would work, would he leave then? Go back to where he came from? Could we be rid of him that way?"

"No," Holly says. "That's the astonishing thing." She tells Jane what Peter said about *others*, about his desire to stay in this world. She tells her too about Peter's words to Barrie before he died. Her mother listens intently.

"So he wants youth," she says at last. "And beauty. But what does he intend to do with it?"

"More of the same, I imagine. I could pity him, under different circumstances. He has no one, he can't go home, and even Tinker Bell isn't loyal to him anymore." She's forgotten that Jane doesn't know about her meeting with Eden. She fills her in as succinctly as possible.

"That *is* interesting," Jane says thoughtfully. "And poor, poor Eden. But where does it leave us?"

"I don't know."

"Well, there's not much else you can do tonight," Jane says. She glances toward the windows. The wind has picked up, an unexpected storm blowing through. Shadows move and shift along the walls. Holly shivers.

"We don't have much time," she protests.

"No, we don't. But we have a little. And you can't keep going like this. You need food. And sleep." Jane takes the crystal glass from where Holly has left it. "And tea."

Holly tries to remember the last time she ate. She can't, and she knows Jane is right. "Food then," she acquiesces.

"I'll make some toast," Jane says.

At the library door she turns back. "Also, those cuts . . . you need to care for them so they don't become infected. What about your ointment? Tell me where it is and I'll fetch it."

Holly shakes her head. "I have it in my bag. But it's too precious. I brought it with me today in case it could help Jack. That and the one vial of blood are all I have left."

"Better save it then," Jane says. "I'll be back with the iodine."

Alone, Holly leans back into the cushions. She's so tired. She closes her eyes, just for a moment, just until Jane returns.

And then there's a pounding at the door.

Chapter Thirty-Seven

Jane and Holly reach the front entrance at the same time. Jane, normally the epitome of grace, fumbles with the lock. Holly stops her before she can throw open the door.

"Wait," she whispers urgently. She stands on tiptoe and peers through the peephole.

It's not Peter on the other side but the last person she would have imagined. Holly nods to her mother to pull back the door.

Standing on the front steps, wild-eyed and windblown, is Nan.

Beside Holly, Jane gives a little gasp. "Goodness, Nan, what is it?"

"Ed's missing," Nan blurts before she's even inside. "He's been missing all week. At first I thought he and his dad were off on a tear somewhere, but that's not Ed. I've been looking everywhere for him. Just now I got a text from his phone, telling me to ask you where he was. So where is he?"

Holly gives Jane a look that says, *Let me handle this.* "I don't know," she tells Nan truthfully. "But Jack is missing as well." The two women stare at each other.

"What else did the text say?"

"Nothing else. Just to ask you where he was."

"Have you tried calling him? Or tracking him using the GPS on his phone?"

"I'm not stupid. It spins, like the phone is off."

What would Peter want with Ed? Nothing Holly can think of. At least nothing good.

"When was the last time you saw him?"

"Five days ago, before lacrosse practice. He told me he might stay with his dad after. Every now and then his dad takes an interest in Ed, enough to have him over, and I guess this was one of those times. But Ed always lets me know when he'll be back. And he's never stayed away this long."

"Have you been to the police?"

"No. Not yet. Ed's dad—he wouldn't like it."

"Why not?"

"He's had some run-ins with the law. Most of them were drug related, but he always manages to charm his way out of them. And he can be . . . unpredictable. Lots of fun sometimes, you know? When he's in the mood, when he wants to be loved, he gives Ed loads of cash or the newest stuff. But when he's not . . ." She trails off. "Ed usually knows to get out of the way. But he'd never not call. He doesn't like me to worry."

"Five days," Jane says quietly to Holly. "That's when Jack disappeared too."

Alarm bells are going off in Holly's head, a terrible suspicion growing.

"His name." The whisper threads past the blockage in Holly's throat, the one that's choking her. "What's his name?"

"Ed's dad? Why would that matter?" Nan says. But one look at Holly's face and she answers. "Peter. His name is Peter."

Chapter Thirty-Eight

Dimly, as if from a long way away, Holly can hear Jane's voice, but it's as if all the air has been sucked from the room, as if she's being held underwater. Holly can see her mother's mouth moving but can't understand the words. She's sitting on the floor, her legs finally having given way.

Jane disappears from sight. Nan is still there, looking at her worriedly, her mouth open and shutting as if she's talking. But Holly can't hear her, either, only the buzzing in her head.

Jane reappears at her side. There's something in her hand. She twists it, then waves it under Holly's nose. Holly gasps and the world comes rushing back in.

"Smelling salts," Jane says. "You're in shock. Here, drink this." She holds a glass to Holly's lips. Holly obediently sips. The liquid is warm and sweet. Tea with honey.

"Better?" Jane asks.

Holly nods. Struggles to stand up, but Jane puts a hand on her shoulder and holds her down. "Sit for a moment."

Nan stares at them. "I don't understand," she says uncertainly. "Do you know Ed's father?"

Jane nods grimly. "After a fashion."

"All this time," Holly whispers. "He's had someone at the house all this time."

Jane waves her off. "That doesn't matter now. Nor does the fact that he could have a veritable army of offspring. The real question is, what do we do next?"

"What can we do? He has all the cards. He has everything except Eden."

"We can't do this alone. Not now." Jane glances at Nan. "Holly, I think you should call Christopher. Meet with him. See if he can help."

"I don't understand," Nan says again.

Jane eyes her. "None of us do, my dear. But that doesn't mean it isn't happening."

Holly calls from the office, on her cell phone, as far away from the window as possible.

"I need your help," she says as soon as he picks up. "I need to see you, but not at the house."

"Why now, after you gave me the slip this morning? What's happened?" His voice isn't friendly.

She takes a breath. "I can't talk, but I promise I'll tell you everything if you'll meet me. Someplace private."

He's silent a long moment. "There's a restaurant on High Street," he says at last. "The owner's a friend of mine. He has a bar in the cellar. I'll be at the table farthest from the door." He gives her the address and hangs up.

Jane wants her to call a ride, doesn't want her to drive, but Holly can't bear the thought of getting in a car with a stranger, not after finding out about Ed. Anyone could belong to Peter now. She leaves Nan and her mother at the kitchen table, deep in discussion.

The drive there is an eternity. Every decision she's made has felt like the wrong one, and enlisting Christopher's aid now is no different. It's like walking down a dark corridor, knowing that every step is taking her closer to disaster, but no more able to stop than a moth can avoid the flame. She'll be burned. She may not survive. But she keeps walking anyhow.

The bar is ancient, the walls covered with newspaper clippings from a different era, the ceiling dark with smoke. There are steps at the back that lead to the basement, an underground grotto with an arched roof and thick stone walls. It's like a tomb. She places her hand against the wall for support as she descends. The stone is cool to the touch, and vibrating. Surprised, she draws her hand back. The vibrations get stronger, louder, until the walls are shaking. The Tube must be passing by.

Christopher's in the back as promised, watching for her. Holly doesn't believe in auras, but she'd swear there was a pool of energy surrounding him, radiating from his body. The tables on either side of him are vacant, other customers kept at bay by the fire he emits.

He nods but doesn't stand when she reaches him. As she sits she can see why he chose this location—there's only one entrance, and no one can come in or out without being seen.

Thanks to the candles in the wall sconces, not even a shadow.

There's a whiskey in front of her, a mug of something steaming in his left hand, which is covered by a leather glove. His right hand is out of sight under the table.

"Not drinking?" she says, nodding at the mug. She doesn't touch the glass.

He shakes his head, his eyes dark and watchful. "I'm working."

There's no time for niceties. She plunges in. "When we spoke before, I didn't tell you everything," she says.

"Surprise, surprise." He cocks an eyebrow. "And now?"

"Now I will."

This time, she tells him who Peter really is. She explains about magic. And Neverland. About Grandma Wendy and Great-Uncle Michael. About Eden. She leaves nothing out. She doesn't spare herself.

"What do you want me to do?" he says when she's finished.

"You believe me?"

He looks at her thoughtfully. "I believe you believe this. I also believe you are in way over your head and it's liable to get much worse if you don't get help."

Holly exhales with relief. A start, at least.

"One thing doesn't make sense. If this story of yours is true, Ed should be growing the same way as your daughter, right? Faster than normal. But nobody's mentioned that to me."

Ed *is* taller than normal, true, but not abnormally so. He's handsome and flush with vitality, but so are many teenage boys.

"Maybe Peter was right," she says slowly. "Maybe it *is* us." At Christopher's blank look, she elaborates. "The Darlings. Maybe there's something in *our* blood." She pictures Wendy of the portrait, then her mother. The glowing health, the seductive smiles, the extended life spans.

"Ed doesn't have that. He isn't a Darling like Eden, so he isn't affected the same way."

"Interesting theory," Christopher says. His matter-of-factness surprises her, makes her take the last step.

"There's something else."

"Why am I not surprised?" he says dryly.

She ignores this. Her hands are in her lap, and she's squeezing them together so tightly the tips must be white. "Peter said something . . . it made me think of you. Not you, exactly, but . . ." She's stammering; she can't find the right words. "He said that Neverland is a shadow place, like a . . . a threshold between worlds. And he said . . . he implied . . . that Captain Hook fought to stop him from bringing people in. From hurting them. And I thought . . . I mean, with your arm and what you do . . ."

"That I must be some long-dead foe of Peter's, returned to vanquish him," he says, deadpan. "Only, of course, better-looking."

At her look, he shakes his head. "You think I haven't noticed the coincidences? Or that I'm too sophisticated to consider them? I've lived enough to know that there's more out there than most people think," he says. "And I'm smart enough to keep an open mind. But who you think I am, or may have been, is a topic we can debate later. Right now we don't have much time. Not if you want to save those kids. Where is Peter now?"

She gives Christopher the address of the cottage.

"What can you do?"

It must be her imagination, but the pool of menace around him grows, expands, until it almost reaches her. Instinctively she leans away. When she looks up, Christopher's smile is gleaming and white and treacherous.

"I'm a man of many talents," he says. "That's all you need to know."

He walks her to her car, stays until she's inside. It's started to rain. Puddles shimmer on the ground, reflecting light and images. Holly locks the car doors and starts the engine. Then, on impulse, she rolls down the window and calls to him.

"Please be careful." There's so much that could go wrong. For Jack, for Eden, for Ed, even for Christopher himself. "You have no idea what he's capable of."

There's a flash of silver by his side, magnified in the water on the ground. Christopher has uncovered his hook. "Don't worry," he says over his shoulder as he strolls into the night. "That's exactly what they say about me."

Chapter Thirty-Nine

At home, Nan and Jane are still at the kitchen table, a pot of tea between them. Jane stands when Holly walks in, relief flooding across her face.

"He listened and he'll help," Holly says, sinking into a chair. She has no desire to share details about Christopher or anything else in front of Nan.

Jane reads her expression. "Why don't you go into the library and rest for a bit," she tells Nan. When the housekeeper hesitates, Jane says firmly, "We'll join you in a moment."

She waits until Nan has left. "I've told her the bare details—that he's someone who was once in our lives and now wishes us harm. She had no idea he was tied to us at all. And no idea who he really is. Her mother had a brief relationship with him and broke it off when she became pregnant with Ed. Apparently he could be quite charming but had"—Jane hesitates—"violent tendencies."

Holly notices Jane shares her reticence to say Peter's name, as if it could call him here. "What do you think she's told him about us?"

Jane shakes her head. "Nothing intentionally. She doesn't care for him at all. But he's been very, very sly. He told Ed I needed a new housekeeper and that Nan should apply. How on earth could he have known that?"

"He's been watching this house the entire time," Holly says. "Even longer than we thought."

Jane shudders. "Do you really think Christopher can help?"

"He's going to the cottage."

"Is that wise?" Jane raises her eyebrows.

Holly recalls Christopher walking into the night, that flash of silver. It gives her courage.

"Maybe not for Peter," she says.

All they can do is wait. Jane toasts crumpets, spreads them with butter and jam, brews another pot of tea. Then, having taxed her culinary abilities to their limit, she sets a tray and carries it into the library, insisting that Holly come and speak with Nan.

"It's not Nan's fault," she says. "Anyone can see she's worried sick as well. She's had sole responsibility for that boy for years—she'd never knowingly endanger him. Or Jack. Besides, you both need to eat."

"I didn't know," Nan says as soon as Holly enters the library. Her face is so tight and pale that Holly immediately dismisses her suspicions. "I swear, I didn't realize he was somebody who wanted to hurt you. But I don't understand why he'd want the boys. He can barely stand to have Ed around most of the time."

There's nothing Holly can say about Peter's intentions that will be reassuring, nothing that will take away the fact that Ed's life is in danger. Instead she stretches out a hand and places it atop Nan's. "It's not your fault. Peter is very adept at using those around him to get what he wants. But I have a . . . a friend. He's very good at finding people. He's looking for them now. If anyone can help, he can."

Maybe it's the warm food and tea, but she believes her own words. Surely if anyone is a match for Peter, it's Christopher.

So when her phone rings and it's Christopher's number, a wave of optimism surges through her.

It's short-lived.

"Are you home?" he asks, his voice grim.

"Yes. Did you find them?"

He hesitates. "I need to talk to you. In person. I'm already on my way."

Jane takes one look at her face and crosses to her side. "It's bad," Holly says, her voice so low she has to repeat herself. "He's coming here."

Beside her, Nan clutches her hand. "What did he say?"

"Nothing," Holly finally manages. "He's on his way."

When the doorbell rings, Jane collects herself first and hurries to answer it. Holly tries to follow, but her heart is pounding and her legs have gone boneless again and all she can think is, *Please, please, please.* She leans against the library wall for support.

And then he's in the room, and she looks at his face, and her voice deserts her. It's Nan who speaks.

"Tell us," she demands, her voice high-pitched. "Did you find them? Please, tell us."

Christopher shakes his head. "I'm sorry," he says simply. "I went back to the school. To the caretaker's cottage. There was a body in the back bedroom. A boy. It wasn't Jack." He turns to Nan. "He has pale skin, curly hair. Facial features similar to yours. I think it was your brother."

Nan lets out a wail and falls to the floor. Holly wants to comfort her, but she can't move, can't breathe. "I took a picture," Christopher says, holding out his phone. "Is it him?"

Holly doesn't want to look, but she can't look away, either. It's a photo of a handsome boy, dressed in a gray sweatshirt. In the picture, it looks as if he's smiling. He's curled on the bed. He could be asleep.

It's unmistakably Ed. And a small red feather has drifted onto his cheek.

Chapter Forty

Help me get her into a guest room," Jane instructs Christopher. He scoops Nan up easily, and they move toward the staircase. Holly wants to follow, but her legs still aren't cooperating. It's not relief or terror or even a combination of those two feelings that keeps her locked in place. It's guilt.

This is her fault. Hers, and no one else's. If she'd told Christopher the truth right from the start, if she'd gone to the police, if she'd done something—done anything—Ed might be alive right now. She can't fathom the world without him, without the space he takes up in it. The brown eyes and the long legs and the laugh and energy—all of those things that say Ed, that hold an Ed-shape in this universe—gone. Leaving a hole that for the rest of her life Nan will have to try not to fall into.

She staggers into the hall. She can hear Nan's sobs, then her mother's voice overhead. "Here," Jane's saying soothingly. "Let me help you." But there is no help. Holly knows that, even if Nan has not yet discovered it. She will.

And then Christopher is coming down the staircase, walking down the hallway toward her. Graceful and sleek and dangerous. *Oh, panther,* she thinks irrationally. *How very, very sharp your teeth are.*

He leads her back into the library, shuts the door. "I'll keep searching," he says. "He has to have held the boys somewhere close. You said he let you look through the house?"

Holly nods. "No one else was there. I'm certain."

"Do you know if Ed used drugs? The kid's arms were a mess. Covered in bandages and track marks."

Holly thinks of Ed's clear gaze, his beautiful skin. The health he radiated on and off the field. "No," she says. "Not a chance."

"Then somebody was using him. Like some kind of science experiment." He hesitates.

"What?"

"I have to report this," he says. "There could be consequences for you, for your family."

"Consequences?" Holly says bitterly. "There's a woman upstairs who lost her brother, a boy she loved so much he was like a son. She'll never see him again. Those are *consequences*. If I'd come to you earlier, or if I'd gone to the police, he might still be alive."

"You don't know that. Peter might have panicked, killed him sooner." He lowers his voice. "He might have killed Jack too. At least right now there's still hope."

"Hope?" she says dully. "What's that?"

"It's what carries us." He nudges her side with his hook, and she realizes she's forgotten about it. It's become normal to her. And then she stops thinking about what that means, thinking about anything, because he's leaning forward. He kisses her, a quick, gentle kiss that breaks through the fog and pain around her like an electric shock. That drags her back into this world.

"I'm not saying it will be okay," he says, pulling back. "I'm saying you'll get through it."

And then he's gone, before she can ask him what the hell he was doing.

Or ask him to do it again.

✳

When Jane comes downstairs, she looks exhausted, every bit of her seven decades, as if she's aged twenty years in this one day.

"She's sleeping," she tells Holly, crossing to the decanter and pouring herself a drink. "I put her in the room next to mine and gave her two sleeping pills."

"You can't hand out those pills like candy," Holly protests.

Jane sniffs. "The child has no family, nowhere to go. Sleep is the best thing for her, and she won't get that on her own." She takes a long look at Holly. "How are you?"

Holly shakes her head. "Numb."

"It's not your fault," Jane says in a gentler tone. "Wendy, myself, you . . . we all did the best we could."

"Right," Holly says. She can't talk about this. She leaves the library and climbs the stairs, stopping outside Nan's room to listen for her breathing before continuing on.

In the nursery, she sits on the bed and looks at the sky, searching for the evening star through the clouds. She thinks of Ed, how he'll never grow up, never get married, never dance at his sister's wedding or give her away. She thinks of all those other boys, the ones Christopher told her about, pictures their gray faces in a twilight room somewhere, sleeping away their youth. Or scurrying down dark alleys, willing to trade everything for one more taste of Peter's drug.

She thinks of Jack. Of that night in the nursery so long ago, when he was in the hospital. Her despair now is a perfect echo. What else, really, does she have to lose? Nothing. Except herself.

And then she thinks of Peter. Of the boy he once was. What was he searching for, that first night he came to the Darling window? What would a boy, tired and lost, facing dangers she can't even imagine, be looking for? Safety. Security. A haven. Somewhere he could get help.

Whatever he found in the nursery room that night, whatever happened between Wendy and her father, it wasn't that.

Slowly, as if she's in a trance, she takes off her clothes. Slips into the white, lavender-scented nightgown. Plaits her hair. Lights a candle. Pulls down the bedsheets and fluffs the pillows. Makes the room as warm and inviting as she can. The type of room a lost child would be drawn to.

And then she opens the window.

It doesn't happen for a long time. Her skin senses the change in the air patterns before her mind does. The hair on the nape of her neck prickles as the candle flickers. She can't bear to turn around, keeps her face turned toward the wall, but she knows he's there. She bows her head and stares at the floor.

"You win," she whispers. "I choose you."

And then someone sits on the bed beside her. Someone leans their head against her shoulder. Someone who smells of springtime and cut grass, of fresh air, who carries the scent of an effervescent joy that is impossible to explain.

"Eden?" She can't believe it. But it's true.

"I don't have much time," Eden says softly. "Bell is keeping watch for me. But I can save him. I can save Jack." She lifts her head up, and Holly can no longer pretend she's a child.

"Tell me where he is," Holly pleads.

"Jack was searching for me. Ed told him his father knew lots of people, that he worked with kids, that he had connections with runaways. He offered to help. So they went to Peter," she says, her voice shaky. Holly pulls her closer, strokes her hair. "And Peter tricked them. He trapped them. He used them for their blood. He used them as bait for me." Her blue eyes fill with tears. "It's all my fault."

"It's not. I promise," Holly says firmly. "But you have to tell me where Jack is now."

"Inside Big Ben," she says. "There's an old apartment there, a room for the guards. Bell showed me. She's been flying me there, through an opening behind the clock face. But Peter made Bell tell him, and he's there now, with Jack." She looks away. "I heard you calling that day."

Holly's sick. If she'd found a way into the tower—if she hadn't lost Jack's trust . . . But guilt and what-ifs won't help Eden now. Or Jack.

She gives Eden one last squeeze, then stands up.

"I'm calling the police."

"No! You can't," Eden says, tugging her back down. "He'll hear them coming. He'll kill Jack before they even get to the top of the stairs. I have a plan. I can get him out."

"No," Holly says. "Absolutely not. If anyone's going, it's me." She thinks for a moment. "Would Tink take me? Could we trust her not to tell Peter?"

"Don't call her that," Eden says sharply. "That's his name for her, and she doesn't belong to him anymore. She's Bell now, and she's with me."

"Then you need to take me there. You and Bell. Call for help, and then disappear." She has Christopher's number programmed on her phone, and she hands it to Eden now. "Do you understand?"

Eden shakes her head. "Peter doesn't want you. He wants me. And if he catches you, he'll use you as bait, the same as he did to Jack."

"Maybe," Holly agrees. "But I'm still going. Not you."

They argue in whispers, heads together, so intent on saving each other they never notice the door opening. Not until Jane's gasp.

"Eden. My goodness. Is it really you?"

She takes Eden's face in her hands, stoops to kiss her forehead. "Oh, my dear girl," she says. "My lovely, lovely girl. You've turned into such a beautiful woman."

"She's thirteen," Holly reminds her mother. "A baby." Rapidly she

314

explains her plan to Jane. She's counting on her mother's support to keep Eden here and safe.

"Can't we call Christopher? Tell him where Jack is?"

Eden shakes her head. "The only way to get in, to do it without being seen, is through the window. Someone has to fly."

"Well then," Jane says. She turns to Eden. "What do you suggest, my child?"

Chapter Forty-One

Y ou can't be serious," Holly says. "There's no way I'm letting her go."
"I don't think you have a choice. You can't make her take you, after all," Jane points out. "And from what she's said, calling in Christopher before you have Jack in hand may make the situation worse. At least hear her out."

Eden's plan is simple. She'll fly with Bell to where Jack is. They'll watch until it's safe to bring him back to the Darling house and deposit him with Holly, calling Christopher to handle Peter once they're clear.

"I can save him," Eden insists. "I'm the only one who can do it."

There are so many things that can go wrong with this plan, so many ways Eden can get hurt. Holly starts to argue, to push back. But then she sees the look on her daughter's face and it crushes her. It's not the look of a thirteen-year-old arguing with her mother. It's an adult face, wise beyond its years, weary beyond all words but still fighting for what is right.

Holly takes a deep breath. But Eden isn't done.

"Bell has a way to save me too. She can guide me to Neverland if we can get away from Peter. She thinks that once I'm there, the aging will stop."

"Neverland isn't what you think," Holly says, alarmed. She recalls

Peter's words, about the *others* waiting there, and shudders. A young, feral army of his own making.

"I know. Bell's told me. But what choice do I have? If I stay here, there's no chance at all. Bell agreed to take me with her, but she can't make it that far on her own. Not yet. She's still sick from him, from what he made her carry. So, I need something from you."

"Anything." Holly will give her daughter the moon and the sky, she'll wrap it in a ribbon cut from her own heart if that's what it takes to save her, but what Eden wants isn't nearly so easy.

"What do you need?" Jane asks.

"A picture," Eden says. "One of only me. A talisman that will remind me of a happy memory strong enough to guide me home. Not home to London or to Cornwall, but to where Bell says I *really* belong. Neverland."

"And what's in this for her?" Holly says, wounded.

"She wants to go home too," Eden says. "She's been here too long, and she doesn't like it anymore. And she doesn't like Peter. She doesn't trust him. She trusts me. If there's two of us, working together, she thinks we can tame Neverland again, the way Hook did." She looks at Holly with those bright blue eyes. "He was always the one, the guardian all along. But you know that now, don't you?"

Holly nods. "What happened to him?" she whispers.

"Bell says he sank beneath the waves and disappeared. But no one in Neverland ever really dies, not really. They just turn up in a different place, she says."

Holly thinks of Peter's words. *Shadows and shades.* The Christopher she's kissed fits neither of those descriptions. He's as real and solid as can be. But then, so is Peter.

"Mama?" Eden says. "Did you hear me?"

Her daughter is standing in front of her, patiently waiting, a miracle all its own, right here and now. Holly reaches out and clasps her hand.

"I said if we do that, if we can keep control, there's a chance I could come back. To visit. But I need a picture."

A chance to keep her safe. And see her again. Holly leaps at it.

"The one by Jack's bed?" she suggests.

Eden shakes her head. "Jack is in that. Even his happiest memories have pain in them."

"Pain?"

"Not just physical pain," Eden says. "Deeper. There's a piece of him missing. Just because you ignore something doesn't make it disappear."

Isaac, Holly realizes. To have a second self and then lose him must be a little like losing your shadow. And maybe that half-memory, that yearning, is why Jack pushes boundaries, takes risks. When part of you is dead, the other part might do anything to feel alive.

"Perhaps one with the two of you?" Jane suggests, drawing Holly back. Holly racks her brain, but she knows how unlikely it is. To find a memory of Eden—let alone a photo—that involves sheer joy is a herculean task. Even Holly's best memories are tinged with shadows: guilt over sleeping with Peter, worry over Jack. Any moments she spent alone with Eden likely came because Jack was in hospital, recovering from yet another surgery. No matter where Holly was or what she did, it was never the right place or the right thing. She was always wishing she were somewhere else.

"Well," Holly begins. And then she remembers there is one picture. A talisman of her own. "Maybe."

There's a low buzzing outside the window.

"Bell says we need to go soon," Eden says urgently. "There's not much time."

Jane steps forward. "You get the photo. You'll need the vial and the cream, yes, in case Jack is injured? Give me the passcode to the safe—I can get those for you."

Holly tells her the code to the locked refrigerated safe in the office, reminds her the cream is in her bag, then hurries to the storage closet.

She slides her fingers through the lining of her suitcase and pulls out the picture of her daughter.

"Here," she says, once she's in front of Eden again. In her hand is the photo she's kept all these years. It's faded and creased, but in the center, sitting on a low tree branch, is Eden. Her face is a soft blur, because she's in motion, the way she always was, but there's no one else it could be. Even with the distortion, anyone can see that her expression is one of pure glee.

"You were two," Holly says. "We were in Cornwall. Jack was sleeping on a blanket in the sun. It was a good day. I'd turned around for a moment, and when I turned back, you were sitting in the tree. I don't know how you got up there, but you were so proud of yourself. You made your own joy. You made mine as well."

"I remember," Eden says, staring at the photo. "Why did I never remember before?"

"Sometimes it's easier to remember sorrow than joy," Holly says. "Sorrow doesn't hurt as much." A lifetime of memories still just beyond her reach, walled off for more than a decade and with enough power now to overwhelm her: Robert's large, gentle hands on the steering wheel. The twins shrieking with laughter in the back seat, the windows down. Eden smiling at her from a low tree branch, the hem of her blue dress dancing in the breeze.

These memories prick at Holly, they pierce her, but the pain they cause is nothing compared to the ache of looking at her daughter. It's almost unbearable, knowing that she has so little time left, just enough to make one more memory. So she makes it the best possible memory she can. She reaches out in an embrace. And when Eden hugs her back, she realizes that her heart, frozen all these years, still has life in it after all. She knows because it is breaking.

Chapter Forty-Two

They stand that way for a long time, only releasing each other when Jane returns. She's holding a tray with three crystal glasses.

"This will only take a moment," she says in response to Holly's look. "And you both must have some. It's a special vintage I've been saving. We may not be together again for a long time, and I've some things I must say."

Holly knows her mother, knows how implacable she can be. There will be no leaving until the drink is gone. So when Jane hands her a glass, she accepts. It's whiskey, neat. Holly looks at Eden and shrugs. Now, with all that they are facing, does not seem to be the time to worry about underage drinking.

Jane raises her own glass high, and Holly and Eden follow suit.

"To the Darling women. The stars are not only above us, they are in us. May we shine brightly, dream deeply, and fly high all on our own. I am terribly proud to know you both, my darlings," she says. "Now drink up."

She tilts her glass and drains it, motioning for them to do the same. The clear liquid is bitter in a way that most of Jane's vintages are not and burns Holly's throat. Eden coughs.

"The vial!" Jane says. "My goodness, I left it in the library."

Holly steps toward the door, but Jane shoos her away. "No, no. Take this moment. I'll be right back." She hurries away.

Now that it's almost time, Holly can't bear to let her daughter go. Even for Jack. She wraps her arms around Eden again and holds her tight.

"I can't let you do this," she whispers. "I thought I could, but I can't." The thought of losing Eden makes her dizzy, makes her weak at the knees.

"There's no time," Eden says. "You have to trust me."

"I do. I do. But . . ." Holly's having trouble finding the words for what she wants to say.

"You're wrong, Eden dear. There's all the time. For you and your mother both."

It's Jane, at the door. Holly blinks and blinks again. Jane looks . . . She can't describe it. Different somehow. Golden. Holly rubs her eyes. Why is her vision blurry?

"Are you feeling well? You both look a bit peaked. Come here. Sit for a moment," Jane says, patting the beds.

It's true. The weakness in Holly's legs has increased. Her tongue is numb. She staggers to the nearest bed, reaches out a hand for Eden, who collapses next to her.

"Mother?" Holly whispers. There's something happening to Jane's face. As Holly watches, it morphs, changes. Time runs backward. Wrinkles smooth and disappear. Age spots vanish. Jane's face swims in and out of Holly's vision until she's not certain if she's looking at her mother or her daughter.

"What did you do?"

"I'm sorry, my darling. What I had to. Or did you think you were the only parent willing to risk everything for her child?"

Only then does Holly see the empty syringe clutched in Jane's hand.

"Sleep," Jane/not Jane says. "Just sleep."

Fatigue is pulling at Holly like a tide, dragging her down no matter how hard she fights. Jane pulls the sheet up, presses cool lips against Holly's cheek. She kisses Eden too. Then she leaps onto the window seat with cat-like grace. At the edge, she pauses.

"I never told you," she says conversationally. "But I did see him. Peter. Only the once. He came to the window when you were a baby. Looked right in at me, waggled his finger as if I were a dog and he the master. You were in my arms, fast asleep. I could have laid you down in your bed, slipped into the sky, and you never would have woken. But I didn't. I couldn't."

Her voice dips even lower, a whisper. "He only came the once. But I've never regretted it. You should know."

She looks back at them for a moment, taking them in. Her eyes are damp and shining. Then she straightens. "Now, my darlings. What is that abysmal saying? 'Faith, trust, and pixie dust'?" She leans out the window and whistles, a long, piercing sound Holly wouldn't have believed her mother could make if she hadn't heard it. "This is the faith part, I suppose."

There's a swirl of wind, a flash of feathers, a glimpse of something—of someone—no longer bloated and stretched. Someone small, sparkly, and gold. Bright bird eyes meet bright bird eyes in perfect understanding. The wind picks up. Jane/not Jane leaps.

And then Holly can't keep her eyes open any longer. The world turns black, and she slides off the edge.

Chapter Forty-Three

Someone is shaking her. Someone is calling her name. She hears it as if from a long way away, at the end of a very black tunnel.

"Holly," the voice says. "Do try and wake up. Decisions must be made. There's not much time." There's something cold on her forehead, on the back of her neck. A biting and sharp scent under her nose. Holly groans.

"Please," the voice says, more urgently. Holly opens her eyes and promptly shuts them again. The room is spinning and she fears she might be sick.

"What did you do?" she whispers hoarsely.

"We can discuss that later," Jane says. "Right now we have bigger problems."

With an immense effort of will, Holly forces her eyes open again and trains them on her mother. Jane is no longer a child, but her face is still youthful in a way it hasn't been since long before Holly was born. And then she sees the rug beyond her mother. Jack is there. His face is white, his lips pale. And she can't tell if he's breathing.

"The vial!" But even before Jane shakes her head, Holly knows it's gone. She tries to run to Jack, but it's like the nightmare she used to have—her legs won't support her, won't let her rise. Her mother heaves her up, and together they stagger to his side. Holly collapses next to him, checks for a pulse. It's faint and thready, but it's there.

"Call an ambulance," Holly orders. She's scrabbling across the room on her hands and knees to reach the phone.

"They won't get here in time."

At the voice, Holly turns. It's Eden rising from the bed, looking and moving much better than Holly herself.

"Peter . . . the drug brings you up so high, but when you crash, it's twice as low. He probably gave Jack too big of a dose if he saw you coming. He did it on purpose."

Holly dials anyway. "Help me," she says when they answer. "My son, he's overdosed on something. He needs adrenaline or naloxone. He needs . . ." She tries to think of what else would help, but she can't. Her mind is a blank.

"They can't help," Eden says again. She stands unsteadily.

The dispatcher's voice buzzes in Holly's ear. "Yes, he's breathing," she says. "Barely. Please, please hurry." But even as she's struggling to answer questions, another part of her is watching Eden make her way to the desk in the corner of the room. Her daughter seizes a letter opener. She brings it back to Jack, kneels beside him, cuts an X into his wrist, his wrist that is already sliced and cut and scarring.

"What are you doing?" Holly cries. But even as she utters the words, she knows, because Eden has turned the letter opener onto herself. She slices her wrist open, cuts deep, so deep that the red blood wells against the white of her skin, suspended for a moment. She presses her wrist to Jack's. Her face grows white, then whiter, the color of paper, of chalk, of bone. And like some gruesome magic trick, Jack slowly flushes, color seeping through his cheeks.

"Enough!" Holly says. "That's enough."

But Eden's not listening. She's swaying, about to collapse. Holly drops the phone, kneels beside her, tears her wrist away. Clamps one hand over it and rips at the hem of her own white nightgown because there's nothing else.

Jane helps hold Eden down, helps bind the wound. They're so busy tending to her that they don't see Jack stirring, revived by Eden's blood, not until Eden herself pushes them off and brushes the hair from his forehead.

"Jack?" Holly says. "Jack, can you hear me?"

He opens his eyes, but it's not Holly that he sees.

"Eden?" he whispers. "Is that you?"

"Hi, Flea," she says. She's smiling, but there are tears too. She reaches out her good hand and pats his shoulder.

"You used to call me that," he says sleepily. "I remember. But I don't think I liked it."

Eden laughs. "It's not a nice name," she agrees. "Jack it is, then." She turns her gaze to Holly.

"They'll be here soon," she says, and only then does Holly remember the dispatcher. She's been caught up in a world that doesn't exist, one where both of her children are with her.

Jane retrieves the phone from the floor and disconnects it. "There really isn't much time," she says. "Not for us." Her voice is light, but her eyes are dark. Ever changing, quicksilver, shifting like the sun chasing shadows across the landscape. It's as if she's been stripped to her core, anything extraneous burned away.

"I should be really, really angry with you," Holly says. "Not to mention that I'm still dizzy."

"I'm sorry about the whiskey," Jane says, deadpan. "It pained me to waste that vintage."

They both look at the children, who have their arms wrapped around each other. "I *am* sorry," Jane says. "But how could I let you or Eden risk yourselves, my darling?"

"He believed you." It's not a question.

"Yes. It was a gamble, of course. I bet on my good health and lack of injuries. I hoped the proteins in Eden's blood would repair my old age

instead, bring me to that adolescent perfection Peter can't seem to resist." She holds her hands up, turns them back and forth beneath the
light. They are slim and perfect, without age spots. "Remarkable, really.
The rush of well-being it brings. I'd forgotten what youth feels like."

"What happened?"

"It was the strangest thing—flying through the air, the silhouette of
Big Ben in the distance. The moon overhead, so bright and clear I could
almost touch it. Like being inside the storybook." Jane's face grows
dreamy. "Then swooping through the tiny entrance behind the clock
face. Peter was sitting in a chair in the center of the room, just staring
out at the night sky. At the stars, I think. The story says he used to be
able to hear them, did you know? That they whispered and sang their
secrets to him."

She pauses, as if seeing it again. "At first I thought he might be a
watchman or a guard—he looked terrible. Wrinkled and gray, with a
single streak of golden hair in the front. Jack was on a small cot next to
him, asleep, and when Peter saw us, he bent over and did . . . something.
Tink . . ." There's a golden chatter from outside the window, a spark of
light that zooms around the room, bouncing off walls and furniture until
it shoots outside again, and Jane corrects herself. "*Bell* dashed over and
knocked a syringe from his hand. He looked at me then, full-on, and his
eyes were terrible. Beautiful and blue but dead. No warmth at all. 'So
you've come,' he said. 'Canny girl. I knew you would.'"

"He thought you were Eden?"

"The blood made me young enough, and I'm not sure he'd ever seen
Eden up close. He reached out and grabbed me. Old as he was, he was
terribly strong, in a ropy, bony sort of way. He started muttering 'Somebody had to choose old Peter. Who better than you? My own flesh and
blood. That must be the secret.' I asked him what he meant, but by then
he'd spied the vial in my hand, filled with a concoction of red food
coloring and sleeping pills mixed together when I'd fetched the whiskey.
'What's this?' he said. 'For me?'"

Jane lifts her chin. "So I gave it to him, as if it were a present. And greedy child that he is, he couldn't resist. He used it on the spot. It didn't take long. His eyelids fluttered a few times, and then . . ." She makes a toppling motion with her hand.

But there's something in her face.

"What?" Holly prompts. Jack and Eden are still entwined, listening as raptly as she.

Jane bites her lip, then shrugs. "For all the magic, for all the beauty his tale brought to the world, it's a rather sordid one, isn't it? Downed asleep on the floor, undone by a simple drug. Not even the hero of his own story after all. But then again, he never was." She looks away.

Holly slips her hand into her mother's. "But you are," she says. "The hero of yours, I mean. And of mine as well. Thank you." Jane's eyes brighten. She starts to speak, stops, squeezes Holly's hand, then pulls her into a full embrace. Jane's arms are firm, not soft, her skin un-wrinkled, but Holly can feel her heart, and it has the same steady beat as always. They stand there, each lost in their own thoughts. Holly hates to break the spell, but she needs to know. Gently, she pulls away and looks at her mother's face.

"Is he . . ."

"Alive? He was when we left, but we didn't linger. I wasn't certain how long the pills would work, if he'd wake in time to follow us. I grasped Jack, who was barely breathing, and Bell clutched me, and we flew out the same way we'd entered. That high, the wind was fierce. I couldn't bear to look down. I just closed my eyes and hung on, terrified I'd drop him. But I didn't, and here we are." She smiles at Jack, then turns back to Holly, her face pensive. "Just before we took off, I called Christopher, so I suppose I can't make any promises as to Peter's health. I've become quite fond of that man, by the way." She leans in, her voice dropping to a whisper. "You could do worse."

Holly's eyes widen in surprise. She's about to respond when sirens thread the air. Still a ways off, but growing closer.

"Decision time," Jane says, nodding toward Eden.

Holly lets go of Jane's hand and crouches in front of her daughter. Gently brushes the hair back from Eden's face and tucks it behind her ear. "What do you want to do?" she asks.

Eden untangles herself from Jack and sits up. The faintest smudge of color is returning to her cheeks. Her body responds so fast to injuries that the cut on her wrist has already started to heal. Yet somehow she looks older than she did when she came through the window this evening.

"I want to stay," she says, biting her lip. "But I think . . . I think I have to go." She looks anxiously at her mother.

If Holly asks, she knows that Eden won't leave. They'll stay right here, in London, or maybe go to Cornwall. In a few months or a year, the neighbors will wonder who the old woman is who loves to jump rope, who chases soap bubbles and feeds the birds and has the most infectious laugh they've ever heard. They'll marvel at how patient Holly's son is with her, how he spends hours sitting on the garden wall listening to her talk. They'll shake their heads at seeing an elderly woman up that high. "Does she think she can fly?" they'll ask. "It's such a long way down."

A year. Maybe two. Holly will keep working, keep trying to find a cure, but in her heart she knows the odds are against her. The only gift she can give her daughter is the hardest one of all—that of letting go.

"I think so too," she says as steadily as she can.

Jane pats her back, her hand small but strong. "Well done," she whispers so only Holly can hear. And then:

"How would you feel about a companion?"

Eden, Jack, and Holly all turn to gape at her.

"Grandma?" Jack says.

"Well, she shouldn't go alone. And I certainly can't stay here," Jane says, gesturing to her body. "Not like this."

"The serum will wear off . . . ," Holly begins.

"Yes. But that's not what I mean. Tonight . . . the danger, the excitement, even the night sky . . . what if Peter wasn't the one I was waiting for all these years?"

"I don't understand," Holly says. "You think there's someone else?"

"Yes," Jane says simply. "Me."

No, Holly wants to cry. It's too much. To lose both of them on the same day . . . But as she looks at her mother, Jane's words from earlier in the evening ring in her head. *I've never regretted it.* She finds the strength to nod.

"I'll keep her safe," Jane says. "I give you my word. And if we can, we'll return."

"You could come," Eden blurts. She takes Holly's hand, tugs her to the window. Holly breathes in the early-morning air and wonders what it would be like. New adventures, new places no one—or almost no one—has ever seen.

"We really are made of star dust, did you know?" Eden says. And when she says it, Holly can see those stars, winking out behind the morning sky. No longer visible, but still there. Places she could almost touch.

But then she thinks of Jane, always chasing the next wonderful thing, when so many wonderful things were right in front of her. Of Jack, who is looking at Eden with such grief on his face, grief she knows he's struggling not to show. He is still far too pale. And, like this, he might not survive whatever Peter left behind in that far-off Neverland.

She remembers Ed, who is already star dust, and Nan, who may never see the stars again unless someone is there to help her navigate her way through the dark. And a very small part of her thinks of Christopher, of blue-black eyes in a scarred face. Of a single kiss and a gaze that's infuriating, challenging, yet tender. Her heart pulls in two, but she shakes her head.

"If I come with you, who will watch the stars?" she says. "Besides, it's not an adventure if there isn't someone waiting to welcome you home. Isn't that what mothers are supposed to do?" She says the last with a look at Jane.

Jack has struggled to his feet and joined them. He cocks his head. "Listen," he says. And over the noise of the traffic, over the sirens, they can just make out tiny bells. Joyous bells. They lift Holly's spirit despite her grief.

"It's time to go," Jane says. She takes Eden's hand and steps to the window. "The house and everything else is in your name. Use it as you see fit."

But Holly knows she'll stay here. She could never sell—how would Eden and her mother find her? Every evening she'll be right here in London with Jack, gazing up at the stars.

The bells are louder, closer, and then there's a light at the window, a tiny sparkling thing. It perches on Eden's shoulder, nuzzles at her hair. "Bell said to tell you, do you know that place between sleep and awake? The place where you can still remember dreaming?" Eden says. She's clutching the photo of herself tightly in her hand. "That's where I'll be every night."

"Then that's where I'll look," Holly says. The tears behind her lashes make everything look softer, as if she's already in a dream.

"We have to go," Jane repeats. She blows a kiss to Holly, to Jack. For the first time since Eden cut herself, Holly looks—really looks—at him. There's something different, more solid somehow, about him. Could what Peter gave him, whatever bit of magic he used, combined with Eden's blood, have changed him? Healed him more thoroughly than anything she's tried before now? He catches her gaze and, to her surprise, reaches out a hand to her, just as the wind picks up.

When the birds come, they're no longer black, no longer starlings. They're doves. They swirl through the room on their white wings, and it looks for an instant like a blizzard of snow, so blinding Holly has to close her eyes.

When she opens them, they're gone. Only the photo of Eden remains, discarded on the floor.

Chapter Forty-Four

Holly sits on a bench in Hyde Park under a very tall, very ancient chestnut tree. She's been waiting for what feels like a long time, but she knows that's her nerves. She left the house early so she could walk here, so she could think, and she still has no idea what she wants to say.

The tree's leaves are turning, brilliant reds and golds that fall gently from the sky, that strew the path below and crunch underfoot. The air is chilly, reminiscent of fall in New York, and she's grateful for the blue cashmere wrap she unearthed from Jane's closet this morning. Light and elegant, it still manages a comforting warmth, as if embodying Jane herself. The blue is the color of the sky, of her mother's eyes, of her daughter's, and Holly wraps it about her as if they are holding her in their arms.

Next to her, Jack shifts restlessly, looking at his phone. When she glances over at him, the top of his head seems unexpectedly far away. She swears he's grown in the last few weeks, although he won't let her measure him. He catches her gaze and guiltily slides his phone into his pocket.

"Go," she says. "I'm fine."

"I can wait. It's just practice."

"Go," she says again. "If you want to make the team, you need to put in the time. You're going to have to show them what you can do, take some risks."

He gives her a long look, as if he knows how difficult that speech was for her to make. "You too."

She smiles, resists the urge to tousle his hair. "Scram."

She doesn't have to tell him again. In one graceful movement, he bounds to his feet and retrieves his stick and helmet from behind the bench. He hesitates for just a second, then squeezes her shoulder gently, a touch so light she's not sure she actually feels it.

"Good luck," he says.

Holly doesn't say, *Be careful*. She doesn't say, *Go easy*. "Have fun," she tells him instead. "See you at dinner." She watches him walk away, follows him with her eyes until the path turns and he's lost from view.

And then she turns her attention to searching the park for a different figure.

At last she spots him. There's no one else it could be, really: that long, graceful stride, that muscled frame, the hint of menace that makes others on the path give him a wide berth.

She rises from the bench and descends the hill to meet him. As he gets closer, she frowns. What is that beneath his arm? And then her eyes widen in recognition and surprise.

"Hello," he says. "You look well." He scrutinizes her. "Lighter somehow." It's such a Christopher thing to say, with no mention of the bundle that he carries, that she laughs.

"I feel lighter," she agrees. "You want to walk?"

"Let's sit for a minute. That okay with you?" At her nod, he positions himself on the bench, long legs stretched out, bundle settled firmly on his lap. The October sun makes a momentary appearance, and he turns his face upward, closing his eyes.

Surreptitiously, she studies him. She hasn't seen him since that night, months ago, when Eden and her mother left. He looks different, more relaxed, as if that tight coil at his center has unwound a bit. The shadows under his eyes are gone. Even his scar seems faded.

"How's Jack?" Christopher asks, eyes still closed. She doesn't mind. It makes him easier to talk to somehow. She shrugs, then catches herself.

"Physically, he's fine," she says, discreetly knocking the bench with her knuckles. She'll never, ever take her son's good health for granted. "No relapses. Not since . . . that night. Mentally . . . he's seeing a really good therapist. He has a lot to deal with. Not just Ed. It's not easy. But she's given him the green light to start school, so he's enrolled in a day school not far from the house. He seems to really like it. And he's trying out for their lacrosse team. Captain's practice starts today."

"So you won't be going back to New York?"

Is it her imagination, or does his breathing subtly quicken? She's not sure. She pulls her eyes away, gazes out over the park. Her own breath is coming more quickly, and she tries to slow it before she responds.

"Doesn't look like it," she says lightly. "We sold the company, Barry and I—it was the right decision." Barry, it turned out, still knows her better than she knows herself. Lauren Lander had been happy to purchase it, so long as Holly promised to make a handful of annual appearances at trade events. "I'll need to go back to sell the apartment at some point, but there's no rush. I've offered it to Nan to use for a bit, if she likes. I'm hoping she'll consider it when . . . when more time has passed."

He nods, eyes still closed. "She's still staying with you then?"

"The house is so big, it just makes sense," Holly says. "And it's good for her to have Jack, I think. Good for him too. I've told her she's welcome to stay as long as she likes." Holly may never be able to assuage her guilt at Ed's death, but she'll spend the rest of her days trying.

"So what will you do now?"

"Oh, I've got some ideas."

Out of the corner of her eye she catches him peeking at her, but when she turns her head, he immediately closes his eyes again. "Yeah?"

"Yes," she says, and feels the start of a tiny, secret smile at his reaction.

Holly doesn't ever have to work again, thanks to the sale of the company and her Darling money. But a London lab space has come up for sale, and she's tempted. She needs something that's all hers, something bigger than mothering Jack or missing Eden. Something she can grow into. The research she's compiled on her children could help others, with a little work. No press conferences, no launch parties, just lots of lab time. Barry thinks she'll be bored. He's trying to rope her into starting a new company, an all-organic skin care line they could run together. She doesn't think so.

But she's been wrong before.

"We can talk about that later," she says. She pokes his foot with her own, and the bundle in his lap shifts slightly. "You promised you'd tell me what happened that night. That's why I came."

"Is it?" he says agreeably. She doesn't reply, but feels her skin redden slightly, and he opens his eyes and looks sideways at her just in time to catch it. "You read the report."

She had. He'd emailed her a copy, almost identical to the one he'd sent to the police. In it, he described how he'd found a small drug operation run by a teacher from Saint Ormond. There'd been a trail of boys, students at the school, used as test subjects. Several deaths linked to the drug, including the brother of the Darling family housekeeper. And then the near fatality of the Darling grandson.

The matriarch of the family, the famous Jane Darling, had left the country suddenly. Her whereabouts were unknown, conveniently shifting the press's focus away from Holly and Jack. Jane had always been quite good at drawing attention to herself. Now, even in her absence, she was the center of attention. Holly didn't mind one bit.

But these are the details she already knows. And that is not why she's here.

"I want your version," she says firmly. "Not the official one."

The silence stretches between them for so long that she's worried he won't answer, but at last he sighs and sits up. "After your mother called me, I managed to talk my way past the guard at the base of the tower he's retired, friends with a few mates of mine—and dash up the stairs. There's no elevator, and the stairwell is ancient, just up and up and up."

He's quiet again for a bit.

"And?" she prompts.

"And . . . the way he was sprawled out on the floor—I thought he might be dead," he says. "I bent over, to see if he was breathing, and he grabbed me so fast, so hard, I couldn't get away."

Holly's eyes widen, and Christopher angles himself to face her. "He looked ancient, all bones and leathery skin, as if he'd run out of whatever it was he'd been using to keep himself together. Like a skeleton. And yet he was strong, stronger than me. He bared his teeth and grinned, like something out of a horror film. I was slashing at him and he was still coming and then . . ."

"What?" Holly's holding her breath.

"He just . . . crumbled. One second he was there, and the next he wasn't. In his place was a pile of gray dust. The weirdest damn thing I've ever seen." He shrugs. "I thought I'd feel something. I thought I'd recognize him. But I didn't."

"That's it?" After years of Peter haunting her dreams, shaping her life, she can't believe he's just . . . gone. She exhales.

Christopher hesitates. "That's what I've been telling myself." He's wearing a white shirt, unbuttoned at the throat, and no sweater or jacket, as if he's unaware of the chill. Holly can feel the heat coming off him. She waits.

"Okay," he says. He takes a deep breath. "Right after that . . . thing . . . disintegrated . . . there was a breeze. I can't explain it, but it was like a whisper on the back of my neck. Like a . . . a vibration, the way a bell rings, that I could feel but couldn't hear." He rubs his neck with his left hand, as if he's still feeling whatever it was. "And then something sparkly and gold was in the air. It brushed over that thing, over its remains, and the gray dust and the gold just kind of . . . floated out the window together. Up toward the stars. Like some kind of ribbon, into the wind."

Bell. It had to be. Holly thinks back to that night, to the lapse between the small bright light zooming about the room and the quiet before it reappeared. But if Bell returned to Peter on her own, was it in forgiveness or vengeance? She finds herself hoping for the former. Hoping that somehow a lost, scared boy was given a chance to start over.

The bundle cradled in Christopher's lap squirms, opens its eyes. Carefully, he sets it on the ground.

"Awake now, I see," he says, and leans over. He's licked in the face for his trouble.

"Are you going to introduce me?" Holly asks.

"Meet Rosie," he says. "Someday she'll be a full-blooded English Labrador, when she's all grown up. Right now she's all paws and puddles." He eyes the puppy ruefully. "Want to walk her?"

Holly bends down and pets the soft black fur. "Sure."

"Good." Christopher wraps the leash around his right gloved hand and stands. He extends the left to Holly, and when she takes it, he pulls her close, so close she can feel his heart beating.

"You must have made a lot of progress," she stammers. "For your therapist to approve a dog, I mean."

"Some," he says. His breath is warm on her cheek. "Probably not enough, because I didn't actually tell her. But I am sleeping better. Also, the plant died."

"Rosie," she murmurs.

He steps back, cocks an eyebrow. "Short for Rosemary. For remembrance."

And then he pulls her really close, close enough to kiss. Which he does. She shuts her eyes and kisses him back.

When she leans against him, the locket she's taken to wearing everywhere swings between them. She'd found it in Jane's jewelry box, and it was the perfect size for the photo of Eden. She knows now why her daughter left it behind. That last night together, horrible as it was, was a happy memory in itself, because Holly loved her daughter enough to let her go.

At home, she's unpacked her pictures from the attic. She's unpacked her memories, her grief. All this time, she thought that it would kill her if she let it loose, but the opposite was true. Holding it in, pretending the bad things never happened, was what was destroying her.

The puppy wriggles between them, and Christopher finally releases Holly from his embrace. She bends to scratch Rosie's ears, this dog named for memories.

"They stay with us, you know. The friends you lost to drugs or in the war. Ed. Isaac. Robert. Even Eden and Jane. They're all still here."

She sees a frisson of shock cross his face as she says their names so easily, those names she once kept locked away. But it's true. In this moment, they are alive to her, all of them. She lets the memories in, lets them settle everywhere. In her heart, in her skin, in the very breath she takes. She'll carry them with her the rest of her days, whatever the future brings. She'll search for them every morning before she wakes, hoping against hope to find that in-between space in her dreams.

But Christopher is waiting for her, inviting her into the present. And as she looks at his face, at the arch of the tree branches overhead, the brilliant colors of the leaves, the memories quiet, still.

Holly takes a deep breath. Lets the cool October wind wash over her. Looks at Christopher's outstretched arms.

She closes her eyes.

And leaps.

Acknowledgments

There aren't enough superlatives to describe my agents, so I will just say thank you, Andrea Cirillo, Jessica Errera, and everyone at the Jane Rotrosen Agency—you are brilliant and amazing and I am so fortunate to have you on my side.

To my fantastic editor, Stephanie Kelly, thank you so much for your guidance, patience, and skill. Your hard work made this book the best it could be, and I am so grateful. And to Cassidy Sachs and Maya Ziv, for seeing it through.

To the team at Dutton, especially Lexy Cassola, Mary Beth Constant, Alice Dalrymple, Tiffany Estreicher, Amanda Walker, Emily Canders, Stephanie Cooper, Katie Taylor, Tiffani Ren, Vi-An Nguyen, and Nancy Resnick, thank you for all your work, expertise, and passion.

To the denizens of purgatory, thank you. Special shoutout to Cindy Pon, Rebecca Burrell, Bryn Greenwood, Kris Herndon, Sue Laybourn, Tracey Martin, Gretchen McNeil, and Clovia Shaw for support, advice, reading, and translation skills.

Mary Akers, much gratitude for allowing me to lean on your marine life expertise. Kelly Jaakkola, Robert Pistone, and Julie Wu, thanks for reading and sharing your expertise on past and future projects.

ACKNOWLEDGMENTS

To the tribe of my heart, Writer Unboxed, you are my writing home. Special appreciation to Brunonia Barry, Kathryn Craft, Donald Maass, Vaughn Roycroft, Barbara Samuel, Mike Swift, Dale Whybrow, and Cathy Yardley for advice, support, reading, and encouragement. Heather Webb, you have crazy editing skills—thank you.

To my holy-moly guacamole ladies, I have mad love for you all. Jan O'Hara, Therese Walsh, and Grace Wynter, you make my writing world run. Thanks for all the help, advice, reads, and late-night-text panic attack support.

Lisa Ahn, you are an editing fairy godmother as well as a friend, and I'm lucky to have you in both capacities. For seeing the path and coaxing me onto it and for leaving me breadcrumbs whenever I got lost, you have my undying gratitude.

To Angela Cheng Caplan, for taking me on an amazing adventure and for being such a fierce advocate. And to Asha Irani, for scheduling superpowers.

To the Shiloh Club: Emma, Felicia, Molly, Olivia—the originals— and Alyssa, Jake, Joe, Julia, Nicole, Sam, Shazain, Zach, and anyone I missed. You are brilliant and talented, even those who spent time in the special chair. Eat chocolate cupcakes whenever you can because you deserve them, read *The Once and Future King*, and do all the fabulous things you are capable of. I hope to hear all about them.

To my family: My parents, Anne and Stan, much love and gratitude for everything. Maureen, thanks for your strong fingers pulling me through. Emma, thank you for the plot twists, and Alex, for the writing advice. I adore you both more than words can say. To Bill, for your belief and love. None of it would be possible without you.

And finally, thank you, dear reader, for taking flight with me.

About the Author

Liz Michalski lives with her family in Massachusetts. She loves reading fairy tales and, sometimes, writing them. *Darling Girl* is her second novel.